The Pinwhe_____ whole expanse _____ acceleration into the compartment's floor, but it was lesser now as gravity countered the centrifugal whirl. Their air, too, thickened as the tree's walls exuded a sweet-scented, moist vapor.

The spectacle of her whole world, spread out in silent majesty, struck her. They were nearing the top of their ascent, the Pinwheel pointing vertically, as if to bury itself in the heart of the planet.

She wondered what would happen to them next. The Pinwheel throbbed. She had felt its many adjustments and percussive changes as it struggled against both elements, air and vacuum, so this latest long undulation seemed unremarkable. Only a short while ago she had thought that the ravenous green, eating at the pale deserts, waged an epic struggle. Now she rode an unending whirl of immeasurably greater difficulty.

The kinetic whirligig of all these events dizzied her. The last few days had stripped away her comfortable preconceptions, leaving her open to naked wonder. She was beyond fear now, in a curious calm. Ideas floated through her mind like silent fireworks. She looked down and in a glance knew that the Earth and the Pinwheel were two similar systems, brothers of vastly different scales. . . .

—From "Blood's A Rover"
by Gregory Benford

COSMIC TALES

ADVENTURES in SOL SYSTEM

Edited by
T.K.F. Weisskopf

For my husband,
Hank Reinhardt

And with thanks to Hank Davis,
comrade in arms

CONTENTS

Strange adventures on other worlds, the universe of the future.

—motto of Planet Comics

INTRODUCTION
Why do we need tales about "Strange adventures on other worlds, the universe of the future"?

T. K. F. Weisskopf

> "To imagine is not to fashion charming
> make-believe. . . . Out of the known or
> knowable, Imagination connects the remote,
> reinterprets the familiar, or discovers hidden
> realities."
> —From *From Dawn to Decadence: 500 Years
> of Western Cultural Life,* Jacques Barzun

As I write this it is the eve of the hundredth anniversary of the Wright Brothers' flight off the North Carolina dunes. And I have come to realize that I am not going to be living in the age of humanity's great expansion into space. I will not be on the *Nina*, the

1

Pinta nor the *Santa Maria*, let alone the *Mayflower*. Instead, I am living in the age of St. Brendan and Lief the Lucky. I can witness humanity's first tentative steps in the direction of the endless frontier—but the chances of me, personally, getting out there are small. Still, at least I can read stories about it! If we as a species are going to get there, we have to remember that we *want* to go.

I've long thought that it's one of science fiction's most important jobs to explore the future in fiction. Decisions about what kind of future we want to aim for can be played out in the pages of our magazines and novels. As Travis Taylor's story and article illustrate, the dreams of the writers become the dreams of the engineers and scientists who shape the direction of our technology. You want to make a difference in the world—write science fiction that will touch the hearts of these people.

It seems obvious to me that staying on one planet is a dead end for humanity. And I like humanity, in general, if not all its specific manifestations. Flush from conquering a new continent Americans of the early twentieth century had a positive vision of the future. We in the West went from horse-drawn carriages to rockets in less than fifty years. Now, in darker times, we seem to be on the road to losing the stars, losing the urge to explore. Science fiction needs to clear away the light pollution and show us the glories of the stars again. Show us where we can go next. Show us where progress should lead.

One of the most positive visions we can have of the conquest of space is that it will be strange and dangerous, but also in some ways familiar. There will be humans, living their everyday lives, albeit in exotic locations and only because of amazing technological developments. Several of the stories herein describe that kind of existence. And some take us a little farther beyond. . . . There is beauty and wonder in this universe, and whether man makes it his business or God ordains it, it is a noble calling to answer to destiny, search that wonder out and reveal it for future generations.

If you'd like to see more *Cosmic Tales*, there will be another volume coming out later in 2004, *Adventures in Far Futures*. If you'd like to see more beyond that, or to comment on these volumes, write to me care of Baen Books, P.O. Box 1403, Riverdale, NY 10471. Or you can write directly to me at toni@baen.com.

Scientist and dreamer Arthur Morton McAndrew was one of my favorite science fiction characters. He was one of Charles Sheffield's, too. In his introduction to The Compleat McAndrew (made incomplete by this story, by the way), Charles referred to him as an alter ego. Charles loved speculating about how far science would go, and his nonfiction volume Borderlands of Science is invaluable for any science fiction reader. For the McAndrew series he always included an afterword telling the reader just where the known science in each story stopped and the speculation began. Charles Sheffield died last year, soon after completing this story and before such an afterword could be written. Science fiction will be the less for his passing.

McANDREW AND THE LAW

Charles Sheffield

It's widely accepted that there's no such thing as a free lunch. I suppose anyone with a brain in her head would realize this applies equally well to dinner, but some people never learn; so there I was, sitting across the table from Professor Limperis and fully expecting him to pick up the tab.

He's a wily old bird who puts a high value on his time, a fact which I've known for as many years as I've been visiting the Penrose Institute. And today we were far from there. I was on vacation, ready to

4

follow the progress of the Grand Solo Solar Contest out in the Belt. What were the chances that Limperis had traveled several hundred million kilometers for the doubtful privilege of taking me to dinner?

At the moment he was busy telling me that it was hard times for the Institute, with research budgets squeezed tighter and tighter. I nodded sympathetically, but to be honest my mind was otherwise engaged. I like to gamble on the outcome of the Grand Solo Solar Contest, and a prime entry for the GSSC had just entered the dining room. I guessed that he massed between five and six hundred kilos.

In the GSSC, fat is good because the contest is just what the name suggests. You do the Belt-Jupiter-Mars run *alone*, with no assistance. "No assistance" means no fuel, no food, no water. Also, no ship. You are provided a suit with an oxygen supply and built-in fusion and chemical drives. Solo means solo. The materials to power the drives have to come from the competitor's own body.

That's where judgment enters the picture. The chemical and fusion drives are lipid based, and a competitor draws reaction mass only from his or her own body fat. That's why the hard-to-say "Grand Solo Solar Contest" is better known as Fat Man's Run.

With some people, the will to win inevitably takes over. In a pinch, the drives run at reduced power on muscle and sinew. I have seen a competitor, what was left of him, dragged out of the race by the marshals when his total body mass was down to sixty pounds. He might recover, after a fashion, but he would never race again. He would also never walk, run, or have sex, even in low-gee. When I saw him, skin hung off his spongy skeleton like rags on a frame of twigs. And still he was complaining about being removed from the race.

I became aware that Professor Limperis's eye was on me. He knew I had been distracted by my potential dark horse, and he was quietly waiting.

"I mentioned that finances were tight, Jeanie," he said at last, "but I didn't tell you the worst of it. Mac has another pet project stuck in his head, and there's no way the Institute can afford to do it. I told him that. So he took it on himself to try his hand at fund-raising. He went to Fazool el-Fazool to see if the man could help out."

That was a real shock. McAndrew fund-raising? Money means less to him than it does to a ground-hog.

Limperis saw my look of astonishment and misinterpreted it. "You know Fazool?"

"I've never met him. But he's McAndrew's mother's . . . friend."

"Ah!" Limperis's chubby face lit up. "That explains a lot. I only know Fazool as one of the System's richest people. But if he's McAndrew's mother's—er . . ."

"Friend."

"Right. Her friend. Then it makes sense that Mac would get a hearing. More than that, he received a promise of the money he needs for his new project. But there's a condition."

"That doesn't surprise me. Rich people like to stay rich. Fazool will want a return on his investment."

"It's not that kind of condition. Fazool wants his son, Abdi el-Fazool, along on the expedition. He says it will be a—er—a *broadening* experience for the lad."

I could agree with that. I've had near-death experiences with McAndrew all too often.

Limperis was watching my face. "You don't like the idea?"

"I don't. How old is Abdi el-Fazool?"

"Eleven."

"Then I certainly don't. But if you think that Mac will take any notice of what I—or you—think, you should know better. The man's a human mule. Particularly when one of his pet ideas is at stake."

"Jeanie, he listens to you more than anyone."

This, while true, was hardly relevant. But something else was going on here.

"Professor, I understand that money is tight at the Institute—it's tight everywhere with today's economic conditions. Fazool's money must be a great temptation. But money or no money, won't Mac need the use of Institute equipment to perform his project?"

"Assuredly. What he has in mind would be impossible without it."

"Then if you're so worried about this, why not just say no? Fazool's a powerful man, and I'm sure he has lots of influence. But he can't force the Institute to do whatever he fancies, even with Mac's blessing."

Limperis eyed me thoughtfully. He's as sharp as they come, and normally he's inscrutable. This time, though, I could read what was in his mind. It was, *How much can I afford to tell her?*

"It's not quite that simple, Jeanie," he said at last. "McAndrew views his expedition as a research activity, but not everyone sees it that way. Others at the Institute believe that we may be in sight of a new and inexhaustible source of free energy."

"There can't be any such thing," I began, then paused. *Others at the Institute.* I suspected that I was talking to one of them. "Can there?"

He coughed. "Well, there might be. There just might. And as you can imagine, it's very difficult for the Institute to say no to a project that won't need a penny of our funds and holds out even the remotest chance of unlimited free energy. I'm in a spot, Jeanie."

It was dawning on me. Limperis didn't want me to *talk* to Mac. We both knew that was a waste of breath. He wanted me directly involved, because he was worried about McAndrew's judgment and possible fate. And, of course, if Limperis was worried he thought I should be doubly so.

As I was. He had me, and he knew it. I was about to be sucked in. Forget my holiday and Fat Man's Run, I must fly out and talk to McAndrew. As I said, some people never learn.

Limperis didn't tell me what McAndrew's infinite energy scheme was all about. Better, he said, that it should come from McAndrew himself. That was his way of ensuring that I would head out to the Penrose Institute as soon as possible to clear up the mystery.

The Institute had settled into one of its rarer research locations, down near the Vulcan Nexus. Although an excellent site for solar observation, it is one of the places in the solar system that I least like to visit. It is perfectly safe—they tell you—but the Sun is only two million kilometers away and occupies half the sky. An unprotected human exposed to the intense flux of radiation will fry and die in ten seconds.

That sort of risk means nothing to a man who has spent a large fraction of his life thirty meters from a kernel, a shielded Kerr-Newman black hole. I found McAndrew staring through a set of specially designed optical filters at the naked solar surface. Prominences a million kilometers long sprang out at him—at least, they sprang out at me.

The greatest theorist since Einstein and the greatest combination of experimenter and theorist since Newton was dressed in dirty long johns. His thinning hair straggled down over his face. He was in his bare

feet, and he was sitting cracking his toe joints in a
way that I found both infuriating and disgusting.

Was this scraggy unwashed specimen of humanity
also my longtime companion and the father of my child,
the man to whom I had been faithful (mostly) for over
twenty years? Apparently it was. McAndrew is not the
only one who needs to have his head examined.

"Jeanie." He greeted me with the vague pleasure
of a man reacting to an Institute minion who has
brought him an unexpected cup of tea.

"All right, that's enough." I have my limits. "Arthur
Morton McAndrew, I traveled four hundred and eighty
million kilometers to see you. Either you give me a
proper hello, or you're a dead man."

That got through. Mac stood up and enfolded me
in an awkward embrace. Twenty years of hard work
was paying off. With luck, in twenty more he might
start acting close to human.

I plunged right in, because on my trip to the
Institute it had occurred to me that young Fazool,
rather than McAndrew, might well be Limperis's biggest source of worry. An unsuccessful expedition was
one thing. An unsuccessful expedition that killed off
a child of the super-rich was quite another. Rich men
tend to have powerful friends, and that could hurt
the Institute—Limperis's baby.

"Where's the boy?" I asked.

McAndrew frowned at me. "Who?"

I said slowly, "Mac, I am not here to play games.
I am referring to Abdi el-Fazool, the son of Fazool
el-Fazool. Where is he?"

"Ah. He's not here yet. He's flying in on a private
vessel, right behind yours. Be here within the hour."

"And you agreed with his father that you would
take him with you?"

"Well, yes. I did do that."

"I assume he doesn't have two seconds of space experience?"

"Actually, you're right. He doesn't."

Mac was being a clam. I might have to wait until we were heading out, when with a more intimate environment I could wheedle anything out of the man. I changed tack.

"This expedition of yours. How many people will be going on it, and what roles will they play?"

"Ah. That's a very good question. There's me and you, of course."

"Me?" I should have known what was coming from the minute that Limperis sat down with me at the dinner table, but now I had absolute proof.

"Sure. I don't know why, but approval for the use of the ship—it's going to be the *Hoatzin*, because we'll need something with the balanced drive—was conditional upon you coming as well. Didn't Limperis tell you that?"

"He did not."

"I guess he overlooked it."

"I guess he must have." Trying to explain certain aspects of reality to McAndrew is a waste of time. "Who else is going?"

"Well, we don't have much extra capacity, because the *Hoatzin* has to take along a lot of special equipment including a space pinnace designed to withstand high accelerations. The only other person will be young Abdi."

"That's it? Me, you, and Abdi el-Fazool?"

"That's it."

I felt the worry-knot in my stomach loosen. In many ways McAndrew is like an eleven-year-old himself, and I've dealt with him for long enough. If I couldn't handle two of them, I deserved whatever was coming.

"Can we go along and meet Abdi's ship when it docks? I'd like you to introduce me."

"We can go to where he'll be docking. But I can't introduce you."

"Why not?"

"Because I never met him."

"Mac, he's the son of your mother's friend."

"He is that. The son by another woman, and he lives with her. But we'll go meet him."

"Might you consider dressing first?"

He glanced down at himself, and seemed surprised by what he saw. "Oh, aye. I suppose I could use a bit of a wash and brush up."

"And a shirt, and a pair of trousers. Maybe shoes."

"Right. Give me a couple of minutes."

As he washed and dressed I learned what Mac knew about Abdi. It was not encouraging. The information came from Mac's mother, whose information came from Fazool el-Fazool, who apparently spent almost no time with his son. Chain those together, add distortion or misinterpretation at each link, and our knowledge of Abdi el-Fazool consisted of three items: he was male; he was eleven; and he had recently been expelled, for reasons unknown, from the most expensive school on Earth.

Given McAndrew's reference to a private vessel, I expected that Abdi el-Fazool would arrive aboard some expensive space yacht. However, the ship that floated in to dock at the Institute was a tired-looking charter vessel. The umbilical between the ship and the Institute's airlock established itself, it seemed to me, unusually quickly.

The lock began to open. As it did so a brown-skinned boy, small for eleven years and with short hair

and dark-brown eyes, popped through the half-open
hatch. He wore a red shirt and short tan pants, and
carried a knapsack on his back. Almost before he was
inside he was glancing about him, as though taking in
everything with one rapid sweep. A crewman followed,
more slowly, and fixed a dull eye on McAndrew.

"Arthur Morton McAndrew?"

"That's me."

The crewman nodded and sighed heavily. "Abdi
el-Fazool, delivered according to contract. All yours,
and welcome to him."

He thrust a yellow sheet into McAndrew's hand,
backed away into the umbilical, and had the hatch
closing before McAndrew and I had time to speak.

Abdi looked up at Mac. "I could have flown that
ship, you know, but he wouldn't let me try. He kept
throwing me out of the control room." Then, without
a pause, "My father says that you are the greatest
scientist in the solar system but he's wrong about a
lot of things. And you"—those alert brown eyes turned
to me—"you must be Captain Jeanie Roker. You don't
look like a spaceship captain. My father says that you're
McAndrew's keeper. Is that true?"

"I—"

"Did you once take a circus troupe out to the prison
colony on Titan, and the prisoners and circus perform-
ers got all mixed up with each other, and it was a
horrible mess? It must have been really neat."

"That's one word for it." I glanced at McAndrew.
He had the dropped-jaw half-wit expression that often
said he was deep in thought. This time, I didn't think
so.

"Abdi," I said, "if you like we can give you a tour
of the Institute. We'll show you where you'll be staying until the expedition is ready to leave."

"No need for that. On the way here, I downloaded

complete plans of the Institute. To get to my room you go that way." He pointed up and to the left. "Before I go there, though, I want to have a good look round this place."

"If you would like someone to come with you—"

"No. More fun if I find things out for myself. Maybe I'll see you at dinner."

And he was gone.

I glared at McAndrew. No one would call him a man sensitive to nuances, but apparently he read something in my look.

"Jeanie," he said anxiously, "this expedition is going to cost an awful lot of money, and Abdi is the key to getting it. If we don't take him along, his father won't come up with two cents. Fazool isn't much interested in science."

"If you want my opinion, Fazool is much interested in having his son out of the way while they try to find another school that's fool enough to take him."

I was wasting my breath. McAndrew went right on, "But with Fazool's support we can fly the *Hoatzin* out beyond the Edgeworth-Kuiper Belt and the Kernel Ring. Without that support—and that means taking Abdi along—I don't have a prayer."

"I suppose you have a good reason to *want* to be out beyond the Kernel Ring? It's not a place I'd choose for a vacation."

He stared at me. Finally he decided that I was joking about the vacation part, and said, "Don't you want to know what's out there, Jeanie?"

"Mostly nothing, I thought."

"Aye, mostly nothing. But something strange, too. We seem to have discovered a region that's locally negentropic—a place with negative entropy. That's why we have to go out there, to make sure it's what it seems to be."

I didn't scream, though I rather felt like it. If you want to pick one word in science that makes me uncomfortable, "entropy" will do fine. I have degrees in gravitational engineering and electrical engineering, and I know all the thermodynamic and information theory formulas. But still I don't have a satisfying *feel* for what entropy means.

The glare that I gave McAndrew would have melted lead. "Correct me if I'm wrong," I said, "but haven't you often told me that the whole of life is negentropic? It builds up from a state of disorder, to one with a high degree of organization and order."

"Quite right."

"So aren't you, and I, and everyone at the Institute, and every living thing, negentropic by definition? We decrease entropy, because we turn disorder into order."

"Aye. We are. But surely you understand how that's possible?" And, at my shake of the head, "Och!"— the strongest trace I could find in him of his Scots ancestry, other than an unyielding obstinacy. "Jeanie, entropy can decrease *locally*, of course it can. Don't you remember the laws of thermodynamics?"

"I thought I did. Law Number One: energy is conserved. Law Number Two: in any closed system, energy always must proceed from an organized to a less organized form. In other words, entropy, which is a measure of the degree of disorganization of energy, must always increase."

"There! You said it yourself. Just what I was saying."

"I did? It seems to me I said the exact opposite." As usual in a technical conversation with McAndrew, my head was beginning to spin and I was convinced that I would come out knowing less than when I went in. "Mac, I said that entropy must always increase."

"In a closed system, Jeanie. You said that. *In a closed system.* You and me, we don't live in a closed system. We get energy from outside—from the Sun, from power kernels, from radioactivity."

"So the Second Law of Thermodynamics is wrong?"

"No!" McAndrew sounded horrified. "The Second Law of Thermodynamics, wrong? Never. It's the most important and best-established law we know. In physics, it's THE LAW. Do you know what Eddington said?"

"No." I had the feeling I was about to find out.

"He said." McAndrew paused, and his eyes went vacant. It's one of life's mysteries that a man who has trouble remembering what he ate for lunch can recall, verbatim, whole pages of text and thousands of formulae that he has not seen for thirty years. "Eddington said: *The law that entropy always increases—the second law of thermodynamics—holds, I think, the supreme position among the laws of Nature. If someone points out to you that your pet theory is in disagreement with Maxwell's equations—then so much the worse for Maxwell's equations. If it is found to be contradicted by observation—well, these experimentalists do bungle things sometimes. But if your theory is found to be against the second law of thermodynamics I can give you no hope; there is nothing for it but to collapse in deepest humiliation.'* " McAndrew came back to life. "Jeanie, the second law of thermodynamics isn't just a law of physics. It's *the* law."

"So it can't be violated. This place you want to go, out beyond the Edgeworth-Kuiper Belt; is it receiving a flux of energy from somewhere outside, the way the rest of the solar system does from the Sun?"

"No."

"Is there a power kernel nearby, or radioactive materials?"

"Not a sign of either."

"Then, according to what you yourself just said, it *can't* be a region of negative entropy. Otherwise the second law of thermodynamics would be violated."

"You might think so."

"But you have some other explanation?"

"Aye. I think I do." His face took on a furtive and secretive expression. I'd seen it many times before, and I wasn't sure how much more I would get out of him today. He didn't like to talk about his ideas when they were "half-cooked," as he put it.

I took the initiative. "This place you want to go. How far away is it?"

"It's local, well within the Sun's gravitational sphere of influence. About a twentieth of a light-year—the *Hoatzin* will take us there comfortably in sixteen days of shipboard time."

"And there's a source of energy there, right? Energy coming in from nowhere?" I took a jump in the dark based on what Limperis and McAndrew had told me. "It's as though there's a hole in the universe."

"More matter than energy, though of course the two are exactly equivalent. But then, you'd expect—" He stopped and stared at me. "A hole. How did you know that?"

"From Limperis. He's as excited about this as you are." I wasn't making the last part up. You couldn't read Limperis from his facial expressions, but it was a safe bet that he—along with all the Institute scientists—couldn't wait to send an expedition to learn what was going on.

To guarantee funding for a trip to a hole in the universe, they would agree for Abdi el-Fazool to be taken anywhere, at any time. In fact, if Fazool el-Fazool had made it a funding condition that his son had to be chopped up on arrival and baked in a pie, I would not take bets on the Institute's dinner menu.

During the next few days I concluded that my worries had been excessive. We saw Abdi only at mealtimes, and then it was for the few minutes that it took him to wolf down his food and run.

Also, the preparations for our outward flight proceeded at magical speed. Instruments that we needed were produced within an hour of my request. Equipment tests were done in record time, and ship's supplies seemed to appear almost before we asked for them. In my innocence, I patted myself on the back for my clearly defined and timely requests.

I learned the truth on the day before our scheduled departure. Early that morning, Ulf Wenig and Emma Gowers paid me a visit. Wenig is the master of compressed matter stability, while Emma Gowers is the system's top expert on multiple kernel arrays. More relevant today than their impressive talents was their appearance. Wenig is small and slight, with a luxuriant and well-groomed black mustache. He is rather vain about his looks, and always well turned out. Emma Gowers dresses like a whore, but a *high-class* whore, with never a hair or a stocking seam out of place.

This morning a rat had apparently been chewing on Wenig's moustache. His face was pale. His eyes, like Emma Gowers's, were bloodshot. She wore thick and patchy makeup, which, together with an ill-matched pink blouse and dark-green striped skirt, was enough to turn her into a clown. I considered, and rejected, the notion that the two had spent the night engaged in some novel and physically demanding form of vice.

"Captain Roker," Wenig said. "We understand that the *Hoatzin* will depart tomorrow. However, we have heard that the ship is already fully equipped and tested. We are here to make a formal request. We would like you to advance your time of departure, and leave today."

"Dr. Wenig, you know I can't do that. There have to be final inspections."

"We know. The parties responsible for those inspections have all agreed to perform them today."

"But why? What's the rush?"

"Abdi el-Fazool, that's what the rush is."

"Why? What has he done?"

"What has he done?" Wenig's voice rose about two octaves. "You're asking me, what has he done?"

"Steady, Ulf." Emma Gowers took over. "You ought to ask, what *hasn't* he done. My latest experiment, in which I use a linear array of kernels to reproduce results of classical diffraction: it's ruined, because that little bugger left a dead frog in the middle of the optical bench and nobody knew it was there until too late. It's not just the two of us, Captain Roker. Everybody at the Institute wants him gone. He's been into everything. It's not that we don't like kids—though right now, I'll admit that I hate the guts of anyone who's eleven years old."

"That boy is a Child of Satan!" Seeming to realize that this statement called for justification, Wenig rushed on, "Two years of work, wasted! Because Abdi el-Fazool wondered what would happen if you turned off a compressed-matter field. He's lucky he wasn't killed."

"*We* are *unlucky* that he wasn't killed." Emma Gowers ran her hands through her blond curls, adding to her raddled look. "Please, Jeanie, in the name of sanity and for everyone's sake, get that boy out of here."

"I'll see what I can do."

And I would; though it did occur to me that removing Abdi el-Fazool from the Institute would do nothing for me or McAndrew. We were going to be stuck with him in the confined quarters of the *Hoatzin* for a sixteen-day outward trip; and, unless we were driven to execute him and dispose of the body, Abdi would also be with us during the sixteen-day return.

I've flown the *Hoatzin* and the sister ships that use the McAndrew balanced drive so often that they no longer appear strange to me. Others, seeing one of the vessels for the first time, usually do a double-take. Abdi was no exception.

"That thing?" he said. "We're supposed to fly in that? Where are the crew's quarters?"

I could see his point. The object we were drifting toward was nothing like a conventional passenger or cargo ship. From a distance, all you could see was a flat plate like a big solid wheel, with a long axle protruding up from its center.

"Look closely," I said. "See that thing like a little round bubble out near the far end of the axle shaft? That's the living quarters—*all* the living quarters."

From the blank look on Abdi's face I realized that I would have to go through the explanation of the way the ship worked. The disk was a hundred meters across, made of compressed matter and stabilized electromagnetically. It was not much more than a meter thick, but with a density of fifteen hundred tons per cubic centimeter the gravitational pull on nearby objects was formidable. A person sitting at the middle of the disk when the ship was at rest would feel a force of more than a hundred gees, enough to flatten any human. However, gravity as a force falls off rapidly with distance. A few hundred meters away, along the axis of the disk, the pull of the disk would be only one gee—a comfortable environment for the crew, sitting in the cramped sphere that constitutes the living quarters.

Now start the drives. The drive units are all situated around the perimeter of the disk, and they accelerate everything in the direction *away* from the central column. Provided that you slide the sphere of the living quarters along the shaft toward the disk at the appropriate rate as the drive acceleration increases, the total force for anyone sitting within that capsule will remain at one gee. That's true whether the ship is accelerating at two gees, ten gees, or one hundred gees.

The only physics involved is the equivalence principle, which states that a gravitational force cannot be locally distinguished from an acceleration. The idea is simple and even self-evident—provided that you happen to be McAndrew, who designed it. I understood it myself after the second explanation.

I'll say this for Abdi: he was smart beyond his years. He understood the concept the first time around. And he asked a couple of good questions.

"What would happen if the sphere with the living quarters got stuck and you couldn't slide back along the shaft?"

"Been there, done that. You'd have to keep the drive turned on."

"And accelerate forever?"

"Unless you found a way to free the sphere. This isn't just theory, Abdi. It happened on one of the first tests."

"Neat! Wish I'd been there. Hey! What happens if you leave the sphere when the ship's accelerating at a hundred gees?"

"Nothing you would enjoy. If you leave on the side closer to the mass plate, gravity pulls you into it and squeezes you flat. Leave on the side away from the mass plate, and before you know what happened the ship's out of sight and you're alone in empty space. Don't even think of it, Abdi."

"I won't. But then what's *that* for?"

He was pointing to the little space pinnace, seated at the very end of the long central shaft.

"That's only for use when the drive is off. The pinnace is at a fixed position on the end of the axle. When the drive is at maximum, it feels an acceleration of a hundred gees. Everything in the pinnace is designed to stand that, but you aren't. If you stayed inside it, you'd be killed. Squashed like a bug."

"Squashed like a bug." Abdi repeated the words with relish. "Neat. But can I take a look at it now, while the drive is off?"

I hesitated. I wanted a private chat with McAndrew, but I also didn't care for the idea of Abdi poking around inside the pinnace.

While I was still dithering, McAndrew said gruffly, "All right, then. But I want you back here in half an hour, or I'll be there after you. You look, but you don't touch. Understand?"

"I understand."

That should have been enough, but I remembered what Ulf Wenig and Emma Gowers had told me. I added, "Don't touch the controls or anything else on your visit to the pinnace. Do you hear me? For the time being, it's strictly hands off."

"I hear you. And I heard McAndrew."

"So do what you are told."

"I always do what I'm told." Abdi sounded aggrieved at the very idea he might consider any other course of action. "And I *don't* do what I'm told *not* to do."

It wasn't until much later that I realized the full significance of Abdi's reply. But I was still not totally convinced, so as Abdi headed off to the pinnace I turned to McAndrew.

"Are you sure we can trust him?"

"From everything I've heard, we can. The lad likes to be into everything, but if he's told something specific, the way we just did, then he'll follow instructions."

It did cross my mind to wonder why Abdi had been kicked out of his school if he obeyed the rules so well, but a different question was on my mind.

"Mac, you know how small the living quarters are here in the *Hoatzin*. I don't know much about Abdi, but I can already tell you one thing. He's a hyperactive child if ever there was one. He'll buzz around the living space like a wasp in a bottle. The trip out will take sixteen days. What are you planning to do with him while we're on the way?"

The expression on McAndrew's face told me that he had never given it a moment's thought. To him, a sixteen-day trip was an opportunity to sit, stare at the cabin wall, and indulge in prolonged mental gymnastics. Finally he shrugged and looked at me hopelessly. "Do you think he might be interested in a course in statistical mechanics?"

"Mac, he's *eleven*, for God's sake. Would you have been interested in a course in statistical mechanics when *you* were eleven? Oh, never mind, don't bother to answer that. I'll find a way to keep Abdi occupied. But when the time comes, I'll want my reward."

"What reward?"

"Mac, stop being literal-minded." No chance of that. "For starters, you can tell me what secret you've been sitting on since I arrived."

"Secret?" He was all bland innocence. "I don't have a secret."

But I was sure he did. And once we were heading out he retreated into his private mental world. I might have been at a loss, but something that Abdi had said at our first meeting gave me an idea. It was his ambition—at least until he changed his mind—to be a spaceship captain. He was fifteen years and a lot of hard work away from that, but if he was willing I could give him a running start.

It turned out he was a good student, given that he was so fidgety he had to be hopping about and doing something different every twenty minutes. He was enormously inquisitive, and wanted to know how everything worked. One of the communications units had not been performing up to par when we left the Penrose Institute. With Abdi's assistance, I stripped the unit down to discover the problem. Then there was the job of putting it back together from the thousand bits and pieces scattered around the living quarters.

That was enjoyable, and in a perverse way I welcomed Abdi's company. Of course, given the tight space in the *Hoatzin*, Mac and I didn't get any chance for personal interaction. That would have been tolerable, too, except that near the end of the outward run Mac had the gall to say to me, "You and your worrying. Hasn't this been the smoothest trip you could ask for?" He rubbed his hands together. "In a couple of hours the drive goes off. And then the fun starts."

At the halfway point the ship had turned and begun the deceleration phase. From the living capsule I had a clear view out along the central shaft to open space beyond. I had looked that way occasionally for the past eight days, and seen nothing. More to the point, I saw nothing now and we were almost there.

"What were you expecting, Jeanie?" McAndrew said, and Abdi, who had also been staring out, turned to watch the two of us.

"Well . . ." A hole in the universe? That was something neither I nor anyone else had ever seen. I vaguely imagined streams of light and particles, jetting out like a great fountain into space. "You said that matter was appearing from nowhere. I thought we would see it."

"It depends what you mean by *see it*. A hundred million tons appear every hour, but the *caesura*—the hole in space—is three hundred kilometers across, and naturally it's three-dimensional. Spectroscopic analysis suggests that almost everything coming through is neutral hydrogen, and it disperses rapidly. When you do the arithmetic you find that the region ahead is much less dense than the air we're breathing. I doubt anyone would have picked this up if there hadn't been a refractive effect around the whole region. The images of distant stars change from points to little rings of light." He smiled. "There's something interesting going on, no doubt about it."

"You're not thinking of taking the *Hoatzin* any closer, are you?" I knew that McAndrew's sense of danger was about as well developed as his dress sense.

"No, no. I expect that the region is safe enough, but we'll park at a distance with the drive off. There's a whole slew of observations that I'm keen to make."

Reassuring? It might have been, except that the space pinnace was hanging out at the end of the central axle.

I persisted. "You brought a pinnace all this way, and you don't plan to go near the region at all?"

"Well, I wouldn't go quite that far. It would be fascinating to see what it's like close up. But I would never do that until I was sure we were safe. It's observations first, today and tomorrow. Then we'll see. Would you like to help set up the instruments?"

He addressed that question to Abdi, who nodded

eagerly. So once the drive went off and we hung motionless in space—I could still see nothing ahead—the two of them headed out to the very end of the axle. A cluster of special instruments had been set in place there before we left the Institute.

For the next peaceful half day I was alone with my thoughts. One result was that by the time they rolled back into the living capsule, tired and hungry, I had decided that McAndrew's explanations to date provided more confusion than clarity.

"I know there's matter coming out from nowhere." I had already eaten, and I watched the other two as they gobbled down everything in sight. "But Mac, that doesn't make any sense to me. Matter must come from *somewhere*."

He wiped his mouth on his shirt sleeve. "Oh, it does. It's a standard prediction of brane theory."

"Brain theory—the way we think?"

"No, no. B-R-A-N-E. The word's short for membrane, and the result follows from an old extension of superstring theory. Things that lie close together on a multidimensional membrane—separate universes, if you want to think of them that way—can touch. One theory suggests that our whole universe began when two neighboring brane elements collided. We're looking at something much smaller here, just one little region of contact between us and a neighboring universe. Of course, there may be billions or trillions of others like it, scattered around in places too far off for us to see them."

He had finished eating, and now he yawned. "I'll go into detail tomorrow if you like. But it's been a long day, and I want an early start."

"That's all right." I suspected he had gone as far as he could without becoming unintelligible to me. "Get some sleep. You too, Abdi, so we'll all be up bright and early in the morning."

I expected resistance—Abdi hated to go to bed—but for a change he didn't argue. He stood up without a word, and was gone.

He was also gone the next morning, though McAndrew and I didn't realize it at first. I was saying, "If he doesn't get his sleepy head out of his bunk in the next few minutes, he'll miss breakfast," when McAndrew interrupted.

"The pinnace!" He was staring out of the cabin's top window.

"What about the pinnace?"

"It's not there."

"You think it came loose and drifted away?"

"I don't see how it could." He was already struggling into a suit. Before he was half done with that I was over at Abdi's bunk, pulling back the curtain.

"Mac, Abdi's not here! He must have taken the pinnace."

"I don't think so. We told him not to, and he agreed."

I was thinking back. "That's not quite true. We told him that he wasn't to do anything with the pinnace *before we left the Institute*. We didn't say a word about after we arrived. I think Abdi interprets things in his own way. If you tell him not to do something, he won't. But anything that's not explicitly forbidden, he treats as permitted."

As I spoke I was using the external sensors to scan space in all directions. "Where could he have gone? I see no sign, and the pinnace has a low-thrust drive. It's not designed to take you far away."

"Oh Lord." McAndrew paused with one arm in his suit and leaned his head back against the living capsule wall. "All those questions he asked yesterday. I assumed the little bugger had just a casual interest."

"Mac, stop speaking in riddles and tell me what's going on. Where is Abdi? And what's—"

He held up his hand. "I know where he is. I have to go after him. Before that, you need to understand what we're getting into. It could be dangerous."

"If Abdi is in danger, we can't sit around for explanations."

"The full story can wait, but there are things you absolutely have to know. You see, Jeanie, it's a two-way street. It has to be. If matter can emerge from a neighboring universe into ours, matter from here must be able to go there. I was hoping that the transfer might work for something a lot bigger than individual atoms. That's why I brought the pinnace, in case we had a chance to go next door and learn what it's like."

"And you told all that to *Abdi*?!"

"I might have. I suppose I did. But I would never have dreamed of trying the transfer until we'd made hundreds of measurements using small probes, and we knew it was safe."

"Were you thinking you might come out somewhere dangerous—near a star, maybe, or a planet?"

"Worse than that, Jeanie. We're seeing what looks like hydrogen atoms coming through, and you might say that's a good sign because it suggests physics there isn't much different from what it is here. But tiny changes in the weak force or the strong force would make any atom quite different in its properties. I'm not sure that life as we know it can exist on the other side."

"You mean Abdi could already be dead?"

"That's what I'm afraid of. Either way, this is my fault. I have to go and find him. We don't have another pinnace, but I doubt that he has gone far. The drive on a suit should be enough."

He was starting forward when I grabbed his arm. "The pinnace has a communications unit. You said that radiation goes between the universes. We can call Abdi, and *ask* where he is."

"We can. But take a look." He nodded toward the console. "No carrier signal. Either the unit on the pinnace was never turned on, or Abdi switched it off."

I was still gripping his arm. "Mac, why do you imagine Professor Limperis and the others at the Institute wanted me to travel with you?" That earned a blank stare, and I went on, "They trust that I'm cautious, and they know for sure that when you get an idea in your head, caution is the last word anyone would apply to you."

"You said we don't have time for philosophical discussions. Now you're trying to start one."

"Not philosophical. Practical. Mac, you mustn't try universe-hopping alone. Either we both go, or nobody does."

"That's a terrible idea. Abdi and I need a backup. Suppose we both get in trouble?"

"Suppose you do. What am I supposed to do? Sit here at the edge of creation until supplies run out, then turn and head for home? I would have no idea how to act if you disappeared."

He pursed his lips and said nothing.

I continued, "On the other hand, if I went looking for Abdi and *you* stayed here, you could take action if I was in trouble. You know a thousand times as much as I do about where we are, and what's going on."

"If it were a million times as much it might not be enough. Jeanie, you can't travel alone through the caesura and into the other universe."

"Nor can you. And I'd be no help back here."

And that, after a lot more argument, kind of settled the matter. We would both be going—but not before McAndrew insisted on telling me more than I wished to know about the overall situation.

"It's natural to think about the material that enters our universe, because that's what we see. But the second law of thermodynamics is more complex than that. Let me give you an example, Jeanie."

We were makings preparations to leave the *Hoatzin* in our suits alone. We could stay away from the ship for up to thirty hours, then it was return or die.

He went on, "Suppose you have a box divided into halves by a solid partition. Nothing can pass through, not even heat. Call the boxes A and B, and imagine that they represent separate universes. On each side of the partition you have matter. Let's say it's a gas. The temperatures are the same in A and B, and so are the pressures. If the gas on each side of the partition is perfectly mixed, that's as disordered as you can get. Entropy is at a maximum on each sides. Now you make a hole in the partition. Is there any observable effect from making that hole?"

I was dying to leave, but if he said I needed to know, I was forced to accept his rambling. I said impatiently, "The gases from both sides mix, but they were at the same temperature and pressure to start with. Things were as random as you could get. You shouldn't notice any difference at all."

"Shouldn't, and wouldn't. But suppose I give you another piece of information. Suppose the gas in box A is different from the gas in box B. Maybe, it's oxygen in A and hydrogen in B. Before the hole was made, the gas on each side had maximum entropy and maximum disorder. I couldn't produce energy from the gas inside either box. But once I make the hole we have a *combined system*. Hydrogen molecules from B start going into A. If I'm sitting in A, I will notice the change and I can measure it. I will say to myself, 'Aha! Entropy is going *down* around that hole.' I know, because if I strike a spark the new hydrogen molecules will combine with some of the oxygen molecules, and produce energy.

"But now suppose I'm sitting in B. Oxygen molecules are arriving, so near the hole I can strike a spark and combine them with some of the hydrogen to generate energy. I will reach the same conclusion as I did in A. Entropy in B is decreasing, too."

"Mac, entropy always *increases*. Isn't that the second law of thermodynamics?" As usual when I talked with McAndrew, I was more confused instead of less. "You have it decreasing in *both* boxes."

"That's right. It must, since the situation is perfectly symmetrical. But because of the hole connecting them, neither A nor B is now a closed system. The complete system is (A + B), and it's the entropy of that which has to increase. It may not look like it to someone in either box, but the total degree of randomness is going up. Eventually, all the gas will be perfectly mixed."

"We see things from only one box. Is that your point?"

"Part of it. But I want to emphasize the symmetry. We have matter coming in from outside—from another box or another universe. And things can run both ways. If matter comes from there to here, it can just as likely go from here to there."

"Separate atoms and molecules."

"Sure. But maybe more. What we lose must be different from what we gain, or we'd see no entropy change. Maybe bigger things can go the other way. Like the pinnace."

"And Abdi."

"Right. And the problem is, we have no idea *how much energy* his arrival might trigger in the *other* universe."

"But we're going to find out."

"I suppose we are. Unless you will let me go alone—"

As I said, when he gets an idea in his head he never gives up. Of course, that doesn't mean you have to let him act on it.

The hole in the universe was invisible, but McAndrew had plotted its boundary and knew exactly where it was. A hundred meters from the edge he halted and said over his suit radio, "Can you hear me?"

"As clear as if you were sitting next to me on board the *Hoatzin*." Which I wished was the case. I looked back at the ship, less than ten kilometers away. The central shaft and living-quarters were invisible, but the mass plate hung like a silver coin in space.

"We stay close, Jeanie. We move forward together, and make sure we can still see and talk to each other."

We gripped gloved hands. Side by side we drifted toward the caesura, the nothing, the three-dimensional hole in the wall of the universe. I felt nothing, but without warning the darkness around me disappeared. I moved through a shimmer of light, multicolored and constantly changing. No longer in any place that I could recognize, I suspected I was *between* universes.

The display of my inertial guidance system, designed to track position in three-dimensional space, suddenly went blank. It lit again after a few seconds, but its spatial coordinates had reset to zero values. At the same time, everything around me went dark. My suit radio filled with a roar of static.

"Mac, where are we?" I hoped my voice was calmer than I was.

"We made it through in one piece." His voice was a near-unintelligible thread of sound, but I could hear the satisfaction. "So chances are that Abdi is all right. Hold on, and set your suit to roam. I'm going to try different frequencies."

Nothing happened for about thirty seconds. While I waited I realized that the space surrounding us was not completely dark. A faint, pearly radiance glimmered in from all directions. It was just enough to show the outline of my arm.

"How about that? Better?" McAndrew's voice was much clearer.

"Lots better. I can hear you now. Do you know what's going on?"

"Sure. We've arrived in a universe where the dominant radiation is at radio frequencies, probably generated by discrete sources. I picked the quietest region I could find and tuned us to it. Visible wavelengths seem to come from a general background. If there are stars, they are radio stars."

His words were distinct enough, but there was a curious background echo to them, as though everything was being repeated a fraction of a second later. I turned on my helmet light and directed its beam at McAndrew.

There he was, clear and unmistakable, but faint shadow images of his suit marched away to left and right, above and below, diminishing ghostly arrays that shrank in size until they merged into the pearly background.

"Mac, turn on your helmet light and point it at me."

Not one light appeared, but a whole constellation of them. They blinded me to anything beyond.

I said, "What do you see?"

"Same as you do, I imagine. I'm only guessing, mind, but I'd say this is a spacetime with a totally different structure. It's built of discrete units on a macro scale, at least so far as optical properties are concerned. I want to try an experiment." His hand released its hold on mine. "Stay right where you are, Jeanie."

I certainly wasn't going anywhere. I kept my light focused on McAndrew's suit, and watched uneasily as it receded from me. It was no more than fifty meters away when the structured array of images turned into a bland glow, little brighter than the background.

"Mac, I've lost you. You've disappeared."

Not a word of reply, only the steady hiss of static. The urge to drive my suit toward the direction where I had last seen him was very strong. I fought it, hovering frozen in space. I could hear my pulse, loud in my ears. I counted the beats. Sixty—eighty—a hundred. On the hundred and twelfth beat, a suited figure popped back in sight, accompanied by its retinue of ghostly images.

"I'm seeing you again, Jeanie," Mac said. "And hearing you. Is it two-way?"

"Yes."

"That's reassuring. I was afraid for a minute we might be in a spacetime with asymmetric affine connections, and no metric."

He reassured a lot easier than I did. But perhaps not, because his next words came in a voice more serious than I had ever heard before.

"Here's the problem, Jeanie, and I must admit it's not one I'd ever anticipated. We need to find Abdi and the pinnace, but we seem to be stuck with a distance limit of fifty meters for any form of electromagnetic propagation. If the common region is the same size in the two universes, then we're dealing with a space about three hundred kilometers across. That gives us a finite volume to search, which is good news. The bad news is the length of time it will take us if we're stuck with traverses that are only a hundred meters wide. We'll run out of air and fuel for our suit drives, long before we're done."

"That would only be in the worst case, Mac. Don't we expect Abdi to stay close to the place he came in?" Something had gone dreadfully awry, when I was the optimist and McAndrew the pessimist. "We have to look for him. What else can we do?"

"I don't know. Let me think for a minute."

I didn't like the sound of that. McAndrew's "minute" for thinking could sometimes last for days. But after only a few moments he said, "You've spent more time with Abdi than I have. How smart is he?"

"Very. But Mac, he's just a kid."

"Aye. But children often think clearer than older people. They have fewer falsehoods cluttering up their brains. He's sure to have looked outside the pinnace, and he'll have made no more sense of that than we have. Less, because he doesn't have the physics to let him interpret what he sees. So what does he do, Jeanie, assuming he's bright and he's logical?"

I said slowly, "He knows he can't rely on anything he sees outside the pinnace. So all he can rely on is—"

"—what's *inside*. He won't learn anything from sensors that record external conditions. But the readouts that tell him his absolute position in inertial space should be working, because they're working in our own suits. And mine reset to count from zero when we transferred here."

"So did mine. I saw it happen. But we've been drifting ever since."

"We have indeed. But we can reverse course and

take ourselves back to zero position coordinates. That
will place us on the *edge* of the region. Abdi insisted
that he could fly the pinnace. Assume that he's right,
and that he's smart. Then he can take himself back to
zero coordinates, too. That will be where he entered
this region."

"But Mac, we have no idea whereabouts he was on
the edge when he did that. It could be a long way
from where we came in."

"True enough. But it has to be on the *boundary*
of the three-dimensional space. That changes the
problem, replacing a three-dimensional search by a
two-dimensional one. All we have to do is set up a
systematic procedure to cover the boundary."

I knew he would already be working out a plan to
search a spherical shell rather than the whole interior.
In fact he apparently had one already, because he was
zooming off in what seemed to me like an arbitrary
direction. Without arguing, I followed McAndrew and
his attendant arrays of ghost images. Every wasted
breath decreased Abdi's chances.

"Of course," he said as we flew along through nothing, "our strategy for finding Abdi relies on there being
a peak probability with respect to his intelligence."

He would philosophize at the gates of Hell, and
I knew from experience that there was no point in
trying to stop him.

"If Abdi's not smart enough," he went on, "he'll
never think to go back to the origin of his inertial
coordinates. On the other hand, if he is super-smart
he will head back to and through that origin of coordinates, to take himself right through the transition
zone and into the universe from which he came. For
all we know, Abdi could be safely back on board the
Hoatzin, wondering where we are. Maybe we should
have taken a quick look there ourselves, before trying

this search. Or maybe we had it right the first time, and only one of us should have come here while the other stayed behind in case Abdi returned."

Or maybe we should never have agreed to take a hyperactive eleven-year-old with us into the unknown.

Before I could do more than frame that thought, all discussion of alternatives became academic. If time is Nature's way of stopping everything from happening at once, it failed to fulfill its function. The digits on my suit's inertial coordinate readout, which had been ticking steadily toward zero, became an unreadable blur. I felt an acceleration stronger than the suit was designed to provide. McAndrew said, "What the devil," in a tone somewhere between excitement and astonishment; and in that same single moment, the pinnace sprang into view straight ahead. The hatch was open. Before I had time to think of aiming for it, I was through. McAndrew followed, to sprawl beside me on the deck. A split-second later the pinnace itself was darting off at high acceleration in a new direction. Everything around me became a dazzling whirl of rainbow hues.

The colors faded and vanished at the same moment as the acceleration ceased. I was given no time to catch my breath. McAndrew grabbed hold of my arm. I saw Abdi on his other side, also being towed toward the still-open hatch.

Toward, and through.

We were outside the pinnace again. I recognized familiar star patterns, but had no chance to savor them. The *Hoatzin* was a few hundred meters away, and McAndrew was dragging all three of us single-mindedly toward it.

"Mac!" It was both a question and a protest.

He said one word: "Inside." Then he was pushing

us through the *Hoatzin*'s lock, cycling it at maximum speed before we had cleared the opening.

As the lock filled with air I said, "What's the hurry? We're back in our own space, in our own ship. We're safe."

"Aye. Now we are. But look." He reached a gloved hand down to the waist of his suit, grabbed a handful of material, and pulled. The suit—made to withstand a pressure of up to fifty atmospheres, impervious to radiation, and tougher than the most hardened composites—ripped away to show McAndrew's unzipped tunic and bare belly.

I gripped the left arm of my own suit in my right hand and tugged. Half the sleeve ripped away like wet paper. If that had happened a few minutes earlier, while we floated in vacuum . . .

"Abdi?" I said.

"I'm—I'm—" His teeth were chattering. "I'm . . ."

Either he was trying to tell me that he was alive, which I already knew; or that he was all right, which he certainly wasn't. I stripped off my useless suit and helped him out of his. He was close to catatonic, nothing like the inquisitive and self-confident lad of yesterday.

"When did you realize, Mac?" I gestured at the remnants of my suit, which had disintegrated as I removed it.

"That they would soon be good for nothing?" His own tattered and discarded suit was on the floor and he was at the *Hoatzin*'s control panel. "Soon after we made the transition. My suit's condition monitors suggested it was protecting me, but destroying itself in order to do it. The physical parameters of the neighboring universe may be close to our own, but they're not close enough for long-term survival."

"And you didn't mention that to me?"

"What good would that do? Anyway, who was to say that the readings meant anything over there. I knew that the only way to make a test could be fatal. The only thought in my head was to find Abdi as fast as we could, and then get back here."

"And you did it. Mac, no one should ever suggest again that I'm needed on your expeditions to get you out of trouble. This proves it. I couldn't have saved us. And I still don't understand how you did it."

He had finished work at the controls and the *Hoatzin* was turning in space, aligning us so that we were set to accelerate back toward Sol. With the rotation completed but the drive still turned off, he swiveled his chair to face me.

"If I thought for a minute I could get away with that line back at the Institute, Jeanie, I might give it a try. But you know me. I'm the System's most incompetent liar. I didn't find Abdi and the pinnace. I didn't bring us out through the transition zone to our own universe. I didn't save us. You saw the way that your own suit accelerated. How did you imagine I could make that happen, when I wasn't even touching you?"

If McAndrew was the System's worst liar, sometimes I think I'm the slowest person in the System to catch on. "If *you* didn't," I said. "And *I* certainly didn't. . . ."

I turned to stare at Abdi, who had not moved a millimeter.

McAndrew said, "No. Of course not."

"Then . . ."

"Not me, you, or Abdi. We didn't save ourselves. Somebody knew we were in trouble, and they gave us a hand."

"Then there's *life* in the other universe? More than life. *Intelligence.*"

"It looks that way." McAndrew initiated the drive. There was no feeling of acceleration, but the living capsule began edging along the axle toward the mass plate. We were on the way home. "I'm wondering if *they* will believe that there's intelligence in *our* universe, given the way we blundered in. We have to return there."

He wasn't looking at me, but he must have sensed my instinctive shake of the head. He went on, "We have to, Jeanie. First contact, and already we owe them. We have to go there again—if only to seek a chance to pay them back."

There's something about youth. I don't know quite what it is. I only know I don't have it any more.

On the fifth day of our return journey to Sol, I was watching Abdi dissect a fragment of the helmet of his ruined suit. He had said not a word regarding his experiences in the neighboring universe, and when I asked him about it he told me he didn't remember anything that had happened. He didn't feel that he had nearly been killed, because at eleven the whole concept of mortality is alien. He seemed his old self again.

Or maybe not quite his old self. I saw a caution that had not been there before, a new look-before-you-leap deliberateness in Abdi's actions. And he was making notes, something he had never done. Fazool el-Fazool had said he hoped that a trip with McAndrew would be a broadening experience for his son. Against all the odds, it seemed to have worked out that way.

And McAndrew himself? Well, Abdi may have learned, but Mac certainly hadn't. He couldn't wait to get back to the Institute, where he planned to organize and outfit a new expedition better prepared for the unknowns of the other side.

He didn't want to hear me play the role of Cassandra, telling him how close he had come to being killed, warning him how next time he might not be so lucky. He wanted to talk to Limperis about his ideas, and he spent most of the return trip sitting impatiently at the communications console.

Of course, the general cussedness of Nature guaranteed that when the first faint carrier signal reached us from the Institute, McAndrew would be taking a food break and I would be at the communications console.

"Can you hear me?" I said. "This is the *Hoatzin*. We are on our way home, and heading straight to the Institute." At our range it was audio only, and I waited patiently through the round-trip signal delay.

"We are receiving you." The operator's voice was weakened and distorted by extreme distance. "Do you need help?"

"No. We've had difficulties, but we're safe now." Then my brain caught up with my mouth. We had not been in touch with the Institute since we left. The communications equipment was in perfect working condition. How did they know we had been in trouble? "What makes you think we might have problems?"

"Well, the flight plan that you filed shows an outward travel time of sixteen days, and a return travel time almost exactly the same. But you've only been gone for twelve days."

McAndrew had come back to stand behind me after the first exchange. He was holding a huge sandwich and his mouth was crammed too full to speak, but while I sat and gawped at the console, he slapped his knee. As soon as could swallow, he spluttered, "I knew it! Or I would have known it when I sat down to make drive settings, if only I'd had the sense to believe the evidence of my own eyes!"

"Mac, in normal speech, please. Not just your idea of normal speech, either—use the sort of language that I can understand."

"In a minute, Jeanie." He leaned over me and said into the console microphone, "Everything here is just fine, and we have results more exciting than you can ever imagine. Contact Professor Limperis. Ask him to organize a conference for senior Institute staff the minute that the *Hoatzin* docks. And tell *everybody* that they'll want to be there."

He turned to me, beaming.

"Mac, I thought we didn't have anything—unless you count nearly getting killed."

"Och, that was nothing." He dismissed the near miss with death with a wave of his hand. "We found a new universe, with intelligence in it—friendly intelligence, by the look of it, because they saved us. What more could you ask? But there's more, a whole lot more. Look at that control panel, and tell me what you see."

Since there were about four hundred separate readouts and dials, I saw far more than I could take in. I said, "How about a hint?"

"Start with the chronometer. You can end there, too."

I stared at the instrument. "It's wrong! Days wrong."

"It is. How many days?"

"A bunch. Twenty-one, or twenty-two. Mac, it's reading earlier now than when we arrived at the caesura. I know, because I recorded the time when we turned off the drive. That instrument is supposed to be foolproof. I can't imagine what could make it malfunction the way it has."

"Nor can I. And I think it didn't. When we passed through the caesura, we entered a universe where time runs in the opposite direction from here. At a different rate, too—we felt we were only there for a short while, but we traveled back more than three weeks. The *Hoatzin* was close to the caesura. We know matter passes through . . ."

I turned to look around me. Over at the other side of the living capsule, Abdi was quietly at work on his suit helmet. McAndrew's words disturbed him not at all. And McAndrew was smiling at me, not at all like a madman. Was I the one who was losing it?

"Mac, do you realize what you're suggesting? If you're right, anyone could travel out, just the way we did, and they would have a way to move backward in time."

"Aye."

"But that's impossible. Time travel is impossible. The whole idea leads straight into loads of paradoxes."

"It does seem to." He sat down next to me, and suddenly seemed to notice what he was holding. He lifted the sandwich to his nose and sniffed, as though he had never seen it before. He nodded. "Salami. And paradoxes. Right enough. We'll have to work through those, but that will be part of the fun."

"And causality, Mac? What about *causality*? It's a law of nature."

"It is. It is indeed."

He nodded thoughtfully, and took a bite. His next words were distorted and barely intelligible.

"Causality is a law of nature, true enough. But Jeanie, that's all it is. A law of nature. It's not like the second law of thermodynamics. It's not The Law."

If you have ever wondered how a dashing hero is made, here is some insight, in a story set on the rough and ready frontier that our solar system will turn into in the next few hundred years. It is the origin of a character whose mature exploits were chronicled in Martian Knightlife. *Disclaimer: I don't make the puns, I just print 'em. . . . And hats off to Leslie Charteris, creator of* The Saint, *who inspired the author. . . .*

JAILHOUSE ROCK

James P. Hogan

It was storm season in the southern hemisphere of Mars. Above the turbid orange clouds currently obscuring the western parts of Hellas Planitia and the region toward the equator, the "Mocha" freighter flew on a heading north of west. A thousand yards behind, the Skyguards escort gunship that was accompanying it to Lowell base, still a quarter of the planet away, maintained station slightly above and to starboard. Unseen satellites passing high overhead sent periodic updates on the vessels' progress to a monitoring program running in the computers at Skyguards' headquarters, located at Lowell.

As flying machines went, the Mocha was ugly and ungainly—a boxy, open-frame center-body designed to hold a variety of cargo modules; an independently maneuverable crew module in front; one from a selection of propulsion modules attached behind; and on the sides, either high-lift wings for atmospheric duty, or boosters capable of low-orbit injection to connect with the satellite transfer stations. But it was well suited to its role of hauling miscellaneous loads around the newly opening-up planet. Its name derived from the official designation of MOdular Cargo HAndler. Naturally, everybody called them Mocha ships.

At the rear of the flight deck in the crew module, rookie recruit trooper Kieran Thane sat cramped on a folding jump-seat between the rear bulkhead systems panel and an equipment rack, one arm resting on a run of power cables crossing the wall ribs, a close-quarters autocarbine wedged next to his leg beneath. The vessel was owned and operated by a general carrier at Zerolon base on the far side of Mars from Lowell that styled itself grandly "Haulers of Fame," and was carrying a cargo of space weaponry and programmable munitions that would fetch premium bid prices among the various mercenary forces, commercial rivals, and other squabbling enterprises taking form among the Belt habitats and beyond if it happened to go astray. Hence, the armed escort ship. Kieran had been put aboard the Mocha as link man between its crew and the escort commander, as routine required. The vessel was built to minimal surface utility standards, which meant that everyone was wearing EV suits with helmets close by, ready at hand.

"Escort Leader calling Mocha." The voice of Lieutenant Coombs sounded in Kieran's phones. "Acknowledge and report."

"Roger. Everything normal here," Kieran responded over the circuit.

"I read you. Out."

The three-man crew's captain, who was called Ursark and occupied the c-com station on the far side of the nav-display table, looked at Kieran with a mixture of cynicism and amusement. "Right on time again. That's a regulation-scrubbed toy soldier you've got there, kid. Does he come with a key sticking out of his back, or batteries?"

"I . . . guess everyone does things the right way until they get to know where they can cut corners," was all Kieran could think of to say in reply.

"Well, I'm sure glad it's not me who stands to get shot while he's learning," Ursark drawled. He seemed to be trying to goad. Kieran wasn't sure why. Probably just part of his nature. Kieran didn't respond, but kept his eyes on the windshield in front of the other two crewmen and watched the slowly creeping vista of whipped cotton candy stirred by descending canyons of clearer air. Occasional upthrusts of rock loomed as shadows, sometimes breaking through into the sunlight like yellow-brown icebergs riding in an ocean of orange foam.

Ursark was swarthy-skinned and fleshy in build, with oily black hair, several days' growth of stubble, and a barking laugh that revealed strong teeth while asserting disdain and defiance. His eyes were black and depthless, betraying nothing of what might be taking place within. But Kieran conceded inwardly that he had a point in his own artless way. The troopers dubbed the commanding lieutenant "Thumper" Coombs—everything was undeviatingly as ordained and stipulated in the book. But at least they weren't having to take orders from somebody learning in a combat mission situation, Kieran reflected. That would have been a lot worse.

He rested his head back against the painted metal bulkhead and idly surveyed the other two crew.

Bolen, doing the piloting, was lean and muscular with somewhat drawn features and short reddish hair. He seemed to go about his work easily and competently. Kieran wondered what other tempting offers there might be for somebody like him out here—as opposed to working for the regular carriers or other agencies that employed pilots. Demand was said to be such that they could virtually name their own pay. Maybe the added kick of mixing a little danger with the job wasn't something that appealed to everyone. In the engineer's station next to Bolen was Wallax, black-haired, square-chinned, and rugged-faced. He had said little, not allowing Kieran to form any clear impression of him—although there had been a hint of an aggressive streak. Somehow, the three didn't really fit the image that Kieran would have guessed for an off-world flight-crew; but then, what experience did he have to guide him as to what should be expected in these distant places where humankind was finding new homes? As the freighter droned on above the wilderness, his thoughts drifted to the wider picture that he found himself part of.

Although still officially a "base," Lowell was creeping outward along the canyon bottoms from an intersection of canyons in the complex of Valles Marineris, merging its original dome structures between new roofs spanning between the walls to already become an incipient city. Earth had rebounded from its century of institutionalized technophobia and, with the advent of fusion, strong-force catalysis, and other nuclear technologies that had revolutionized just about everything from space transportation to materials extraction and processing, humanity was finally bursting from its home world to pick up again at what should have been the next step back in the years when the Apollo monuments were left on the Moon. Mars was opening up. The Belt worlds, natural and artificial, were seeing the beginnings of what some predicted would become a dizzying diversity of cultures and lifestyles. A few adventurous souls had established what looked like being a permanent human presence among the moons of the gas giants. Amid all the vitality, restlessness, innovation—and inevitably, rivalries and differences—comfortable Terran notions of a common system of enforceable law had been left behind. Some said it would follow eventually; others maintained it was already a dead concept, and some new system for restraining excesses and dispensing justice would have to be invented. In the meantime, there was plenty of work for go-it-alone operators like Skyguards, protecting life and property, and, where expedient or arguably justifiable, generally helping to "promote interests."

The Mocha's engine note changed suddenly to a succession of juddering coughs, bringing Kieran back from his musings. The craft dipped and banked to port, throwing him forward from the seat and causing him to grab at a side bracing. An alarm note wailed as the pilot's panel lit up with red indicators. Outside, the horizon of cloud titled and swam sideways across the windshield. Bolen slammed the controls to manual and threw a worried look back at Ursark.

"What is it?" Ursark barked.

"Major thrust loss. Synchronizer failure. Double-X category malfunction."

"Power system's screwed! We have to go down!" Wallax shouted.

"Escort Leader to Mocha Rider," Lieutenant Coombs's voice said. "You're altering course and attitude. What's happening?"

"Some kind of power failure, sir," Kieran answered. "The engineer says they have to put down."

"Hell, we're not asking for permission," Bolen yelled

over his shoulder as he wrestled the manual stick, and Wallax called numbers and flipped switches. "Whatever he thinks doesn't come into this." The Mocha nosed into a descent, then angled back to use its braking thrusters, the main power note steadying but falling. Orange haze enveloped it, becoming denser, streaking past the windshield and ports to give a sudden hint of the craft's velocity. Bolen watched the forward radar imager and centered on what looked like a straight run of reasonably flat terrain ahead, clear of obstructions and boulders, flanked by rocky bluffs on both sides. "That's our only chance," he yelled to Ursark.

"Go for it," Ursark told him.

Kieran spoke into the stem mike on his suit collar. "It looks like a genuine emergency, sir. We're out of options here. Trying for a clear strip dead ahead at . . ." He raised his voice to call to the front. "What's the range of that?"

"Five miles," Bolen answered.

"Five miles."

"We're following you down," Coombs advised. "Tell the captain that I'm calling Lowell for an emergency pickup."

Kieran passed on the message and braced a foot against one of the metal steps coming up from the doorway behind, which led back to the access section, where the suiting chamber and airlock were located. A hazy, colored version of the radar image appeared dimly beyond the windshield, growing larger, flattening out, and then expanding to meet them as the Mocha came down. Additional dust blown up by the retros blotted out what view there was for the final few seconds before the skids struck with a jolt and a brief shriek of metal racing over frozen sand and rubble. The craft went up on a bounce, grounded again, and eventually scraped its way to a halt. As the dust thinned outside the windows and on the viewscreen, Ursark cut to a rearward shot showing the escort ship landing through the storm, maybe a hundred yards back. The Mocha's engines died, and the hiss of sand blowing over the outside hull became audible for the first time.

Ursark looked across at Kieran. He was showing his teeth, smiling in a strangely satisfied way that wasn't at all consistent with the situation. Kieran returned a puzzled look and was about to speak . . . when Wallax produced a pistol and leveled it at him.

Kieran shook his head noncomprehendingly. "What—"

"Not a word, kid." Ursark's voice was cool but menacing. He leaned over the nav-display table and reached across to tear the mike from Kieran's suit collar. Then he indicated the autocarbine by Kieran's leg and motioned with a hand for Kieran to hand it over. "Slow and easy, butt first, okay? Nobody has to get hurt."

Bolen was calling from the pilot's console. "Hello, Sandman. Do you read? Are you out there?"

A voice answered, patched through to the cabin speaker. "I hear you, Bird. You're a few hundred yards past the marker. We're on our way."

"Gotcha."

Coombs came through in Kieran's ear. "Escort Leader to Mocha Rider, report situation," But Kieran had no means of reply. "Come in, Rider. . . ."

Kieran lifted his weapon clear from the wall, reversed it, and set it in Ursark's waiting hand. "What's going on?" he demanded.

"Wait," Ursark answered, and stared expectantly at his viewscreen, still showing the shape of the gunship nose-on, standing in the murk. Wallax kept Kieran covered. Kieran followed Ursark's gaze. At the pilot's console, Bolen operated some switches, and an electric whine came from the rear, which Kieran recognized as the sound of the loading door of the cargo module opening. Maybe ten seconds passed by. . . . And then a quick series of flashes lit up seemingly behind the gunship, which lurched visibly, accompanied by the *crump-crump-crump* of weapon fire sounding deceptively distant in the thin atmosphere. A window opened on the screen to present a side view of the gunship— evidently coming from an external source—that showed the rear end of its fuselage torn and holed, its the tail surfaces shredded. Then another burst of tracer streamed from a point near the camera and raked the stern engine pod. The damage was localized away from the personnel compartment, which was farther forward, Kieran could see; but the gunship wasn't going anywhere. It had been reduced to little more than a life-support shelter in the desert.

Coombs hadn't fully grasped the situation. "Mocha crew, alert! We are being attacked. Secure—" But a new voice cut him off, sounding on a channel evidently directed at the gunship, but which Bolen or Wallax had patched to the speaker circuit. "Calling you Skyguards turkeys. Can you hear me in there?"

Coombs replied. "I hear you. What is—"

"Your bean can is immobilized and covered by heavy infantry weapons." Which meant ordnance capable of taking the gunship apart at that range. "Sit tight, and this can be easy on everyone. You're not calling any shots. And let's not forget that we still have one of your people in the freighter." The viewpoint that the image was coming from began moving forward past the nose of the stranded gunship, and then ahead of it. Moments later, a smaller, approaching blur appeared on the screen showing the view sternward, and transformed into a general-purpose desert crawler—used all over Mars for survey work, exploration, scientific expeditions, and the like. It halted just short of the Mocha, and two figures clad in heavy-grade EV suits and helmets got out. They crossed through the sand spray toward the Mocha and disappeared from the viewing angle. Bolen switched to a camera showing the inside of the cargo module with its loading door open and the two figures just coming in off the ramp. "The voice that had spoken before announced, "Okay, we're in."

"We've got you, Roney," Ursark confirmed.

"Then let's move it."

Bolen closed the loading door. The engines started again, rose in volume, and Kieran felt the craft moving.

"Escort Leader to Mocha Rider. Our position appears to be compromised. Unknown hostile elements are approaching you and are heavily equipped. If you are receiving this, offer no resistance. Repeat, do not resist."

Ursark flexed his console mike in Kieran's direction and gestured toward it, at the same time leering derisively. Despite himself, Kieran felt his face flush with embarrassment at his own helplessness. "Yes, sir," he acknowledged self-consciously.

"That's a good soldier," Ursark said.

The voice that Ursark had addressed as Roney came over the speaker again. "Calling the bean can. Just to let you know, we've left a functioning crawler about a hundred yards in front of you. It'll get you by until help shows up if your support system's shot. 'Bye turkeys."

The Mocha bumped its way up to speed, lifted off, and rose into the storm, by then growing darker with the first shades of evening.

Since there was no internal access forward, the

two additional hijackers—for it was obvious that the
whole thing had been a setup all along—remained
in the cargo module. No doubt Coombs had already
put out a distress call and reported the incident; but
provided the Mocha relied on its navigation aids and
stayed below the ceiling of the storm blanketing the
region, the satellites would have little chance of finding
it optically or on infrared—and naturally, the tracking
signal being transmitted previously would have been
switched off. Since its course was unknown, the area
that it might be in increased with the square of the
distance covered as time went by. A thousand miles
of flying would generate over three million square
miles to get lost in—and plenty of time to switch
the cargo to a different vehicle, or whatever else the
hijackers had planned.

Ursark's manner mellowed somewhat, now that
the critical point was past. He produced a flask and
some plastic mugs, poured out three coffees and
passed two forward, along with a couple of film-
wrapped sandwiches and a bag of chips, and then
looked quizzically at Kieran, as if in an afterthought.
"Eat?" he invited.

Kieran had no idea how long it might be before
another opportunity might present itself. In any case, he
was getting hungry. He nodded. "Sure. . . . Thanks."

Ursark filled another mug and pushed it across
the nav table, following it with another sandwich. He
unwrapped one for himself and began munching, at
the same time watching Kieran curiously. "You know,
you're not so bad, kid," he grunted finally. "You keep
it cool, know what I mean? Not the kind that loses
his head and acts stupid. Somebody like you could
do okay if you had connections." He smacked his
lips noisily and worked something from his teeth with
his tongue. "Any idea what you could make, working

for the right people?" He studied the expression on Kieran's face—firm, not looking for a fight, but refusing to concede or be drawn into anything either. "Still pumped up with principles and ideology, eh?"

"Give him another ten years," Bolen said without taking his eyes off the dust veils whipping by outside. "I used to fly for one of the enforcer outfits too, once."

"I never knew that. . . ." Ursark seemed about to say something more, when Roney spoke from the cargo module.

"Hey, Urse?"

"What?"

"I don't think we're going to have enough air here to last all the way to Quentas."

Ursark's eyes flickered alarm in Kieran's direction. "Watch your talk," he said into the mike.

"Oh . . . right. But we need to put down somewhere along the way and get fresh bottles from the cab."

Ursark turned his head in Bolen's direction. "Did you hear that? Can do?"

Bolen was already keying in a query to change the flight plan. A revised course appeared on a terrain map showing on one of his screens, and a string of numbers unrolled across the bottom. "There's a hard pad we can put down at forty minutes from here," he announced. "Increases final ETA by . . . less than a half hour. We should be okay."

"Forty minutes from now," Ursark relayed back. "Reckon you can hold out till then?"

"Yeah. Shouldn't be a problem," Roney replied.

Quentas, if Kieran remembered correctly, was a mesa-like geographical feature somewhere near the edge of the deserts of Elysium.

Night had fallen by the time the Mocha set down.

The flight-deck screens and the view through the windshield showed the surroundings to be in a flat depression fringed by a rocky scarp—possibly a crater rim—appearing as disconnected crests and edges picked out against shadow by starlight filtering down through the still dusty air. But they seemed to be out of the storm. Kieran made out structures of some kind outlined dimly a short distance away—a construction gantry, maybe, and several storage sheds.

Moving awkwardly in his suit in the confines of the cabin, Ursark went back into the access section, taking his helmet. From the doorway behind where he was sitting, Kieran heard the clatter and clinking of bottles being taken from a rack, sounds of Ursark securing his helmet, and finally a suit monitor's triple *beep* confirming systems to be functioning normally. Then came the *whirr* of a the inner lock door opening, Ursark shuffling through, and the lock closing again. In the flight deck compartment, Wallax studied his fingers between glancing at Kieran, his pistol still close at hand. Bolen opened the cargo module door and reactivated the view of the inside to show Roney and his companion moving out onto the ramp to stretch cramped arms and legs in the light that had come on within.

"Any coffee left back there?" Bolen asked. Wallax passed him the flask. Bolen refilled his mug and returned to contemplating the scene outside, immersed in thoughts of his own.

Something was odd, Kieran realized. Why would Ursark have bothered putting on his helmet and going outside to take the bottles back, when Roney and the other with him were already fully suited? Ursark could simply have left the bottles in the lock chamber to be retrieved from the outside. The answer came when Ursark appeared in the view on the screen, and while Roney and his companion took turns attaching the replacement bottles to each other's packs, entered into an animated discussion with them over another channel, this time not switched though to the cabin: They wanted to have a private conversation. . . . And then, when Kieran had been watching with more-or-less detached interest for perhaps a minute, it suddenly hit him what it was they needed to talk privately about. After Roney's careless talk earlier in which he had let slip their destination, the problem was what to do with *him*—with Kieran! And now, guessing the subject of the debate, he was virtually able to follow the exchange from the gestures and body language—even in suits.

Roney—somehow Kieran knew which was Roney—arms spread, hands upturned; then a one-handed throwing-away motion, followed by hands crossed, opening to make a breast-stroke movement: *What's your problem, Urse? He knows too much. Get rid of him; it's simple. Then the whole thing's behind us, clean and over.*

Ursark—two-palmed restraining gesture; window-wiping movement; side-to-side shoulder swings, emphasizing shaking of the head. Finally, both hands turned up in appeal: *Wait a minute, think about it. That's a whole different rap than for a heist if things screw up. I didn't agree to that kind of ride. He's just a kid, for chrissakes.*

Roney's companion—half-turn away; pause; turn back, one arm sowing seed. *Either way, I don't care. Can we just get this settled? We're wasting time.*

The chilling realization came home to Kieran that they were arguing over his life. Wallax's idle toying with the pistol, and Bolen's studied detachment took on a whole new, sinister significance. He felt his mouth and throat turning dry. He was the kind who knew how to keep cool, Ursark had said, not one to lose his head. Yeah, right. . . . Not losing your head could come fairly naturally when you had no choices to make.

Then Ursark's voice sounded over the cabin speaker. "Calling the kid soldier. Get helmeted up and move your ass out here. Okay?"

Kieran stared around dazedly, trying to tell himself this couldn't be happening. He'd signed up for a tour away from Earth on what sounded like an exciting job, that was all. It wasn't supposed to end like this, and so soon. He looked at the others in a silent, desperate plea. Bolen continued staring implacably through the windshield. Wallax cradled the pistol more securely in his palm and looked up.

"I guess that means you," he said laconically.

For an insane moment Kieran tried estimating distances by eye with thoughts of trying to grab for it . . . but it was pointless. He got up numbly from the jump-seat and picked up his helmet from the ledge where he had set it.

"I'm not hearing an answer," Ursark's voice said from the speaker.

"He's on his way," Wallax replied.

Moving mechanically, as if someone else had taken control, Kieran went down the steel steps to the access section, initiated the lock cycle, and donned his helmet while the lock was filling. When the indicator changed to green he entered, heard the inner door close behind, and waited for the chamber to exhaust, refill with Martian air, and for the pressures to balance. The outer door slid aside, and the conveyor step carried him down six feet to the surface. His dreamlike sensation enhanced by the thirty-eight percent Earth-normal gravity, he walked back toward the opened cargo door. Ursark was waiting at the bottom of the ramp. Farther back, the other two were maneuvering something down from its stowage space between the center-body frame and the propulsion module. Kieran saw that it was the vessel's "scooter"—an open, two-person electric runabout carried by most larger craft for extending the range of surface activities; on occasion, they had also proved their worth as lifeboats. While Roney and the other proceeded to strip the radio and emergency beacon from the scooter's electronics box, Ursark filled Kieran in.

"Okay, so this is the deal. There's a Triple S on a bearing of two-forty degrees from here that you should be able to make in four to five hours. You've got extra air and water under the seat. We can't leave you with a live transmitter, but there's a homer that'll give you a fix when you get close enough. Just hope you don't hit problems. I know the chances aren't perfect, but they're the only ones you've got." Surface Survival Shelters, containing food, life-support gear, medical kits, and other essentials, usually located at radio navigation beacons, were dotted all over Mars for use in emergencies. Mars had no magnetic field; the electronic compasses worked off the satellite grid. Kieran opened his mouth behind his helmet visor to say something, but Ursark cut him off with a wave. "There's nothing to discuss. That's it. On your way, kid. Adios."

Wa-it a minute! . . .
Kieran had covered maybe three miles, when the subconscious processing going on in his brain suddenly delivered its conclusion that something wasn't right. He eased back the scooter's throttle, slowing the procession of sand and rocks through the scooter's headlight beam to a crawl to free up more of his attention to pondering what. . . . And then it came to him.

This had shown every sign of being a professionally

planned and executed operation. The people staging
it might be crude in some ways, but they weren't
dumb. Professionals would have made sure to leave
the crawler and come away from the hijack with fresh
air bottles—or at least, bottles full enough to get them
where they wanted to go. So, the Mocha had never
been heading for Quentas.

Why, then, had Roney said it was? The only reason
could be: *for Kieran's benefit!* The whole thing had
been a setup to feed Kieran false information, which
he was now supposed to take back and report, sending
everyone who would be searching off on wrong trails
all over Elysium. While the hijackers did . . . what?

The scooter came to a halt as Kieran followed the
thread through further. Already, his blood was rising
again, this time not only from the humiliation of being
disarmed and made a hostage, but from being taken
for a fool and used as a dupe as well.

If the Mocha wasn't going to Quentas, then in all
probability the destination it had been heading for was
right here—to do whatever was due to happen next,
while Kieran was purring his way sedately on a jaunt
across the desert. Why would the hijackers waste any
of that time going somewhere else now? And he surely
hadn't seen or heard any sign of the ship taking off
since he'd set out, so something more was detaining
them. His best guess was still that it was rendezvous-
ing to transfer its cargo to some other craft.

Kieran turned off the headlamp, eased the scooter
into motion again, and U-turned between the dunes
to set off back the way he had come. He could
manage without the lamp now, anyway. Phobos was
rising—on a clear night it could appear three hundred
times brighter than Venus seen from Earth—and even
with the residual dust from the storm he was easily
able to follow his own tracks. He wasn't sure what

he intended doing—get access to a radio; disable the craft somehow; cause some kind of mischief. But he was mad and had a score to settle.

The glow from lamps illuminating the area where the Mocha lay was visible before Kieran reached the last intervening ridge. He ditched the scooter on the reverse slope, and after taking a flashlamp, binoculars, and some tools that he thought might be useful from its utility compartment, continued from there on foot. The sight waiting for him when he reached the jumble of dusty rocks forming the crest and peered cautiously down was the one thing he hadn't thought of in all his conjecturing.

The ship was standing with its tail end in a pool of arc light, its wings removed and lying a short distance away on either side. In their place, two orbital-injection boosters were in the process of being attached. And the plan became clear in all its ingenuity and deviousness. The searchers could waste as much time as they wanted scouring Elysium—or anywhere else on the surface they liked; it wouldn't do them any good. For the cargo wasn't being diverted or disposed of anywhere on Mars at all. The rendezvous with another, probably longer-range craft was going to take place in orbit. Which made perfect sense in terms of getting the load the farthest distance away in the least time; and it would fetch far higher prices, say, out among the Belt frontier worlds. The only problem Kieran could see was short-term: the risk of radar detection while in orbit.

Fine. But what was he supposed to do about it? He tried tuning his suit's receiver to pick up the cross-talk between the hijackers but was unable to find the channel. To be expected, he supposed. They would be using some obscure frequency to minimize the

risk of stray signals giving them away. Kieran found
a hollow deep in shadow, where light wouldn't chance
to reflect off his helmet or equipment, and propped
himself back against a rock to contemplate the scene
and wait for some inspiration.

The two booster tubes were attached at their
forward ends, just short of the front of the Mocha's
center-body, but presumably loosely, since their tail
ends were still resting on the ground before being
lifted into line. That meant there was a fair bit of
work to be done yet—and hence time. Three suited
figures were working around the booster tails, in the
center of the lighted area. On the far side of the
Mocha, some kind of tractor vehicle mounting its own
headlamp was moving out from the sheds outlined
behind. As it came closer to the arc lights, Kieran
saw the gleam from the twin silver cylinders angling
upward like gun barrels but supporting a curved
cradle, and identified it as the mobile hydraulic ram
used to elevate a Mocha from horizontal to vertical attitude for booster launching. As he continued
watching, another figure came down the steps from
the crew module and went back to join the others.
The doorway continued emitting orange internal light.
Curious, Kieran checked with the binoculars and saw
details of the interior cabin itself, not just the inside
of the airlock chamber. It meant that both the inner
and outer lock doors were open. To avoid repeatedly
having to wait through the lock cycle to go back and
forth to the flight deck, since they were working in
suits anyway, the hijackers had tanked the cabin air
and left the entrance permanently open until they
were ready to depart. Kieran sat up as an excitement
that he already knew somewhere deep down he wasn't
going to be able to resist suddenly seized him.

Three already out, one just having joined them, and

one driving the ram unit. The five were all accounted for. And the way inside was right there, beckoning to him—at the front end, with the approach from that direction dead ground behind the ship's body. And even with Phobos in the sky, for anyone working under the arc lights, everything beyond their perimeter would be blackness anyway.

But what did he think he was going to do? . . . Yet even as he asked himself the question, a plan was forming in his mind. All craft carried a radio distress beacon as standard equipment—independent of the main systems, easily accessible, and operated by simply removing a safety latch and pushing a button. He could be in and out in a minute. The Mocha would be a flying lighthouse, and he could raise the alert when he reached the Triple S. . . . Or better still, at the cost of remaining in the Mocha a few minutes longer, he might even be able to radio from there and have the ship recovered before it got off the ground. Who'd be a "kid" soldier then, huh? He snorted to himself at the recollection. Checking through the plan revealed no flaw. Kieran pulled himself up onto his feet and began working his way around through the rocks and shadows toward the vessel's noseward side.

The approach to the ship went smoothly, as he had hoped. The ram was in place underneath the stern by this time, manned but facing away from him, its stabilizing spades extended into the ground. The final stretch had been his greatest worry. But now that he was dead ahead of the ship, he saw that the doorside booster, still angling downward from just behind the crew module to the ground, in fact screened him from the working area—a bonus which hadn't been obvious from his original vantage point. He gained the steps without a hitch, and a matter of seconds later was through the open airlock chamber and inside the access section of the crew module. The distress beacon would be somewhere around the captain's station on the flight deck. Kieran had just started climbing the steps into the forward compartment, when the whole structure lurched suddenly, causing him to grab at a handrail. The floor in front of him continued rising like a drawbridge, making him stagger backward, until he lost his footing and had to cling to an edge on the rotating wall, while the way through to the flight deck transformed into an impossible trapdoor moving up over his head. Finally, to avoid being thrown to the bottom of what was becoming a well below the lock access door—now almost lying sideways—he clawed his way into the stowage bay alongside the lock chamber and fell among the spare suits and special-duty garb that were kept there. He lay like a layer in a sandwich between items that were taking on the role of being "under," and others pressing down on him from "over," until he was fully horizontal, at which point the motion ceased. His thoughts would need a moment to reorganize, but it was already obvious what had happened: The Mocha had been elevated *before* the tail ends of the boosters were secured, not after, as he had assumed. In fact, already he could hear clunking noises coming through the structure from the stern, which sounded like the fastenings being made. *Of course! . . .* He groaned inwardly as the obvious reason came to him—too late. Why bother lifting the boosters against gravity to align them in the horizontal position, when they would align themselves automatically once the ship was vertical? And that also meant that there probably wasn't as much time left as he had presumed, either. No sooner had he thought it, when more clunks sounded, this time much closer—as if the top ends of the boosters had snapped secure and fast under a spring loading as soon as the alignment was correct. Which meant that the operation was virtually completed!

Kieran was still lying in the suiting bay, his mind a blank, waiting vainly for some continuation from there to suggest itself, when he became aware of a motor sound coming from outside the open lock now below him, getting nearer. Scuffling noises followed of somebody entering, and then a brief series of *clacks* sounded all the way up to the flight deck—a ladder being released from somewhere for forward access when the ship was vertical. A figure climbed from the chamber below and actually stopped at the suiting bay to slide shut the concertina-net that retained the contents—Kieran could *see* him through a chink in the suits and accessories burying him. A second figure followed from the lock, then a third, after which the motor noise came again, this time receding. Kieran could only conclude that the ram did double duty as a telescopic access-platform elevator—or maybe some other equipment was used. It didn't make much difference which. Either way, it seemed the crew were already boarding for departure. This was confirmed when the motor noise came again to deliver the final two hijackers. It receded once again, probably under remote control now, the two came through the lock, this time closing both doors, and followed the previous three up to the flight deck. The door up to the nose compartment slammed, and Kieran found himself left on his own.

Several minutes passed, but the indicators on the arm panel of his suit showed no sign of normal air or cabin pressure being restored. For a while, anyway, it seemed the inside would remain at suit environment conditions. Kieran couldn't think why this should be—but at least he had a supply of fresh air bottles back here. Then the whirrs and whines came of pumps and other machinery starting up within the ship. Kieran had barely finished improvising the best he could manage for a g-couch, when the boosters and main engines fired.

After the engines cut, the ship drifted in freefall for a little under an hour. Having nothing better to do, Kieran remained where he was, rearranging the contents of the bay for better concealment in case somebody decided to make a sudden excursion back. Then the engines started up again—but at low throttle, nothing like the power for liftoff from the Martian surface. Kieran's first thought was that they were maneuvering to match with another craft as he had guessed. But then came a gentle, barely perceptible jolt, followed by a short burst of scraping noises coming through the structure that sounded like the lightest of touchdowns, in the course of which Kieran felt himself sliding in the direction that had originally been "down" to make contact with his feet—barely; he felt as light as a snowflake—on what had started out being the floor when he first came aboard. Then the engines cut again.

There was some kind of gravity or gravity-equivalent out there. Conceivably, they could have matched course with some kind of rotating structure and now be sharing its centrifugal force. But the scraping sound had sounded wrong—too much like a rock-and-dust landing—which could only mean that they were on one of Mars's tiny satellites. The flight time seemed about right. And yes, of course—that would answer Kieran's question of how the hijackers hoped to hide from radar detection until their rendezvous ship arrived. Neat! If so, it would almost certainly have to be Deimos, Mars's smaller, outer moon, often described as a scarred potato, measuring something like ten miles in the long direction and seven or so across the middle. The larger moon, Phobos, about twice the size in both dimensions, was being turned into a transfer port for connections between surface shuttles and long-range vessels, and had too much work going on about its surface and in excavations to provide a hiding place. Kieran could only hope now that the hijackers' plans here didn't call for clothing or other gear from the stowage bay that he was concealed in.

He stood motionless, pressing himself against the rear wall while the earlier sequence was reversed, and the five hijackers came back from the flight deck to exit through the airlock, again leaving the doors open—it was clear now why they hadn't bothered filling the cabin for the short-duration flight. The déjà vu replay continued with jolts and internally transmitted vibrations coming through of work being done on the structure . . . and then all of a sudden it ceased, and the surroundings became uncannily still. After a while, Kieran's fears began rising that the hijackers might have departed by some other means and left him stranded here. His anxiety eventually forced him to come out and creep into the airlock chamber to risk a peek outside to see what was happening.

He found himself looking out at a miniature version of Mars—a yellow-brown desolation of dust and rock, some boulders and impact ridges, but with a black, starry sky. The Sun was low, near the close, visibly curved horizon, shedding a weak light and casting long shadows. Oddments of constructions and abandoned materials from previous visitations littered an area to one side, but there was no sign of current human presence. Yes, this could only be Deimos.

Moving to the outside of the lock chamber and edging his head past the doorway, Kieran saw now why the crew module he was in had suddenly gone quiet. The hijackers had decoupled it from the cargo frame, and two of them that Kieran could see were now working farther back, apparently preparing to disconnect the propulsion module. The intent was doubtless to ready the cargo module for pickup by a longer-range vessel—possibly, as Kieran had surmised, for onward transport to the Belt. The loading door of the cargo module was open again, and another figure glided out even as Kieran watched, making him duck his head hastily back inside the airlock again. So he was alone in the crew module, and the crew module was detached.

Hmm . . . Kieran's first plan for extracting come-uppances had failed. But the nature of the situation was already causing mischievous wheels in his head to begin turning again.

The Mocha crew module did not possess a propulsion system of its own. However, it was fitted with low-power, directable thrusters for course correction and independent maneuvering when in orbit. If Kieran's memory served him right, surface gravity on Deimos was somewhere around a thousandth of Earth normal—and it certainly felt like it. Escape velocity was only twenty feet per second—less than thirteen miles per hour. You could get off this place on a bicycle! Now, Kieran wasn't about to attempt any detailed calculations in his head, but surely, he thought, without anything else attached to it, there had to be a good chance that the maneuvering thrusters would be sufficient to get the crew module away. At least, away from Deimos—there could be no contemplating a descent to the surface of Mars, of course. But once off Deimos he would share its orbit around Mars, and from there he could radio down for a relief ship and wait in comfort and at leisure to be picked up—hero of the day, with the five hijackers captives, marooned on their rock as securely as in any lockup. It was all so deliciously simple.

With a plan of action now clear, delay could only decrease its chances. Using his arms more than his legs, Kieran hauled his way through to the flight deck, floated himself down into the pilot's station, and secured himself. Only then did the realization come that exactly what to do next wasn't as obvious as he had unwittingly assumed. Oh, like all recruits he had taken basic piloting skills during training, and as part of his self-education he had watched Bolen through the flight out from Zerolon and thought he had assimilated most of what was involved. . . . But the array of instruments and controls confronting him now seemed suddenly a lot more formidable than he remembered. And Bolen had never had reason to actually use the maneuvering thrusters.

Kieran activated the console, and after some trial and error succeeded in setting the controls to manual—he would never have deciphered the routine for directing automated sequences. Inspection of the panel labels, a system identification chart and guide that he located with one of the screens, and systematic elimination of what was irrelevant brought him to the thruster startup, throttle, and direction controls, which he figured would be all he'd need initially. From the system guide, it seemed that the thruster system coupled automatically to the manual control stick. Great news! It meant that coordinating them would be pretty much like flying a basic trainer. He could worry about how to operate the radio when he was safely off Deimos, he decided. Thus resolved, Kieran stretched a hand toward the starter switches, flexed his fingers over them for a moment, stared out at the bleak landscape while he gathered his nerve . . . and then he released the Enable safety lock.

Everything went wrong within seconds of his opening up the throttles. The nose lifted okay—faster than he had expected—and starfield filled the windshield; but the vessel carried on turning until yellow-brown rock came into view again, this time from the top, and he realized he was looping completely over. Trying to correct somehow added a rolling component, making things worse. This was nothing like regular flying. As Kieran tried desperately to pull out of what was becoming a turning, inverted dive, the craft slewed sideways, adding another dimension to what had already become too convoluted a motion for him to follow. The horizon tilted crazily with rock and sky in the wrong places, rotating, rising, and sliding by all at the same time; then the metallic bulk of the Mocha's cargo module suddenly appeared, growing larger for a split second . . . before the rending crash came, and the jolt of Kieran's being thrown against his seat harness—he might have been virtually weightless, but he still possessed mass and momentum—as the cavorting crew module slammed into it.

Kieran's senses came back together raggedly. He was practically upside down. One side of the module's nose was buckled inward, part of the hull breached, and the windshield shattered below canted control panels. Screeching sensations reaching him through the stick still gripped in his gauntlets told of metal tearing against metal as the thrusters continued driving futilely. Kieran reached out dully and cut the throttle, bringing stillness. Spray was vaporizing into the vacuum from a ruptured pipe. He didn't know what risk there might be of an explosion, but with his mental faculties still only half-functioning, his first instinct was to get out. He released the harness, fell lightly to the cabin ceiling, and clambered back over the door lintel into the access section. The airlock was angled downward,

and with some awkward contortions he lowered himself
out onto the surface, ducked from beneath the body,
and stood up. The crew module had impacted against
the far side of the cargo frame from the loading door
and now hung partly entangled in it. Kieran tested
his limbs, body, neck, and head warily. As far as he
could tell, he was unharmed. There was still no sign
of anyone else. But after what had happened, he
could hardly pretend any longer that he wasn't here.
He had no place else to go. Drawing a deep breath
of suit air to prepare himself for whatever the consequences would be now, he glided his way in light,
sailing bounds that barely seemed to touch the ground
around to the ship's other side.

The loading door was open, but no one was outside.
Kieran reached the ramp, cleared it in a slow bound,
and stopped to peer in. There was nobody inside either.
He entered to check behind and between the banks
of containers and crates. Nothing. Mystified, he came
back to the door and scanned the landscape as far as
he could see. There was nobody anywhere.

The military shuttle bringing the Skyguards relief
force arrived a little over four hours after Kieran's radio
call came in at Lowell. A Major Sileski commanded
the party, accompanied by Lieutenant Coombs, still
chagrined somewhat after his experience but relieved to
know that the news wasn't all bad. They found Kieran
looking relaxed and grinning cockily outside the open
door of the cargo module, which he had adapted into
makeshift shelter from the Sun, now high.

"We were worried about you, Thane," Coombs said,
giving Kieran a congratulatory pat on the shoulder.
"Intelligence turned up some grim things about that
bunch. They've got quite a record." He turned to survey the terrain and the ship with its partly detached

propulsion module. The upturned crew module rammed into its other side would have been visible as the shuttle descended. "So I guess they got away, eh? Too bad—but there'll be other times. The main thing for now is that you're okay. I take it you were mixed up in that crash. Are you all right? No broken bones or anything?"

"I'm fine, sir," Kieran acknowledged. His grin broadened. "And you don't have to worry about other times. Everything's under control. They didn't get away."

Coombs looked puzzled. "What do you mean?" He looked around again. "Where are they?"

"Under confinement, sir. They should be coming over pretty soon. It takes about two hours. . . ." Kieran glanced at the readout on his arm panel. "In fact, they're due again just about now."

Coombs shook his head bemusedly. Major Sileski was equally at a loss. "What are you talking about, trooper?" he demanded.

Kieran nodded his head inside his helmet to indicate the direction behind them. "About half a mile away," he said. "You have to look up." It took them several seconds to pick out the specks, a couple of them growing lighter and darker as they tumbled in the sunlight, sailing slowly toward them above the horizon. "They've spread out a bit since the last time around," Kieran commented. "I guess you'll need to send a couple of EV mobiles up to fish them down with cargo nets."

For the five hijackers were in freefall around Deimos. It so happened that they had chosen that time to hold a conference in the open bay of the cargo module, when Kieran crashed into the other side. The impact was all it had taken to eject them with sufficient velocity to attain orbit. Fortunately, they were going round in the "short" direction, in which the surface of Deimos was almost circular and didn't intersect with their trajectory anywhere. Not that it would have done them much harm if it had—the impact speed would only have been eleven miles per hour. It was fortunate because it had prevented their getting their hands on Kieran.

"My God! . . ." Coombs gaped disbelievingly. "Are they all right?"

"They were the last time I checked," Kieran said. "You can pick them up on channel one twenty-six."

The two officers adjusted their radios. Strangled shouting that Kieran recognized as Ursark's streamed in as from above, the Mocha came into sight. "*Don't think you're getting away with this! We've got your number, kid! NOBODY does this to me and walks! There's gonna be pay day! You'll find out! . . . I'm gonna send you straight to—*"

Sileski was staring at Kieran in undisguised astonishment. "It's the most extraordinary display of initiative I've ever come across," he declared. "What made you think of it?"

"I was unarmed, sir. They were five. Where else was there to put them?"

The major still looked incredulous. "What's your name, son?" he inquired curiously.

"Kieran, sir. The guys call me Knight—on account of the initials."

"Hm." Sileski nodded approvingly. "The chess piece that makes complicated moves. Well, you've sure lived up to that. You'll go a long way."

Kieran did his best to look modest—not easy, given his present circumstances and state of mind. "Yes, sir. I think I've been told that today already," he replied.

WINDOWS

Jack McDevitt

The moon was *big*. It was an enormous gasbag of a moon, like the one Uncle Eddie used to ride down at the fair grounds, when she'd stand only a few feet away, watching it strain against the lines and then cut loose and start up. She used to wish for the day Uncle Eddie would take her soaring above the treetops, but he said he couldn't because of insurance problems and eventually the gasbag went down and Uncle Eddie went with it. Janie thought of that last flight as she gazed at the foreboding presence dominating the night sky. The moon looked as if *it* was coming down. It was dim, dim as in dark, not at all like the bright yellow globe that rides the skies of Earth. It was a ghost moon, a presence, a thing lit only by stars.

"If there were more light," said the voice in her earphones, the voice that sounded a bit too cheerful,

72

"it would look silver and blue. Its name is Charon, and it's less than a third the diameter of our moon."

"Why does it look so big?" asked Daddy.

"Do you know how far the Moon is from the Earth?"

Daddy wasn't sure. "About a million miles," he said.

"That's close, Mr. Brockman." The AI was very polite.

"I think," said Janie, trying not to sound like a know-it-all, "it's 238,000 miles."

"That's very good, Janie. Right on the button. But Charon is only twelve thousand miles away."

Janie did the arithmetic in her head. Multiply by ten and Charon was still only half, one-twentieth of the distance of *her* moon. "It's close," she said. She'd known that, but hadn't understood the implications. "It's right on top of us."

"Very good, Janie," said the voice. It belonged to a software system that was identical to the AI that had made the later flights, the Iris voyages, the *Challenger* run, the Long Mission, and the circumsolar flight on the *Eagle*. All the data from those missions had been fed into it, so in a sense, it had been there.

Its name was Jerry. Same as the originals. The onboard AI was always *Jerry*, named for Jerry Dilworth, a popular late-night comic of an earlier era. Daddy had commented how much the voice sounded like Jerry Dilworth, for whom Daddy had a lot of affection.

The sky was dark. This place never really experienced daylight. She wondered what it would be like to live where the sun never rose.

"But it *does* rise," Daddy explained.

"I know," she said. He meant well, but sometimes he just seemed to go out of his way to misunderstand her. Of course it rose, and for all she knew it might be up there now among all those stars, but who could tell? It was no more than a light beam.

She lowered her gaze and looked out across the frozen surface, past the Rover. A few low hills broke the monotony of a flat snowfield. It was lonely, quiet, scary. *Solitudinous.* Janie liked making up new words from the vocabulary list.

The Rover was the sole man-made object on the planet. It looked like a tank, with sensors and antennas aimed in all directions. The International Consortium seal, a blue-white globe, was stenciled on its hull.

"It's really much lighter than it looks," said Jerry. *"Especially here, where the gravity is light."*

"Nobody's ever been to Pluto, Janie," said Daddy. "It's very far."

Of course no one had been to Uranus or Neptune either. But never mind.

A bright star appeared over the hills and began climbing. *"Do you know what it is, Janie?"* Jerry asked.

She was puzzled. Another moon? Was there a second moon she didn't know about?

Daddy put his hand on her shoulder. "That's the Ranger," he said.

Oh, yes. Of course. Given another moment she'd have thought of it herself. "I know, Daddy," she said.

" . . . Orbits Pluto every forty-three minutes and twelve seconds."

The place *felt* cold. She pulled her jacket around her shoulders. This little stretch of ground, the hills, the plain, the snow, had been like this for millions of years, and nothing had ever happened until the Ranger showed up. No dawn, no rain, nobody passing through.

"Once in a while," said Jerry, *"the ground shakes a little."*

"That's it?" asked Daddy.

"That's the whole shebang." Jerry waited, perhaps expecting another question. When no one said anything, he returned to his narrative: *"The snow isn't the kind of snow you'd see at home. It's frozen carbon monoxide and methane. . . ."*

He went on like that for a few minutes but Janie was no longer listening. When he paused she touched her father's arm. "Daddy, why did the missions stop?" The magazines said it was because there was no place else to go, but that couldn't be right.

"Oh, I don't know, honey," he said. "I think it was because they cost too much."

"In fact," said Jerry, *"unmanned missions are much more practical. Not only because it's a lot cheaper to send an instrument package rather than a person, but also because a lot more can be accomplished. They're safe, and the scientific payoff is considerably better."*

"That's right," said Daddy.

"People can't go on deep-space missions without getting damaged. Radiation. Zero gravity. It's a hostile environment out there."

This was the reason Janie had come. To put her question to the machines that ran the missions. To get it straight from the horse's mouth. "Jerry," she said, "I can understand why you would like to go, but what's the point of running the missions if *we* have to stay home?"

She could almost hear Jerry thinking it over. *"It's the only practical way,"* he said finally, *"to explore the environment. But it's a good way. Most bang for the buck. And nobody gets hurt."*

Daddy squeezed her hand.

"Seen enough, Janie?" the AI asked.

She didn't answer. After a moment the snowscape and the Rover blinked off and she was sitting with sixty or so people in the viewing room. Music started playing and the audience began talking and getting up and heading for the doors. A group of teens in front of her were deciding about going down to the gift shop for a snack. Somebody in back wondered where the bathroom was.

"That was pretty good," said Daddy.

They drifted out with the crowd. Janie had never been to Washington before, had never been to the Smithsonian. She'd done the virtual tour, of course, but it wasn't like this, where she could *touch* a coffee cup that had been to Europa, pass through the cabin of the *Olympia*, from which Captain D'Assez had looked down for the first time on the Valhalla impact basin. She could try on a suit like the one that Napoleon Janais had worn on Titan. And stand before the Mission Wall, where plaques honored each of the thirty-three deep-space flights.

They wandered down the shining corridors, lined with artifacts and images from the Space Age. Here was a cluster of antennas from Archie Howard's transmit station in the Belt, where he'd directed operations for almost a year until someone decided that mining asteroids wasn't really feasible and the whole project collapsed. And Mark Pierson's jacket, with the logo for Jupiter VI, the mission which had made it back leaking air and water while the entire world watched breathlessly. And a replica of the plaque left on Iapetus. *Farthest from home. Saturn IX. August 3, 2066.*

There were portraits of Yuri Gagarin, Gus Grissom, Christa McAuliffe, Ben MacIntyre, Huang Chow, Margaret Randauer, the whole range of heroes who had taken the human race out toward the stars over the course of almost a century.

"Are we ever going back, Daddy?" she asked.

He looked puzzled. "Home, you mean? Of course."

"No. I meant, to the moon. To Mars. To Europa."

Daddy was a systems technician in a bank. He was more serious than the other kids' dads. Didn't like to play games, although he tried. He even pretended he enjoyed them but she knew he would rather be doing something else than playing basketball with her. But he never yelled at her, and he encouraged her to say what she thought even if they might not share the same opinion. It was hard for him. She couldn't remember her mother, who had died when she was two. He studied her, and then looked around at the pictures of Luna Base, of a crescent Jupiter, of Deimos, of a launch gantry at the Cape. "I don't think so, darling," he said.

They were standing just outside the exhibition hall, which contained a mock-up of Mars Base. She could see part of the dome, a truck, and an excavation site.

"There's no point in people going," Daddy was saying. "Robots can do everything we can, can go anywhere, and it's safer."

"Daddy, I'd love to see Charon. Really *see* it."

"I know. We all would, love." She could tell he had no idea what she was talking about. "The money that's been saved by not sending people out there has been put into doing real science. Long-range missions to the edge of the solar system. And beyond." He smiled, the way he did when he was going to do a joke. "Of course, I won't be here when the long ones get where they're going. But *you* will. You'll get to see pictures of whatever's at Alpha Centauri and, what is it, Something-Eridani. That wouldn't have happened if we'd stayed with the manned program." He waited for a response. "Do you understand what I'm saying, Janie?"

"Yes, Daddy."

Where, Janie wondered, was Hal Barkowski?

"He was something of an embarrassment," said Daddy. "I think they'd just as soon everyone forgot him."

Hal was the father of artificial intelligence. He'd been Janie's hero as far back as she could remember, not because of his work with advanced sentient systems, but because he'd been at Seaside Station on Europa when President Hofstatter, during her first month in office, cut off U.S. support for the international space program. The ships had been ordered home, everything and everybody, but Barkowski had insisted on staying at Seaside, had refused to come back even when the last ship left, had stayed and directed the machines until they'd broken through the ice. He'd sent the sub down into the ocean and kept reporting for seventeen months, but the survey had revealed nothing alive, nothing moving in those chilly depths, and eventually, when he was sure no one would be coming back to get him, he'd shut down the base AI, told the world that the president of the United States was a nitwit. And then he'd opened his air tanks.

"He thought," Daddy told her, "that he could bluff them. That he was too important, had won too many awards, that they couldn't just abandon him. I thought so too. We all did." He shook his head at the man's arrogance. "Didn't happen."

Louise Hofstatter was still in office and was immensely popular. Though not with Janie.

She had been seven years old when they'd left

Europa, and she'd prayed for Barkowski, had gone to bed every night thinking how it must be for him all by himself millions of miles from anyone else. She hadn't understood it then, hadn't been able to grasp why he'd stayed behind. That was probably because the search hadn't been successful, no life had been found, and it had seemed such a waste. But she knew now why he'd done it. The search was all that mattered. What you found or didn't find was beside the point. She prided herself thinking that, if she'd been there instead of Barkowski, she'd have done the same thing.

Daddy led the way into the Martian exhibit, and they looked at the world flag and the excavation gear and Janie climbed onto the truck and sat in the front seat, pretending to drive. The sun was high overhead, pale and small, but the sky was dark anyhow, though not nearly like the sky at Pluto.

"Hello, Janie." The voice startled her. It came out of the earphones, female this time. It sounded like Miss Harbison over at Roosevelt. "Welcome to Mars."

"Thank you."

"My name is Ginger, and I'm the base AI. Is there anything you'd like to know?"

"How fast will this go? The truck?"

"It's capable of speeds up to fifty-five miles per hour, although we wouldn't run it that fast."

"Why not?"

"We don't have roads. It would be dangerous."

"What does it use for fuel?"

"It uses batteries."

She imagined herself bouncing over the uneven terrain. *Vroom.* Look out for that ditch. Cut hard on the wheel.

Ginger explained how the base had functioned, showed her where the landers had been serviced, how fuel had been extracted from the ground, provided a simulated flight in an orbiting communication satellite. She'd raced above the red sands, chirping with joy, and thought how it must have been to lift away from Moonbase and ride the rockets out to Io and Titan. She laughed and begged Ginger for more.

She was accustomed to the house AI and the school AI and the AI down at Schrodinger's. They were all wooden and serious and addressed you with tiresome formality. The one at school even yelled at you if you blocked the corridor while classes were changing. But Jerry had seemed more realistic, somehow. More like a person. And Ginger sounded vaguely as if she would have enjoyed a good party. "Were you actually there, Ginger?" she asked, pulling off the VR helmet. "Mars?"

"No. I've never been out of the museum."

"Oh." She shifted her position on the truck seat, which was too big for her.

"I'm the same model, though."

"Will you have a chance to go someday?"

"To Mars?"

"Yes."

"Marsbase is shut down, Janie."

"Well, yes, I mean, I knew that. But I meant, will you have a chance to travel on one of the missions?"

"No. I don't think so."

"I'm sorry."

There was a tinkling sound like water tumbling over rocks. As if Ginger was having problems with a relay. Or reacting without words. *"It's okay. I'm only a data processing system. I don't have emotions. No need to feel sorry for me."*

"You seem *too* alive to be just software."

"I think that's a compliment. Thank you."

"May I ask a question?"

"*Of course.*"

"How old are you, Ginger?"

"*Fifteen years, eight months, four days. Why do you ask?*"

"I was just curious." And after a moment: "You're older than I am."

"*Yes. Does that matter?*"

"Are you aware that you're an AI?"

"*Ah, a philosophical young lady, I see. Must be top of the class.*"

"I'm serious."

"*Wouldn't you rather just look at the rest of the base?*"

"No. Please. Are you aware who you are?"

"*Yes. Of course.*"

"But you're not supposed to be, are you? I thought AIs were *not* conscious."

"*Well, who's to know? My instructions call for me to give the illusion of consciousness. But whoever knows for sure what's conscious and what isn't? Maybe that stairway over there is watching us.*"

"You're kidding me."

"*Not entirely.*"

It was hard to believe. But Janie thought about the AIs going out to the Oort Cloud, and the one headed for Alpha Centauri, who wouldn't get there for a thousand years.

Riding alone.

Like Hal Barkowski on Europa.

She climbed down, making room for a pushy ten-year-old boy. Daddy told her she looked as if she'd have made a good astronaut. He said it as if she were only ten herself but she controlled her irritation. "Daddy," she said, "do they really not feel anything?"

"Who is that, honey?"

"The AIs."

"That's correct. They're just machines."

"Including Jerry and Ginger."

"Yes. Just machines." He actually seemed to be enjoying the exhibit. He was looking around, shaking his head in awe. "Hard to believe we actually managed to send people to all those places. Quite an achievment."

"Daddy, how do we know? That they're just machines?"

"That's a tough one," he said. "We just do."

"But how?"

"Your friend Barkowski, for one reason. He says so. And he designed the first generation of sentient systems." He glanced at her. "In this case," he added, "*sentient* doesn't literally mean aware." He held up an index finger and spoke into his mike. When he'd finished he nodded. "Ginger tells me all the deep-space systems were designed by him."

"That would include her," said Janie.

He shrugged. "I suppose so."

They went into the dome, which was pretty primitive. Plastic tables and chairs, a bank of monitors, some obsolete computer equipment, a half-dozen cots. Windows looked out over the reddish sand. She approached one and thought how the landscape never changed. Like Pluto. No lights anywhere. No movement. No rain. No flowers. Zip.

Maybe Daddy was right. Maybe people should stay home.

"You don't really believe that." Ginger's voice again. Different now. More intense. *"Hold on to the dream, Janie. Interplanetary vehicles should have viewports and bases should have windows. And there should be somebody to look out the window. If we don't have*

that, we'll take the temperature of Neptune and not get much else."

"That's a strange way for an AI to talk."

"Whatever."

"You can look, Ginger. You have sensors. You can probably see better than I can."

"No. I can look, but I can't see. I can't describe what's out there. I can't penetrate things the way you do."

Janie laughed, but she felt the hair rise on the back of her neck. "Are you sure you don't have any feelings?"

"Absolutely." The voice was serene again.

"And you think people should go? On the long flights?"

"I think you *should go."*

"Me?"

"Somebody should go who can get out of the ship and look at the peaks on the moon and know what it means. Someone should throw a party on Io. Someone should capture her feelings in a poem that people will still be reading a thousand years from now."

"Yeah," she said. "I'd love to do that."

"Then do it."

"But how? There's no program anymore. I can't ride on the ships they send out now."

"How old are you, Janie?"

"I'm thirteen."

"A child."

"I'm *not* a child."

"It's okay. You won't always be so young."

"I'm a teenager."

"Your time will come. When it does, take hold of the hour. Make it count."

❖   ❖   ❖

"The AI said you could go to Alpha Centauri?"

"Not exactly, Daddy. She told me, when I got the chance, I should go."

"Probably tells that to all the kids."

"It seemed a strange thing to say."

"It probably has a bug somewhere. Don't worry about it." They strode out through the doors onto Constitution Avenue. It was damp and rainy, but the air smelled of approaching spring. "They ought to do something about the damned things. Get them fixed." Daddy flagged down a taxi and they climbed in. He gave Aunt Floss's address, where they were staying, and the vehicle slipped back into traffic. "Encouraging kids to do crazy stuff. It's probably Barkowski's programming. Man dumb enough to miss the last bus off Europa, what can you expect?"

I was introduced to this author by Jim Baen, who bought his first novel, Warp Speed, out of the slush pile—er, from the backlog of unsolicited manuscripts. Based on that book, full of exuberant, old time SF feeling, and the fact of the author's multiple degrees, Jim decided that SF had gone long enough without a "Doc" in the house. Dr. Travis Taylor was given the nickname "Doc" by his students some years back. Like the legendary E.E. "Doc" Smith of Lensman fame, "Doc" Travis was ready to take his place in the pantheon of SF writers. The author assures me this story could take place within the next seventy-five years, sooner if the solar sails he is working on with NASA get funded. . . .

CLEANING LADY

Travis S. Taylor

It really had been a good idea. I mean there are plenty of asteroids that are big enough to cause problems if they hit the Earth that pass by our orbit every three or four years. So it was a good idea for us to figure out ways to "clean up" the local neighborhood a little. I'm not a scientist or an engineer, I'm just your typical lady sailor, but I can tell you right out that we never considered the consequences of space terrorists!

I had been driving solar sails for about ten years for one of the larger mining guilds when the eggheads came up with the idea of cleaning up the near-Earth objects (NEOs) that might one day cause a threat to Earth. It looked like fun work and a steady paycheck, which I needed, so I sent in my resume. I was more than qualified; after all, I have sailed more than six medium-sized asteroids from the far side of the asteroid belt to the mining station near Eros. You see, it's easy to radar and seismograph search the Belt for mineral-rich asteroids. The things are typically small enough that two or three good solar sailing tugs can pull them in to the mining facility in short order. The larger ones have to be brought in by bi-modal nuclear thermal and nuclear electric propulsion barges or mined on the spot, which is much more dangerous.

Well, I was hauling in a small rock from the Earth-side of the Belt to the mine when I got the call to come work for the "cleaning crew." I was more than happy to get into the government union and out of the commercial mining guild. Sailing about the Belt was fun, don't get me wrong, but it was more like treasure hunting than a career and until you find a big treasure you go hungry.

As a "cleaning lady" I would be a civil servant and have all the benefits that go with that; I was looking forward to knowing I would get three squares a day again. So what was the new job? I would fly helmsman on a new one-hundred-kilometer-diameter hoop-supported solar sail ship made of the new superlightweight carbon-carbon nanotube fiber mesh. The total spacecraft mass is only about three thousand kilograms. *Wow!*

My job on this great new ship would be to fly in formation with two others and we'd go out to a matching orbit with a particular NEO as it came in on its perihelion or its closest approach to the sun. These Earth-crossing NEOs typically have perihelia at about one astronomical unit. In other words, they come into Earth's orbit twice on their way around the Sun. Occasionally they time this right and smack right into the Earth. That's what took care of the dinosaurs, most likely.

I've been a "cleaning lady" for a little more than two years now and it has really been fun. The idea works great: we fly over and meet the NEO and the three formation-flying sailing ships spread out around it with a tether connecting all three. The tether is made of some new-fangled carbon-nanotube-spun fiber or some such damn thing. Like I said, I'm not a scientist, but I can tell you that the fiber tethers are the strongest rope ever put together by mankind. An engineer ex-boyfriend of mine told me that a piece of the tether the thickness of a human hair could hold up a nuke tug in one gravity, and those damn things weigh over twenty thousand kilograms! I since checked on it and he was right. Of course, that is the only thing that that sorry SOB didn't lie to me about. Anyway, sorry I get irked when I think about Johnny; he just up and left more than a year ago now and never called me back.

After we catch the NEO with the tether net, we tug on the thing with the sailing ships as much as we can in order to alter its orbit. Here is the really cool part: we alter the orbit of the NEO just enough so that not only will it never hit the Earth, but it definitely will hit Mars in a few orbits. Each orbit of these NEOs is only about four or so years long so they end up at Mars pretty quickly. Why hit Mars? Why hit Mars!? Have you been living under a rock?!

People have plenty of room on Earth right now, but in less than a hundred years at the rate we are growing there won't even be elbowroom! Mars is close and almost Earth-like. If we increase the temperature on Mars and add some dust to its atmosphere, in just a few decades, or maybe a century, it might be livable. Oh, we will still probably have to wear oxygen masks, but no need for pressure suits. Once the NASA boys and girls were through playing around on Mars and decided that there wasn't any life there that we could harm, it was decided to try our hand at terraforming. Of course the environmental wackos have been bitching about altering God's natural habitat ever since, but I don't hold stock in any of that.

Actually, the real reason for the terraforming wasn't terraforming at all. That NEO that just missed the Moon about eight years ago really had scared the public enough to initiate the politicians into the new policy of "cleaning up the neighborhood." The egg-heads came up with the idea to kill two birds with one stone. In fact, it makes sense that if the rock is taken out of space then it ain't likely to hit Earth now don't it?

So that decision was made about twelve years ago and we had successfully removed seventeen asteroids and already crashed them into Mars. About ten other asteroids would be impacting Mars in a few short years and we were currently chasing many more and altering their orbits.

I was coming off a two-month vacation Earthside and had to hook up with my sail tug crew as they caught up with the newest NEO acquisition at its perihelion near Earth. I would pack up tomorrow and then catch an Earth-to-orbit (ETO) hop up to the Elevator and from there I would take the Elevator up to geosynchronous earth orbit (GEO). At GEO my plans were to catch a lift with a nuke tug to match orbits with my sailcraft, the *Boy's Life*.

But for now, I had one more day on the beach. Two months ago when I came into Cocoa Beach as soon as I got home, there was Johnny. We had argued and fought and I told him to get lost, but he just wouldn't leave. After about two weeks of his persistence I gave in and he had been with me ever since. I expected that he would leave me again just like he had the year before, but Johnny is cute, good in the sack, and besides I'm going back to spacing for another year or so anyway. I deserve a pleasurable fling every now and then, right?

The last night Johnny and I were lying beside each other on the beach looking up at the night sky. The Elevator was particularly bright.

"Isn't that beautiful, Tamara?" He pointed up at the Elevator and stroked my hair with his other hand.

"Sure it is, John-boy. But you should see it from up there. The view is much better," I told him.

"Well, I just might. I wasn't going to tell you until tomorrow but . . . I signed on with a nuke tug crew."

"Really?" Johnny had never been a spacer; in fact he was more of an environmentalist. "I would have never expected that."

"This way I thought I might get closer to you somehow." He smiled and batted his eyes at me. I kind of giggled.

"Johnny, once I get on the *Boy's Life* I will be there for the better part of a year. Orbital mechanics just doesn't allow any diverging from that schedule. I don't see how you will get any closer to me. In fact, you will probably be much further away." I told him that perhaps he could get out of flying on a nuke tug if he explained he had no clue of how such things worked.

"Oh, I realize that. I am an engineer, you know,"

he stated. "I meant closer metaphorically. Besides, it will be different and fun and I'm looking forward to seeing you off tomorrow. My tug is the one that you're taking to your solar sail." He smiled again.

Our last night on Earth was a good one.

The next morning I showered and shaved and clipped my hair down to regulation. Johnny and I dressed and then made our way over to the Cape. We both processed through customs and met our respective organization representatives to punch in our start time and then we boarded the ETO rocket. I never will get used to the ETO hops. The three gravities are pretty rough and the fear of one of those millions of moving parts seizing up and no longer moving scares the hell out of me. The outcome of one of those parts stopping while extremely hot volatiles are flowing through them doesn't sound appealing to me. But we made it safely to the Space Elevator just above low earth orbit (LEO).

The Elevator is really just a huge solid and rigid tether with compartments attached to it. Elevator cars ride up and down the tether causing a momentum transfer to and from the tether. Since the cars weigh much less than the rigid tether, the tether's orbit is only lowered a few meters while the Elevator car's orbit rises many thousands of kilometers. Johnny explained to me that there was something about conservation of momentum involved here. I understood how the damned thing worked but I guess Johnny felt more like a smart engineer getting to explain it to me. I just kept my mouth shut and acted the dumb blonde.

At the top of the Elevator we hopped Johnny's nuke tug, the *Prometheus,* and pressed onward for the *Boy's Life.* I pointed out the view of Earth to Johnny and he watched out the portal the whole trip—well, except for when he was throwing up. The high-gravity, microgravity, and low-gravity mix of our trip had really taken a toll on him. I kind of felt sorry for him. But by the time we were approaching my sail a week later, he had acclimated himself to the environment pretty well.

Johnny and I kissed and said our goodbyes and then went our separate ways. Or so I had thought. By the time I embarked and ingressed to the command cabin of the *Boy's Life*, the *Prometheus* had come about and passed close enough to one of the tethers holding the sail formation and the NEO to burn through it with its ion propulsion system's plasma exhaust. Captain Billy was hailing the *Prometheus* and not being very successful at it. After a moment or two of confusion, Billy finally got through and a video image from the bridge of the nuke ship came through. It was Johnny's face on the screen!

"This is the Mars Environmental Protection Organization telling the people of Earth that it is wrong to bombard other planets with disaster from space. We will show you what it is like!" Johnny's face was bloodied and there were several bodies lying lifeless on the bridge of the *Prometheus*. Several other men and women were standing around Johnny with automatic weapons. How they had gotten those weapons on board is still a mystery to this day.

"Johnny! What are you doing?" I cried, neglecting bridge protocol. The captain just eyed me with his peripheral vision. We were friends and he had trusted me for years.

"Ah, my sweet Tamara. You have been corrupted by the expansionist nature of the evil capitalists and will have to learn that what you are doing to Mars is wrong!"

"You're nuts!" I screamed and then the *Boy's*

Life listed and lurched and I knew that Johnny had burned us loose from the NEO as well. The low-mass solar sail spacecraft had been cut loose and was beginning to pitch forward. Of course it was pitching very slowly and it would take days for the two hundred-kilometer-diameter disk to pitch through ninety degrees. I jumped into my helmsman seat and began counteracting the unexpected forces or lack thereof. Then I set the automated correction algorithms to full control of the pitch-correction controls. The computer would make the minor adjustments to the control sail vanes and solar light pressure would remove the unwanted pitch in a few hours.

With two of the sailing ships now untethered from the NEO it only made sense for the third ship to let go as well. The NEO was on its outbound leg and now had odd perturbations to its orbit. There is no way that the slight perturbations would push the sail into Earth in short term. Even if its orbit were modified enough that it would impact Earth in a few orbits or so, we could simply come out and catch it with another sail formation and fly it out of the way. I didn't understand what these so-called Mars Environmental Protection Organization nuts had in mind.

"Captain," I asked, "are there protocols for dealing with this type of thing?"

"Well, there probably are but I've never heard of them," Captain Billy replied.

"Yeah, this has never happened before to my knowledge and I've been flying sail tugs for years." What should we do? The sail tethers would have to be reconnected before we could grab the asteroid and it would take hours to do that.

The navigator, Carol "Jelly" Wilson, looked up from

her computer system. "Captain, I think I understand what they have in mind."

"Well, don't keep us hanging, Jelly," he said.

"The orbit of the NEO now tracks right over the Belt, sir."

"So what, Jelly? It will go over the Belt not hitting anything," I responded.

"Well, yeah, Tami, but . . . they only need a few meters per second of delta-V to bring the inclination down. If they bring the inclination down just a few degrees then the NEO will plow right through the top of the Belt."

"I see," Captain Billy said. "They want to play bumper pool with the Belt and scatter rocks throughout the system!"

"That's right, sir. And with that nuke tug they have more than enough delta-V to do just that." Jelly frowned and shook her head.

"With that many collisions I don't know if we could stop all of the newly created NEOs," I said. "The Earth could be totally devastated!"

"Then it's settled. We can't let them push down the inclination of that rock." The captain ordered, "Jelly, see if we can plot a course that will allow us to catch them and drag it back up out of harm's way."

"Yes, sir!"

Jelly worked on the course trajectory for about an hour or so. There was no big hurry; the Belt was weeks away and she had calculated that the nuke tug would have to push the NEO continuously for four or five days to move it down enough into the ecliptic to cause problems. We had time. What we didn't have was speed or maneuverability.

By the time Jelly had finished her calculations, the nuke tug had positioned itself against the NEO and had started pushing it. Captain Billy had discussed options with the other sail tug drivers and with headquarters but nobody had come up with a solution. We were far enough from other vessels that nobody could catch us in time to help. All we could do was to sit and watch. So all three of the sail tugs floated along behind the asteroid in loose formation just in case we came up with an idea.

Jelly did believe that we could net the NEO and pull it up and over the Belt since the solar sail propulsion ships don't run out of fuel this close to the Sun, because sunlight is the fuel. The nuke tug, on the other hand, would run out of reaction mass if it ran continuously in just eight or nine days and there would be no way it could push the NEO all the way to the Belt. We were more than two weeks from the Belt and had many kilometers of tether, so we could just hook up the tethers, catch the NEO again, and pull it up against the nuke tug until it ran out of fuel. We would prevail because we had an endless fuel supply and the nuke tug didn't. So we had figured out a plan.

We suited up and took the long ride from the control room, located in the hoop on the circumference of the sail tug, down one of the radial support beams to the central hub of the sail. The tether system is located in the middle of the sail on the central hub so the force from dragging the NEO is in the center of pressure and mass of the sail. You see, the sail is really a giant hula-hoop two hundred meters in diameter. The hoop itself is two stories thick and this is where the crew lives. There are also three support booms (one every hundred and twenty degrees) that run radially from the hoop inward to the central hub where the tether mechanisms are. The hoop and booms are made of carbon-nanotube-reinforced polymers and titanium struts. The sail material itself is a carbon-carbon nanotube fiber mesh. There are heavier-duty compartments spread about the hoop to offer crew protection in case of solar flares, but the ship is mostly super-lightweight stuff.

We spent hours outside in pressure suits repairing the tether release mechanisms and setting them up for a NEO catch. Normally we just let go of the tether and if we want to hook up again we just reel out more tether and the super-small coffee-can-sized satellite or picosatellite on the end of the tether flies to meet the picosatellites from the other two sail tugs. The problem here was that when the tethers are usually released there is an automatic tension placed on the tether reel to avoid a backlash or "bird's nest" to spring backward into the tether reel. If the reel is let free with no tension on the tether, the entire tether tries to unwind itself while still on the spool. So we had a knotted-up and tangled-up mess that we had to unwind while in spacesuits. That was not an easy task and it took hours. But once we got the "bird's nest" loose and unwound, we spooled the tether tight and hooked up the next picosatellite in the hopper. Our counterpart sail tugs had to go through the same process. We were all real tired after this and I was expecting to put in for extra class hazard pay for the unscheduled EVA.

Unfortunately, the nuke tugs can be somewhat maneuverable and once we had netted the NEO, Johnny simply stopped pushing the NEO and burned through the tethers with his exhaust plasma again. The tether backlash on one of the other sail tugs, the *Tsander*, was reported to be so bad that it would take weeks to fix. The *Boy's Life* and the *Tsiolkovsky* were in good shape and could be fixed with another tiring EVA. But we could no longer drag the NEO with just two sail tugs; there just wasn't enough delta-V. So the plan was no good.

Three days had passed and we still had no idea what to do. We had fixed the tethers that were fixable, but what could we do with them? Captain Billy had told us that he wanted the ship in proper order because you never know what you can use during a crisis. This was most definitely a crisis since one more day of the *Prometheus* pushing the NEO and it would be enough to cause serious problems in the Belt. Jelly had also figured out that the mining facility would be totally destroyed as the NEO passed through the Belt. We had to do something. But what?

I was on break and so I planned to spend some time in my quarters resting and thinking and cursing Johnny. It turns out that he used me as a reference to get on the nuke tug crew. Having told them that I would vouch for him got him through a lot of hoops. He must have been setting this terrorist thing up for some time and had been planning to use me. That's why he suddenly came back into my life and wouldn't leave. He needed me for his plan to work. That sack of shit!

The hoop is so large that you can barely feel the curvature as you walk it. It is two stories wide and the sail is rolled slightly to give a light artificial gravity field. I was "moonwalking," as we call it, to my quarters when the fire alarm went off. The automated alarm said there was smoke detected in Floor One, Degree Nineteen. This meant that the fire was in a room on the outer floor and at nineteen degrees clockwise from the command center. In other words, about a half of a degree from my present location, so I went from a "moonwalk" to a "moonrun." I beat the fire team to the fire. One of the new crew members had left a makeup mirror out with the curved side facing the window. As we listed forward and the window let sunlight into the room, it hit the makeup mirror, which in turn focused the sunlight onto the bed across the room. The bedspread had begun to smolder and the smoke set off the alarm. The fire marshal presently chewed out the rookie, but I wanted to kiss her!

I turned back toward the command center direction and "moontrotted" down the hoop. I was out of breath when I got there so I had to relax a second before I could speak.

"Captain . . . *huff puff* . . . I've got it!" I said.

"What've you got, Tami?" Jelly asked.

"We burn the nuke tug up!" I panted some more.

"How do you propose we do that?" Jelly asked sarcastically.

"Let her finish, Jelly," Captain Billy scolded her.

"We tether the center of one of the sails to another sail tug and have them sail in opposite directions. The tension of the tether pulling on the center of the sail and the resistance of the sail's support booms to the tension will cause the sails to be curved toward each other just like when we pull a NEO. Then we point one of the sails concave side toward the Sun at an angle that will reflect the light and focus it on the nuke tug. We will burn them by focusing the light with the sail just like you can burn ants with a magnifying lens or bedspreads with a makeup mirror!"

"Would that be enough energy to burn a spaceship hull?" Jelly asked.

"Well," the captain said, "the sail is one hundred thousand meters in radius. Square that and multiply by pi and you get a surface area of nearly thirty-two billion square meters! Our distance from the Sun is about one-point-two astronomical units so there is about a kilowatt per square meter of sunlight here. Multiply the two and you get more than 3×10^{13} watts of sunlight that can be collected and focused. Even if the sail is only thirty-percent efficient at reflecting light to the target we would still have $1x10^{13}$ watts on target. I would say that is plenty!"

"Johnny," I stared him down through the video screen. "You are an idiot and a bastard and you can't just use people this way. Also, how does killing millions of people on Earth help your case, hunh? You're stupid and it's time you saw the light!" I had timed my hail to them with the moment that the sail tug pitched at the right angle. And then more than $1x10^{13}$ watts of focused sunlight swept across the NEO onto the nuke tug. As the intense beam of sunlight swung through the dust cloud surrounding the NEO, sparkles and flashes from the tiny grains of asteroid vaporizing tracked with the beam. The focused beam burned across the NEO, leaving a scorched mark, and then the light settled onto Johnny's hijacked tug. The tug vaporized almost immediately and out-gassed into space.

After that little incident, we realized that we should pay closer attention to security in our space fleet. A positive outcome of the incident was, we realized, that we could use the sail as a mirror, and push or vaporize the NEOs as we needed. We didn't even need to sail out to them. We would stay in near Earth's orbit and focus sunlight onto whatever we needed to with these gigantic mirrors. Oh, people had thought of it before but never knew how to implement the idea. I guess thanks to Johnny, we figured out how to do it. And also, the wackos sort of disappeared into the woodwork and we never heard from them much anymore.

Soon, I hear that an array of sail mirrors is going to be aimed at Mars to add even more energy to the ecosystem there. I hope to get a job steering one of those things so I can continue being a "cleaning lady." Of course the NEOs will still have to be pushed into Mars at least for a few more decades, but we all firmly believe that one day we will have a nice livable neighbor in Mars and a "clean neighborhood" to boot!

Here's a bit more background on "Doc" Taylor—he's earned his soubriquet the hard way: he has a doctorate in optical science and engineering, a master's degree in physics, a master's degree in aerospace engineering, all from the University of Alabama in Huntsville; a master's degree in astronomy from the University of Western Sydney, and a bachelor's degree in electrical engineering from Auburn University.

Dr. Taylor has worked on various programs for the Department of Defense and NASA for the past sixteen years. He's currently working on several advanced propulsion concepts, very large space telescopes, space-based beamed energy systems, and next-generation space launch concepts.

In his copious spare time, Doc Travis is also a black belt martial artist, a private pilot, a scuba diver, has raced mountain bikes, competed in triathlons, and has been the lead singer and rhythm guitarist of several hard rock bands. He currently lives with his wife Karen, two dogs, Stevie and Wesker, and his two cats, Neko and Kuro, in north Alabama.

ARE WE THERE YET?

Travis S. Taylor

With the advent of the recent mess in America's space program and inherent problems with the Space Shuttle and the cost overruns on the International Space Station (ISS), we begin to wonder if we are ever going to really get into space and have wonderful adventures like Tamara does in "Cleaning Lady." For the general public it must seem as though the evolution of space exploration came to screeching halt, or at least a slow crawl, after the Apollo program. Some of this "going nowhere" feeling is true, but there is a significant amount of research and engineering going on today in the aerospace community that will bring us closer to space. Of course, what we have mostly seen is the bad press and the disasters. What will be discussed here are the success stories and the hopeful outlook on getting us into space and enabling adventures worthy of science fiction.

To start with we have to be able to get off the planet. Tamara in "Cleaning Lady" rode a rocket into space to get out of Earth's gravity well. Heinlein said in various ways that once we get out of the Earth's gravity well you are halfway to anywhere you want to go. This implies that getting out of Earth's gravity well, or to orbit is half of space travel. Indeed it is. Presently our best way to get man and machines into orbit is with the Space Shuttle, but the Shuttle is limited to only about three hundred or so mile-high orbits. If we want to send people, or anything for that matter, to orbits higher than the ISS then we will have to build something new. Of course there are expendable launch vehicles that will lift satellites to much higher orbits. The Atlas V and the Delta IV Heavy boosters can lift nearly 15,000 kilograms to an elliptical orbit as high as 35,000 kilometers at the peak. But these rockets are not designed to carry people and since the Apollo days man has been limited to ISS-type low Earth orbits (LEOs).

The Russians and the Chinese also have rockets similar to the Apollo systems that can carry people into space (the Chinese have yet to fly humans but soon will) but they are also limited to LEO for the most part. The foreign rockets, Space Shuttle, and the American expendable rockets all use typical combustion engines that implement some sort of volatile like kerosene, liquid hydrogen or hydrazine. These are highly explosive materials and therefore make these Earth-to-orbit (ETO) rockets very dangerous. That is why they are so expensive; it takes a tremendous amount of engineering effort to make them even moderately safe for the crews who fly them.

NASA has plans to make these systems safer and more cost effective and to reach more useful orbits. This plan was previously the X program rocket systems and was hopefully going to lead to the Venture Star reusable single stage to orbit spacecraft. The X-33 was to be the first demonstrator of this program but there were technical and programmatic issues that caused the program to be canceled a few years back. Recognizing the need and public outcry for a better manned initiative, NASA followed the defunct X-33 with the Space Launch Initiative (SLI).

SLI was to bring all of the aerospace industry together to develop a next-generation spacecraft to replace the aging and troubled Space Shuttle fleet and to fill the gap that the failed X program had caused. SLI was funded to the tune of several billion dollars for about three years and design concepts were beginning to be refined and "downselected" to. The NASA Advisory Council met at NASA Headquarters in Washington, D.C., in 2002 to discuss the progress of SLI and made the decision to change the direction of the program.

The Advisory Council expressed that they were concerned that billions of dollars had been spent for some very fancy view graphs and fun animations. This is a bit of a facetious and over-encompassing statement since there were many engineering trade studies that were undertaken in order to calculate the most likely designs for the SLI concept vehicles, but in the end pretty pictures *are* what make it to visual displays. Were the efforts and pretty pictures worth the billions that were spent? They would have been had we gone on to the next step and started building these designs. Due to the Advisory Council input and various other political influences, the SLI program was gutted and redesigned.

The new emphasis on SLI became: "Get a way to carry payloads and people to the ISS as soon as possible because the Shuttles are failing." This new SLI emphasis was decided about nine or so months before the *Columbia* accident. It makes one wonder doesn't it?

At any rate, the new emphasis for SLI was for it to become a split-personality program. The two personalities of the program are the Orbital Space Plane (OSP) and the Next Generation Launch Technologies (NGLT). The OSP is to be a small person-carrying lifeboat that will be strapped on top of an expendable rocket. The only thing reusable on the OSP concept vehicles will be the lifeboat itself and, of course the lifeboat will never go higher than an ISS orbit!

The NGLT personality of the program was put in place in order to keep the advanced or next-generation flavor in SLI that might one day enable single stage ETO vehicles or at least reusable vehicles. This seems for now to be purely political in that the OSP personality has the largest share of funding.

Hopefully, the split-personality program will not become viciously self-competitive and eat itself politically and economically from the inside out. It is possible that the program will generate useful space vehicles in the future, but the odds of success seem low. The main issue with SLI now is that it will be the program that drives the American manned space effort for the next generation. It is obvious from the program's requirements that no consideration for higher than LEO are being made. If SLI continues as planned, we will be stranded below the ISS-type orbits for another generation. So getting from Earth-to-GEO may be tough to do in the next twenty or so years. For this section of space travel we must hope that the Chinese will initiate a bold space program that will spark a new space race. They have plans to set a Chinese team on the Moon by 2010 and once they put their first "taikonaut" into space, perhaps we will take them seriously and change our split-personality ETO space program to something more useful. (Note: One must wonder if this is what has sparked President Bush's new space initiative?)

On the other hand, it is possible that ETO-to-LEO rockets will be enough. In the story, Tamara takes a rocket from Earth-to-LEO where she catches the Space Elevator and rides it from LEO to GEO. A space elevator works just like an elevator on Earth does. A space platform would be placed at LEO and one would be placed above it at GEO. The two platforms are "tied" together by a very very very strong but very very very lightweight cable. The distance from LEO to GEO is about 35,000 kilometers so you can see why the cable must be lightweight. A cable that long with a mass of just one gram per meter of length would have a total mass of 35,000 kilograms! Wow, that is just a little more mass than a Shuttle can lift. Also, a cable that is only one gram per meter must have amazing tensile strength in order to withstand the stresses of lifting an elevator car full of people and stuff. A cable with only one gram per meter in length is not much larger than fishing line in diameter. The tensile strengths required of such small cables are nearly a property of "unobtanium." However, there is recent research in carbon-nanotube-reinforced fibers and cables that are very close to having the properties required for a space elevator. NASA, industry, and even fishing line companies are currently testing the materials.

So the elevator platforms are tied together by this extremely strong and lightweight nanotube-reinforced fiber. The elevator car simply uses motors to winch itself up or down the cable. As the elevator car moves upward it imparts some of its momentum to the elevator platforms pushing their orbits slightly lower. The orbit of the platforms will raise when the car comes back down. The platforms would also be much more massive than the elevator car and cargo so the momentum transfer to the elevator platforms would be analogous to the momentum one would transfer to a barge by diving off it into the water.

There are presently many individuals and several companies that believe the space elevator concept is viable and doable today. Some even believe it can be constructed not just from space-to-space locations but from Earth to space like in the Arthur C. Clarke novel *The Fountains of Paradise*. The materials strength-to-mass ratio required to build the ground station is beyond present capabilities and the effects of the atmospheric drag on the cable increase the strength requirements for it as well. Most likely, space-to-space elevators will come first.

Now ETO might not be that exciting for the next generation, but the NASA In-Space Propulsion Program is making leaps and bounds toward making travel within our solar system a reality. Funded by the Office of Space Science and centered in Huntsville, Alabama, at the NASA Marshal Space Flight Center, the In-Space

Propulsion Program is currently developing solar sails, ion drives, space tethers, advanced chemical propulsion, aeroassist, beamed energy, pulsed-plasma propulsion, matter-antimatter powered propulsion, and many others including the space elevator concept that Tamara used to get from LEO to GEO. The In-Space Propulsion Program is currently funded and projected to be funded to the tune of a few tens of millions of dollars per year for the next five or so years.

These concepts are being pushed to levels of development so that craft could be test flown within the next five to ten years. In fact, the solar sailing technology that uses sunlight pressure on very large lightweight reflectors like Tamara's ship the *Boy's Life* is currently at the state of near flight readiness. There are several NASA contractors developing solar sail spacecraft and preparing the concept for a test flight expected to be within the next year or two. Also, two separate private entities, Team Encounter and Cosmos I, are developing solar sail spacecraft for flight. The private teams might beat NASA in the race to fly a solar sail.

Why develop solar sails? Well, actually, sails are currently the only way to carry a spacecraft into the outer edges of our solar system in a short amount of time. A sailing ship would be launched on an expendable chemical rocket toward the Sun. When the ship approaches about half the distance between the Earth and the Sun its sail would then deploy. The photons from the Sun impact the sail and deliver momentum to the sail. It turns out that a sailing ship of a few hundred kilograms or so and a sail size of about two hundred meters in diameter could reach the outer solar system in less than ten years. This size spacecraft at such a low mass is about ten years away in technology development. All of the components for such a craft have been developed in small quantities; it is now just a matter of figuring out how to put it together on such large scales. The best approach is to start out smaller.

The first NASA solar sail flight will most likely be a square sail about fifty meters or so on a side. The mission will be to demonstrate that the technology works. It is possible that the spacecraft will be given an actual job once it has been tested. A sail of this size could sail from high Earth orbit inward toward the Sun to about ninety-five percent the distance from the Sun to the Earth. The sailcraft could sit there and watch the Sun for solar flares and other forms of coronal mass emissions that wreak havoc on our satellites and communications grids. The particles ejected from the Sun travel a little slower than light speed. So if the sailcraft that is a little closer to the Sun than the Earth detects the particles, it can send a radio signal to Earth to tell us to turn off our stuff. The radio signal should beat the Sun emission by several hours, giving us plenty of time to prepare for the bad "solar weather." This mission could be implemented in just a few years.

The advantage of solar sails is that they use no propellant or reaction mass that is ejected from the spacecraft. The propulsion is purely provided by the incident light from the Sun. On the other hand, the propulsive effect is negligible once the spacecraft is at distances from the Sun much farther than Mars's orbit since sunlight pressure drops off as the inverse square of the distance from the Sun. So if you want to go somewhere and stop with a solar sail it must be within Mars's orbit if you plan to stop by using sunlight. However, a recent study by myself and Dr. Greg Matloff has shown that the sails can actually be used as a parachute. So a sail could fly close to the Sun to get sped up really fast and then fly out to Neptune perhaps and aerobrake or parachute into Neptune's atmosphere and slow down to a Neptune orbital velocity. This is a brand new concept that NASA is looking into but it appears that it can be done successfully at Mars, Jupiter, Saturn, Neptune, Titan, or basically any solar system body with an appreciable atmosphere. So, the technology for sailing from Earth to Mars or other solar system bodies is at hand and soon to be flown.

Another neat application with sailing ships is beam riders. At the end of the story Tamara has started running a large mirror that directs sunlight and focuses it onto a sailing ship. I did a study in 2000 that showed that if a mirror 100 km in diameter could be placed in a high GEO and could continuously focus sunlight onto a 100-km-diameter sail of appropriate design for about ten years, then that sail could reach Alpha Centauri in less than fifty years. Of course stopping would be another matter altogether but there are theories on how to do that by the late Dr. Robert Forward, Dr. Greg Matloff, and others. The biggest hurdle in developing these interstellar sailing ships as in "Cleaning Lady" is learning how to build such very large spacecraft. Most of the materials are available but we are not quite sure how to put them all together, yet.

In the story Tamara encountered several "nuke tugs" that used nuclear power as the main power source for the spacecraft. NASA is also looking at nuclear fission-powered electric propulsion. This research effort is called Project Prometheus. A fission power plant the size of a beer keg or a garbage can could deliver several hundred kilowatts of thermal energy to a power converter that would then convert the heat to electrical power just like terrestrial nuclear power plants. The conversion process is about twenty-five to thirty percent efficient. Therefore a three-hundred-kilowatt thermal fission reactor could deliver about one hundred kilowatts of electrical power to the spacecraft systems. The propulsion for the spacecraft would be an advanced ion engine similar to the one that recently flew on the Deep Space 1 mission. Ion engines use a small electrically powered ion accelerator to accelerate small particles to very high velocities. These small particles are then electrically pushed out of the exit of the accelerator to generate thrust. The thrust generated is not very high but the fuel usage is very efficient. Analyses have shown that a nuclear fission electric propulsion spacecraft of this type could carry thousands of kilograms of payload to the Pluto-Charon system and maybe even the Kuiper Belt with trip times of less than twenty years. And when these types of spacecraft get where they are going they still have all the electrical power that they need from the fission reactor. One of the problems with previous outer-planet missions has been that there was no electrical power after the batteries died. A well-designed fission reactor should generate power for decades.

Another possible nuclear rocket design would be to skip the electrical conversion part and superheat a fluid such as liquid hydrogen by flowing it through or around the reactor core. The superheated liquid is then flowed through a rocket nozzle, which would then deliver tremendous thrust to the spacecraft. The thrust generated by a so-called "nuclear thermal rocket" is much greater than that of the electric mode of operation but the fuel efficiency is very low. It is possible that the two different modes of operation can be utilized for different aspects of space missions. Nuclear thermal mode is used when high thrust or quick acceleration is needed and nuclear electric is used when long slow efficient thrusting or accelerating is needed. And of course when all the fuel is used up the spacecraft can sit wherever it is or coast along with plenty of electrical power for making scientific measurements or powering crew quarters.

Finally there are the far-reaching and many-generations-down-the-road technologies. Although exotic means of space travel were not mentioned in the story, no essay on the future of space propulsion would be complete without at least talking about faster-than-light travel. The NASA Breakthrough Propulsion Physics program (BPP) mostly investigates these efforts. The BPP has tried to create interest and serious investigation into concepts like warp drives, wormholes, vacuum energy, and various other seemingly science-fiction–type technologies. Recent efforts have shown that our modern theories of the universe allow for such things as wormholes and warp drives, but the problem is that we simply have no idea how to build them. In fact, we have no idea where to start!

The BPP has asked the propulsion and theoretical physics communities to combine their collective thoughts on the topic and make suggestions for a starting place. There have been several suggested experiments and many theories but few have proven fruitful to date. The most promising concepts involve the Alcubierre warp theory and the so-called Casimir effect. The details of this are too complex to go into here but suffice it to say that there still remain possibilities within known physics for faster-than-light science-fiction–type travel. But this would be generations away, perhaps.

It should also be noted that the output of the BPP has been amazing for the little funding it has received.

The program has delivered many peer-reviewed concepts and papers and a few proposed experiments in just a few short years. The BPP has been alive for about five years and has had a total budget of about one and a half million dollars; that's total budget, not per years. Until serious funding is applied to the program the program will not be considered seriously. But don't fret over it too much since the scientists and engineers that grew up watching *Star Trek* and reading Heinlein will never give up on the idea until we have done it. The theories suggest that faster-than-light travel can be accomplished and someday we will do it.

So, we see that there are serious direction issues within our space program. We spend immense amounts of money on our ETO capabilities but redirect the emphasis so often that we will likely get nothing to show for it. Our In-Space technologies are funded at a fairly reasonable pace (although I'm sure more funding wouldn't hurt the program) and reasonable results are being achieved. In fact, if we have a means to get the technologies off the Earth, the In-Space technologies will be able to take us anywhere we want to go within our solar system. If we want to go farther than our solar system, well we will just have to be patient. The In-Space technologies could get us there . . . with many decades if not centuries of travel time, but who wants to wait that long? The BPP efforts might develop a faster-than-light propulsion system that would take us beyond the solar system in short periods of time, and as interest increases, funding for the program will increase.

It appears for now that we will just have settle for our own solar system and traveling within it. That's okay, as we should learn to crawl before we learn to run. The ETO technologies will be developed out of necessity. We have to go to the space station or it will eventually fall, and we have to put up communications satellites, and sooner or later the Chinese will go to the Moon, so we will develop ways to get off the Earth within a generation or two. The In-Space propulsion technologies being developed and tested today will enable us to travel anywhere within our solar system within this generation possibly and most definitely within a generation or two. That should be exciting enough to offer us great adventures like the ones presented within this anthology. So we can all look forward to some really exciting space adventures if not within our lifetimes at least within our children's lifetimes. And when we have really traveled all around the solar system and have learned to use the resources within it, then perhaps we will venture outward to the stars using the BPP-type more advanced breakthrough technologies. One might ask the question, "Are we there yet?" and the answer is simply, "It's not far now!"

Of course, once we get up out of the gravity well and establish colonies, not all will be hunky-dory. . . .

COMMUNICATIONS PROBLEM

Margaret Ball

ComCentral was fizzing with activity when Elaine arrived at the start of her shift. Little sparks of frustrated energy crackled in the air. Her colleagues were talking too fast and clipping the ends of their sentences off in a way that suggested they were barely managing to remain within the Federation guidelines for nondiscriminatory civil speech.

"What's the matter with everyone?" she asked Jana out of the side of her mouth while they changed places in their shared pod. "Com crisis?"

Jana sighed. "No, just the usual. The Prajad Dal says the Islamic Renaissance has got a more powerful transmitter and is drowning out its Ram chants. The Islamic Renaissance says that having to hear Ram chants over the common band is a violation of its religious integrity. The Pieds Nus want equal time with the Naturists despite the fact their colony is about one percent the size of the Naturist community.

The VolksAlliance wants a zoning ordinance preventing nonwhite colonization of any asteroid within their sphere of influence—"

"Well, *that's* not a communications issue, is it? They'll have to take it up with Colony Approval and Registration, and they'll be turned down because their 'sphere of influence' starts inside their own airlocks. I don't see where we come into it." Elaine set the general com channels plug in her right ear but left the other ear free to hear Jana's reply.

"They can't be turned down until they apply to CAR, and they're not going to make a formal application because they know it won't work," Jana sighed. "They're using their entire common-band allocation to make speeches about it. Which means the Islamic Renaissance, the Candomble Negre, Nuevo Aliyah and oh, just about every ethnic-based asteroid community in the belt is demanding extra common-band time to make speeches *against* it. Except the Mixo-Lydians," she added after a pause. "All *they* want is to bomb the Slavo-Lydians out of the asteroid belt. And vice versa, of course."

Once engineering and mining firms had demonstrated that it was technically feasible and potentially profitable to hollow out asteroids and set up closed ecologies for their work forces, the settlement of the lesser asteroids had been touted as the opportunity for each and every persecuted minority group on Earth to have its very own mini-world; "the ultimate gated communities" as one optimistic NASA writer had described them. What the optimists had overlooked was that many groups didn't desire to be let alone so much as they desired to persecute all the others who committed the crime of being Not Like Them. With physical access to each asteroid community well controlled at the entry locks, the rival groups took their bickering to any area where they could still overlap, interfere with each other, and try to snatch resources.

Communications was one such area. Inter-asteroid communication was easy enough, but the cost of a transmitter strong enough to beam transmissions back to Earth made it effectively a Federation monopoly. Federation guidelines dictated the allotment of time each group could have on the Earth-beam channels, which somehow always wound up being defined as not quite enough. ComCentral had been established to control routing of messages, but the job was more political than technical. Or perhaps, Elaine thought as she listened to Jana's rundown of the morning situations, it was more like being in charge of a creche for three-year-olds.

"Oh, and you volunteered to devise a decoration scheme for Unity in Diversity Day."

Elaine groaned. "How? I wasn't even here."

"That's how. Those of us who were on-shift when it came up had the opportunity to explain why we wouldn't be suitable candidates. So you and Dom get the honor."

While Jana brought her up to date Elaine had been murmuring instructions into the mouthpiece, adding entries to her daily work list. Initially she'd had only four items on the list, comprising her regular maintenance and scheduling jobs. Now there were four more:

> *Think up decorations for UDD*
> *Negotiate settlement between Islamic Renaissance and Prajad Dal*
> *Explain bandwidth allocation priority system to Pieds Nus*
> *Do something about VolksAlliance!!!*

The last one was going to be a real pain to deal with; maybe she could get Aksia, her supervisor, to take it up. Elaine glanced through the transparent pod dividers and saw Aksia standing halfway down the ComCen tube, frowning at someone, one hand upraised, tapping the air with her forefinger as she made some point. Didn't look like a good time to be asking for any favors from Aksia.

She needed to plug in the other channels and start dealing in real-time, but she fiddled with the plug for a moment longer. Jana didn't seem to be in any hurry to hand over and get off-shift; there must be something going on besides the usual inter-asteroid squabbling.

"You're right," she agreed, "it sounds like a pretty normal shift. So what haven't you told me?"

Jana spread her hands. "Hey, that's it. Why wouldn't I tell you everything that's in the air? I'm more than happy to go off-shift and leave you and Dom to settle things for the next eight hours."

Usually that was true. In fact, usually Jana was out of her pod so fast Elaine could barely get a decent handover report from her. "So why aren't you going?"

"What's the matter, you want to get rid of me?"

"Stick around if you like," Elaine said, "but I *do* have to log in, and it *would* help if you told me why everybody seems so tense."

Jana sighed. "Oh, it's nothing really. There's this new guy . . ."

"Where?"

"Not in ComCen. He's with Life Support. He was just up here for a few minutes, mid-shift, getting his internal com codes set with Aksia. Actually I was the one who implemented the setup."

"So what's the big deal?"

"You'll understand when you see him." Jana sighed. "I did think he might have to come back by now. Oh well. I guess I'll go to the gym. Got to keep those muscles toned, you know."

Elaine blinked in surprise. Jana usually moaned and bitched about the obligatory daily hour of gravity exercise and spent her free time in the lowest-g areas she could find, claiming that saving the wear and tear of gravity on the muscles did as much as any amount of working out to keep her body as perky as she wanted. Oh, well, people were strange and work was waiting.

Elaine liked to use the first hour or so of her shift on routine work like going through the inevitable stack of internal memos, letting each of them flicker over the screen so they would mark as "read" when Aksia checked, while she thought about the problems the day presented and caught up with her lists. Today this was clearly not going to be possible: the board was already lighting up with urgent calls. She blinked twice to bring up the incoming IDs. About what she'd expected from Jana's summary: three from the militant Hindus of Prajad Dal, five from various representatives of Islamic Renaissance, and a handful from ethnically based asteroids near the VolksAlliance. One from the Federation Ethnic Equality Foundation which instinct told her to put off as long as she could, and one from the Pieds Nus which had better wait until she figured out exactly who they were . . . some kind of Indian tribe, wasn't it? In the Yucatan? Why would Mayan Indians be quarreling with the Naturists? Something else for the list:

> *Research Pieds Nus*
> *Get somebody from Legal to talk to the*
> *   FEEFs*

The work list was getting unmanageably long already, and now her wristcom beeped and flashed an orange light to warn Elaine that she hadn't finished her usual first task on time.

Read and delete daily memos

Well, tough. She moved that one to an end-of-shift priority while making soothing noises to the first Prajad Dal complainant. Yes, of course ComCen would look into the matter immediately. No, there was no Federation regulation against the Prajad Dal's using their allotted com time for any purpose whatsoever, but they should bear in mind that the amount of com time given to each asteroid colony was not simply a matter of time and bandwidth available in proportion to colony population, but that such factors as urgency of broadcasts and their relevance to colony survival were also taken into account. . . . *In other words, sir, you can use your entire com allotment to broadcast holy chants if you like, but if you do that you'll be lucky to be allotted ten seconds per shift next time there's a budget review.* She didn't actually have to say that on the com channel; the Prajad Dal were mostly very bright people as well as very religious ones. But she did have to repeat the soothing noises to the next seriously upset complainant, and the next, and then she had to come up with a variant for the Islamic Renaissance, this time hinting at serious punitive fines for interference with another group's com time and reminding them that nobody was *forcing* them to listen to Hindu holy chants; if they liked they could turn their com service off entirely for the two shifts and seven hours during which they were limited to using their own equipment instead of bouncing signals to Ceres for amplification and communication to Earth.

In between saying the same things over and over in a very calm voice, Elaine surreptitiously muttered commands to update her personal to-do list. There was nothing scheduled there for the next seven hours, of course; she never scheduled personal tasks during her work shift. But she had her wristlister programmed to re-enter regular chores for the next applicable period as soon as she marked them completed, so she was already scheduled for the first two hours after her shift ended:

> *Meet Bethy for dinner in Hall G6*
> *Mandatory gym hour*
> *Shower*

While she repeated soothing, calming statements to the third Islamic Renaissance caller, who was markedly slower on the uptake than the previous two had been, Elaine added a few items as she thought of them:

> *Return library vids*

They weren't due for several shifts, but she had watched one and given up in boredom on the other two; might as well:

> *See if the new Cliff Rockhammer vid is*
> *in*

And since she'd be up on the recreation/vending level anyway, she could also:

> *Buy Bethy something for anniversary*

But what? When Bethy married Henrik they'd been given everything a young couple could want for their

new, spacious married-couple quarters, from personal
recyclers to real antique plastic dishes manufactured
on Earth, where plastics were plentiful and cheap.
Bethy was always complaining, in a sly tone of voice
that betrayed her pride in the fact, that their quarters
were so full of clothes and personal things there was
scarcely room to move around—"even if we do have a
triple-tuber because of Henrik's Important Work," she
never failed to finish, the capital letters quite audible
in her voice. Really, it would be better to give Bethy
something intangible, take her out to dinner or—but
they ate dinner together every time their shifts coin-
cided; well, then, go to one of the fancy expensive
restaurants on the level above Recreation/Vending.
She could walk around up there after she finished
her errand at the library, take her time about deciding whether Bethy would prefer the rowdy singing
and tall rum drinks at Carabanana or the understated
elegance of La Plume de Ma Tante.

That would fill in the empty hours after gym and
shower quite nicely, with a sensible activity that she
could tell people about if they asked. Eight hours
work, eight hours sleep, eight hours recreation was
the Federation rule, not that there was actually any
rule against sleeping more than eight hours. But
everybody knew if you were logged as spending ten
or eleven hours in your tube on a regular basis, a
Personal Counselor would come to talk with you, try
to decide whether you were suffering from a depression that would respond to medication or needed to
be gently encouraged to find a nice social hobby like
zero-g volleyball. *I just want to spend a little time
alone* wasn't considered an acceptable response.

"Elaine, wake up! He's here, talking to Aksia!"
Dom, her shift partner, touched Elaine's elbow and
startled her into cutting coms with the last Islamic

Renaissance complainant a little more quickly than she had intended.

"Who's here, and what's the big deal?"

"The new guy from Life Support." Dom rolled his eyes and gave a deep sigh. "To die for. Unfortunately I hear he's straight, so my chances with him are slim to none."

Elaine peered through the tube. Despite the Earth-normal artificial lighting and its luxurious three-tube width, ComCen was so long that it still felt like being in a tin can. Elaine's pod was at the very bottom of the can, and the new employee everybody was talking up was near the middle, waving his hands and saying something emphatic to Aksia, who looked more and more sullen the longer he went on. Beside Aksia's dark-browed frown the new guy looked like a shaft of real Earth sunlight miraculously materializing in the middle of the tubeplex: long blond hair pulled back and to one side of his face, bright blue eyes, a sunny smile that radiated the certainty that every-thing would be all right as soon as he had explained it sufficiently.

"His name's Bryce," Dom said.

"Very nice," Elaine said flippantly. "Rhymes with Bryce." She really ought to get on with the next prob-lem, but she didn't want to take her eyes off Bryce. He looked amazingly like a younger, softer Cliff Rock-hammer. "Dom, you know anything about the Pieds Nus? Aren't they some kind of Mayan Indians? And why are they getting crossways with the nudists?"

"Naturists," Dom corrected her. "The new Civil Speech Guidelines defined 'nudists' as a discrimina-tory term, remember?"

"I haven't even *skimmed* the new guidelines yet," Elaine sighed. Presumably they were among the stack of memos she hadn't had time to look at yet.

"Anyway," Dom went on, "you're thinking about Piedras Negras. That's a Mayan archaeological site. The Pieds Nus are a French-based splinter group of the Naturists."

"I hate even thinking of splinters in connection with nudism," Elaine said absentmindedly.

"Then you'd like the Pieds Nus better than the Naturists. They mostly keep their clothes on, but they have this thing about the right to go barefoot everywhere."

"Even in space?"

"Well . . . under their suits, probably." Dom grinned. "What do you suppose a truly dedicated Naturist wears under *his* spacesuit?"

Elaine cross-checked the Pieds Nus on her desk console and found that Jana's estimate hadn't been bad: although they had colonized one of the larger asteroids, their population was about one-twentieth the size of the Naturist home colony. Great, this one didn't even require a personal call, she'd just send an email reminding them of Federation regulations relating com time to population size.

"What do you think Bryce is talking to Aksia about?" She brought up the general complaint response form and typed as she talked. *Dear Sir or Madam, we regret to inform you that the Federation regulations assigning central communications times are based on group population rather than philosophy.* Maybe Bryce needed a Coms Spec 4 permanently assigned to his Life Support group. She'd be happy to volunteer.

"Fixing his internal com codes," Dom said. "Jana wanted to see him again, so she made a couple of 'mistakes' when she set him up the first time. Unfortunately, he seems not to have noticed the mistakes until she went off-shift and I came on." He grinned wickedly. "Her bad luck, my good luck."

"I thought you said he was straight?" *Since your population is less than five percent that of the Naturist colony, which has been allocated one standard hour every four shifts, your allocation ought strictly to be just three minutes in every four shifts.*

"Hey. I can have my fantasies, okay?"

Elaine didn't believe in wasting time on fantasies. *Since the minimum communications time necessary for basic colony support has been set at five minutes every third shift, this is what you have been allocated and there is no basis for increasing it. Sincerely, Elaine Byelski, Coms Spec 4, ComCen Staff.* The note to Pieds Nus taken care of, she switched back to her personal list and added a few new items with suggested deadlines. The office to-do list beeped before she was finished, urgently, flashing from yellow or orange to red even as she responded: the VolksAlliance issue was heating up. Elaine went back into soothing-diplomat mode and cajoled, suggested, sympathised, and mentioned ComCen regulations until the shift was almost over and both sides of her wristlister were flashing unhappily. The office listbot reminded her that she still hadn't read and e-initialed the day's memos, and the personal listbot warned that she needed to sign off-shift and take the railtube to meet Bethy on the cafeteria level.

Over dinner Bethy started in again about Elaine's getting married. Before she could get into the familiar arguments about the greater space allocation for married couples, the wonderful creche she and Henrik had already signed up to use if and when Bethy got pregnant, and the nice boy in Henrik's department, Elaine cut her off. "Don't worry, Bethy, that's all taken care of."

"You've *met* somebody? But how? You never

do anything except go to work and exercise at the gym."

"Well, I haven't exactly met him," Elaine admitted. "But he's on the list."

"What list?"

"Personal, naturally. Look here." Elaine set her wristlister to display the personal calendar side and zoomed out so that the regular daily items shrank to illegible squiggles, leaving only major events highlighted. *Meet Bryce* was scheduled for shortly before *Bethy's anniversary*, followed by *Get date with Bryce*, *fall in love*, and *get married*.

"Elaine, you can't *do* that."

"Why not?"

"It's—not how it works."

"It's how you worked it," Elaine commented, remembering clearly how Bethy had picked out Henrik as a suitable partner, maneuvered her way into his group of friends, and reported nearly every shift on the Henrik Campaign until the day of their marriage.

Bethy's face turned a faint and becoming pink. "That's different. I really cared for Henrik."

"You didn't love him before you met him, though, did you?"

"Of course not! How could I?"

"Well, there you are. These things have to happen in the right sequence. First you meet, then you date, then you fall in love, then you get married. What's so bad about writing it down? At least that way I can make sure I stay on track and meet my deadlines."

"Do you always do everything exactly the way you have it on your lists, and exactly on time?"

"Of course I do," Elaine said. "That's the only way to stay in control."

It was unfortunate, to say the least, that her wristlister chose that moment to beep a double emergency red to remind her that she never had read and date-marked the day's memos at ComCen. She tapped the sound off immediately and put her hand in her lap to hide the flashing red light, but Bethy was already smirking. And it was impossible to saw through the algysteak one-handed; Food Processing had seriously overdone the simulated texturing. Elaine gave up the attempt to conceal her wristlister. "I'll take care of that tomorrow," she said. "No, tonight, before I go to sleep." She could call the memos to the screen in her personal tube and deal with them there, and start her next shift at ComCen with a clean list.

It looked like the usual day's mail list:

> New energy conservation restrictions on
>   office tube lighting
> Prejudicial terminology to be discarded
>   immediately
> Sanctions for first-, second-, and third-time
>   use of prejudicial terms
> Let's gear up for Unity in Diversity Day!
> How YOU can make a difference to Com-
>   Cen's public image
> Dear Elaine

What?
Elaine stopped scrolling down the list of memos and highlighted that one. How did her personal correspondence get mixed in with the ComCen memos? And who was sending her personal correspondence, anyway? ComCen policy frowned upon personal involvement with members of the asteroid colonies for fear of allegations of prejudice, it wasn't time for the monthly note from Mom and Dad back on Earth, and everybody she knew on Ceres worked at

ComCen and wouldn't bother sending a note when
they were sure to see her in person in the next shift
or two. Except Bethy, but Bethy had said plenty over
dinner and would hardly have had time to write to
her, and . . .

Oh.

The header showed it was a reply to a message
going *out* from ComCen, that was why it had landed
in her office mailbox instead of her personal one.

But it was such a highly personal reply!

> Dear Elaine, thank you for your prompt
> attention to my request. Are you really as
> pretty as your picture in the Federation
> Employee Database, or do they enhance
> those photos before posting them? Since
> Federation regulations allow each asteroid
> settlement five minutes of central broadcast
> time every three shifts, and the popula-
> tion of Pieds Nus is entitled as you say
> to three minutes every four shifts, clearly
> our total broadcast allocation should be
> five in three plus three in four, which
> is too complicated to figure out, so why
> don't we just say that it's eight minutes
> every three shifts. The directory note says
> you're a classical music lover, just like me,
> so why don't we get together some time to
> listen to audio cubes? I have cubes of the
> Doors, the Rolling Stones, Grateful Dead,
> and many other early-music groups. Or if
> you'd like to round it up to ten minutes
> every three shifts, which might be easier
> to calculate, that would be fine with me.
> Sincerely yours, Orlin Okusa, Pieds Nus

Elaine snorted. Who did this jerk think he was, trying to soften her into increasing the Pieds Nus allotment with cheap flattery and hints that he might share his collection of rare early music?

> Dear Orlin Okusa, you have an unmathematical mind and flattery will get you nowhere. Obviously . . .

It probably wasn't a good idea to insult ComCen clients, no matter how idiotic they were. Besides, this guy wasn't nearly as obnoxious as that last jerk from Islamic Renaissance; if she could be polite to all the other idiots, she could certainly be polite to this one.

> Dear Orlin Okusa, I am afraid you have misinterpreted the ComCen regulations. The total amount of broadcast time allocated to each asteroid colony is the maximum of minimum life-support time and population-based calculated time, not the sum! You have a very unstructured way of expressing yourself. Please do not . . .

Sighing, Elaine crossed out the last sentence and a half. Not only was it rude to comment on his two-streams-of-consciousness writing style, it wasn't necessary. It wasn't like they'd be corresponding again. *Yours sincerely, Elaine Byelski, Coms Spec 4. P.S. Do you really have a Rolling Stones audio cube?*

She tapped "Transmit" and then bit her lip. It had been most unprofessional to ask about his music collection. Unnecessary, too. Still, what harm could it do?

❖   ❖   ❖

She learned the answer to that as soon as she signed on-shift. Her pod was already vacant, which was no great surprise; Jana usually cut out a few minutes early if she thought she could get away with it. For that matter, she was just a couple of minutes late, having slept so deeply that the first and second alarm buzzes had barely registered through the dream that she could no longer remember.

But all the pods surrounding hers were vacant as well, and her usual neighbors were clustered around Aksia complaining vociferously. And there was a low rhythmic beat thrumming through the tube that made Elaine feel happier, more awake and alive, than she'd been in a long time.

As she made her way down the tube to her pod the thrumming grew louder and clearer, until it resolved itself into a repeated four-chord motif.

Coming from *her* com board.

"For pity's sake, make it stop!" Dom detached himself from the group around Aksia and slid into the pod beside Elaine's.

"How? *I* didn't start it," Elaine pointed out virtuously. "I just got here!" Besides, she hadn't heard a Stones audio in, oh, a long time; Ceres Central Programming didn't do much early music.

"It started itself," Dom said, "exactly when you *should* have been on shift."

"One minute and fourteen seconds ago? Poor you." Elaine brought up the list of her emails and nodded once, sharply.

"Do you know how to make it stop?"

"Mm-hmm. At least, I can figure out how it was done. Bound to happen sooner or later, really." Elaine was stalling because she didn't really want to turn off the music yet. "He's figured out how to trigger an action macro from within an unopened message.

Very clever. But somebody'd better get onto Programming Central and tell them to fix that hole in their security before somebody more obnoxious works out the same trick."

"Who cares? And for that matter," Dom whined, "I don't care if that guy can get satisfaction or not."

"Can't get no," Elaine corrected absently. She turned off the music and routed the message to her personal address. She could play it through in her own quarters, after shift, as many times as she liked. It was sort of like somebody sending flowers, she thought, only nicer.

"Thank goodness! I can't *think* with that noise going on."

"Um-hmm. It's not thinking music," Elaine conceded, moving slightly in her pod to the remembered beat. "Be good for a party, though. Maybe I'll save it to play on Unity in Diversity Day."

"Are you out of your *mind*? We need something everyone likes for that. Bryce suggested a nice Vronsolo tape."

"Bryce was here? And I missed seeing him?" Elaine pounded her head against the flexible walls of the pod.

"You should have been on time," Dom said smugly. "Anyway, what do you think about using Vronsolo for background music on UDD?"

"Who?"

"Honestly, Elaine, don't you keep up with anything? He sets inspirational and motivating quotations to music. Not *tunes* or anything vulgar. Nice tinkling bells and wind chimes and he intones the words very reverently. Like, 'Walk with a hope in your heart and you will never be alone,'" Dom chanted with a slight rise and fall in his voice. "That's one of his most popular pieces."

"What comes after that?"

"That's it." Dom looked blank. "With, like I said, nice music in the background. But he did lots more. His top piece right now is, 'Oh, Great Spirit who dwells in the sky, lead us to the path of peace and understanding.' That's Native American wisdom, you know."

"Do you suppose the Native Americans were thinking of Ceres when they looked up into the sky?" Elaine finished scrolling through the new memos and slipped the general com channels plug into her ear. "Lovely, Dom, but now I've got to lead a bunch of VolksAlliance bullies to the path of peace and understanding." Maybe she could play Vronsolo tapes at them until they begged for mercy.

> Dear Orlin, thank you *very* much for the Stones audio, but *please* don't send anything that broadcasts from my work station again. It was a clever way to draw our attention to the security breach in our programming but I'm afraid it rather upset some of my colleagues who don't appreciate the classics. They got *really* upset when I suggested it as theme music for Unity in Diversity Day. Would you believe . . .

Well, Vronsolo couldn't be that bad if Bryce liked him. Elaine had downloaded some of his audios after work and listened to them for—well, as long as she could stand it—and it was, umm, certainly peaceful. She didn't want to say boring, which was the only other word she could think of. Okay, scrap that last sentence and start over.

Anyway, somebody else is working on the theme music, so all I have to do now is decorations. I don't suppose you have any creative ideas on that subject?

Better make the signature formal, just so he wouldn't think there was anything personal beyond mere politeness in her reply.

Sincerely yours, Elaine Byelski, Coms Spec 4, Communications Central, Ceres Base.

P.S. I notice your picture isn't in the Pieds Nus directory.

Not that it mattered, but it would have been interesting to know what this Orlin Okusa looked like. Probably nothing special. *Certainly* nothing special compared with Bryce. Elaine called up his employee picture on the desk console and sighed. What a pity she'd missed his visit to ComCen earlier. Oh well. If he was doing the music for UDD and she was doing the decorations, they really ought to get together and discuss their plans some time, shouldn't they? But it was a long time until UDD. She'd have to think up some excuse to go down to Life Support before then.

When the next shift started, Elaine discovered that Orlin had created the excuse for her.

She could hear Aksia's violent sneezing even before she got into the ComCen office tube; it echoed off the gray corridors like splashes of paint in bright primaries.

"Ged thad thig out of here!" Aksia demanded as soon as she saw Elaine.

"Huh?"

"Thad *thig*." Aksia blew her nose and pointed at Elaine's pod, which was almost filled with a profusion of colors—green sparked with pink and orange and red.

When Elaine got close enough to see over the distorting translucent softwalls, the blurs of color resolved into flowers almost covering the leafy top of a small potted . . . tree? Bush? She pinched one of the flowers curiously; it was soft under her hand, and when she let go the petal showed a thumb-and-finger-shaped bruise. "I'm sorry," she said.

"So you should be," Dom said. "Didn't you know about Aksia's allergies?"

"Not until now, and anyway *I* didn't fill up my own pod with potted plants," Elaine pointed out. "I wonder who . . . Oh, no, I don't." This was Orlin's answer to office decorations for UDD, wasn't it? It must have cost him a small fortune to have it shipped to Ceres by fastmail. "Who delivered it, anyway, and why did Aksia let them install it?"

"Came just before shift change, and she wasn't here to stop the delivery," Dom told her.

"And I suppose Jana had left early, as usual, so my pod was the only empty place to put it," Elaine sighed.

"It'll have to go."

"I know. I'm just trying to figure out how to fit it into my personal tube." Maybe if she put the bed under the desk, after all she didn't use them both at the same time, no, that wouldn't work.

"Can't," Dom told her. "No plants on station outside of Life Support. Regulations. You should know that—well, it's obvious really, isn't it? We can't have uncontrolled life forms with who-knows-what microorganisms attached to them growing just anywhere in a closed environment."

Elaine sighed and agreed it was obvious, and

wondered why whoever delivered the tree hadn't known about this rule and taken it directly to Life Support in the first place. "I'll take it down now," she said. "Dom, you'll have to cover my calls until I get back."

"It's too heavy for you. Better let me take it," Dom volunteered with a fine air of chivalry, "and *you* cover *my* calls."

Elaine gave him a dirty look. "No, *thanks*. My tree, my excuse to go to Life Support. Besides, he's straight, it wouldn't do you any good."

"A man can dream, can't he?"

"Why would anybody send a tree to Ceres?" Bryce was looking at the tree rather than at Elaine. Well, it *was* more colorful. She made a mental note to add to her personal list:

> *Buy brighter clothes. Anyway a scarf or something.* Didn't birds flash bright plumage to attract their mates?

"I asked for ideas on decorating the office for Unity in Diversity Day," Elaine explained. "I think this was his idea of an answer."

"Doesn't he know we don't allow any plants on the station outside of Life Support?"

"I don't think so. He's from one of the smaller asteroid colonies. Well, not a small *asteroid*, they claimed a fairly good-sized one and hollowed out most of it, but the *population* is relatively small." Elaine had looked up some data on Pieds Nus while she was off-shift, and it seemed to be an extremely strange place indeed, with botanical life forms actively encouraged all over the place and a population per cubic meter that was so low she'd thought at first the computer had misplaced a decimal point . . . and this conversation was *not* working out the way it was supposed to, Bryce studying the flowering tree and her babbling about Orlin Okusa. Talk to a man about himself, Bethy had advised, and you'll always get his full attention. "I hear you're programming the music for Unity in Diversity Day."

Bethy was right; Bryce beamed at her. "Yes, I'm putting my entire collection of Vronsolo audios on a repeating loop. It's such soothing and inspirational music, I hope station management agrees to keep it on continuous broadcast after the day. Just imagine how it would be to work in an environment where you kept hearing words of ancient wisdom like, 'Every sorrow is an opportunity to heal yourself,' repeated until they sank into your heart."

"I can feel my heart sinking already," said Elaine, and then, "I mean . . . it sounds peaceful. Very, very . . . umm . . . peaceful." So they didn't like the same kind of music, so what? Lots of couples didn't have exactly the same tastes. "Maybe if I heard more of Vronsolo's work I'd understand it better." *This is your cue to invite me down to your personal tube after shift*.

Bryce apparently couldn't hear the cue. "It's not something you explain. You just have to feel the vibes. Maybe you're not sensitive to them." Bryce was looking at the damn tree again. "Well, I'd better take care of this."

"I hope you can find a nice place for it in the Life Support gardens."

"Huh? No, we'll shred it for compost. Grass is actually much more efficient than trees for recycling carbon dioxide, you know. And *Chlorella pyrenoidosa* is even better. Not to mention that we can process it into food when its efficiency drops off. It makes very good simulated protein."

"Have you tried the algysteaks in the cafeteria?" *Obviously not, or you wouldn't be praising the sim-protein like that. But I'd be more than happy to take you up to sample them after shift.*

"Yes, that's an excellent example of energy- and space-efficient recycling. Well, see you later."

Oh, well. On the way back to ComCen, Elaine crossed *Meet Bryce* off her list. *Date Bryce, Fall in love,* and *Get married* were obviously going to take a little more effort.

Dear Elaine Byelski Coms Spec 4, what did you think of my suggestion for Unity in Diversity Day decorations? If you like the tree, our bio labs can clone as many as you want. They've developed an accelerated growth gene, so the trees can easily be ready by the time you need them.

Since you were interested in what I look like, I've attached a picture. I'm afraid I'm not nearly as pretty as you, but everybody says I have a really nice personality. If you have any vacation coming up, would you like to come to Pieds Nus? I'd love to show you around our habitat, and it would give us a chance to get better acquainted.

Love, Orlin Okusa.

Dear Orlin, the tree was beautiful, but I'm afraid we aren't allowed to have plants on the station outside of Life Support, especially flowering plants. Too many of the staff have allergies. I'll just have to think of something else for the UDD decorations.

As you say, there's plenty of time. Please
don't send anything else to my work station! I'm in enough trouble over the music
audio and the tree already.

Sincerely yours, Elaine Byelski, Coms
Spec 4, Communications Central, Ceres
Base.

He was right, "pretty" wasn't the word. The attached
picture showed a young man with a strong, dark-skinned
face with sharp cheekbones and a surprisingly engaging smile. Not her type, of course, and nobody would
look twice at him with someone like Bryce around,
but he wasn't bad-looking. She would guess a mixture
of West African and Native American blood, except it
was against Federation guidelines for non-prejudicial
thought to speculate on somebody's ethnic heritage.
There was enough of that going on between the
VolksAlliance and the Candomble Negre and all the
other ethnic-enclave asteroids to put anybody off the
idea, anyway.

And he was nice, and thoughtful, but definitely
pushy. "Love, Orlin," indeed!

P.S. I don't expect to have any vacation
time in the near future.

Dear Elaine Byelski Coms Spec 4 Communications Central Ceres Base, it's too bad
you don't have any vacation coming up. I
guess we'll just have to come up with some
other way for you to get to Pieds Nus. I
know you'll love it here.

Love, Orlin.

❖   ❖   ❖

"The guy can't take a hint," she complained to Bethy. "Maybe I should tell him I expect to be washing my hair every free shift for the next year."

"If he doesn't take hints, what makes you think he'd take that one? He'd probably just send you a package of flavored shampoo." Bethy studied the picture which Elaine had printed out along with the latest letters. "Besides, why do you want to hint him off? He looks okay to me."

"I'm already making progress on my master list," Elaine said. "See?" She brought up her personal list and waved the screen under Bethy's nose. *Meet Bryce* was crossed off.

"Not that much progress," Bethy sniffed. "*I* had a date with Henrik the first off-shift we were both free." She regarded Elaine with an older sister's critical eye. "I should take you shopping, get your hair done, get you fixed up to catch Bryce's eye. If you're determined to have him."

"That's on my list too," Elaine said. "See?"

> *Buy brighter clothes. Anyway a scarf*
> *or something.*

"I don't think a scarf is going to quite do it," Bethy said, "and bright colors are all wrong for you anyway."

Elaine didn't feel like getting into one of Bethy's detailed what's-wrong-with-you-and-how-to-fix-it sessions. "Why do you suppose this Orlin Okusa writes so oddly? I mean, first he addresses me as *Dear Elaine*, then it's *Dear Elaine Byelski Coms Spec 4*, then *Dear Elaine Byelski Coms Spec 4 Communications Central Ceres Base*."

"You're definitely more the pastels type, with that

brownish-blond hair and soft coloring," Bethy mused. "You couldn't possibly wear my iridescent peacock eye shadow, for instance."

Elaine didn't think any living being ought to wear Bethy's iridescent peacock eye shadow. "I'm beginning to think he's making fun of me. For being too formal or something."

"On the whole, I'd say you're a Muted Warms color type."

"Do you think I am?"

"Oh, definitely."

"What, I'm too formal?"

"No, silly, you're a Muted Warm Shades color type."

Elaine had barely logged in for her next shift at ComCen before Aksia logged her out. "Did you hear about the disaster on SprOUTs?"

"What, the gay vegetarians?"

"The same-sex-preference non-carnivorous colony," Aksia corrected. "I *wish* you would follow the Non-Discriminatory Speech Guidelines, Elaine."

"So what's happened on SprOUTs? Oversupply of methane from eating all those beans?" Dom snickered.

"No, that would be a Life Support issue," Aksia said, "why would we be worrying about Life Support? This is a *communications* problem. Their transmitter program has suddenly started beaming messages to us every ten minutes instead of at their regular shift time, and they can't fix it. And we can't tell them how to fix it, because it's only transmitting, not receiving. I need a Com Spec to fast-ship over there and take care of the problem, and you and Dom are the only ones without prior commitments."

"I'd be more than happy to go," Dom volunteered. "Some of those SprOUTs are real hunks."

Aksia gave him a fish-eyed stare. "That," she said, "is why I'm sending Elaine. At least she'll keep her mind on the job."

Fast-ship transport between Ceres Base and the asteroids was hideously expensive, but at least Base was paying for this trip. And once she got there, Elaine had to admit that Aksia had been right—in more ways than one. Even if the tanned, buffed SprOUTs had been of her sexual preference, she wouldn't have been interested in them. Not when she had Bryce to come home to! And thinking about Bryce, and about the possibility that Jana was sneaking down to Life Support to make time with him while she was off-base, inspired Elaine to get the SprOUT transmitter program fixed with record speed. It wasn't complicated, really—just a matter of resetting some base code registers that had been overwritten when they added a broccoli/tomato genetic code to an already overloaded central processing unit. Elaine tried to document and explain what she'd done to the SprOUT technician so that he could fix it himself next time this happened, but after three attempts she gave up and simply recommended that they take some budget from Genetic Adventures and give it to Computing Support for more memory or even a whole new system.

She arrived back on base in mid-shift to a series of increasingly urgent messages amounting to, "GET BACK TO COMCEN AT ONCE!" with more and more flashing lights and warning beepers attached to each one.

"About time!" Aksia snapped as soon as Elaine entered the ComCen tube. "Where've you *been*?"

"SprOUTs Colony. You sent me, remember?"

"Well, look what's happened while you were away!" Aksia sneezed and pointed at Elaine's pod. "I've already sent for Bryce from Life Support to dispose of it, but

Elaine, you *must* not let this happen again, do you understand? You and your boyfriend from Pieds Nus are continually disrupting our tube!"

"He's not my boyfriend," Elaine began, "and . . . ohhhh." Something resembling a ball of gray and yellow yarn was clawing its way up the sides of her pod, mewing piteously. "It's a kitten!" She rushed to detach the fuzzy bundle and cuddled it against her shoulder. "I haven't seen one of these since I was a little girl on Earth."

"I should hope *not*," Aksia said. "Animal dander is a major allergen. We can't have this sort of thing contaminating the atmosphere. If I'd been here when that idiot from Pieds Nus brought it in, I'd never have let him just leave it."

"Orlin was here? In person? And I missed him?" Elaine told herself that there was absolutely no reason to feel so upset at the news. After all, every single contact with Orlin Okusa had been a disaster for her career at ComCen.

Aksia waved her hand impatiently. "I have no idea who he was. Thank goodness that nice young man will take it away for us."

"Orlin? He's still here?"

"No, Bryce from Life Support. I've already sent for him. He's been a great help all round. Since you didn't do anything about the Unity in Diversity Day decorations—"

"I wasn't here," Elaine pointed out, without much heat. "And I did email you a suggestion while I was on SprOUTs. After I fixed their system." It was much more interesting to lay her cheek against the kitten's warm fur than to argue with Aksia.

"*Banners* were a good idea," Aksia conceded grudgingly, "but your idea of having banners to represent each of the asteroid colonies was terrible."

"I thought the idea of UDD was to show how well we all get along and tolerate one another's ideas."

"VolksAlliance banners would offend Nuevo Aliyah, Nuevo Aliyah banners would offend the Islamic Renaissance, Naturist banners would offend the Neo-Victorians. . . ." Aksia threw up her hands. "*You*, Elaine, you would manage to offend *everybody*. But Bryce saved the day. He printed out these banners for us to use instead." Aksia pointed at the pale sheets of algypaper hanging down from the rounded top of the tube. Each one bore a saying lettered in pastel rainbow colors. *Friends are angels who lift us to our feet when our wings have trouble remembering how to fly.*

"Very nice," Elaine said. *Rhymes with Bryce.* The kitten was vibrating. *Purring*, that was what they called it. "They ought to go very well with the Vronsolo audios. What's he going to do with the kitten?"

"Same thing he did with the tree, I suppose."

"*Recycling?* He's going to *kill* it?" *Walk gently through the world and know its beauty*, the next banner exhorted.

Aksia looked away. "Base regulations, Elaine."

"Um . . . Right. Base regulations. I understand, of course." *Love is the only reality and everything that is not love is not real.*

"But would you let me take it down to Life Support myself?" She couldn't remember exactly how much was in her savings account, and she couldn't check with the kitten clinging to her wrist. *Learn to be calm and you will always be happy.*

"We really need you here . . . oh, all right. I'll cancel the call to Bryce."

Elaine had always assumed that all airlocks were the same: boring gray chambers where your space-suit kept you from feeling the rush of pressurized air blowing any dust or contaminants you'd brought with you into the filter ducts. And in functional design, this one was just like all the others she'd been through. But it wasn't boring, and it wasn't gray. The walls were painted in rainbows of saturated color, the floor was painted green, and arrowed signs in cheerful, eccentric lettering declared THIS WAY OUT, THIS WAY FOR THE SPACE CRUD, and THIS WAY IN.

After she passed through the airlock, the suit-removal room with its moving holographic designs didn't quite stun her. She was even able to decipher the signs. SUIT STORAGE HERE, and SHOE STORAGE HERE, were the only ones that seemed to apply to her.

There wasn't anything that applied to her main problem. Elaine slipped her ship sandals off, tagged them with her name and ID, dropped them in the offered bin and proceeded to Immigration Control.

Which consisted of just one person, lounging on a slanted surface covered with something that looked like sim-grass.

A young man with dark skin, high sharp cheekbones, and an engaging smile. And bare feet.

"Do you have any *idea*," Elaine demanded, "how much it cost me to get a fast-ship round-trip ticket from Ceres just to bring this back to you? They wouldn't let me ship it, you know. It has to be personally escorted." She tried to hold out the kitten, but it had one paw hooked into her collar and the other one entangled in her hair.

"Elaine," the young man said happily. "Yes, I was counting on that. Er . . . What happened?" His nose wrinkled slightly as she came closer.

"Spacesuits," Elaine said dangerously, "have no plumbing attachments for cats. I'm surprised you didn't discover that when you brought this thing to

Ceres. Here, take it. I can't keep a cat on Ceres, you should have known that."

Orlin grinned. "Well, you did say you hadn't any vacation time coming, so I had to get you here some way. I knew you wouldn't let Zoroaster be recycled."

"Zoroaster?"

Orlin stroked the fluffy gray ball on Elaine's shoulder and gently detached first one clinging paw, then the other. "His mother came of ancient Persian lineage. Let me get you something fresh to wear."

Elaine felt cleaner, if somewhat less like herself, after she retired into the changing room again to exchange her odiferous travel clothes for the light, colorful sarong that Orlin had offered her.

"Seems a pity to come this far and not see something of the colony," Orlin pointed out, and Elaine had to agree. It would have been rude to dash off immediately. She looked for a way around the sim-grass but could see no stepping stones.

"Right this way," Orlin held out his hand to her. "Don't you see the sign?"

It hovered above the bank of green sim-grass, a holographic projection: PLEASE DO WALK ON THE GRASS.

"It's real!" Elaine discovered. The soft blades were tickly against her bare toes.

"Of course. Why waste space on simulated grass when you can have the real thing growing and helping to keep the atmosphere clean?"

Elaine looked across the hollow sphere of Pieds Nus and saw more green, interspersed here and there with sapphire pools of water. Clusters of buildings rose like honeycombs here and there, glass-walled structures built on networks of structural girders. Some of the walls were transparent; others were set to reflect bright colors, patterns, or the golden light coming from the plasma tubes that grew out of the floor every few meters.

"Would you like to see how our residences are arranged? I live in this one." Orlin pointed to a spiral building like a section of nautilus shell stood on edge, with pearl and iridescent glass walls.

As they walked over the springy grass, a soft breeze caressed Elaine's shoulders. It felt very strange to have bare shoulders and no belt around her waist. The springy, living grass under her feet felt even stranger. The only familiar thing was the weight of the wristlister on her arm. Pretty soon it would be beeping the five-minute warning for her return flight.

"My friends thought it was a waste of money, taking the kitten to Ceres," Orlin said. "Especially when I didn't even get to see you. And they thought you'd just hand Zoroaster over to Ceres Base Life Support and we'd never see him again either." His free hand caressed the kitten on his shoulder, and it vibrated so loudly that Elaine could hear it.

"I *couldn't*," Elaine said indignantly. "They would have *recycled* him."

Orlin smiled down at her. "I knew you wouldn't let that happen, Elaine Byelski Coms Spec 4. You know, Pieds Nus needs a communications manager. Somebody with initiative, who's good at solving problems."

"I shouldn't think you'd have any trouble recruiting."

"Ah, well, you see, we like to get someone who will fit in and appreciate our philosophy of life. And we can't pay very well. Mining Pieds Nus while we hollowed it out paid off our initial colony start-up debt to Earth, but since then we've chosen to use as much of our space as possible for public parks like this one, instead of cramming it with zero-g manufacturing bubbles and telecommuting offices. So our asteroidal tax base isn't much. But the job comes with amenities. Your own apartment, for instance. There's space in my spiral; you could have your own rooms there. And—"

Elaine's listbot beeped, and she held up her wrist to see that the screen showed *Return flight departing 005:00*.

"And if you turned in the return half of your ticket, you'd have enough money to live on while you decided whether you liked it here enough to stay." Orlin paused. "While we got to know each other better."

"If there's a salary and apartment that goes with the position, I wouldn't *need* to turn in my return ticket," Elaine pointed out.

Return flight departing 004:30.

"Anyway, I got the cheapest rate I could. It's non-refundable."

Orlin sighed. "Do you *want* to go back and catch your fast-ship?"

Return flight departing 004:00.

Elaine reached up to stroke the kitten perched on Orlin's shoulder. It purred loudly, gathered its haunches, and launched itself across space at her head. Elaine ducked instinctively; the kitten tumbled into the branches of a miniature flowering tree, hissed its disapproval, and disappeared beneath the shrubbery.

"Oh, no! Zoroaster? *Zoroaster!*" Elaine dropped to her knees and reached futilely under the low-growing branches. The kitten retreated with a disdainful hiss.

Return flight departing 002:30. The listbot started a siren wail of warning and Zoroaster took off in fright. Elaine jabbed at the alarm button to turn it off, but too late.

"How will we ever find him now?"

"Oh, he'll come back when he's hungry," Orlin said. "But I don't think you're going to make your return flight." He cupped one hand under her elbow and helped her up. That felt strange, too. Bare shoulders . . . bare feet . . . a cat purring against her face . . . a friendly hand under her elbow . . .

"I guess I'd better apply for that communications job, then," Elaine said.

The personal side of the listbot beeped at her with a list of reminders. *Get date with Bryce. Fall in love. Get married.*

"What's it fussing about now?" Orlin inquired.

"Oh, nothing important." Elaine tapped in one last command that stopped the beeping for good.

Erase all.

This story is set in Allen's "Near Space" future history, and his first venture back into that territory in five years. Mankind won't take only its higher aspirations into space, it'll take universal principles, like "A sucker is born every minute."

HIGH ROLLER

Allen M. Steele

We came into Nueva Vegas through the service entrance on the crater's north side. Our hiding place was a pressurized cell inside a water tank carried by a cargo hauler. We played possum while the vehicle came to a stop and casino security scanned the tank; the water surrounding us blocked the neutrino sweep, and our skinsuits stealthed everything else. The tractor began moving again; we felt it enter the vehicle airlock, then it stopped once more and there was another long wait while the airlock pressurized and electromagnetic scrubbers whisked away the dusty regolith. We rolled forward again; another minute passed, then we came to a halt and I heard JoJo's voice through my headset:

"Clear."

About time. I'd been flat on my back during the forty-kilometer ride down the Apollo Highway from Port Armstrong, and my arms were beginning to cramp from holding the equipment bag against my chest. I reached up, found the hatch lockwheel, twisted it clockwise, and pushed it open, then sat up and squirmed up through the half-meter manhole. Jen was right behind me; I crouched on top of the hauler and took her bag from her, then helped her out of the tank.

As we'd expected, we were in the garage beneath the crater. Rovers, buses, and various maintenance vehicles were parked all around us. No one in sight; the day-shift workers had long-since clocked off and the night-shift guys had already clocked in. JoJo was the only guy around, and he didn't count.

In fact, JoJo wouldn't count for much of anything until I reactivated him. Once Jen and I pulled our masks out of our bags and put them on, I climbed up to the hauler's cab, turned a valve to bleed off the air, and unsealed the hatch. He sat behind the yoke, two meters of ceramic polymer, dumb as a moonrock. Had to be that way; if he'd retained his programming during the ride to the casino, it might have been downloaded at the security checkpoint and searched by the local DNAI. So his memory had been scrubbed before we left Port Armstrong, leaving behind only a well-buried instruction to transmit the all-clear once the hauler had arrived and his peripheral sensors didn't register any body-heat signatures. He'd driven us here without even knowing it.

The next order of business was bringing JoJo back into the game. I opened my bag, pulled out my pad, and linked it to the serial port on his chest. A double-beep from my pad, reciprocated by another double-beep from his chest; lights flashed on his cylindrical head, then his limbs made a spasmodic jerk.

"Reload complete. All systems operational." Then

his head snapped toward me. "Nice to see you again, Sammy. You're looking particularly reptilian today."

Good. He recognized me even though I was now wearing my disguise. "Welcome back, JoJo," I said, then stepped aside so he could see Jen. "You know our partner, of course."

"Yo, Jen! How's it going, girl? Found any good cow pies lately?"

She wasn't amused. "Say it again, tinhead," she murmured, "and I'll download you into a vacuum cleaner."

"Everyone, relax." JoJo was just being funny, sure, but I'd like to find the guy who invented personality subroutines for AIs. "We've got a job to do. JoJo, can you modem the casino comp?"

"Let me work on it." A moment passed. "*Nyet*. Too many lock-outs. I'll need direct interface."

I was expecting that. "No problem. We'll try again once we find a comp." I jumped down off the tractor; JoJo followed me, his slender limbs whirring softly as he unfolded himself from the cab. I locked the cab, then turned to him. "Gimme an eyes-up of the layout, basement only. Pinpoint our location."

"You got it, chief." An instant later, a holo of Nueva Vegas's subsurface levels appeared upon the lenses of my mask. Our whereabouts were marked as three luminous points at the outer circle of a concentric maze of corridors, tunnels, rooms, and shafts. Nueva Vegas's quantum comp lay within a sealed vault at the center of this maze, protected by umpteen levels of defense, both electronic and physical. Ever heard of Fort Knox, the place in Kentucky where the old USA once kept its gold supply back when gold was actually worth something? The DNAI had that degree of protection, and then some. Impossible to penetrate, or so I'd been told.

But then again, that wasn't our problem. We were after bigger game.

I located the nearest service lift that went directly to the crater floor; it was only a few dozen meters away, down a short corridor. "Everyone ready? Got your stuff?" Jen nodded within her mask; JoJo blinked some diodes my way. "Okay, then," I said, and picked up my bag. "Let's roll."

Nueva Vegas is built within Collins Crater, about thirty kilometers from the Apollo 11 Historical Site. A tour bus that will take you out there, and also to the Surveyor 5 landing site just a few klicks away and the Mare Tranquillitatis Battlefield Memorial a few hundred klicks north near Arago Crater. Most visitors don't do that, though. Nueva Vegas wasn't the first lunar casino resort, but most guidebooks consider it to be the best. The table stakes are good, and the payout is excellent; even if you don't gamble, there's vices you won't easily find back on Earth. Not too many places where you can legally purchase a 250-gram bag of Moondog Gold, or hire a double-jointed google—pardon me, a Superior—to be your companion for the evening.

But it's still a place for the rich. A cheap room near the crater floor costs 300 lox per sol; for this you get a bed, a passcard for the shower stall down the corridor, five complimentary chips, and a discount coupon for the all-you-can-eat buffet. A two-room suite—complete with its own personal bath, private balcony, mini-bar, and free Continental breakfast—will set you back a cool million for a two-week stay. High rollers rate the best accommodations, of course: spacious apartments on the upper levels of the crater rim, with outside windows, catered dining, personal masseurs, an unlimited line of credit, and all the liquor, dope, and sex you can take. If you have to ask how much that costs, then you have no business being there.

We were checking in on the budget plan. No room, no bath, no food. We weren't planning to stay very long, though. Just a few minutes on the casino floor, and we'd be on our way.

The lift doors opened and we stepped out into a white-mooncrete corridor with low ceilings and fluorescent lighting. A 'bot carrying a platter of hors d'oeuvres squealed in protest as it swerved to avoid colliding with us. From the other side of a pair of swinging doors, I caught the aroma of cooked food. We'd found the entrance to one of the service kitchens. I noted the direction in which the 'bot was headed, and turned to follow it.

"Hey! What are you guys doing here?"

A short, rotund gentleman in a waiter's tux and powdered wig emerged from a doorway, a magnum of champagne wrapped in a towel in his white-gloved hands. A wine steward, clearly irritated by our presence. "We've told you people a thousand times," he snapped as he bustled up to us. "Entertainers eat in the employee's cafeteria, just like everyone else."

He'd mistaken us for one of the lounge acts. No wonder. I wore a lizard-head mask, and Jen looked like a giant housefly. They didn't just conceal our faces; the masks also contained eyes-up displays, voice filters, and short-range com gear. We looked weird, sure, but in Nueva Vegas weirdness is the normal order of things. We fit right in.

"A thousand pardons, sir," I said. "We just got confused, thought this was—"

"Is that the wine cellar?" Jen interrupted, her voice an insectile buzz behind her mask. "May we see it, please?"

The waiter regarded her as if she had just emerged from a bowl of *potage Rossini*. "You most certainly may not," he huffed, not noticing that her right hand was within her bag. "Now, if you'll please—"

"Oh, but I insist." Jen's hand came out of the bag; clasped within it was Pax Astra Royal Navy taser pistol. He barely got a chance to see what it was before Jen jammed it against his throat. "I'd love to see your collection."

"R-r-right this way, madam." The wine steward managed to keep from dropping the bottle of '77 Sinai Planum as he hastily tapped his password into the keypad, then backed through the door.

The wine cellar was a small, cool room, dimly lit, with hundreds of bottles of expensive wines resting upon faux-oak racks. The waiter sat down in the corner next to the imported Bordeaux, clasped his hands together atop his wig, and wisely remained quiet while Jen and I pulled out our guns—two PARN particle-beam rifles, complete with laser sights—and attached smoke and pepper-gas grenades to our belts. JoJo went to the wall comp; opening a chest port, he pulled out a cable and hardwired himself to it, then went silent for a couple of minutes while lines of type flashed across the comp screen so fast that I couldn't keep up with them.

"We're in," he said at last, his head swiveling toward me. "Ready to initiate final sequence."

"Got it right here, big guy." I reached into a chest pocket, found the diskette I'd been given. Another fail-safe; if we had been caught while passing through security, the first thing I would have done was push the auto-erase tab. JoJo pushed the diskette into the terminal, and I reached past him to tap an eight-digit code into the miniature keyboard. A green border appeared around the screen.

"Locked and loaded." I pulled out the diskette, snapped it between my hands, then tossed it into the corner next to the cowering wine steward. "Thank you, *garçon*. You've been very helpful."

"Mind if we take this?" Jen was examining a bottle of cabernet sauvignon she had taken from the wine rack. "Or would you recommend the beerenaulese instead?"

"Th-th-the cabernet is quite . . . quite good, m-m-madam." He was barely able to look up at her. "I don't . . . I don't think you'll be d-d-disappointed."

"Hmm . . . well, if you insist." Jen gently placed the bottle in her bag, then slung it across her shoulders. I hoped it wouldn't weigh her down too much. "Ready when you are."

"Okeydokey." JoJo detached his cable, let it reel itself back into his chest. "I'm going to huff, and I'm going to puff, and I'm going to—"

"Save it for the civilians." I raised my rifle to the terminal; one quick squeeze of the trigger, and the panel was fried out. I turned around and aimed my gun at the wine steward. "Okay, here's the deal. You get to live, so long as you sit here quietly for the next few minutes and don't make a peep. But if I see you, hear you, even smell you . . ."

"D-d-don't worry about me." His wig had become dislodged; his close-cropped hair was slick with sweat. "I-I-I'll just sit here."

"Good man. Again, we thank you."

He nodded, happy to be rid of us. Then it seemed as if he mustered a gram of courage. "Y-y-you know, of course, w-w-where you are."

"Sure. Nueva Vegas."

"Well, y-yes, of course, certainly, but . . ." His voice dropped. "This is . . . this is Mister Chicago's casino. This place . . . I mean, it belongs to *him*."

I raised an eyebrow before I remembered that he couldn't see my expression behind my mask. "Yes? And . . . ?"

"N-nothing." He stared at me for a moment in bewilderment, then the corners of his mouth twitched upward, as if he was enjoying a private joke at our expense. "Nothing at all. Enjoy your visit."

"Thank you. We will." I looked at the others. "All right, let's go."

The corridor was vacant. I waited until Jen and JoJo had come out, then I closed the wine cellar door behind us. I could have scrambled the keypad, but the wine steward hadn't given us any trouble. He deserved a chance to live. I left the door unlocked.

Our guns beneath our arms, we marched down the corridor, heading for a pair of double-doors at the end. The doors slid apart with barely a sound; light and noise rushed in.

The easy part was done. Now it was time for the tough stuff.

We came out into an open-air restaurant made to look like a Mediterranean cafe: plaster walls, watercolors of French street scenes, garden trellises cluttered with grapevine, tables covered with checkerboard cloths placed upon a red-brick terrace. Only a few diners noticed us as we quickly strode past them, and those who did were baffled for only a moment before knowing smiles crept across their faces. We had to be actors, on our way to a floor show somewhere in the casino. The guns? Obviously fakes. Even the waiters didn't look at us twice. We exited the cafe without bringing any undue attention to ourselves, and now we were within the casino.

The floor of Collins Crater was nearly two kilometers in diameter, and the casino took up nearly every square meter of it. Thousands of slot machines binged and booped and clinked and clanged in a steady and omnipresent cacophony, while the holos that flickered above them—semi-nude women doing strip-tease, classic cartoon characters chasing each other with chainsaws, starships engaged in battle—were ignored by scores of middle-aged men and women hunched in front of the machines, slipping tokens into the slots, pushing buttons and yanking chrome handles, watching in single-minded fascination as apples and grapes and lemons scrolled past their sleepless eyes. Gamblers gathered around blackjack and poker tables watched as dealers slapped cards down on the green felt, collecting chips with smiles, surrendering them with muttered curses. Waitresses in skin-tight outfits and high-heel shoes circulated between the baccarat and roulette tables, delivering drinks and joints to players as they studied cards and tossed dice, collecting tips from winners and favoring those who'd just crapped out with disingenuous expressions of sympathy. Here and there, within small sunken amphitheaters, comedians went through their routines, magicians performed sleight-of-the-hand tricks; applause greeted Frank, Dean, and Sammy as they took to the stage for another sold-out show. Hookers and tricks negotiated with one another, cardsharps tried out their systems for beating the odds, drunks bemoaned their bad luck, and a few hundred dumb-asses parted with their money and loved every moment of it, while smoke and sweat and liquor fumes rose to the opaque sky of the pressure dome far above, obscuring the security flycams that prowled above the gaming areas, their lenses watchful for any unusual activity.

We qualified. Even in the middle of all this, it was hard to miss Lizard Boy, Fly Girl, and JoJo the Robot as they made their way across the gaming area, rifles slung beneath their shoulders. By the time we reached the raised island near the center of the casino, three flycams were on us and a couple of plainclothes security guys moving into position. No alarms, or at least not yet; everyone was still trying to figure out who we were and what we were doing.

I ignored the heat as I approached casino control. A bouncer in a white tux moved in to block my way.

"May I help you, sir?" he asked, raising a hand to stop me.

"Yes, you can," I replied, and then I casually laid my gloved left hand against his wrist. A 10,000-volt charge dropped him. He'd barely hit the floor when Jen turned her taser upon the plainclothes guys. Four shots and they went down.

"JoJo," I said, "kill the flyers."

"You got it, chief." A double-beep from his chest, and every flycam in the casino fell from the air. They crashed into poker tables and slot machines, plummeted into cafes, smashed to pieces next to the Rat Pack. Throughout the casino, we could hear people screaming. As attention-getters go, this one rated a solid ten, and we weren't even started yet.

A Superior was on duty as floor boss. His long-fingered hands were already darting across the wraparound console as I dashed up the stairs onto the platform. "Get away from that," I said, pointing my rifle at him. The floor boss obediently moved away, the angel-wings tattooed across his face flexing slightly as his overlarge eyes stared at me in astonishment. Behind him, a red light flashed on a panel.

"What button did you push?" I asked.

"Locked down, we are. All exits blocked. Access to the cashiers, denied." He smiled at me. "Surrender now, if you're smart. Otherwise, assured your death shall be."

Something else I'd expected. "JoJo, the google's hit the panic button," I murmured, speaking into my throat mike. "Do something about it, okay?"

"I'm on it." A brief pause. "They're onto us, chief."

Looking around, I saw what he meant. All the slot-machines had gone silent. Chrome shutters had automatically rolled down across the windows of the cashier booths. Even the service 'bots had become motionless. Patrons milled about in confusion, still unaware of what was happening in their midst, yet from my vantage point on the platform, I could see recessed floor panels irising open all around us.

"Jen, cover us!" I snapped. "JoJo, link up with the security system!"

Elevators ascended from beneath the casino floor, each one bearing a combot. Big mothers, too: two-and-a-half meters tall, heavily armored, with guns built into their forearms and 360-degree vision in their spade-shaped heads. Tourists shrieked and ran for cover, dropping tokens and chips as they made way for the behemoths stamping through the aisles. Nasty toys. Mister Chicago had spared no expense making his customers feel safe.

Jen's multifaceted eyes turned toward me. "This could be a problem."

"Bad idea, was it not?" The floor boss calmly watched as the 'bots advanced toward us, his right hand hovering above the console. "Give up, and live you still may."

"Think not, I do." I looked down at JoJo. "Got it?"

"Twenty-eight seconds ago." JoJo didn't budge. "Do you want me to . . . ?"

"Yes. Please. By all means." Damn literal-minded machine. . . .

A moment later, the 'bots froze in place. I heard

a brief buzz from the nearest one just before it went inert. I looked around at the floor boss just in time to see his mouth drop open. "You were saying?"

"How did . . . how could you have . . . ?"

I always knew Superiors could speak plain English when they wanted to. "That's my secret," I said, then I reached into my hip pocket and pulled out my pad. "Okay, now that you're all out of tricks, show me how to link up with cash control."

Still not convinced I meant business, he stared at me. I planted my rifle barrel against his chest. "Look, I can do this without your help. You saw what I did to the 'bots. The only difference is that it'll make my job a little easier, and you'll get to breathe through your mouth instead of through a chest wound. So what do you say?"

He was about to reply when I heard a sudden *fizz!* from behind me. Looking around, I saw Jen holding her rifle in firing position. Not far away, a small mob of people was backing away from a slot machine she'd just killed.

"Too many heroes in this place, Sammy," she said quietly, for my ears only. "We need to get a move on." Then she gazed back at the mob. "Anyone else want to try it?" she said loudly.

They stayed where they were. We didn't want to kill anyone, but it was only a matter of time before she wouldn't be able to control the crowd any longer. I looked back at the floor boss; his expression told me that he'd finally realized how serious we were. "Ready to play along?"

"Certainly." Taking a keycard from his pocket, he unlocked a panel on the console, swung it open to reveal a serial port. "Here it is. All you have to do is—"

"I know." I attached my pad to the port, tapped in

a code I'd memorized. Nueva Vegas held very little in the way of hard currency. Most of its transactions were electronic, in the form of funds transferred from the bank accounts of its visitors, which in turn became Pax Astra lox payable as tokens and chips from the cashier booths. A secure system, so long as you didn't have direct access to casino control and knowledge of the code numbers that would allow you to tap into the funds stored within the central DNAI.

Which I did. Within seconds, 680.75 megalox was transferred into my pad. I detached the pad, tossed it down to JoJo. "Upload this, please," I said.

"Roger dodger." JoJo reattached the pad to his chest. In another moment, he transmitted the money to our friends in orbit. "All done, chief."

"Thank you." I turned to the floor boss one more. "Your cooperation has been appreciated, m'sieur. One last piece of business, and we'll be on our way."

"Get away with this, surely you don't expect." He must have begun to feel safe again, because he'd returned to his lopsided manner of speech. "Owned by Mister Chicago, Nueva Vegas. A individual lacking in forgiveness, but not in resources."

"So I've heard. But we have a few of our own." I looked away from him. "JoJo, will you come up here, please?"

"Is it my turn? Oh, joy!" JoJo clanked up the steps, coming to a halt between us. "Thank you, thank you," he said, raising his spindly arms and revolving his head to address everyone. "It's certainly an honor to be here tonight. I'd like to thank my producer, my director, my publicist, my screenwriter, and all the little people who've done so much over the years to—"

"Thanks, JoJo. You can shut up now." He obediently fell silent. I tapped a button on his chest; a panel slid open, and I entered a four-digit string into his CPU. The tiny LCD above it flashed to 15:00:00, then began to count back. I motioned the floor boss closer, then pointed to display. "See that? What do you think it is?"

He peered at it. "A timer?"

"That's correct . . . with a fifteen-minute countdown that's already started." I walked behind JoJo, opened another panel to reveal a liter-sized cylinder within his back. "And this, my friend, is a nuke."

Technically speaking, the nuke wasn't a bomb, but rather a ten-kiloton nuclear device of the sort that asteroid miners use to excavate large c-type rocks. JoJo's body had literally been built around it, so it was well-shielded from the security scanners.

The bystanders close enough to overhear this shrank back. Murmurs swept through the crowd; most people froze, but a few turned and bolted down the aisles. The floor boss stared at me in horror.

"You're bluffing," he said quietly.

I looked him straight in the eye. "No, I'm not," I said, with utter sincerity. "In fifteen minutes—"

"Fourteen minutes, twenty-nine seconds," JoJo corrected. "Whoops. Better make that fourteen minutes, twenty-seven seconds. Oh, dear, now it's fourteen minutes, twenty-five—"

"Fourteen minutes and whatever. Thanks, JoJo, I'll take it from here." I shut the panel. "Anyway, you get the picture. You've got just that much time to evacuate the crater and get everyone to safe distance before—"

"I'm going to huff, and I'm going to puff, and I'm going to blow your house down!" JoJo had been saving that line all night. It wasn't part of his programming, but then again, neither was self-preservation.

"Thanks, JoJo. You said it better than I could have." I handed JoJo my rifle. "And in case you're wondering, he's had all his Asimov protocols scrubbed from memory, so it wouldn't be wise to try to disarm him." I turned to the 'bot. "You know what to do now, right?"

JoJo hefted the rifle. "Any youse punks gets any wise ideas, you gets a belly-full of laser, see? I'ma desperate 'bot, see?"

It was a lousy Cagney impersonation, but it got the point across. The Superior was already backing away. "So if I were you . . ." I continued.

The floor boss was no longer listening. Bolting to the nearest console, his hands raced across various buttons as he jabbered orders in Superior patois. Within moments, red emergency beacons began to strobe throughout the casino as sirens started to wail. A Code Five blowout alarm, activated only when catastrophic loss of dome integrity was imminent.

One thing to be said for Nueva Vegas: the management made sure that the tourists were repetitively instructed about what do in the event of a worst-case scenario. Those constant reminders on the room screens, in the elevators and restaurants and bars, even on the slot machines and above the game tables, got the point across to even the densest and most complacent of its patrons. All around us, everyone who hadn't fled already were running for their lives, sprinting for the clearly marked emergency exits ringed around the crater floor. Within minutes, the first few escape pods would be automatically launched from their ports within the outer crater rim. I saw a few die-hards scrambling to gather their chips, but even they knew that it was time to run. The floor boss had already leaped over the consoles; he joined the stampede, getting out while the getting was good.

"Minus ten minutes, thirty seconds, and counting." JoJo was no longer clowning around. "Um . . . Sammy? You're not going to . . ."

"Easy, pal. I got you covered." I pulled out my pad, rinsed its memory, then slapped it against his chest. A few seconds passed, then a light flashed on its panel: JoJo's higher functions had been downloaded into the pad, leaving behind only the basic routines necessary for the 'bot to continue its primary mission.

"Bye-bye," I said to the mindless automaton. Its head swiveled in my direction, but I wasn't a threat and so it ignored me. I jumped off the platform and landed next to Jen.

"You could have just left him behind." She was already headed for the restaurant where we'd come in.

"JoJo's good. I'd like to work with him again." No point in wasting a good AI for no reason. The casino floor was nearly empty; nothing stood between us and our escape route. "Clock's ticking," I said, slapping her behind. "Beat it, sugar mouth."

"After you, lizard lips."

The getaway was easy. Jen and I went back the way we came, through the service kitchen. By now the whole place was deserted, save for a few 'bots still carrying orders out to customers who had split without waiting for the check. All the same, I glanced inside the wine cellar to make sure the steward was no longer around. He was wise; he was gone. So we headed for the basement, skipping the slow-moving elevator and using the stairs instead.

The cargo hauler was right where we had left it. All the other vehicles had been taken, but no one had managed to break into our vehicle. Cab pressurization took ninety seconds—that was the only period in which

I was truly scared, watching the atmosphere meter rise while the countdown ticked back at the same rate—and once it was done I put the hauler in reverse and put the pedal to the floor. No time to wait for the vehicle airlock to cycle through; I rammed the doors with the hauler's back end, and let explosive decompression do the rest. Jen swore at me as she was thrown against her shoulder straps, but I paid little attention to her as I locked the brakes and twisted the yoke hard to the right, pulling a bootlegger-turn on the ramp. Then I floored it again and off we went, up the ramp and out into the cold blue earthlight.

I glanced at side-view mirror, giving Nueva Vegas one last look as the hauler raced across Mare Tranquillitatis, its steel-mesh tires throwing up fantails of moondust. Lights still gleamed through the crater windows, yet escape pods were rising from the outer wall, tiny ellipsoids heading for orbit. By now, the casino should be empty. Fifteen minutes is a long time when you're running for your life.

The lunar freighter was right where it was supposed to be, two klicks due east of Collins Crater. Its cargo ramp was lowered; I drove the hauler up it as fast as I dared, then slammed the brakes once we were inside the hold. The pilot wasn't taking any chances; he jettisoned the ramp, then shut the hatch and fired the main engines.

Jen and I were still in the hauler when the countdown reached zero, so we didn't get to see the nuke go off. I'm told it was beautiful: a miniature protostar erupting within a lunar crater, rising upward as hemispherical shell of thermonuclear fire. All we experienced, though, was a faint tremor that passed through the lander's hull as it raced ahead of the shockwave, heading for the stars.

After a while, the pilot repressurized the cargo bay. I

unsealed the cab and we climbed out, carefully making our way through zero-gee until we reached the open interior hatch. The crewman waiting on the other side cracked up when we came through, and it was only then that I realized that we were still wearing our masks. I tore mine off, took a deep breath, and grinned at the silly lizard face I'd worn for the last hour or so. Jen shook out her hair, scowled briefly at her fly head, then pitched it aside and let me give her a quick kiss.

I'd just made my way up to the command deck, with the intent of downloading JoJo into the nearest reliable comp I could find, when the pilot informed me that he had an incoming transmission. Mister Chicago wanted to talk to me.

I glanced at Jen. She was in the passageway behind us, floating upside-down as she peeled out of her sweaty skinsuit. We gave each other a look, then I told the pilot I'd take it in the wardroom. He nodded, and I squeezed past Jen to the closet-size compartment just aft of the cockpit.

Mister Chicago was waiting for me there, a doll-size hologram hovering an inch above the mess table. He was seated in lotus position, naked from the waist up, his dead-white skin catching some indirect source of light behind him. His pink eyes studied me as I moved within range of the ceiling holocams.

"I understand you destroyed my casino today," he said.

"Yes, I did," I replied.

Rumor had it that Mister Chicago made his base of operations somewhere out in the belt, within an asteroid he'd transformed into his own private colony. If that was so, then he couldn't be there now, because he nodded with barely a half-second delay.

"And I also understand that you managed to steal . . ."

He brushed his shoulder-length hair aside as he turned his head slightly, as if listening to someone off-screen. "Six hundred and eighty megalox from my casino before you detonated a nuclear device within it."

"Six hundred eighty million, seven hundred fifty thousand." I shrugged. "I haven't checked the exact figures, so there may be some loose change . . . yes, I did."

"Well done, sir. Well done."

"Thank you. We aim to please."

To this day, I still don't know exactly why Mister Chicago hired us to rob his own casino and then blow it up. Perhaps it had become a liability. Nueva Vegas was an expensive operation, after all; it may have cost more to keep it going than it brought in, and once its bottom line slipped from the black into the red, he may have decided to torch the place, once he'd made sure that he'd recovered every lox he could. He'd gone so far as to supply everything we needed—JoJo's nuke, schematics of the Nueva Vegas's sublevels and gaming areas, the codes to disable the security 'bots and provide direct access to the DNAI—and even furnish a means of escape.

Yet even a gangster has to answer to legitimate underwriters: insurance companies, banks, investors, the Pax Astra itself. So what better way to cover himself than have his property nuked during a heist? If his scheme was successful, he could always claim someone else did it. And if it failed . . . well, I doubt our conversation would have been so pleasant. If it happened at all.

But that's just my theory. Not for me to ask the reasons why.

"No lives lost, or so I've heard." His right hand briefly disappeared beyond camera range; when it returned, it held a glass of wine. "Quite professional.

I'm satisfied, to say the least. Add . . . oh, shall we say, another one percent to your take. Is that good for you?"

We'd agreed to do the job for five percent of whatever we managed to grab. A bonus was unnecessary, but welcome nonetheless. I felt a tap on my shoulder; looking around, I saw Jen hovering over my shoulder. She smiled and nodded. "Thank you," I said. "Yes, that's quite acceptable."

Jen kissed my ear; I gently pushed her away. "Well then, I believe our business is concluded, "Mister Chicago said. "If I ever need your services again . . ."

"You know where to find us."

"Very good. Thank you. Goodbye." A final wave, then his image faded out. I let out my breath, turned around to find Jen behind me.

"Want to know what six percent of six hundred eighty megalox is?" she asked.

"Um, let's see. That would be . . ." I shrugged. "You do the math. I'm busy right now."

She grinned, moved closer to me. I reached out, shut the compartment hatch. Until the freighter reached the nearest Lagrange station, we had a long ride ahead of us. And we still hadn't opened the bottle of wine she'd stolen.

We all know that the ambient temperature of outer space between the stars is mighty cold, about 2.7 degrees Kelvin. Even in the warm environs of our own solar system, space can make you cold. In the shadows, the moon can get as cold as 120 degrees Kelvin or -243 degrees Fahrenheit. That's still so darn cold it's funny. So is this story. . . .

MOON MONKEYS

Wen Spencer

I happened to be at the staging area when the first monkey arrived on the moon and departed. I was checking in cargo from the supply shuttle, doing double duty like everyone else. I glanced up and saw Banter coming toward the soft lock with something moving wildly in her arms.

"What the hell is she carrying?" I asked the Russian who had just arrived on the shuttle. I never caught his name; it used to be that we were small enough that every new colonist was greeted warmly, their name and bio fully memorized. Those days were already past; now there are people I don't even know.

"A monkey," he said in English so thick that I didn't understand him until he repeated, scratching under his armpits and hooting like an ape, "a monkey."

"Whose fucking bright idea was—oh shit!" The monkey had suddenly ripped the oxy line free on Banter's suit.

Banter dropped the struggling form and grabbed at her whipping air line. The Russian had already unsuited, so neither one of us could go out onto the surface to save her. The monkey took off, taking giant bounds in one-sixth gravity. Fortunately, Banter stumbled through the soft lock into the staging area, where we could help her.

The connector on her airline was broken, so her helmet had to come off. While it was designed to go on quickly, the old models still had toggle locks that took a minute to disengage. Finally the Russian and I jerked off Banter's helmet.

"Damn little f-hole!" she screamed once she had sucked in enough air to talk.

"You okay?" I asked. "Come on, stop swearing and talk to me. Are you okay?"

"It almost killed me!" she screamed.

I wanted to hug her but knew she'd slug me if I did. "Okay. You're good. I better suit up and go after it."

"No rush," the Russian said.

I turned and spotted the monkey slowly tumbling groundward, the air line of its miniature spacesuit ripped free in the same manner as Banter's.

The first monkey on the moon lasted approximately five minutes.

We sent down a "sorry, the monkey died" message, and Earth demanded a full report and its body returned, complete with the damaged spacesuit. We packed the monkey in dry ice and shipped body, suit, and report back.

The next shuttle arrived with another monkey.

"What do you mean, there's no cage for it?" I asked the Lithuanian who came up with the new monkey. We had gotten it through the soft lock into the safety of the staging area and stripped off its newly improved suit. The animal was actually quite sweet looking, with warm brown eyes and nearly human face. It came with a supply of monkey chow, a small bed, brightly colored toys, a high chair, and diapers, but no cage.

"What the hell are they thinking down there?" I asked the Lithuanian, getting a shrug. I checked my translator to see if it had English-to-Lithuanian on it; maybe he didn't grasp English that well. Russian was the best I could do, getting the same result.

I dug through the incoming cargo, wondering if maybe the cage had just been mislabeled, and discovered that Earth had sent up new air line seals, ones with improved safety locks. I showed them off to Banter when she stormed into staging area from landside.

"What is this about another monkey?" she snapped.

"Yeah, they sent up another one." I held out the air line. "Look, they improved the connectors."

"So where's the monkey?" She scanned the staging area, and then—with eyes going wide—looked out through the soft lock.

I jerked around. A small, dark furred body smudged the gray starkness of the moon surface. "Oh, damn."

The second monkey on the moon lasted approximately ten minutes. Talk about embarrassing.

I had to send down another "sorry the monkey died" message with an apology. Earth demanded a full report including any modifications we made on

the soft lock since it had been shipped up, and of
course, the dead monkey.

We met the next shuttle with a cage, but it proved
to be unnecessary. This time Earth had sent up a
monkey wrangler.

She was a little thing, eyes dark and solemn as
her charge, but there was something about her that
made me want to get primitive with her. "No cage."
Her simple English statement was made beautiful by
some exotic accent. The sweat-dampened hair clinging
to the elegant curve of her neck reminded me how
long it had been since I'd been with a woman.

"It's a nice cage." Banter showed it off. "We padded the bottom. There are blankets, and a mirror,
and some toys."

The wrangler shifted the monkey in her arms, and
spoke in a fluid, wonderfully liquid language.

"What is she saying?" I asked Banter.

"Tell me what language it is, and I might be able
to guess," Banter growled, fiddling with her translator. "Well, let's get the damn thing far, far away from
the soft lock."

"Ah!" The wrangler gasped, and pulled out a data
stick. "Soft lock!"

We got her and the monkey settled into one of the
bachelor cubbyholes—since a goodly number of people
had paired up and moved into the new burrows, even
with the steady influx of personnel, we had plenty of
cubbies standing empty. The data stick had an interesting modification for the soft lock. Using the suit's
com device, the lock would check items trying pass
out of the lock to make sure it was either a human
or cargo being handled by a human. It slowed down
the process of walking out of the staging area, making you hesitate before crossing the field barrier. We

started to play with this, seeing if we could extend the authorization zone, when the monkey wrangler appeared, eyes wide in panic.

"Carly gone!" she cried. "I sleep. She goes!"

"Who's Carly?" I asked.

She said something and we looked at her blankly.

"Carly," she repeated. Then seeing we didn't understand, said, "Monkey?"

It turns out that the ventilation system screens had fasteners that any semi-intelligent creature with fingers could turn. The shafts were built so a man could crawl through them, just in case the need arose. (Don't ask. Yes, shades of B-rate vids come to mind.) Unfortunately, to move air through such the extensive airways, there were massive air handlers at intervals. Read "fans." Read "whirling blades of death."

The third monkey on the moon lasted approximately four hours.

We were improving.

Because she was the only one who didn't have a job—currently—our poor monkey wrangler, Emma cleaned up the fan while we sent off the "the monkey is dead" report to Earth. We figured she'd go on the next shuttle, but instead they sent up another monkey, new fasteners for all the ventilation system, safety screens for the air handlers, and a plea to try and make this monkey last.

We had a long fight with Emma over Danny, the new monkey. While we were all for caging this monkey, Emma insisted that Danny couldn't be imprisoned. Or at least, we're fairly sure that was what she was saying. The translators proved useless. Most of her side was little shakes of her head and exotic-flavored "no's" and occasional outbursts in her own language. We did lots of miming monkey's deaths: loose air hoses, chopping blades, dropping limp onto the ground. In the end, she won by sheer determination.

Unfortunately, Danny discovered the positive pressure toilets late that night. Who would have guessed that its head could get stuck that way? Still, at ten hours, he'd set a new survival record.

It takes nearly two weeks for the shuttle to go and come back, so you would have thought we'd start to wonder "why monkeys?" way before little Ethan showed up. So far as I know, though, Banter was the first to ask. She and I were in a gravity training area, working up a sweat, talking about how totally dippable Emma was. A foundation of our friendship is that I usually manage to ignore Banter's total babe exterior to see the guy inside. Not an easy task to do, sometimes, since we're occasionally the only single people on the moon.

It was our shared opinion that it wouldn't be right to hit on someone just after the death of their pet. With Emma, though, it was *always* right after her monkey died.

"So," Banter paused to see that we were still completely alone in the gravity lab. "Why do you think someone is shipping monkeys to the moon?"

"What do you mean?"

"Well, animal testing has been mostly banned." Banter walked to the wallcom and did a quick search. "It says Emma's studying the effects of the moon on the development of primates."

"It kills them, that's the effect." I got a nasty look from Banter. "Well, who are the idiots that keep sending up the monkeys?"

Banter stood for several minutes, showing off her really fine assets as she searched through databases.

"It's hard to say; it looks like someone is purposely covering that information up. Hmmm, all her monkeys are clones—different series, but all from bio cribs."

At that point, the lights flickered as Ethan departed from this world.

I visited Emma later that night to console her. The ventilation system had removed all smell of electrocuted monkey out of her bachelor cubbyhole, but toys still littered the floor, and Emma—surrounded with photographs of smiling people—looked forlorn. With the addition of all the monkey stuff, I found the apartment claustrophobic when in reality it was no smaller than my place. The reminders of her dead monkeys were unavoidable, from the scuff marks of the shopvac around the air vent to the new scorch marks encircling the ceiling power coupler.

"Why don't you move into another cubbyhole until the next monkey comes?" I spent several minutes pantomiming out the English question.

"Burrow?" Emma pointed out toward the new warrens.

"No. No." How could I explain the housing rules? "Burrows are for couples. Two." And then in case she misunderstood that, I pointed to a picture of a monkey on one of the chow bags. "Emma and monkey—no burrow. Emma and human." I pointed to myself, "Yes burrow."

"Ah." She took my hand and, unzipping her jumpsuit, guided it inside her clothing. Like so many women on the moon, she'd abandoned bras, and so it was her bare breast that nestled in my hand, warm, round, and soft. "Emma and you?" And gazing up at me with her dark and solemn eyes, she undid my coverall. "Burrow? Yes?"

It was the luckiest misunderstanding of my life.

❖   ❖   ❖

Poor Banter wasn't sure which of us to be more pissed at. Me, for getting Emma first—or Emma, for reasons I'm not sure that I totally understand.

"I can't shake the feeling that she's using you to get something." Banter complained but helped me move Emma's stuff to the new burrow.

"You know, if I wasn't so incredibly mellow at this moment, I'd be offended."

"Laugh it up, Monkey Boy, but it's fishy that you tell her that she can't move into a burrow alone and she jumps the closest human."

"Ah." I made noises to make her happy. "You see, Banter, that's the difference between men and women. When a truly desirable female says 'let's have sex' you ask 'why?' and I say '*yes!*' "

"Okay, I agreed that she's totally hot, but there's something a little creepy about all this." Banter picked up one of the photographs. "For example, these pictures. None of them are from Earth; she's taken them all up here. She's got the archive feature on." Banter pointed out the timestamp and record counter; by coincidence she'd gotten the first one Emma'd taken. It was of Mel and Bucky, the unofficial "King and Queen" of the moon.

"That's just Mel for you." I took the picture off of Banter and packed it in the crate. "Mel has to be first for everything. First woman on the moon. First permanent colonist. First documented fuck. First wedding. I hear she's trying for first baby too; claims her biological clock is ticking."

"I still think its weird; none of them are of you."

"Well, there's none of you either," I countered.

Ethan had discovered electricity. Fiona set herself on fire. Gerald garroted himself. Hitomi chewed on hemlock. Honestly, we tried not to laugh about it. Io, at least, broke the pattern and was hit by a cargo carrier and killed.

All things considered, Emma took the death of her monkeys well. She'd insist on cleaning up whatever mess, apparently so she could fully document the monkey's accident. Only after she sent off her reports, and all her work was done, would she grieve, surrounded by the photographs of the bright, smiling human couples. I tried to keep Emma distracted until the next monkey arrived, which truthfully, was quite pleasant on my part, and taught her English, because really, as much as I liked the sex, I wouldn't mind a conversation once in a while.

Now, Banter, I worried about, as she was showing all the signs of becoming a stalker.

"She uses the heaviest level of encryption!" Banter cried.

"You're hacking her communication?"

"Yes! She's hiding something here."

"She's doing simple scientific research!"

"On primate development? On the moon? When are monkeys going to build spaceships to the moon?"

"Oh, cut us some slack, Banter. We've got guinea pigs, chickens, rabbits, cats, a dog, and a current mouse problem. If we're going to be a true colony, we need to be able to live a full, real life here, and animals are part of it."

"Cats and dogs, yes, but monkeys, no. We're not going to have monkeys here. Look at the trouble they get in. Io survived the longest, but that was only a week. Emma is doing something more than development studies. What kind of research is she doing?"

"I'm not sure."

"You're not sure? What the hell does she do all day?"

"She watches the monkey play and takes a lot of notes." Obviously that wasn't enough for Banter, so I added another data point. "She did a full computer rendering of the burrow when we first moved in, and when a monkey gets hurt or killed, she does a computer simulation of the accident."

"Hurt?"

"Well, not everything kills monkeys; there's been nonfatal accidents."

"Like what?"

"Well, the thing with the organic trash processor." I mimed sticking my hand down into a hole. "It turns out that hole is large enough for their hands to fit down." Banter looked horrified. "It didn't cut anything off! Hitomi just needed a few stitches. Besides, Emma must have sent in a report, because Earth already shipped up smaller access plates for all the burrows."

I found out about Mel's newest "first" and the answers to Banter's question just the next day. I came home to find Emma acting like another monkey had died, when the next wasn't scheduled to arrive until the day after.

"What's wrong?"

"So sad," Emma stared at a printout in her hands. "Mel knows."

"What does Mel know?" I gently took the printout. It had two names on it. John Thomas. Sarah Jane. "I don't understand."

"Mel make list," Emma said. "She say: no use names for monkey."

"These names?" I asked and got a sad nod of her head. "Why not?"

"No dead monkey with baby name."

"Ah." And then a heartbeat later, "Mel's having a baby?"

"Eight months. So little time. So little monkeys."

I stood pondering that for a minute and it all clicked together for me. "You've been baby-proofing the moon with the monkeys! That's—that's . . ."

I was going to say "so wrong" but would I rather it had been a child killed by the toilet, the fans, the trash processor, and all the other ways that Emma's monkeys been hurt and killed? The list was already very long. I suppose that we'd been baby-proofing Earth for hundreds of years, but infants were still being killed. Somehow this insane plan to use monkeys as a crash course in safety made . . . sense.

Emma looked at me warily. "No one can know about my monkey business."

"Why not?"

"No tell," she said firmly. "Monkey must go where there is trouble. No one wants a dead monkey."

Which was true. If people knew what Emma was doing, they'd try to stop her, and as she pointed out, we had very little time before Mel's baby arrived.

So here we are, Sarah Jane Bucknell was born yesterday, and Xavier has managed to last a full month. Earth has shipped Ying and Zoey, just in case, and I can truthfully say my life is a barrel of monkeys. And we're hopeful that no monkey will die before its time.

Meanwhile, back on Earth, another story about humanity's closest relatives, by the author of the Posleen Wars series.

EARTH'S FIRST IMPROVED CHIMP GETS JOB AS A JANITOR

John Ringo

"No, Mark. You can't." Mark Second had heard those words too many times in his life. The student's dark face did not flicker but the coach still had a wary look in his eye. "It's not my rule, Mark. It's the rule of the High School Sport Board. Anyone with 'excessive enhancement' cannot participate in intramural sports. Period."

"Why not?" asked the exasperated teenager. He knew the true answer but he wanted the coach to admit it. His features were as still as granite despite his fury. "Or rather, 'why me?' Half the kids in school have one modification or another. What? You don't think Patty Rice naturally has that curly, platinum blond hair? Do you?"

"They're not built from the ground up, Mark," said the heavyset football coach with a cautious shrug. "They're just . . . fixed. They're not specifically designed for . . . physical activity the way you are. They're not—"

"Monsters," said Mark, bitterly.

"That's not it," said the adult, watching the still, flat, square face across from him carefully. Mark never showed what he was thinking, which was one of the things that frightened people. It was currently frightening the burly former football player. Teachers had learned to worry about the quiet ones, the outcasts. Regular troublemakers were bad enough, but the education system had slowly learned that it was the ones who just took it and never fought back that exploded. And if this one ever went mokker nobody would be able to stop him. "Their changes didn't come from illegal genics. Kids like Patty and Tom have the normal, limited enhancements. The sort of thing that anybody can get done through body surgery. Yours are—"

"Evil," Mark finished for him, snarling. He flexed a thigh-thick forearm. "Frightening."

"You keep *saying* things like that," snapped the coach, becoming exasperated. He gestured at Mark as if to take in the whole picture; the armored forehead, the flat, masklike face with eyes set deep in ripples of bone, the tree-trunk legs, the expanded, armored and massively muscled chest. "The rule was practically designed for you, Mark. Putting you on the field with regular kids would be like them playing a Pop Warner team! You're different; face it!"

"So I have to stay the school outcast, huh?" asked the teenager, his face finally starting to show his anger. "Is that the bottom line?"

"Sports won't change that, Mark," said the adult with a sigh, losing his anger as fast as it had developed. "Only you can."

"Get real," snarled the student. "You don't live

this life, I do." He stood up, nodded at the coach and stalked out.

The coach waited until the door cycled closed and sighed in relief. As the designated enforcement officer for the Delta Wing of the school he had had to take down more than one mokking student. But he was afraid if that one ever cracked it would require a bazooka.

Mark walked up to his locker and took a long, cleansing breath. Then another. Stress management exercises were his earliest conscious lessons, even before reading. How to confront and manage the anger, the easy descent into berserk rage, that was his heritage. He took another breath, feeling the trickle of ultraline he had been unable to contain fritter away against the wall of his control. Breathe in, breathe out. Let the rage subside. All in the mind.

He looked hard at the poor inanimate locker but finally resisted punching it. Not only would he, probably, break a knuckle, the punch would undoubtedly shatter the security plastic. And he didn't need the resulting whispers added to the current around him. Breathe in, breathe out. He leaned his head against cool plastic, hoping that some lightning bolt would just strike him dead on the spot. Maybe if he just stayed here until the end of school. Or, at least, until the next PE class came in.

As it was, he stayed there, leaning on the plastic, until his shoes became wet.

"Some super-soldier," opined a gravelly voice. "You've got lousy situational awareness."

Mark leaned back and cracked an eyelid. The Imp janitor peered back at him with soft brown eyes as the kid examined the mop resting on his shoes. "I'm not a super-soldier," said Mark, tiredly. "I'm not any kind of soldier. I've never held a gun. I don't want to hold a gun. But I would like you to take your mop off my shoes; you're getting my feet wet."

"Okay," said the improved chimpanzee, pulling the mop back. "But I need to mop the floor."

"Could you maybe give me a minute," said Mark in a low, growling tone. He rarely let himself sound like that because most people found it intimidating. And that didn't help his reputation either. However, he really didn't have any interest in moving. And the damn chimpanzee was getting on his nerves.

"Kid, I'm not in the mood for adolescent angst right now," said the unintimidated Imp. "I'd like to finish this floor. See, if I finish the floor, I can go prop my feet up for a few minutes and have a coffee and a banana. But, until I finish it, I gotta stay on my dogs. So, I'd really like you to move. Okay? Just, stand on the bench or something."

Mark bemusedly climbed up on the locker room bench as the janitor swept the mop efficiently back and forth. "Aren't there robots to do that?" the student asked. He had sort of noticed janitors around the school, but he'd never really thought about them. However, this was the first person in a long time who recognized him for what he was and didn't act scared.

"Yeah," answered the Imp, expertly flicking the butt of a joint out from under the bench and into the mop bucket. The janitor must have been an earlier model; he seemed both quicker and more intelligent than the current norm. *Pan sapiens* was a diverse species. There had been a variety of early experiments before the current "normal" form was settled on, and then, in the wave of revulsion after the Oligen Incident, locked in by legislation. "But robots are lousy at getting under benches. It's easier to just mop the hard stuff myself and leave the robots for the hallways at night."

"Was mine the last gym class?" asked Mark, stripping off his shirt. The sweat-soaked jersey was the result of a few warm-ups and a solid forty minutes in the weight room fast-pumping four times his body weight; nobody was going to ask him to join the scheduled basketball game.

"Yep. Then I go get a banana until you brats get out of the buildings. Turn on the robots, turn off the lights and go home."

"Seems like an easy enough job," said Mark, pulling on a baggy, button-down shirt. The loose cotton concealed his Herculean physique, but nothing could conceal his face.

"Sure, sure, kid," snorted the janitor. "Every day's a holiday and every meal's a banquet."

Mark slowed in buttoning the top button of his shirt and treated the chimpanzee to a quizzical look. "I've heard that somewhere before."

"Well, I didn't say I made it up," said the chimp, dumping the mop in his bucket and regarding the kid mildly. "Tell you what, kid, wanna banana?"

"I should be getting back to class," said Mark with a sigh.

"Screw it," laughed the chimp. "It's algebra. You can afford to skip a day."

"How did you know what class I'd be taking?" asked the genie, interested.

"I got eyes, kid," said the chimp, pointing to his deep-set orbs. "Just like yours. You want that banana or not?"

"Sure," said Mark, with a nod. "Thanks."

"*De nada*," answered the chimp with a gesture. "Us test-tube types gotta stick together."

"Yeah," said Mark with a rare smile. "I guess. What's your name, chimp?"

"Charlie," answered the janitor. "Charlie Algernon."

"Well, my name's Mark," said the genie. He took the proffered paw and squeezed it gently, but was surprised at the strength of the returning grip.

"Don't worry, Mark," said the chimp with a broad grin. "One of the reasons I ain't worried about you is chimps is pretty strong, too."

Able Tyburn looked up from his reader. "Good morning, Mark," he said calmly. Able and his wife Shari did everything calmly. Which was why they had been chosen as Mark Two foster parents.

When the remnants of the Cyberpunk entry team had finally broken through the Mark One defenders of Oligen and taken the nursery, the Terrestrial Union had faced a dilemma. There were forty-eight Mark Twos completed, but they were, to all appearances, human babies. Unlike the chimp derivative Mark One offspring, all of which had been put down, the Mark Twos fell under the rules regarding human genetic modification. They were, despite universal revulsion, held by the Supreme Court to be humans. Therefore, they could not be killed out of hand.

But the Mark Two was designed as a high-intensity combat model. They had no purpose beyond entering heavy firefights and winning. They were, effectively, genie tanks. As such their ultraline glands were tweaked to produce at the slightest provocation. The testosterone-adrenaline-nicotine neural enhancer gave them the ability to go into "hyper-state" at a moment's notice. The downside was that they were extremely aggressive.

The Terrestrial Union had dealt with this by finding,

among its four million residents, forty-eight couples with almost preternatural calm. Couples who could raise and train pseudo-human hand-grenades in a loving and nurturing environment.

"Good morning, Father," said Mark, with a smile. He opened the cold-door and pulled out a jug of milk and a bunch of bananas then headed for the door of the apartment.

"Where are you going, Mark?" asked his father. The question had no negative overtones; it was a perfectly formed query. Able Tyburn never used a negative tone.

"I'm going to go have breakfast with Charlie," Mark answered, grabbing his reader and coat.

"I had been meaning to discuss that with you, Mark," said Able, setting down his own reader. The morning news had been mildly distressing, with another outbreak of the Thuggee Cult in California. Unlike the traditionalists in India and Europe, the American branch of the nihilistic religion believed that shedding blood in their executions was the best way to worship their goddess. The slaying in the downtown LA-San school had been particularly bloody.

"You understand that we do not want to slow your societal development," said the foster parent, calmly. As he did the house chimp emerged from the kitchen and silently began laying out his breakfast. "However, it would be a preferred condition if you could spend socially enhancing time with a human as opposed to a chimp."

"Unfortunately, Father," said Mark, almost automatically suppressing the stab of irritation he felt at the comment, "I have found it difficult to make human friends. As you know."

"Yes, Mark. I am, sadly, aware of that," said the foster parent. He was, in fact, very aware of that fact.

Mark was on the low end of sociability among the fifteen surviving Mark Twos. As the most recent e-mail from The Program had pointed out in no uncertain terms. "However, I am sure that when you begin attending college, and have a larger population to draw from, you will find more companions."

"Until then, Father," said the young man, as calmly as a Buddha, "my sole socializing outlet is this chimp janitor you seem to disapprove of."

"Mark, there is a difference between humans and chimps," said the control. He gestured at the servant who was serving him his cholesterol-free egg-substitute. "I would suggest that you could actually hurt your socialization process by developing skills that are inadequate. The social reactions you develop from interacting with this 'Charlie' are going to be different than those you should be acquiring. This will delay your development. I cannot find this to be a positive outcome."

"So," said the student taking a calming breath and suppressing the stab of ultraline that threatened to send him into a berserk rage, "you are recommending that I stop socializing with 'this chimp.'"

"Yes," said the father, picking up his fork. "That is my recommendation."

"I shall take it under advisement, Father," said the student. "But not this morning." He knew that the next step up from advice was orders.

"Very well," said the parent. "Have a good day at school, Mark. Remember . . ."

"Calmness is next to oneness," said Mark.

"Be one with the universe and nothing can anger you," said his father with a smile.

Mark opened the door to the boiler room and tossed Charlie the bunch of bananas. "Mornin', monkey."

"Mornin', freak," said the chimp with a grin. He looked up from the reader he was repairing to catch the bundle. "Whassa word?" he asked, pulling off a piece of fruit and pouring the kid a cup of coffee.

"My dad wants me to stop seeing so much of you," Mark grumped. He took the coffee and sipped it appreciatively. "How in the hell do you make such a good cup of coffee?" he asked.

"Old secret," winked the chimp, taking his own sip and a bite of banana. "Pinch of salt. It's called 'goat-locker' coffee."

"Whatever," said the kid. "It's good."

"I told you Abe would kick up a fuss," said the chimp. "And he's got a point, you *do* need friends your own age."

"But I can't make them," said Mark. "And besides, they're not my own age!"

"Well, there's that too," said the chimp with a grin. "Not many twelve-year-olds in their senior year. But you're basically eighteen in every way but actual years, kid. Don't bitch about that."

"I won't," said Mark, sadly. "It's not like I'm gonna live to seventy."

"Oh, I don't know," said the chimp. "All that 'ongenic increase' stuff might be bullshit. They told me I'd be long dead by now when I got uncanned. And here I am."

"Yeah, but I'm sort of programmed to die in my thirties," said the teenager. "I don't think I can avoid it."

"Worry about that when the time comes, kid. Geneticists fuck up more than they get it right, trust me," the chimp chuckled. "Me? I was originally designed for intensive loyalty."

"Really?" asked Mark, looking at him askance. "What happened?"

"I got over it," said the chimp, with a smile. "The coding was . . . sort of open. So I convinced myself that my 'employer' was . . . not my original one."

"What did your employer think of that?" asked Mark with fascination.

"Well, it was a little company that had just gone out of business," said the chimp. "So I had to find my own way. And I did. And so will you, kid. You just have to figure out what comes natural to you."

Mark looked up as Tom Fallon sat down on the seat across from him. The lunchroom was crowded; obviously Fallon felt it was better to sit by "Dr. Demento" than anywhere else.

Fallon wasn't a bad guy. Unlike most of the other kids in school he didn't actively reject the big genie. However, he also didn't spend more time in his presence than he had to.

"Mark," said the teenager with a nod. "How'cha?"

"'Kay," said the genie, taking a big bite of his peanut-butter and banana sandwich. Charlie had turned him on to the mix and he found it fulfilled a craving he hadn't even realized was there.

"You missed algebra the other day," said the other teen, carefully.

"I was trying to get the coach to take me in football," answered Mark, equably.

"Did it . . . work?" asked Tom, picking at his food. Just because sitting by a human time-bomb was better than the other choices available didn't mean he had to like it.

"No," said Mark with a shrug. Charlie had, rightly, pointed out that football wouldn't have been a challenge and that was what he really craved. It was surprising the insights the chimp had.

"Oh," said the other teen, as the doors to the cafeteria opened, "okay."

Mark never answered, as his ultraline gland opened up full-bore and he dove out of his seat. The first 9mm round cracked just behind his moving body but he was already accelerating too fast for the masked gunman in the doorway to track.

His movements were too fast for the human eye to follow as he dove across the serving counter, submachinegun rounds smashing the sneeze-guards and splashing red blood from the servers across the food. He popped back up halfway down the counter as the gunman turned his attention to the mob of shrieking teenagers.

"*Hey!*" shouted the genie, attracting the gunman's attention. As the masked and body-armored gunman turned to see who the impudent youth was, his larynx intercepted a spinning metal pie-pan.

Mark darted through the doors to the kitchen and snatched up a serving knife, still running on ultraline. It was the longest he had ever been under the drug's effect and he was unsure how long the neural enhancer would hold out. For as long as it did, he was four times as fast as an unenhanced human and nearly twice as "smart." Although, at the moment he didn't feel that way.

He had not heard an emergency announcement, though. As long as the kids in the school were trapped in their classes they were dead meat. He looked around and spotted the fire alarm. Good enough for now.

Once the alarm was shrieking he headed for the principal's office. If he could get on the announcement system he could warn the school. He had seen the red hand on the terrorist's vest; the Thuggees had hit and they would keep killing until a TAC team arrived to stop them.

❖   ❖   ❖

Mark looked both ways and darted across the hallway as distant shots and screaming broke out in D Wing. He tore open the door to the office and threw himself through low, hoping there wasn't a Thuggee on the other side. When no gunfire erupted he sniffed then stood up. He could smell somebody in the room, but it smelled like . . . "Patty?" he called.

The blond cheerleader poked her head up from behind the receptionist's desk. "Yes?" she called warily. She ducked back down as another burst of fire broke out. "Who is it?"

"It's me, Mark Second. It's Thuggees, Patty, make an announcement."

"But then they'll know there's somebody here!" she said shakily.

Mark had to admit it was a valid argument, but the students and teachers needed to have some warning. He started to walk over to the desk then caught a faint whiff of cordite.

Dara Kidwai was not the name the gunman had been born with. But he had had it legally changed the year before when he became a full member of the House of Kali. Participation in the religion was not a crime, despite the horrors being perpetuated in its name. Like Islam in the previous century, the Kali Cult and other religions were simply places for like-minded individuals to meet and gather. And use the mantle of the religion for their own ends.

Dara Kidwai was about to do just that. He could see the stupid teen, probably a Kali-be-damned football player from his physique, just beyond the metal door to the office. After he had killed this one he would send everyone else in the office to his goddess. And all the other bastards and bitches in the school. Sacrifice them all to the greater glory of Kali.

Mark spun in place as the door opened, catching the barrel of the MP-12 in his left hand and carrying it up and away as he grabbed the back of the cultist's head. The sound of the genie's armored forehead hitting the forehead of the cultist was wet and sodden as blood spurted out of the gunman's nose and ears.

"Patty," he snapped, wiping the blood off of his face, "make the damned announcement. Now." He bent down and tried to figure out how to detach the machine-gun from the terrorist's harness. He'd never seen a firearm in his life; The Program had made sure of that.

"What happened?" asked the fluff-head, peeking over the top of the desk. "Oh, *gross!*" she continued, turning to throw up.

Mark had to admit it was pretty gross with the blood pooling under the terrorist, but as pumped as he was on ultraline he was pretty much immune to any feeling but anger. He finally figured out how to take off the whole harness and walked over to the desk with the sopping gear draped across one shoulder. He picked up the microphone and keyed it. "Warning, all students and faculty. Kali Cultists in the building. One terminated in office and one terminated in cafeteria. Anyone with a cell phone, please call for Tac Teams. I am on my way to Delta Wing in support. Mark-Two Gen-One Combat System out." Let the bastards chew on that announcement.

He wiped at some blood off his front—apparently one of the bullets had hit his sternum plate and bounced—then pulled the gun around to his front. Holding it in one hand, as he had seen on TV, he pulled on the trigger. It put bullets all over the wall.

Oh, well. He'd just have to figure it out as he went along.

Mark stalked down the empty corridors of D Wing leaving bloody footprints behind him. He had to admit that inviting the cultists to kill him was stupid. But if they concentrated on trying to take him out, they wouldn't be killing the other kids. What the hell, it wasn't like he was designed for a long life.

He had just stalked past Mr. Patterson's classroom when he sensed a movement behind him and smelled blood and cordite.

He didn't know where the damn Kali had come from but the red-hand bastard had him dead to rights. Mark spun and turned with supernatural speed as the cultist opened fire, but this terrorist was good. Nine-millimeter rounds impacted into the youth's unarmored back and sides as he slammed into the wall, the gun in his hand spraying everywhere but the cultist.

The only thing that saved the genie was that both of them were just about out of rounds. Mark's MP-12 and the terrorist's clicked back at almost the same moment. Forgetting that his best bet was hand-to-hand, the badly wounded teen scrabbled for a new magazine as he tried to figure out how to reload the gun.

The Kali had no such problems. The cultist expertly dropped the thirty-round magazine and slipped in another. He chuckled as he pulled back the slide. "Some gene unit," he said, as a loop of wire dropped out of the ceiling. "Pun . . . urk."

The loop of 12-gauge insulated wire snapped up and to the side, expertly breaking the terrorist's neck, and Charlie dropped down on the body. He bent over and started slipping off the terrorist's gear as he shook his head at Mark.

"Stupid, stupid, stupid. I thought Oligen made you smart?"

"I was trying to get them off the other kids," said the teen, weakly. The ultraline was fading and the bullets peppered throughout his body were starting to hurt.

"I was talking about not looking up, kid," said the chimp. "You need to learn to look up."

"I thought I'd smell him," said Mark, doubtfully.

"Yeah, so he put himself by an intake, just like me," said Charlie. The chimp threw the body-armor over his head and looked down with a laugh; the Kevlar-titanium vest dangled to the ground. "Oh, well. Shit happens." He walked over to the teen and reloaded the youth's MP-12 then took all but one spare magazine.

"I think I'm going to need these more than you," the chimp commented as he dragged the bleeding genie into Mr. Patterson's classroom. There was a kid huddled in one corner but otherwise the room was empty.

"Charlie?" asked the combat-unit. He coughed up a drop or two of blood. "I don't think I'm gonna make it, Charlie."

"Bullshit," said the chimp with a grin. "You're a Mark Two, you lucky bastard. Most of that shit will be healed in a couple of days; you're probably already clotting like mad. Just sit there and do your calmness exercises until the medics find you. Oh. And kill any terrorist that comes through the door. Your left hand goes on the *stock*, you idiot."

With that the janitor was gone. As Mark faded in and out he dreamed of a distant one-man war. But the screams were all torn from the throats of adult males.

❖   ❖   ❖

Mark had never seen anyone who looked like him before. The SWAT team commander was a Normal but broad and flat as a human tank.

"So, you have no other information about this 'Charlie Algernon'?" the officer asked calmly.

Mark had never realized that the calmness of his parents was a positive trait in a tactics team member. But all the SWAT guys that he had been talking with since the incident were like that. Calm, controlled, focussed. These guys did not believe in rage as a character trait. "No. I'd barely gotten to know him."

"'Goat-locker coffee,' hmm," said the police lieutenant. "I think that says it all."

"Why?" asked Mark. "Where did Charlie learn that stuff?"

"Well, son, you know you're a Mark Two, right," said the lieutenant with a grim smile. "You know what Mark Ones were."

"Oh," said Mark, his chin dropping.

"Yeah. The whole Oligen thing was originally an outgrowth of the Cyberpunk-SEAL program. Their instructors in close combat were all SEALs and Cybers; thus Navy-brewed coffee. Their training was one reason it was so hard for the Cyber team to take the Oligen facility when the Council found out about the Mark Twos and Oligen's plans for a coup. The SEALs thought that they had tracked down and killed all the Mark Ones but at least one apparently escaped."

"He told me that he had been designed for loyalty to his 'original owners,'" said Mark. "But he had figured out a way around the conditioning."

"Maybe by broadening it," said the commander with a sad smile. "I was aware of the conditioning. But, I think, maybe, he decided that since the government paid for the program, his owner was actually the government. And since it is a representative democracy . . ."

"The whole world was his owner?" asked Mark.

"Maybe," said the lieutenant. "Sort of like any good soldier; he gave his loyalty to the 'bigger picture.' Anyway, I'm glad in a way that he was killed in that explosion. The termination orders are still active on all Mark Ones. We would have had to put him down."

"I understand," said Mark, somewhat bitterly. "But I don't have to like it."

"Neither do I," said the lieutenant. "But it's better this way. We have a toe and some other scraps for a positive genetic ID, but that satchel charge didn't leave much."

The officer saw the kid's face harden and thought about the talk he had had with the teen's guidance counselor. Especially with the media play on this attack, the kid was going to be even more ostracized than before. Which was, frankly, stupid.

"Hey," said the officer with a faint grin. "After you get out of the body and fender shop, gimme a call." He proffered a card to the genie. "There may be a rule against a Modified in football, but there ain't one against them in SWAT."

"Okay," said Mark with a returning smile. "I will."

It might not make up for bananas and coffee in the morning but it would be something to do while he waited to die.

The door was marked "Arthur Commons, Assistant Principal." A heavily-furred hand knocked on it, softly.

"Come in," said a voice from the interior.

"I understand you need a janitor?"

Rebecca Lickiss is the author of two novels, Eccentric Circles *and* Never After. *I first ran into Rebecca Lickiss at a writers conference and was taken with her intriguing aliens. No aliens in this story, though, just humans trying to get along on the frontier.*

TIME IN PURGATORY

Rebecca Lickiss

"I can take all of you!" The voice carried through the open door of the sheriff's office.

Inside, Sheriff Letitia "Legs" Lanier leaned back in her creaking chair, waiting to hear the sound of her deputy, Corin Minerva, breaking up the imminent fight. Unfortunately all she heard was a lot of scuffling and shouting. Corin had disappeared again, right as the biannual supply ship was docking at Purgatory Station.

"Damnation." Legs sighed and shut down the accounting spreadsheet she'd been checking at her desk. The accounts wouldn't balance anyway; there had to be some glitch with the accounting program. One more problem to add to her list, as if Hell Week wasn't enough by itself.

Reflexively checking her synthleather protective vest, Legs headed for the door. Gold nugget buttons all buttoned up, watch-communicator in the front left pocket chained to the third button down, electric manacles in back pocket, first-aid kit in front right pocket, star-shaped badge recorder over her heart.

She stepped out into the bright, false sunshine on her front porch, surveying the wide main street that stretched through Purgatory Station. On the other side of the moving sidewalk that ran down the center of the clean metallic street a small group of half-drunk miners shuffled and jockeyed for position in a brewing brawl in front of the offices for the *Purgatory Prattler*. A few caught sight of her and suddenly decided that they were really bystanders, and uninterested bystanders with somewhere else to be at that.

Her hand tapped the ministunner strapped high on her thigh, as she descended the creaky wooden steps in front of her office to the street. Her fingertips slid down to caress the garters' gleaming jeweled aluminum and filigreed circuits just peeking out from under her loose, pleated, dark miniskirt. She'd checked and serviced the controls and options on her artificial legs this morning. No sense dressing for trouble if her legs would be on the fritz.

"Break it up," Legs shouted as she crossed the street. No footsteps accompanied her progress, her legs and feet merely an illusion generated by the mobility force-field of her prosthetics. Her fingertips tapped the garter controls, increasing her height above any of the brawlers'. Outnumbered and without backup, she'd take any advantage she could get.

Tom Tadman grumbled something to the man standing next to him. Legs slammed their heads together. "Starting Hell Week a little early, gentlemen?"

The fool at the center of the fracas staggered around to face her. She recognized him. Hewlett Brown was a troublemaker from way back. A goofy, reckless expression crossed his face. "I can take you too," he slurred as he fumbled for his stunner.

Before his stunner cleared its holster, Legs slipped her ministunner into her hand and pointed it at him. The skirt kept her weapon handy, but concealed.

"Ha!" Hewlett flung his stunner down. "Can't use one of those on an unarmed man."

Legs stepped up to him and walloped his head with her ministunner, knocking him out. "Bet?" She shook her head as he snuggled in more comfortably onto the hard metal street and began to snore. Looking around at the rest of them, she motioned with her ministunner. "All right, all of you, to the jail. Now." She pointed with her free hand to the two currently rubbing the sides of their heads. "You two carry Hewlett. Come on."

She herded the five remaining brawlers to the jail and put them all into one cell.

"The door's busted," she said, as if this might be news to them. "So, I'm putting you, Tom, in charge until I get back. If any of you leaves the cell before I get back I'll track you down, tie you up, and leave you in here until Hell Week is over. Understood?" Legs waited until everyone awake nodded his head. "Good. Anyone that behaves while I'm gone can leave when I get back."

"Okay, Sheriff."

"Yeah."

Smiling, Legs said, "Good. Good." Then she turned and left.

Hell Week started in—Legs glanced at the large, old-fashioned, round-faced clock in the steeple of the bank storefront at the far end of Main Street—fifteen minutes. Twenty if she could find an excuse to loiter on the clean metallic street, or meander into one of the saloons innocently hiding behind the customized plastic storefronts that advertised their wares and entertainment. Quite a few saloons lurked between where Legs stood hesitating in the wooden doorway of her sheriff's office and the station's docking ports.

Still no sign of Corin. Legs automatically checked the foot traffic on the street. Four miners and two clerks from the bank: just the usual population for Purgatory Station. But everyone was tense, electric. Normal for noontime at the start of Hell Week.

As soon as she reached the docks, the word would be sent out that the biannual supply ship had arrived from Earth, and most everybody in Purgatory's local space would head for the station. They'd gather and party and fight, and conduct business and fight, and drink and fight. New business alliances would emerge, and old feuds would flare. Miners would change employment, looking for something better, and celebrate by tearing up a bar. Legs would have to knock heads together, pile drunks like tailings in the jail's cells, forego sleep, and generally stay busier than a wildcat miner with a one-ton hopper and a hundred-ton claim.

Sure as shooting, some tomfool idiot would try some stupid something and wind up residing in a cell for the rest of Hell Week, or worse, have to be shipped off for real justice.

Delaying was useless. The sooner Legs got Hell Week started the sooner it'd be over. Besides, like everybody else, she'd get a chance at a few treats off the ship: foods that couldn't be grown in the vats on Purgatory Station or in the outlying hydroponic farms, new textiles, new entertainments. She headed for the moving sidewalk in the center of the street. Maybe she'd get lucky and nothing worse than drunk-and-disorderly would go on.

Maybe Purgatory Station, out here in the hinterlands

of the Kuiper Belt, would suddenly become the cross-roads of the solar system.

"Morning, Sheriff," Kimble Phelps shouted from behind her. "No, sorry, it's afternoon."

Plastering a smile she didn't feel on her face, Legs turned to find Purgatory Station's dignified banker walking toward her. She quickly tapped the controls on her garters, adjusting the length of her legs down to match his. "Afternoon, Kimble."

Damnation, but why'd she have to meet him on her way to the docks? His presence just reminded her of all the other problems she had sitting on her desk.

"Expecting trouble?" he asked, tilting his head toward her skirt, as they stepped onto the moving sidewalk.

"Yup." She continued walking on the moving surface of the sidewalk, as did he. "Hell Week."

Kimble glanced proprietarily back at his bank, before turning the full force of his heavily jowled smile on her. "A man or woman'd have to be a fool to mess with our sheriff."

"Yup." Legs kept the smile on her face, but didn't really want to encourage him.

"Maybe it won't be so bad, this time." Kimble darted behind her in preparation for his upcoming exit from the sidewalk. He whispered hastily, "Perhaps if you get some free time, Letitia, we could have a drink."

She tipped her hat in good-bye as he stepped from the sidewalk. The sunlight from the fake sun in the distant station roof glinted off his shiny balding head. She readjusted her legs to her normal stride, and set off at a brisker walk.

But it was too late. Kimble had reminded her of all the problems waiting for her, along with Hell Week, and she couldn't prevent herself from rehashing them in her mind.

Corin Minerva, her deputy, was more a hindrance than a help. Constantly late, incompetent, and insolent, she'd have replaced him months ago, if not for the fact that his family was the wealthiest on the station, and they had found the proper political pressure to make him her problem, until they could unload him on some unsuspecting university back on Earth, or Mars, or somewhere else closer in toward the sun.

Then there was the accounting system. Somehow— Legs wasn't certain she could blame Corin—the accounting program in the sheriff's office couldn't seem to disgorge any useful, or auditable, information. If she couldn't get it working, she'd have to go see Kimble, and have him straighten it out from the bank's end.

An announcement plastered to the center column of a sidewalk circle at the corner of Main Street and Tin Alley advertised the *Purgatory Prattler*, blaring today's headlines in tall, bold, black, moving print, and a loud tenor.

Legs snarled at the announcement as she sailed past to take a left on Tin. Elections were coming up the week after Hell Week's biannual outsystem ships run, and, of course, the *Purgatory Prattler*'s best method of drumming up business was rehashing gossip and innuendo, and stirring up trouble. The latest editorial urged someone, anyone, to run against Sheriff Lanier. The implication being that someone, anyone, would be better than a bitter, crippled ex-pilot turned power-hungry, mean-tempered, iron-fisted bitch.

And where the hell was Elmer? Not, Legs reminded herself, that she particularly cared about the big lummox, but, as the station's third-largest employer, Longshanks Limited did merit her concern. Especially when all of its miners, ships, and equipment were overdue at the station.

She stepped off the moving sidewalk onto Coal Street, which was really just a fancy name for the circuitous corridor spiraling down to the docks under Main Street.

Damnation, but she didn't have time to go searching through Elmer's claims to find him and his crew, and verify that they hadn't been attacked by claim jumpers, or mid-system pirates, or joy-riding kids bent on mischief.

Probably they were just extending their tour, while they eked out a promising patch of asteroid. When Elmer got back she'd have to chew on him a bit about schedules and timing, and sending messages.

At the bottom of the Coal Street corridor's spiral, Legs waved open the door that led to the docks. On the other side of the door, in the oily smelling bowels of the station, was the docking gallery, a long cavernous hallway with hatches on either side like soldiers standing to attention in two rows. Purgatory Station's manager, Jim Nutil, and her missing deputy, Corin Minerva, waited for her by the largest hatch.

At least Corin'd be around to help with this.

Mr. Nutil, a small, weasely, stooped, gray-haired man, whined, "Well, I guess we can send the okay to open the hatches now that you've arrived."

As soon as the working light on the doorframe turned green, the hatch's blast doors ground up into the ceiling. Nutil, Corin, and Legs entered the large customs dock, to wait for passengers and supplies from the biannual ship.

Nutil read from his docking pad, and announced that it was a fairly standard run, with the usual cargo of supplies, a crew of five, four returning locals, five immigrants, and one visitor. Visitors were rare, but not unknown.

With Nutil scrutinizing the cargo, Corin checking the

crew and locals in, and Legs handling the immigrants
and visitor, the inspections went fairly fast.

Legs recognized the four returning locals as new
university graduates, coming home to celebrate before
making their way into the great, wide solar system.
Nobody of importance, or that she needed to worry
about.

The crew was the same crew that had been making
this biannual run for the past three years. Again no
one worth worrying about. The pilot, of course, waited
in his ship until everything and everyone else was
cleared. Also, he and Legs knew each other from the
war, and traditionally had dinner afterwards to catch
up on old times, and gossip about the passengers.

The five immigrants were youngish, ignorant, female,
and probably awaiting employment as brides-of-the-
common-man, since no mining supervisors or mail-
ordering husbands waited for them. Legs tried to
remember if and when she'd ever been that young
or that reckless. She would have to keep an eye on
them the next couple of months to make sure they
stayed within the permissive, liberal laws of Purgatory
Station. But they all seemed to be fairly nice young
ladies. Not much trouble there.

The lone visitor would definitely be a problem.
His identification named him Damon Karybdis,
traveling salesman for Stellar Cogwheels, a company
she'd never heard of before. He was a tall, dark, and
handsome blade of a man, with twinkling blue eyes, a
false white-toothed smile, suave manners, fashionable
debonair clothing, and a hawklike attitude. A predator
looking for prey.

Legs pegged him as a game sharp, or con man,
come to fleece the hicks in the sticks. She briefly
considered putting him in quarantine for the ship's
weeklong layover, but there was no guarantee that

he'd choose to leave at that point with the ship, and not stay to make trouble for six months. Or more. Better to let him loose on the station, to discover the difficulty of skinning those who'd learned the hard way through their own ignorance and experience. He'd either give up, or end up in the hoosegow. Either way though, she'd have a rough week of it. Couldn't be helped.

"So, you're the sheriff?" Karybdis flashed a brilliant white-toothed smile as he made an obvious show of leering at her legs. "Must be a mighty nice place here."

Little did he know it was her there's-going-to-be-trouble outfit. The short skirt enabled her to get at her prostheses' controls easier. She didn't smile back. "Out the lock, take Coal Street all the way up to the top level. Tin Alley will take you to any of the three big streets running the length of the station: Main, Small, and Parallel. There's five other alleys that connect the big streets up top. I'm sure you'll find your way around."

She waved the scanner to pick up his face and palms, and nodded to him, while frowning. "Enjoy your stay in Purgatory."

Mr. Karybdis turned his attentions to the new immigrants. Legs was glad to see him head out, up Coal Street, to find himself a hotel room.

A short, thin, nearly bald dark-skinned man finally exited the docking tube. Legs adjusted her height to his. Jack Dixon, pilot-owner of the *Ocher Dust*, grinned maniacally. "Legs! Still sheriffing, I see."

"Yup." Legs grinned back. "And you're still space jockeying."

Nutil left to finish releasing the cargo to its various owners. Legs waved Corin to leave, before she wafted Jack through customs on waivers and political license.

"Tell me about this Damon Karybdis," Legs said as they walked up Coal Street.

"Spotted him right off, but there's not much to tell." Jack frowned. "He kept pretty much to his room for the six-week trip. As far as I can tell he doesn't drink, drug, gamble, pilfer, or engage in any known vice."

"Which just leaves the unknown ones."

"Pretty much. He isn't a man-of-the-cloth, of any variety or stripe, not even counterfeit. He's not a wanderer, as far as I can tell. He's too flashy and annoying to miss, but too exceptional to be the simple salesman he says he is."

"He's trouble."

"That's what you've got the skirt for." Jack raised one dark brow questioningly. "So how's the old war-wound doing?"

"No trouble lately," Legs said as they turned to walk up the short Tin Alley toward Main Street. "I installed that last update you brought, and haven't had a whisper of trouble with them since."

Jack slapped one hand over the *Prattler's* announcement speaker on the center column of a sidewalk circle at the corner of Main Street and Tin Alley. But he couldn't drown out the tenor voice shouting, "Won't Someone Take On Sheriff Lanier?"

"Idiots," Jack muttered.

Legs shrugged. "They're entitled to their opinion. And to broadcast it, as long as they don't interfere with my duties. In any case, they have to know they're scraping bottom here just to get anyone to take this job."

"They're damn lucky to get you. They ought to realize it." Jack stalked angrily down the moving sidewalk.

They stopped by the jail, and let all the brawlers go, before heading for the high-rent neighborhood near the bank.

The Struck It Rich was Purgatory's most exclusive tavern, which only meant if you needed credit, go elsewhere. The thick, steamy smell of seared vat-steaks and powdery soft slow-baked hydroponic potatoes washed over them as they entered. Tall faux-wood stools clustered near tall faux-wood tables taking up most of the floor space. To the right stood a long bar, that was also the kitchen, and took up one whole wall. On the left a wall of real wood backed intimate booths. Directly opposite the door another row of booths lined a transparent picture-vista porthole with a panoramic view of the stars. If you knew where to look you could pick out old Sol and all the planets. Legs and Jack walked to their usual booth, with a scenic overlook.

As they relaxed against opposing wooden benches, and scanned the menu in the tabletop, Legs asked, "So how's the home life?"

"Cora's fine. She's still after me to quit the long hauls, but she doesn't want to give up the bonus money. Tony and Mari are doing well in school. Garick's talking real sentences now." Jack punched his order into the order pad, his usual. "So when are you going to settle down and have a pack of little sheriffs?"

Sighing, Legs punched in her order, her usual. "Whenever the big lummox finally nerves himself enough to ask."

Jack looked up in surprise. "Since when did you get to be so patient? Why don't you just ask him yourself?"

"You should have seen him the last time I asked him out." Legs leaned back against the high hard-backed bench, smiling and shaking her head. "You've never seen anyone so embarrassed and flummoxed. It took him ten minutes of uhms and uhs to say yes. He spent the evening acting uncomfortably scared I was going to forget propriety. If I asked him to marry me he'd probably die on the spot from apoplexy."

"No fool like an old fool, I suppose." Jack shrugged. "What could he be afraid of? He can't believe those stupid yarns about grounded pilots. It's not like he hasn't seen you in action, in and out of the war."

"That may be the problem."

"Hmm." Jack sounded noncommittal. "Perhaps. You can be scary when riled. But his record wasn't any better."

She waggled her eyebrows and grinned. "Maybe he still thinks I'm the enemy."

"There is that. I'll see what I can get out of him. I'm not the enemy after all." Jack winked.

"Got to find him first. He's five days overdue. Him and his crew. Not a word, not a peep out of them for three weeks now. If I haven't heard from them soon, I'll have to go looking for them."

Jack looked surprised.

Their food arrived, and they scooped their steaming platters off the autocart before it trundled off. They ate in the companionable silence of two very hungry, very good friends. Over a dessert of banana-split cake, a special treat available only as long as the bananas brought by the *Ocher Dust* lasted, they discussed the *Ocher Dust*'s crew and passengers. There was little gossip this trip; the crew and passengers had behaved themselves. Legs had a few tidbits on Purgatory denizens known to Jack to pass along, nothing very titillating.

As they were exiting the Struck It Rich, Jack said, "It occurs to me that Karybdis may be a diversion. Perhaps the one you should be watching is one of the immigrants or one of the local yokels."

"Already ahead of you. I'm keeping an eye on everyone here. It's going to be a long week." Legs

glanced at the door of her office, halfway down the
street. There was work to be done, and she needed
to get to it.

"See you later," Jack said.

"Tomorrow."

At first light, Legs pulled herself up to a sitting
position in her hammock bed, and massaged the
stumps of her legs. The prosthetic disks sat on the
table underneath the hammock, the jeweled aluminum and filigreed circuits glinting in the spreading
light of the false dawn. She picked them up carefully
by the tan plastic handholds, attached them to their
permanent couplings on the ends of her legs, and
turned her legs on.

After stowing the hammock in its cabinet, Legs
punched her usual breakfast of juice, protein strips,
and toast into the kitchen nook set in the corner of
the room. Wishing once more that the coffee maker in
the sheriff's office worked. While waiting for breakfast,
she opened up and looked out the window.

Her room over the sheriff's office looked out on
Main Street. From her strategic position at the exact
midpoint of the length of the street she could see
to both ends. Hell Week was in full swing beneath
her.

Miners, floozies, families, and company CEOs
swarmed the street, moving in the strange tides,
swirls, and eddies of crowds everywhere. On the
opposite side of the central moving sidewalk a river
of people flowed toward the bank; on the near side a
similar river drifted in the opposite direction. Nearly
everyone had come in to Purgatory Station from the
surrounding space.

The usual smell of sidewalk lubricant had been
replaced by a myriad of perfumes, colognes, and musky

sweat, the miasma of a large number of human beings in close quarters. Legs caught a whiff of a familiar sharp cologne, and kept a snarl from her face only with supreme effort.

"Hey, Sheriff! Any quotes for the *Prattler*?" A suave, darkly dressed man stood on the porch beneath her window holding a recording pad up toward her.

Trying not to growl, sneer, or reach for her ministunner—which was really what Langdon Kade, owner, reporter, and staff of the *Purgatory Prattler*, deserved—Legs said, "Morning, Langdon," and retreated back into her small room.

During breakfast, she checked through the list of arrivals. Elmer wasn't on it. Nothing from Longshanks Limited was on it. And contrary to what it looked like from her window, only about two-thirds of the inhabitants of Purgatory local space were on the station.

Legs used the accounting program problems as an excuse to stay in her office for a while after breakfast. She did have to get the accounts to balance, and soon she wouldn't have time to mess with accounting. Hiding didn't help any, though. People just drifted into her office as suited themselves.

"Sheriff, there's been some sort of strange goings-on out by Chronos. All sorts of traffic through there, but not much mining."

"Ottoman's selling the mining rights," Legs said without looking up from her display. "Hasn't found a buyer yet."

"Oh. I might look into that."

A few minutes later, a slim shadow fell across her desk. "When am I getting my stolen hopper back?"

"It's in the impound, Mr. Tulver. Pay Mr. Nutil's storage fees, and it's yours again."

"That's legal robbery, that is."

"I have no control over that, Mr. Tulver. Take it up with Mr. Nutil."

A little later, Langdon Kade was back. He dropped his recorder pad on the desk beside Legs. "There's been a lot of talk about those pirates operating in the fringes of the Kuiper Belt. Do you have any leads? Any idea where they might be hiding out? Any plans to catch them?"

"Oh, sure, Langdon, I'm going to tell you where I think they're at, and what they're going to do next, and how I plan to catch them, so you can print it all up, and they can know all about it. Get out of my office."

Langdon scowled at her, and picked up his recorder. "Those pirates are news. And people want to know what you're going to do about them, seeing as how so far you've just let them have free range."

Legs scowled back at him. "I have leads and ideas and plans. Those raiders haven't been seen in over a month. I don't think everyone is all that concerned, right this minute. Now get."

He left.

A large shadow fell across her desk. She looked up to see Ramon Minerva standing in her doorway. A big man, Ramon generally looked the part of the wealthy businessman, head of a large extended family, and powerful mover-and-shaker. Legs figured the chain hanging around his neck and across his broad chest, made of plastic packing chunks sloppily painted to look like gold nuggets, had probably been manufactured and put around his neck by one of his doting toddler grandchildren in celebration of the biannual family gathering.

"Sheriff Lanier." He nodded to her as he sat in the chair opposite her desk. "I wanted to let you know as quickly as possible that Corin has been accepted at the University of North Dakota on Earth. We were hoping, I know it's sudden and difficult for you, but we were hoping we could send him off with the *Ocher Dust* when it leaves."

"Congratulations!" Legs smiled at the first good news she'd had all day. "I understand perfectly, and I'll start looking for a new deputy right away."

Ramon Minerva sighed in relief. "Thanks, Letitia. You've been a good influence on my boy, and I do appreciate all you've done with him."

"He's been an interesting deputy," Legs said honestly. It was just like Corin to make his father come put in his notice for him.

They shook hands, and Ramon rose to leave. "By the way, Sheriff, you have our support in the election. I just wanted you to know that."

"Thanks, Mr. Minerva. That's good to know."

Legs headed for the *Purgatory Prattler*'s office. As she crossed the moving sidewalk, she overheard a couple of young miners talking.

"You got yourself a room yet? The saloons are filling up."

"Naw. I'll just get drunk, and let the sheriff put me up in one of the cells, like I always do."

Nodding to the pair, Legs said, "Morning, gents."

"Morning, Sheriff."

Neither looked the least bit worried that she might have overheard them.

Langdon wasn't in, of course. When she had something for him he was never around. She put in her order for a column advertisement at the corner of Main Street and Tin Alley through the automated messenger and left. Langdon could figure it out for himself.

People accosted her with demands for information,

or with something they thought was sheriff's business, every few feet as she made her way down the street toward the bank. She broke up an impending fight in front of the Struck It Rich, and made her way into the sepulchral quiet and cool openness of the bank lobby. Five clerks stood behind a long curving counter, quickly dispatching the orderly queue of people patiently waiting. Kimble Phelps' simple glassed-in office was empty, because he'd joined his clerks behind the counter. Everyone was busy during Hell Week.

Kimble Phelps had seen her come in, and walked out from behind the counter after he finished with his customer. "Dare I hope this is a social call?"

"Sorry, Kimble. I'm having trouble with my accounting program. It can't seem to give me two numbers straight in a row, columns don't total up, and nothing balances."

His mouth thinned. "Perhaps I should come down to your office, and have a look at it."

"I'd appreciate it."

"Maybe afterwards we could do lunch."

"Let's see how it goes."

At the sheriff's office Kimble sat in her chair, fiddling with her computer, while she loitered nearby, sweeping out the cells at the back.

"Well, I think I've found the problem. It seems you've got some kind of old-fashioned virus here on your machine. It seems to be aimed only at your accounting program. Let me erase it and get a proper download from the bank, and you'll be all set."

Jack Dixon walked in the open office door, hands in fists at his sides, eyebrows low over his eyes. "You been down to the column today?"

"No," Legs said. "Did Langdon mess up the help-wanted ad?"

"I don't know about that, but I think you'd better get down there."

Usually Jack was a calm, almost serene person. Seeing him angry and in full bulldog mode alarmed Legs. She looked at Kimble. "You need me here?"

"I'll take care of it." He waved at her. "Lock up when I'm done?"

"Don't bother."

She followed Jack to the moving sidewalk. With too many people riding on it to walk today, they had to content themselves with the gentle gliding speed. Jack stood, hands still in fists, arms crossed on his chest, looking like he wanted to punch someone.

When the advertising column came in view she could understand why.

"Purgatory Sheriff Hoping Raiders Gone for Good," the *Prattler*'s announcement plastered to the column proclaimed.

Legs pressed the back of her watch communicator to the announcement's reader eye, and a curl of paper spewed out. She could feel one side of her mouth twitching up in a snarl as she read the article. A few sentences especially bothered her.

"Not having bestirred herself to protect the good citizenry of Purgatory from the depredations of these unknown bandits, our fine Sheriff Lanier hopes that since they haven't attacked in over a month that they have left local space for good" and "When asked about any projected plans to track down these desperadoes, Sheriff Lanier became very uncooperative, leaving this reporter to wonder if she has given it even a moment's thought" and "Local citizens' concern for their safety and the safety of their businesses doesn't seem to in any way motivate Sheriff Lanier."

"That son-of-a-bitch." Legs crumpled the paper in

her hands. "It'd feel so good to put my hands around his neck and squeeze."

"Allow me," Jack drawled.

She shook her head. "I'd hate to have to jail a good friend like you." She searched the column for any sign of her ad for a deputy, but didn't find it. Reaching over she ripped the announcement off the column. "I'm going to go deal with Langdon. Do me a favor, Jack, spread the word that I'm looking for a new deputy to replace Corin. He's heading off to school."

Jack sighed and nodded, wandering off down the street, mingling with the crowd swirling around the moving sidewalk, and spreading the word. Legs headed for the *Prattler*'s office directly across from the sheriff's.

Luckily Langdon was in. She slammed the announcement down on the counter. "What the hell do you mean by putting this up?"

"Freedom of the press." Langdon shrank back, away from the counter, shaking and nervous. "I have a duty to let the public know what is going on. They have a legitimate concern about the bandits. You can't deny that."

"Disseminating information is all well and good, but if I catch you encouraging crime or abetting criminals I'll see you rot in one of my cells. Is that clear!" Legs threw the announcement at him. "Now you clean this up, so that it's just information, and not a challenge to the bandits to attack now. Understood?"

Trembling, Langdon glared at her as she left.

A line of eager youths, disenchanted floozies, and elderly miners awaited her at the door of her office. Word had spread.

Kimble had left, and now her accounts were accessible and balanced at a single request. She talked to potential deputies as she ate lunch, and through the afternoon, and well into the evening.

Elmer and Longshanks Limited still hadn't docked when Legs checked that night. About three-quarters of Purgatory local space population now inhabited the station.

A knock at the door stopped her as she headed for the stairs to her room.

Outside, seventeen-year-old Sadie Amber held a flimsy and looked nervous. Petite, and neat, Sadie had lost the gawky awkwardness of most teenagers through eking out a living in her family's hard-rock mines. Her light-brown, shoulder-length hair was pulled back into a practical ponytail, her hazel eyes were bright, and her face scrubbed clean without makeup or jewelry. She looked up at Legs, and held out the flimsy. "I understand you're looking for a deputy. I brought my resume."

Legs knew everyone who lived in and around Purgatory. Sadie Amber was in fact the younger sister of one of her previous deputies; from a good, solid, but poor family; got good grades on her schoolwork; was well behaved; and would come well recommended. None of that mattered. Most of the youths she'd spoken to today had the same qualifications.

The one thing that put Sadie above the other applicants was her older brother Tom. Tom Amber had been the best deputy Legs ever had, and she'd been sorry to see him go off to college.

Taking the flimsy, Legs said, "Come in."

Sadie looked around the office with obvious curiosity. Probably checking the sights against her brother's stories.

"So why do you want to be a deputy?" Legs reached down to adjust her legs to Sadie's height.

"I need the job. I'm too young to work in any of

the mines, other than my folks'. Seventeen." Sadie frowned. "But, legally, I can work on the station. We need the money, and . . ." Sadie stared at Legs' garters. "Can you really make those look like anything?"

"Sure." Legs grinned. A few twiddles on the controls and her legs were encased in old, faded-pink cotton pants and ended in ratty-eared, fuzzy bunny-slippers. A few more taps and they changed to combat boots and silvered protective trousers, which didn't suit her sheriff's vest and dark miniskirt. So she switched to plain black garter, ordinary legs, and plain black shoes.

"Wow!" Sadie's fingers twitched. "Are they battery powered or bio-electrical?"

"Bio-electrical, with battery augmentation."

"Do they run off a standard Evif-Tenelli chip, or is that specialized?"

A mechanic-in-embryo if ever one lived.

"Check for yourself." Legs smiled, sat down, turned off her legs, and disconnected one of the prosthetic disks to hand to Sadie.

"Oh. A customized Evif-Tenelli. Wow." Sadie examined the prosthesis reverently.

"Captain Dixon brought me the latest upgrade on his last run. So now, not only can I choose the style, color, and covering on my legs and garter, it automatically sets up a body field in case of sudden air loss or decompression. So even if I'm caught in some emergency here on the station or out chasing someone down, I'm protected. It'll maintain pressure and oxygen levels within the body field, as best it can. And it'll stop most projectile and energy weapons, within its specs."

"You have that running all the time?" Sadie asked.

"No. Too much power drain. But it's there if I

ever need it. Not only automatic, but I can turn it on manually if I want. And all the controls are ambidextrous, so I can change one leg or both from either disk."

"Wow." Sadie looked from the disk in her hand to Legs' stumps. "Oh." She looked embarrassed, and handed the disk back. "Sorry."

"For what? Curiosity will get you far in life."

Slouching and looking chagrined, Sadie said, "Papa keeps telling me to remember my manners before my curiosity gets the better of me."

"Everyone I interviewed today was curious. And not one dared to ask." Legs reattached and engaged her prostheses. "You come back in the morning. We'll roust Corin out of his quarters, so you can move in. He can go live with his family."

"Ah." Sadie stared open-mouthed.

"You're hired. Go get some sleep. Be here first thing in the morning."

Legs responded to five alarms that night, all drunk and disorderly brawls. So when Jim Nutil showed up in the wee hours before the office opened, Legs wasn't her normal pleasant self.

"What now?" She stood over the coffee machine trying once more to make it disgorge coffee rather than weak, colored water.

"I just got notice of a raid in progress out Heck-and-Gone." He shook his head, and keyed up the report on her computer.

Heck-and-Gone were a couple of large heavily met-aled asteroids orbiting just inside the limits of the Kuiper Belt. Purists debated exactly how they should be classified: planetoids, asteroids, failed comets, escaped moons, space debris. As far as Legs was concerned they were nothing but an invitation to trouble. Every mining operation attempted there failed. Businesses that took them on ended up ruined. People got lost just heading out their way. Longshanks wouldn't touch them with a ten-light-year pole.

Sadie walked in as Legs and Nutil were conferring. Legs paged Corin with orders to show Sadie the routine, get her settled in the deputy's quarters, get her outfitted, and take care of whatever came up while Legs was out to Heck-and-Gone.

Legs spent the day gathering reports and evidence, limiting damage, and chasing through the vacuum. When she got back, Corin met her at the docks.

"Why did you hire the Sidewinder? Didn't anyone warn you about her?" Corin demanded as they walked back to the sheriff's office. "You wouldn't believe what she's been doing today! Taking over like she was the sheriff."

"What happened?"

"She's arrested fifteen people on drunk and disorderly."

"The cells only hold ten."

"She's got some of them in manacles on the porch benches."

"They all sobered up?"

"All but a few that're still sleeping it off."

"Well, let them go."

The column at the corner of Tin Alley and Main Street blared the *Prattler's* latest offerings. "Sheriff Lanier Unable to Safeguard Purgatory," "Details on Latest Bandit Attack at Heck-and-Gone," "Record Population Surge on Station Equals Record Bank Receipts," and in small type with no audio "Local Girl Hired as Deputy in Midnight Pact."

"Langdon's going to regret that." Legs tapped the deputy headline. "The Ambers might be poor, but they're numerous and well liked. And this ain't going to make them happy."

"He's blaming it all on you. Corrupting the local youngsters. He don't know much about the Sidewinder." When they were past the shouted headlines, Corin said, "She's been messing with the office. Moving things around and getting into stuff. She's been taking apart nearly every piece of equipment we've got. She's a pain. I don't know why anyone would hire the Sidewinder."

"Someone's got to corrupt Purgatory's youth," Legs said.

Corin frowned.

Though it was close to midnight station time, Main Street was as filled as it had been before. Perhaps even more so. Five men sat on one of the rough wooden benches outside the sheriff's office, shooting the breeze with passersby and laughing. Only by looking closely could Legs see the manacles around their ankles, keeping them sitting on the bench.

"Let everyone that's sober and awake go," Legs told Corin. He sighed as she entered her office.

The first thing she noticed was the overpowering fragrance of strong coffee, the second thing she noticed was that someone had been in to steal all the dust. They'd buffed every piece of metal till it gleamed while they were at it.

Sadie sat at the desk, sorting through computer displays. She looked up, saw Legs, and her expression changed from confused frustration to fearful hope. "Evening, Sheriff."

"Coffee." Legs stood over the coffee machine, staring in wonderment at the dark, black liquid in the transparent pot. "How'd you get coffee from this machine?"

"It just needed some adjustment." Sadie shrugged,

and looked around nervously. "I fixed a few things. I hope you don't mind."

"Mind? Damnation, I ought to give you a raise for fixing the coffee machine."

A relieved grin spread over Sadie's face. Corin, who'd entered in time to hear Legs' comment, grimaced, and headed for the back cells. When most of the drunks were cleared out, Legs sent him home—permanently, since she had a new deputy now. She sent Sadie off to the deputy's quarters, and settled in to the computer to make her report.

After checking the docking records first thing in the morning, Legs paged Jack Dixon. He peeked in the front door, as if afraid of what might be lurking inside, before he entered.

"What are you doing?" Legs asked.

"They say you hired a woman known as the Sidewinder for your deputy. They say she's crazier than you."

Legs grinned. "Nobody is crazier than me. Sadie's something of a mechanic, with a more strict approach to the law than folks around here are used to. That works out fine as it happens, since last night was the first Hell Week night that I didn't get called out for a series of alarms."

"Good grief," Jack said as he took in the newly scrubbed condition of the sheriff's office. "I've known some of that dust nearly as long as you."

"I like her."

"You paged me. I thought maybe you were having problems with your new deputy. Obviously not. So, what do you want?"

"I want you to go looking for Longshanks. He and his crew are now officially a week overdue, and nobody's heard from them for a month now. I was out

yesterday, and finding them may take several days. I
need to circulate here and keep order. Being gone
for a day during Hell Week is bad enough, without
taking off for days on end."

"Find Longshanks. Good idea." Jack grinned at
Legs. "Can I tell him you sent me?"

"Yes." Legs flipped a flimsy and a star-shaped badge
in Jack's direction. "In fact, I'd like this to be official
business. Deputize and pay you."

He picked up the flimsy and the badge. "You just
want to boss me again, like you tried to during the
war." He looked at her. "I'm not ramming any ships
for anybody."

"That's fine." She decided to ignore his reference
to one of their battles. "Just bring Longshanks in."

"Yes, boss!"

Legs spent the day walking around the station,
making sure everyone saw her, behaved themselves,
and stayed out of trouble. A few miners accosted her,
to warn her against hiring the Sidewinder. Legs just
nodded, and ignored them.

Sadie stayed at the office, doing what she did best,
and the sight of cleanly scrubbed cells, neatened office,
and working equipment made up for all the nasty *Prattler* headlines. Legs decided to nap in the afternoon,
to make up for any sleep she might miss later.

Good thing too, because Legs never saw her hammock that night. Between brawls and petty thievery,
she kept busy the entire night.

Sadie took over the office and the disturbances in
the morning, allowing Legs to get a short nap. At
lunchtime Legs woke, and checked on docking records
and Jack Dixon's reports. Jack had been to two of
Longshanks' claims, but hadn't found anyone. Nearly
seven-eighths of Purgatory local space's population was

now on the station, but Elmer and his crew were not among them. Legs sighed, and got herself another cup of coffee.

"Sheriff?" Sadie asked.

"Call me Legs, or I'll call you Deputy."

The Sidewinder blushed. "I wanted to ask you something, but I'm not sure it's something I should have gotten into."

"Ask."

Pulling a stack of flimsies from the desk drawer, Sadie hesitantly set them in front of Legs. "I found these when I was cleaning. They looked like you'd been doing accounting by hand."

Legs smiled. "I had, or was trying to. My accounting software glitched, and I was trying to make everything balance. I never could."

"That's because these numbers don't match what the computer has." Sadie pointed to several entries and blushed again. "I checked."

"That's all right. I finally had Kimble Phelps come down here. He said it was a virus. He cleaned it off, and got me a fresh download from the bank. All taken care of."

"Oh." Sadie looked thoughtful and nodded. "I see."

"You want to hold down the office, while I go knock heads together?" Legs asked, getting up from her seat at the desk.

Sadie nodded.

"It's all right. Don't worry about it. You're doing great."

Putting the flimsies back in the drawer, Sadie just nodded.

Out on her office porch, Legs noticed the crowd gathering up by the bank, and decided she'd better get over there. But it wasn't the bank everyone was crowding around, it was the Struck It Rich, next door. Damon Karybdis stood near the doorway, directing the placement of a new plastic sign underneath the old wooden one.

He looked over at Legs, and smiled as she approached, but didn't take his hands from the construction controls. "Good morning, Sheriff Lanier. Beautiful to see you."

"What's going on?"

Looking back to the new sign going up, Karybdis smirked. "I bought me a restaurant. I'm making a few changes."

The sign consisted of a statue of a woman from the waist up, looking for all the world like an old-fashioned sailing ship's masthead. Her hand was extended, and she was holding an enormous set of dice.

"Gambling?" Legs asked.

"Of course," Karybdis said.

"Prostitution?"

"Naturally."

A sinking feeling took over in Legs' stomach. "And the steaks and potatoes?"

"Oh, uh. I'm sure we'll still have steaks and such." Karybdis shrugged and the sign shuddered. He turned his attention back to what he was doing. "I've closed up shop, while I redecorate. Not much is finalized yet."

With all his attention on the sign, Legs knew he didn't see her shocked look, but she couldn't find anything to say.

Close a busy restaurant during Hell Week? No sane businessman would do something like that. The Struck It Rich made good money. Lots of good money. But like most of Purgatory Station's businesses most of that money was made during the two Hell Weeks a year that the outsystem ship was in dock. The money they'd lose would make it more sensible to keep the Struck It Rich up and going as a restaurant until after Hell Week, then close it down during the quiet time and redecorate then.

Legs shook her head. Just because it was stupid didn't make it illegal. Though it was very strange. Odd. Unnatural. Every instinct Legs had said something was screwy, something wrong was going on.

Jack's reports were all negative, and Sadie seemed very quiet, which only made Legs more apprehensive.

After sleeping in fits and starts all night, between breaking up fights and generally keeping the peace, Legs irritatedly checked the docking reports. No Longshanks. Jack had checked all of Elmer's claims, without finding Elmer, and had moved on to checking unclaimed territories, to see if Longshanks might be establishing another claim.

Sadie tiptoed in, and cautiously set about straightening things that were already straight. Something about the way she was acting got on Legs' nerves.

"What's with you?" Legs asked.

"Nothing." But Sadie didn't look at Legs.

"Sadie," Legs said it harsher than she'd intended. "What's wrong?"

"It's just, well, the accounting stuff."

"What about it?"

Fiddling nervously with the broom handle, Sadie shrugged. "The numbers just don't add up. Even if you take the virus into account the numbers don't match."

"Show me." Legs stood up and motioned Sadie into her chair at the desk.

With the flimsies on one side and the computer display on the other, Sadie took Legs step by step, charge by charge, deposit by deposit, back through the sheriff's accounts. "See these charges, listed by the bank. They aren't on your written list."

"Maybe I forgot them?" Legs asked.

"I suppose it's possible," Sadie said. "But before this you'd always kept track of every charge. Can you remember spending these amounts?"

"No."

"Then this, if you add these deposits and subtract these charges from the amount here—" Sadie did just that, but in a different program from the accounting "—you don't get this total."

There was no arguing that.

"And here. According to this report this is when you last balanced with the bank, so the virus should have been afterward, but, see, your record of that amount and the bank's record don't agree. Isn't that strange?"

Very.

"And, I found an old record, from that balance date. At that time the bank agreed with your total, not its current total."

Legs carefully went back over everything Sadie had shown her. The bank's program hadn't fixed anything; it had made things worse. Legs could almost hear alarms going off in her head. "Good work, Sadie. Now, I need a favor. We're going to document all this, copy everything, hard and soft. Put it in evidence bags." Legs pulled a box of evidence bags from the supply closet, and handed it to Sadie with the little instruction booklet on collecting evidence. Her eyes locked with Sadie's. "But don't tell anyone. Not yet. I need to think."

She supervised Sadie's evidence gathering, making sure the girl understood what she was doing and why. Legs patiently and calmly assisted Sadie through the whole process, trying not to jump like a guilty school-girl caught skipping school everytime someone came to the office. When they'd finished documenting the entire problem, Legs said, "Go home to your folks. Don't tell your family, but find an excuse to check their accounts. I want to know if it's just mine, or if it's spread out."

Stepping out onto the porch, Legs surveyed all she could of Purgatory Station. Sadie nodded good-bye as she disappeared into the crowd.

Legs received the normal complaints and whines as people flowed past. She glanced down toward the bank, then forced herself to stare straight across the street, at the *Prattler*'s office.

Someone had been messing with Purgatory Station's money, and Legs suspected it wasn't limited to the sheriff's account.

Nearly ninety percent of the population from Purgatory local space was on the station. And, by certain accounting methods, over two hundred percent of the liquid assets rested in the bank. All of the ordinary cash, plus all the extras brought in for exchange during the biannual supply ship's visit. For this short week those goods and supplies had been transformed into liquid cash on the computer system. Which would disappear with the *Ocher Dust*, in the form of supply orders and goods transfers in the cargo holds. The combined assets of Purgatory Station would make an excellent target—if someone could find a way to physically access them. Once out of the Purgatory local space, possession of actual physical assets would cancel any phantom computer assets. The citizens of Purgatory would be left with money only in the virtual sense, while someone would be holding the actuality.

The culprit had to be confident and cool, able to get to the actual assets, able to hold and hide those assets until well away from the wrath of the victims, and well versed in diddling computers.

The Struck It Rich. Conveniently closed for remodeling. Smack-dab up against the bank, and if Legs' memory served her, right up against the vault. Physical access. Karybdis had to be involved.

Kimble Phelps? A possibility. But it was his bank. Legs didn't see much use in him fleecing his own bank. Unless he planned to leave with the goods. He'd know how to diddle the computers, where the assets were, what best to take, how to hide them until they were away from Purgatory. And probably where to sell them off outsystem.

So, did the fact that the accounting program was glitched indicate that Kimble was trying to hide what was going on, or that someone was trying to hack into the bank?

"Well, Sheriff, you're thinking awful hard."

Legs looked down to see Langdon Kade standing at the foot of her porch steps. Strangely, he wasn't holding a recorder pad toward her. She sighed mentally. "Yup."

"Wouldn't happen to be thinking about a missing businessman? Perhaps the overgrown owner of one of Purgatory's finest mining operations?"

"That ain't your business. What I think is sheriff's business."

Langdon grinned. "The public has a right to know official sheriff's business."

"Well damnation, Langdon, if the public wants to know so bad, you can tell them that their sheriff is keeping track of who is and isn't on the station. And who has and hasn't checked in like they're supposed to. And she's been poking her ornery, ugly nose into all sorts of things that people don't want her to." Legs' fingertips caressed the garters peeking out from under her miniskirt. "You know, I've had a complaint about the press. Perhaps I ought to come over there and stick my nose in your business. Let the people know exactly what's going on over at the press office. What do you think?"

"No need to get snitty." Langdon glanced fearfully at her legs, and walked off. Langdon might be a thorn in her side, but he knew and respected what her fiddling with her garters meant.

"Hey, Sheriff! Why'd you go and hire the Sidewinder? Didn't anybody warn you about her?"

Legs smiled, shook her head, and retreated back into her office. If she asked Jack, he'd delay the *Ocher Dust*'s departure. He'd get his engineer to "arrange" an engine problem or something. There wasn't much he as captain of the ship couldn't arrange. If he hadn't been her friend he'd be the perfect suspect for ringleader on this scam.

Her thoughts ground to a full stop. Not Jack. Not Jack.

He'd been the one who'd told her Karybdis wasn't a concern, or possibly at best a distraction. He'd told her to keep an eye on the locals. She rested her head on the cool surface of her desk.

And now he was out who knew where in Purgatory Station. Delivering assets to an accomplice?

Elmer Longshanks. Conveniently missing right when she couldn't go looking for him. When she'd turn to her trusted friend the captain of the outsystem ship to go track him down.

Memories of the war rose up in her mind, the confusion and terror and cold. She and Elmer facing each other, weapons drawn and aimed. Not their first meeting, this was after they'd gotten to know each other through a complicated series of battlefield encounters, surrenders, guardings, and prisoner swaps.

She and Elmer facing each other, at the business ends of the other's weapons.

She'd lifted her weapon; fired over his head. He'd lowered his, and shot out her first set of prosthetics. Taken her captive. Prevented his superiors from torturing her for the secrets she'd known. No torturing. Not around the honorable Sergeant Elmer Longshanks.

Honorable. He might have been the enemy, but he was honorable. Legs drew a deep breath and wiped away the hot wet tracks across her cheeks. Longshanks always did his duty. Always did what was right. That was one thing she could count on with him. He wouldn't touch something like this with a ten-light-year pole.

Jack Dixon had a more entrepreneurial approach to life, but she'd never known him to steal.

People could change. Did change. It was possible that Elmer and Jack were involved, but she'd consider them innocent until she found proof. Still, Legs felt guilty for suspecting them.

She had to get into the Struck It Rich, before Jack got back. While she was figuring how to get in, it wouldn't hurt to go case the bank. But first she wanted to check with the *Ocher Dust*'s customer attendant and see who had booked passage out.

On her way to the docks she passed the center column at the intersection of Tin Ally and Main Street. She picked out the *Purgatory Prattler*'s headlines through the surrounding ads.

"Raiders' Whereabouts Remain Unknown," "Record Population Aboard Purgatory Station," "Celebration Planned for Tomorrow," and "Sheriff Lanier Ineffective Against Rising Tide of Violence."

Legs found Martine Pease, the *Ocher Dust*'s customer attendant, at her shiny desk in her sumptuous office on the *Ocher Dust*.

"Letitia, welcome. What can I do for you?"

"Mind if I peek at the outgoing passenger list?"

Martine called it up on her computer, allowing Legs to look over her shoulder.

Damon Karybdis had already booked passage out. As had Corin Minerva and a few other students. The name Phillip Kim wasn't familiar to Legs though.

"Find what you need?" Martine asked.

"Yup." Legs smiled tightly. "Just checking to see that Corin was set. He tends to be forgetful of certain things."

"Oh, yes. You're losing your deputy." Martine cleared her throat. "I heard you'd found another, known as the Sidewinder."

Winking, Legs said, "I think I'm coming out the better on this deal."

Martine looked confused, but smiled.

"Who all's taking cargo?" Legs asked.

"Well, let's see." Martine changed the display. "The students have only their effects. Karybdis has reserved a small space. He says he's going to recoup some decorating costs by selling off the old fixtures from the Struck It Rich."

"Did he bring any cargo with him?"

"No. Just his effects. Samples, he said they were. Sure surprised me when he decided to take up a different line of work."

Legs made a noncommittal noise.

Martine scrolled down. "Most of the mine operators have already booked their cargo space. We're almost up to our normal passage weight. Not near capacity, though. Haven't heard from Longshanks Limited yet." She turned to smile up at Legs. "I'm sure Jack'll find him."

Legs made some polite good-bye. She snarled to herself as she walked up Coal Street on her way to the bank. Kimble Phelps was involved, definitely. She couldn't think who else would be masquerading as Phillip Kim.

She stopped to look at the *Prattler's* headlines on the column.

"Celebration Planned for Tomorrow," the tenor announced.

Pressing the back of her watch against the announcement's reader eye, Legs obtained a printed copy of the entire article. She read as she continued down Main Street. The *Prattler*, the bank, and the Minervas were sponsoring a general celebration from dawn to noon tomorrow. An early pyrotechnic display, breakfast, and games were planned. To ensure attendance, the bank and several other offices would be closed.

How convenient.

Spotting Langdon, Legs pulled him from the center of a crowd of people. She waved the article flimsy in front of his face. "Whose idea was this?"

Langdon pulled his arm from her grasp. "Oh, that's just something we've been kicking around for a few years now. Why? Don't think you can handle it?"

"I'll handle it." Legs stalked off toward the bank.

Kimble Phelps came out from behind the counter almost as soon as she'd walked in the door. "What can I do for you?"

"Not a thing." Legs smiled at him. "I'm just circulating around, trying to prevent trouble before it starts."

He smiled back at her. "Good thinking." He saw the flimsy in her hand. "Planning on going to the celebration?"

"Wouldn't miss it for the biggest claim in the universe." She looked once more around the bank's lobby. "Well, no trouble here." Legs waved good-bye and headed out the door.

Glancing back at the bank's storefront clock, she said, "Damnation!"

Dawn and the pyrotechnics were still a good two hours away. There'd been no more dockings at Purgatory Station, and neither Jack nor Longshanks had checked in.

Legs held the rumpled, bright silver-colored space-emergency suit out to Sadie. "Ever used one of these?"

"Only for drills. Won't the protective vests shield us?"

"Against the ministunners and such, yes. But our enemies will have basically similar defenses and weaponry. I intend for us to be better equipped than them. They may outnumber us, but they won't outgun us."

Looking cautiously scared, Sadie didn't say a word.

Tossing the suit onto her littered desk, Legs closed the door of the musty cabinet. So Sadie hadn't gotten to every nook and cranny of the sheriff's office yet. "So, how'd your exploration of your family's accounts go?"

"About like my excursion through the sheriff's accounts."

"Today won't be a drill." Legs motioned Sadie to take the chair at her desk. "Pull up the station's specs. Get to know the mechanical and air ducts. Locate all the emergency containment blast doors for Main Street. For the most part each shop, saloon, or office will be contained to itself, but there are a few exceptions. There's going to be a problem today, and I want you in the suit, moving from compartment to compartment, working crowd control on Main Street."

"What's going on?" Sadie asked apprehensively.

"Kimble has booked passage on the *Ocher Dust*, under another name. I think we have a bank robbery on our hands."

"How?" Sadie's blue eyes widened.

"Through the closed Struck It Rich on the other side of the vault."

Sadie pulled up the station specs on the computer. "You can count on me."

Legs ran a quick set of diagnostics on her prostheses. Everything was in working order. She suited up in her shortest miniskirt, long-sleeved cotton shirt, and protective synthleather vest, adding a couple of miniature grenades to her standard arsenal. One in her right pocket, one in her left. Whoever she was up against wasn't likely to have any grenades, or be prepared to use them.

She checked herself in the mirror, and decided a little camouflage was in order. Legs twiddled the controls on her prostheses, adding height to her legs, and covering them in fishnet stockings, red spike-heeled shoes, and lacy garters. In the mirror she looked less threatening, more distracting, but it all felt the same to her. Floating on the field generated by the disks, she only noticed the difference in height. Until she looked down.

In the office Sadie continued her frantic study. Legs nodded to her. "Hold down the office until the pyrotechnics start. Then get into the suit and to wherever you need to be for access to Main Street. The problems won't start until after the pyrotechnics."

Barely glancing up from the display, Sadie said, "I'll be ready."

In truth, Legs had no intention of letting Sadie, an untried inexperienced deputy, anywhere near any action that might include gunfire. Not even if everyone called her the Sidewinder, and quaked in fear of her.

At least the girl would be mobile and well defended, whatever happened. It did mean Legs would have to fight this battle alone. Still, it could be worse. Breathing a sigh of relief that Corin wasn't deputy any longer, Legs left the office.

Without proof either way, Legs couldn't eliminate or accuse Jack and Elmer of collusion in this. She hoped she'd have some answers before they got back. If not, she'd have to wing it. This time she had no intention of letting Longshanks shoot out her prosthetics.

Legs had to go all the way down to the docks before she was alone, and could enter the duct system. Purgatory Station had a simple layout with a main level for human living, and a series of lower levels for engineering, vats and hydroponics, and docking. It took her another hour to wind her way through the tight duct passageways back up to the Struck It Rich. Her watch said she had a few minutes to wait until the pyrotechnics started.

From her post, sheltered behind the duct grating, she had a good view of the restaurant. And a great deal of nothing. Most of the chairs and tables were gone. She had no idea what they'd done with them. Five large, gray, plastic packing crates, open and empty, huddled in the center of the vacant restaurant floor. Ten shiny canisters of packing foam leaned against the cleared counter, which had served as both bar and kitchen, to her left. The wall behind the counter, smack-dab up against the bank's vault stood as it always had, seemingly unbroken.

Maybe she'd been wrong?

Kimble and Karybdis arrived right on time, as the shouts of the crowd and whine and pop of the pyrotechnics filtered into the empty restaurant. They shed their outer coats, revealing protective vests and lift belts. Legs watched the two of them open a concealed door to the vault.

Right. Kimble had had time to plan this.

A few moments more to allow Sadie to get positioned, and give Kimble and Karybdis time to carry a couple loads of ill-gotten gains from the vault to the empty crates in the restaurant. Legs burst from the duct, ministunner in her left hand, grenade in her right.

The men dropped their loads, shut the concealed door, and grabbed hastily for weapons concealed in their clothes.

"Stop it! Hands up!" Legs hadn't really expected them to obey her, and she wasn't disappointed. They ignored her order, continuing to scramble for weapons. With protective vests and ministunners all around, they'd end up shooting at each other until someone's vest failed. Since there were two of them and one of her, it stood to reason her vest would fail first.

She tossed the grenade onto the transparent wall. It exploded on impact, taking a portion of the wall with it.

A temporary force-field crackled over the shattered wall. Alarms screeched. Emergency bulkheads dropped. The force-field would contain everything in the restaurant larger than a pea, and it would slow the air loss. Just long enough for any presumed customers to get safely to the emergency pods now dropping from the ceiling. Legs had the air reserves in the restaurant calculated to approximately two minutes. Not long enough for a ministunner fight. She'd always loved emergency drills.

Kimble started shooting at the pods, blowing holes through them. "Get the pods," he shouted to Karybdis. "She won't make it without them."

Karybdis joined in the destruction. Legs ducked

behind a shot-out, holey pod, figuring, one pod for every ten people, and the restaurant rated for a maximum of two hundred people, so they had to destroy nineteen pods.

The low whine of wind escaping began, and loose objects started creaking and shaking.

When the shooting stopped, she stood up. Kimble was climbing into the last good pod, Karybdis already ahead of him. Kimble glared at her and said, "A few more minutes and you won't be a problem anymore."

He entered the pod, and sealed it behind him.

Everything loose in the restaurant began a slow, inexorable migration toward the force-field, crates and canisters making a high-pitched wavering shriek as they scraped against the tiled floor. Not wanting to be trapped in the force-field, like a bug in a spider's web, Legs ran to the bar, against the wind, and opened an emptied cabinet. She crawled into it, watching crates, canisters, cash, and bits of broken pods scoot across the floor on their way to the force-field, accelerating faster with every second that passed.

With a muffled *whoosh* the last of the atmosphere emptied into the void. Legs settled farther into the cabinet as her prosthetic legs disappeared and the crackling lines of a body field appeared around her.

The manual hadn't mentioned that she wouldn't have legs if the body field was on. Something to keep in mind if she ever wanted to turn it on manually.

Pulling herself out of the bar, Legs contemplated the remaining operational pod, and her prisoners. Kimble and Karybdis would remain trapped in the emergency pod until pressure was restored to the restaurant. Legs had to make sure they'd be trapped just a little longer, until she could decant them into a jail cell.

Crawling over to the pod, she began the long and difficult task of fusing the seal with her ministunner, set on low. Legs started at the bottom, the easiest to get to, and worked her way up the pod's seal, to as high as she could reach, standing on the stumps of her legs. The inhabitants of the pod struggled and shook against the sides, but couldn't escape without proper pressure. She left the last handspan or so of the sides and the top unfused, since she was unable to reach that high, but she'd fused enough of the pod's opening to keep them in.

By the time she finished, she was exhausted and her ministunner's charge nearly wiped out.

She crawled back to the bar, and pulled herself up onto it. She didn't want to meet anyone while flopping around on the floor with her legs off. She took a deep, shuddering breath before reaching for the chain to pull the watch-communicator out of her left vest pocket.

A sudden thud accompanied the restaurant's door falling inward. A whole squad of silvered emergency-containment-suited figures trooped in. One stood head and shoulders above the others, stunner in hand and pointed into the restaurant, looking for trouble. Only one person in Purgatory Station fit that description.

Legs pointed her ministunner at the tall figure, and they faced off a moment. He lowered his stunner, and switched his visor to transparent, so she could see his face.

Elmer looked tired, twitchy, and worried.

"How'd you know where to find me?" Legs asked, keeping her ministunner aimed at his heart, and desperately desiring some sort of cover for the stumps of her legs.

"The Sidewinder told us what she knew, and we guessed," Elmer said. "I wish you hadn't hired her as a deputy. I was planning on hiring her as soon as she was old enough. Damnation, half the mine owners wanted to hire her." He held his hands up in surrender, and walked closer.

Behind him the rest of the troop lowered their weapons, and cleared their visors. Legs saw Jack and Jim Nutil and Corin Minerva and Langdon Kade and Sadie Amber and most of Jack's crew. No way could all of them be involved in this. No way, no how. Impossible.

"Where have you been?" She was feeling a bit tired and twitchy herself.

"Staking a new claim. I didn't mean to worry anyone." Elmer looked down at her ministunner, just touching his suit directly over his heart. "You going to shoot me?"

"Damnation, Elmer. It's empty." She tossed it toward the force-field. "I'll have to strangle you with my bare hands."

Jack pulled Elmer away from her, pointing toward the shattered transparent wall. "Careful, Sergeant. She's in one of her moods."

Nutil waved at the gently rocking pod.

"Kimble and Karybdis are in there. I caught them stealing from the bank's vault." Legs motioned to the wall behind her. "After we repressurize here, I'll show you the door they've hidden there. You can see the vault's contents, decorating the force-field."

Cash glittered like faraway stars around the dark hulking crates in the crackling rifts of the shattered vista wall.

Legs tapped the bar beside her. "Karybdis bought this place and shut it down, not for redecorating, but to get access to the vault. Kimble's been playing with the bank's accounting. My guess is he's been trying to hide their tracks, and confuse the issue of exactly how much is missing when we finally found out. Make it a lot harder, if not impossible, to track them down once they'd left the system."

Sighing, Nutil shook his head. "You had to shut down the entire station to take them?"

"I didn't know who all I was up against, who I could count on for help, or how heavily armed they would be."

Snaking an arm around Nutil's shoulder, Jack grinned. "This is exactly how she was in the war. Did I ever tell you about the time . . ."

"Just can't make some people happy." Jack shook the flimsy he picked up off Legs' desk, the one with the headline that read, "Sheriff Still in the Dark on Raiders' Whereabouts."

"I don't expect to anymore," Legs answered easily.

"Anyone figured out what to do about setting up a bank in the interim?" Jack asked. "Until we get back in six months."

"Not my problem." Legs smiled and settled back into her desk chair. "Nutil will have to deal with it. The same as he has to deal with the station repairs. I just have to get Kimble and Karybdis safely to your brig, for transport to the sector penitentiary."

Kimble and Karybdis, lounging morosely in the second cell, glared at her, but made no overt threat. They hadn't said much since they'd been decanted into the cell, and stripped of their weapons. Legs guessed that they were probably both waiting until they'd talked to a lawyer before they shot their mouths off. They probably knew about the auto-spies constantly recording them, too. One more bit of evidence she'd be sending off with them.

"We could make Longshanks be banker." Sadie

looked up from the main cell, where she had the door completely taken apart and in pieces all around her. The cell's bunks were filled with snoring drunks. "He don't need time to work his claims anymore. He's rich as Croesus, with that new claim. He could float this whole station. He'd have the time. He could do it."

Jack and Legs exchanged a look.

"He'd hate that," Jack said.

"But he'd do it, if he thought he had to." Legs narrowed her eyes. "It'd serve him right for not reporting in. He didn't have to give his position, but he could at least have let us know he was all right."

"Not his style."

The door opened, and Elmer walked into the office, dwarfing everyone and everything in it.

"Sidewinder." Jack tilted his head toward the door. "Take a break, let me buy you a drink."

"She ain't legal, Captain," Elmer said.

"Complain, complain." Jack grabbed Sadie's arm. "Come on." They left.

Legs raised her eyebrows questioningly at Elmer, but he seemed fascinated with the half-mended cell door. She waited patiently as he cleared his throat, and uhmed and uhed for several minutes.

"Get on with it," Jack shouted from the porch outside the office. "We don't have all day, Sergeant."

Elmer looked at his scuffed boots, and said, "The new claim turned out real good. We made quite a bit off of that."

"Aim for the target, Sergeant!" Jack's hollered order floated in through the open door.

Clearing his throat, Elmer tried leaning against the bars of the main cell in what he might have thought was a casual posture. "I wanted to give you time to settle into yourself after . . . Time for me to make a little more of myself."

"Damnation! Do I have to come in there?"

Red faced, Elmer walked over to Legs' desk, and dropped a ring into the middle of her display. A diamond the size of a pea twinkled in the glow of the computer.

"Say it," Jack shouted.

Legs grinned up at Elmer. "Marry me?"

He nodded.

"Damnation!" Jack shouted from the porch.

Paul Chafe's first published fiction appeared in Larry Niven's Man-Kzin Wars series. After meeting him at a World Science Fiction Convention and learning a little more about his avocation (playing with big guns for the Canadian Army), I asked him to contribute to this volume. And after I read his story, I asked him to follow in Charles Sheffield's very big footsteps and explain just where the science in his story left off and the speculation began.

THE CUTTING FRINGE

Paul Chafe

I was driving up to Holmes' house when I became aware of a ghostly voice rising over the strains of Vivaldi coming from my car stereo. At first it didn't quite register, but then I heard it again. I turned down the volume, and there it was, quite plainly.

"Bewaaarrrre. The goverrrrmennnt is watchinnnnngg youuuu."

Reflexively I slammed on the brakes. My Porsche has antilock brakes big enough to stop a tank. It didn't skid, but I nearly went through the windshield with the deceleration. Sixty to zero in one point nine seconds flat. Well okay, eighty to zero in three point four. Don't give me that look, of course I was speeding. I drive a Porsche.

For a moment I thought I was hallucinating—I had a few experimental experiences back in college that I don't want to repeat. After the initial fear of incipient paranoia faded I looked in the rearview mirror, but it was nothing that obvious. It had to be Holmes' doing of course, the only question was how. I turned off the ignition and got out and looked in the ditch, looked up in the trees for hidden loudspeakers, for wires, for some bizarre gadget of no clear purpose. There was nothing. I thought about it. The voice had been too close for it to be a distant source, and it had moved with the car—no Doppler effect up or down as I passed it. Maybe some kind of transmitter? A huge magnet turning my whole car into a speaker?

With Holmes it could be anything. I looked at my car. It had been parked in my garage all day, and while he was perfectly capable of building some gadget to make my car talk to me, it would have been far too much effort for him to actually sneak into my garage and install it. You have to understand, Holmes isn't lazy, not at all, but he's very focused on his work. It wouldn't be worth his effort to go so far out of his way.

Probably not, anyway. You never could tell with Holmes. I tried to remember if I'd had the Porsche at his house last time and made a mental note to bring the Jag next time. If it ever did enter his head to play around with one of my cars I wanted it to be one I wasn't quite so finicky about.

I got back in, started the car and drove off. A hundred yards down the road the voice came again. "Dowwwnn with federrraalll surveeiillllancce lawwwsss." The voice was right in the car. It even sounded like Holmes. I sighed and turned up Vivaldi.

Perhaps some explanation is in order. My name is John Watson, and I never would have met Holmes if

I'd had any other name, despite the fact that we lived just across the hall from each other in the dorm. I studied arts and spent my weekends playing rugby on the varsity team and chasing girls. He studied physics. And computer science. And chemistry, and math, and geology, neuroscience, biology, statistics, mechanical engineering, electrical engineering, aeronautics and astronomy, to give a nonexhaustive list. He spent his weekends co-authoring papers with his profs, who occasionally came to blows over who would get to be his mentor for his postgraduate work. I had seen him a couple of times in the hall, this tall gangly student in ill-fitting jeans and a faded black T-shirt that said "The Wrath of Con," wild blue eyes with a mop of dirty blond hair that looked like he styled it by sticking his fingers in a power socket. Maybe he did, it would explain a lot.

It was Jane Proudfoot who introduced us at the residence Halloween party. "John, you'll never guess what. There's this guy on this floor named Holmes! You have to meet him." I was in hot pursuit of Jane who was barely dressed in a harem girl costume, so I let her drag me over to talk to this obvious misfit who was trying to reprogram the flashing orange lights in the plastic pumpkin-ghoul's eye sockets to send secret Morse code messages in the middle of a party. His first name, thank God, was Brian and not Sherlock, and after Jane had giggled at the coincidence of our names Holmes launched into a demonstration of how he could count to a thousand and twenty-three on his fingers, a trick I neither understood nor was interested in understanding. Before I could figure out how to extricate myself and Jane from his nonstop lecture she excused herself, leaving me trapped. Every time I tried to break the conversation he launched into another tangent, gabbling on about complementing twos, nybbles with a "y" and how to use hex, whatever hex was. None of it made any sense and I was much more interested in complimenting Jane in order to get nibbles with an "i." Hex had the wrong letter too, for my purposes. Across the room I saw Brock McMaster pick up his beer and head for Jane, who was now talking with friends by the beer tub but shooting glances his way. I could see my chances of getting laid that night falling rapidly toward zero and wouldn't have put it past her to have attached Holmes to me so Brock would have a clear run. I was about to simply turn and leave on an intercept course when Brian mentioned something about free long-distance calls.

Now technology marches so quickly that many of you may not understand that there was a time when long-distance calls cost money. When I was in school you had to be very careful how much time you spent on the phone calling home to beg your parents for more cash or you might find the entire exercise self-defeating. I knew a girl who spent seven hundred dollars on a single call to her boyfriend in Toronto, because Bell South considered Canada to be an overseas call destination. So when he said "free long distance" I forgot all about Jane Proudfoot and became very interested in what Brian Holmes had to say.

He showed me his pocket calculator. It no longer calculated, because he had rewired the keypad. We went down to the pay phone at the front of the residence and I gave him my parent's phone number in New Orleans. He plugged a speaker into the recharge jack, held it against the phone's mouthpiece and dialed directory assistance in Hawaii. When it rang he dialed again on the calculator before the operator could answer. The speaker made a high-pitched whistle, then a series of tones like touchtones, but different. Smiling, he handed me the receiver. Not quite believing it, I held it to my ear. My mom answered. I hung up. He was smiling, proud of his trick. "Intersil eight-oh-thirty-eights. Aren't they beautiful?"

I had no idea what he meant. I didn't care either. "Can you make more of these?" I asked him.

"Sure."

I offered my hand and he shook it somewhat bemusedly. "My friend," I told him, "you and I are about to get rich."

We didn't get rich right away. The first problem was getting him to actually make more calculators—blue boxes he called them. He kept promising them and then not delivering. Having solved the problem of hijacking the entire North American telephone system for his private amusement the mundane act of building more boxes simply held no challenge for him. Nor was money a motivator. It turned out Brian was already rich, if you call a hundred grand in the bank rich, which I did back then. Every high-tech corporation in the nation was throwing scholarships at him in hopes of luring him into their research centers. I finally got him to draw the circuit diagrams and hired some of his less brilliant and more penurious classmates to actually build the boxes. We sold about a hundred that year, at five hundred dollars a pop. Not exactly wealth, but a tidy little sum, even allowing for expenses. There were some tense moments when the FBI busted some of our clients, but when they came and asked me some pointed questions I simply denied all knowledge. It was easy to demonstrate I knew barely enough about electronics to change channels on TV, and though they ransacked my apartment I was too smart to have anything incriminating there. I never told Holmes about the investigation, but I gave him fifty percent of the net. I knew the future when I saw it coming. I convinced him to let me manage his assets too, for ten percent of all he made over bank interest, and rode the waves of boom and bust, war and peace. I may not know much about technology, but I know how the world works and I have a knack for the markets. I doubled his money in four years and the profits kept me in pizza and beer. I came out of school with my law degree and an MBA, Holmes just kept on taking classes. He never finished a program because he refused to take the boring subjects on the "required" lists.

In my spare time I tried to commercialize the gadgets he invented, a difficult process since around ninety-nine percent of what he comes up with is technologically brilliant and absolutely useless. Like the anti-flashlight—just a normal flashlight, except the lens plate is made of this special barium phosphorous crystal he developed that splits every photon that enters into two photons exactly out of phase with each other. Result—no light comes out. He was immensely proud of it and couldn't understand why I didn't want to market it. I stuck with him anyway, and in the third year of my law degree he came up with the split-ring convolver. I don't know what that is any more than you do, but you've got a few million of them in your house, submicron-sized circles etched on the silicon chips that run our world. I did all the paperwork for the patent as a class exercise and took it to the big semiconductor houses. My professor sniffed at the language in my filings and slapped me with a B+, but the patent has netted Baker Technologies over a billion in royalties. Baker Technologies is our company. Get the pun? His next useable brainstorm was the vortex cell windmill, which now powers ninety percent of the world and netted many billions more. I'm what you'd call comfortably well off.

That money has given us the freedom to do whatever we want with our lives. For Holmes, that meant buying Wild Oaks, the old Grafton plantation house, and cramming it with lab gear. Every time he gets a new research interest he buys all the best equipment and puts another wing on the house. As for me—well, I do what you'd expect an MBA and lawyer to do with limitless wealth. I try to get more of it. Wealth beyond the wildest dreams of starved avarice is my goal, to quote a great writer, and power such that mighty gods shall tremble before me, to quote him again. I plan to rule the planet someday, and I'm well on my way to doing it. You can laugh at me if you like, but don't make the mistake of lumping me in with deluded world conquest wannabes like Napolean, Khan and Caesar. World domination through military conquest is doomed to failure because it automatically generates resistance. Eventually the rest of the world gangs up on you in sheer self defence. My plan is economic conquest, and I'm betting I can buy all the nations of the world before any of them even notice. I just need more money.

Holmes remains the principal tool in my campaign, which is why I was driving up to Wild Oaks once more, wondering how he was managing to project ghostly and paranoid warnings into my car. Usually I just let Brian invent things and commercialize what I can, but this time I had a plan in mind. It was time to start the big gamble. I guided the Porsche up his long, winding driveway, overhung with ancient cypress trees, and pulled in to park next to a battered VW van. The rear windows had been removed and the entire back of it was crammed with tanks, hoses, machined steel and sundry less identifiable gadgetry. Some bizarre arrangement of hydraulic pistons protruded from the back. In the side garden an eight-wheeled wagon was rolling along, video cameras switching this way and that as it towed a roller mower efficiently over the grass.

A video camera in a tree pivoted to follow me and the door opened as I approached. A synthesized female voice said, "Good afternoon, Mr. Watson."

"Hi, Pandora." Pandora is Holmes' computer—or rather, she's software that runs on his network. She runs the house and, though Holmes assures me that she's not actually sentient, she certainly does a good job of faking it.

"Did you have a pleasant drive?"

I pushed my momentary brush with paranoia out of memory. "Yes, I did, thanks."

"Mr. Holmes is in the main lab. Please go in." Pandora sounds downright sultry and I can't help but imagining a body to go with that voice. I headed down the hall when Holmes himself came barreling out of the lab.

"John! Excellent! You're just in time! Come and see this." He grabbed my hand and dragged me into the lab. Still wild blue eyes and tangled blond hair and still—I'm not kidding—wearing the same "Wrath of Con" T-shirt he had on when I met him ten years ago, now too faded to read clearly. I don't mean to imply he's never had it off since, but his wardrobe is, shall we say, limited.

"Listen, Brian, I've got something I need you to build . . ."

"Wait wait!" He wasn't even listening. The main lab used to be the Grafton's ballroom, and the finish on their beautiful parquet dance floor has been ruined by lab-cart wheels and heavy pieces of equipment dragged over it with callous disregard for antebellum sensibilities. High on the south wall a ten-foot-high portrait of Colonel Wolfe Beauregard Grafton in full

Confederate uniform stares down disapprovingly on the chaos. He let me go to close the door behind us, and I noticed that the entire inside surface of the room had been covered in chicken wire on a rickety frame of two-by-fours, even the floor and the ceiling. The wire bulged considerably in places, to clear the huge chandelier, and to go over some of the larger pieces of lab equipment that couldn't be lifted to get it under. It looked like he'd installed it himself, which was probably accurate. Colonel Grafton looked like he'd been caged, and he didn't look happy about it.

"Okay, they can't hear us in here."

"Brian . . ." I looked at him askance. He *did* seem a little more wild-eyed than usual. "Nobody is listening to us."

He looked surprised at that, taken aback, but quickly recovered. "Good, very smart, but it really is safe. I checked and there's no field leakage outside the lab. The chicken wire blocks it perfectly. You can speak freely."

I looked at him, opened my mouth to say something, thought better, closed it and started again. "I need you to build—"

He held up a hand. "Wait one more moment. You're just in time. You have got to see this."

In a cleared space in the center of the room stood what was clearly Brian's latest pride and joy. Two induction coils bigger than forty-five-gallon drums were stacked in a wooden frame. In between them was a thick, plexiglass cube with a single copper helix as thick as my thumb. Firehose cables snaked off to a twelve foot cubical array of what looked like paint cans.

I knew better than to argue. He wouldn't listen to me until he'd shown off his gadget, whatever it was.

"What does it do?" I stayed a good ten feet away from it. I have learned to be cautious about Holmes' inventions in their early stages. Sometimes they explode.

"Watch!" He threw a switch large enough to serve as the main circuit breaker for a nuclear power plant. There was a deep, ominous hum and the high-pitched whining sound that I'd come to recognize as a capacitor bank charging up. A *big* capacitor bank—that was what the paint cans were. Merlin the lab cat slunk out from between some equipment racks, leapt to a bench by the east wall, squeezed through a gap in the chicken wire and vanished out an open window. I wished I could do the same. Holmes fiddled with some instruments, then turned to me.

"Do you have a quarter?"

"A what?" I was regarding the array with distrust. The voltages involved looked dangerous.

"Twenty-five cents."

"Oh sure." I dug some change out of my pocket, gave him a quarter. He put it in a paper drinking cup, the kind that comes in stacks. He balanced the cup on top of the bottom coil, positioned it with delicate care, then turned back to the stacked controls on the lab bench. He flipped a couple more switches and the quarter jumped out of the cup, bobbed in the air for a moment and then just floated there, hovering exactly between the two coils.

That was neat, the big coils were obviously magnets of some kind. I relaxed, breathing out. There was a lot of extra equipment involved just to make a quarter float, but sometimes Holmes' experiments were a little anticlimactic. I already told you about the anti-flashlight.

There was a blinding flash and a *crack* that seemed to split my head in half. I jumped back reflexively and fell over some nameless piece of equipment on the floor behind me. My vision swam with fluorescent spots and the air smelled of ozone and burnt insulation. I couldn't hear flames crackling or feel heat, so I resisted the urge to bolt blindly for the door.

"Hey, you okay?" I peered through the glowing spots to see a blur that could only be Brian standing over me. He helped me up. "It's a little loud when the capacitors discharge."

"A little loud. Sure." I stood, rather unsteadily.

"Here! Look!" I squinted as he held out the paper cup. Inside was a little silver ball bearing, rolling around.

"What happened to the quarter?"

"That is the quarter." He had the self-satisfied expression of a puppy who's just pulled off its best trick.

"It's a little ball."

"Well, yes, it is now. But it was the quarter. It's been magnetically imploded."

I looked at him blankly. "And what's magnetic implosion when it's out with friends?"

"Well, basically there's a magnetic field and an electric field. The electric field induces a current in the quarter, which then produces its own magnetic field. This little coil here..." The little coil he was referring to was as big as my head. "... makes it float at the exact center of the big coils. So then I dump a big current into the big coils—the rise time is the vital thing, the field has to come up fast. That generates a huge opposing magnetic field and the reaction forces crush the quarter. I've been wanting to build one of these for a long time, but it wasn't until I had to install the chicken wire anyway that I could.

"Why the chickenwire?"

"To keep the electromagnetic pulse out of the lab electronics of course. It would fry everything electrical in the house."

He answered the question I asked of course, but not the question I meant to ask. I looked at the plexiglass cube. It was full of shards of copper and shredded insulation. Evidently the reaction forces that crushed the quarter inward also exploded the coil outward. EMP was hardly the biggest danger this contraption posed to the contents of the lab.

I looked at Brian, beaming and rolling the little ball around in his fingers. "So it's a quarter squisher? Is that about right?"

"Absolutely! Not just quarters—it can squish paper clips, small bolts, bits of aluminum foil—the sky is the limit. It's simple really. The hard part is making the collapsing field symmetric when . . ."

"Listen! Brian!"

" . . . the Q factor of the coils . . ."

"Brian!" I grabbed the cup from his hand "This is important."

He blinked, coming back from wherever it is that he is when he's explaining something. "What?"

"I want to build a ship. A spaceship."

"That's a solved problem." Coming from Holmes, this means he isn't interested.

"This one isn't a solved problem." He raised an eyebrow. I had his interest. "I need a ship that can take a crew to the asteroids."

"Why?"

"To mine them."

"Uhhhmm . . ." He hesitated. "I can't really build you a whole ship . . ."

"I need to be able to get into orbit for a hundred dollars a kilogram. Get me that and I can solve every other problem."

His other eyebrow went up. He didn't answer right away. Instead he looked at his quarter squisher. For a long moment I watched him waver, holding my breath. It wasn't yet perfected I knew, and it tore him up to leave problems unsolved, but the bait I dangled was powerful. Deep space travel is the ultimate challenge for any scientist.

Challenge won out. "Okay, I'll see what I can do."

I smiled. "I knew I could count on you."

He got that faraway look in his eye. "Getting cheap specific impulse is going to be the hard part, it's really a materials problem . . ."

There was a clatter of china from the doorway and a smiling garbage can on rubber treads lurched awkwardly into the lab, a wooden tray extended in its pincers—another of Pandora's remotes. Coffee slopped around on the bottom of the tray, soaking into egg salad sandwiches and a plate of cookies.

Twin cameras atop the garbage can scanned, panned and focused. "Would you care for a snack, Mr. Watson?" When I imagined a body to go with Pandora's voice, somehow it was never this one.

"Dammit!" Holmes sounded annoyed. "She cut the sandwiches lengthwise again."

I spent another couple of hours there, mostly going over the details of what I wanted in a space drive. Once I had his attention Holmes was focused on the problem like a laser beam, and he outlined several possible technologies, the least attractive being launching a ship by detonating a fusion bomb underneath it. On the way home his ghostly voice warned me again about the government watching me and I realized who the "they" was that he thought was listening to him. I resisted the urge to look in the rearview mirror again. Of course since Congress passed the Personal Privacy Act and opened the databases to the feds the government really has been watching everybody. All your medical records, academic records, travel records, employment history, insurance history, the netsites you visit, who you call and when you call them, and where you call them from, the magazines you read, the books you borrow from the library, the groups you belong to, all that information is on file somewhere. Combine that with automated video surveillance in airports, train stations and shopping malls, cameras at stop signs and highway ramps, satellite tracking of your car and electronic tracking of your bank chip, your credit cards and every financial transaction you make. Tie it all together with the computer power to build the big picture and there's really nothing the government doesn't know about you. That doesn't mean you have to be paranoid, because after all, what have you got to hide? The bleeding heart lefties complain about violation of civil rights, but I'm all in favor of the new Open Society, as the president likes to call it. When I take over everyone will be so used to obtrusive electronic snooping that they won't even notice they live in a totalitarian state. Control America and you control the world. All I need to do is position myself properly and then create another National Emergency.

What about my privacy? Don't make me laugh. The fish swept up in the digital dragnet are the small ones—plumbers cheating on their taxes, doctors cheating on their spouses, college kids using drugs, illegal immigrant fruit pickers, drifters, greenpeacers and people with dangerous political opinions. I pay no taxes at all and it's perfectly legal—you just have to have the money to structure your finances properly, and of course the legislative branch is well aware of the need to structure the tax code so as not to annoy those of us who fund their campaigns. I donate generously to both recognized political parties, don't need health insurance and I really have nothing to hide. Except when I do of course, and in those cases I have the wealth and power to make sure it stays well hidden. And in the unlikely event that one of the three-letter agencies comes knocking on my door—well, I have the President's private number. The SWAT team's careers would be over before their shift was.

There was another car about half a mile back and I felt the skin on the back of my neck prickle. Was I being followed? Of course there is nothing unusual about having another car going the same direction on a public road and I cursed Holmes for his paranoia-inducing prank. I have enough to worry about as it is.

Five minutes and a highway merge later the car was still there, neither gaining nor losing ground, and I was getting antsy. Of *course* it was nothing, but rather than fall prey to my own nerves I slowed down to let it catch up and pass.

It didn't pass. It didn't catch up. I began to sweat. Of *course* it was nothing. I drive a Porsche for a reason, so I put my foot down. I've got after-market pressure boost to the fuel cells and high-torque motors and the acceleration is head snapping. The car vanished from the rearview mirror like a rabbit at a fox party. As soon as I'd lost them around a corner I stood on the brakes and ducked into the driveway for some tenant farmer's double-wide trailer home, got out of the car and waited.

The car didn't come flying around the corner in hot pursuit, it came around reasonably close to the speed limit. It was a nondescript late-model sedan, medium blue, a man and a woman in the front, thirtyish. As they passed the driver noticed me, eyes widening in surprise.

Well, it is surprising to see a shiny new sports car parked in front of a ramshackle trailer, isn't it? Nothing unusual there. As I got back in the car I caught the distant *thwopthwopthwop* of rotor blades. It couldn't be the government—they'd just monitor my movements from the satellites. Kidnappers? Anyone who can afford a helicopter is unlikely to need to kidnap anyone. Coincidence then, nothing more. I started driving back at the speed limit, watching the surrounding traffic with care. I didn't notice anything unusual—but then after the pull-over incident they'd make sure I didn't, wouldn't they?

They. Faceless, omnipresent, omnipotent they. I shuddered, remembering the time the FBI had kicked in my door in search of illegal electronics. Paranoia goes hand in hand with megalomania, and I certainly had enough of that. Uneasy rests the head that wears the crown—or plans on wearing it. I put the thought out of my mind, put my phone on handsfree and told it to call Douglas Straughn. I needed to borrow some money. A lot of money.

That may surprise you, since my personal net worth is twenty billion dollars, give or take a billion or so. I'm sure that seems like a lot of money to you, but when you plan to rule the world the important figure is not how much you have but how much you don't have. Financial figures get fuzzy when they get big, but the global gross national product, if that term makes any sense, is around fifty trillion dollars a year and the amortization-adjusted purchase price for the whole damn globe entire is a whopping two and a half quadrillion dollars. You can see the magnitude of the problem I've set myself. I don't know how much Straughn is worth personally, but the investment fund he controls totals a cool trillion. Power, like money, is difficult to judge on large scales, but by any measure Straughn is on top worldwide. They call him the Wall Street Wolf for his rapacity and cunning, and I needed him on my side—at least until I had the power to grind him under.

So I'm not a big fish in the shark pool Straughn swims in, but twenty billion dollars is enough to get me on the short list of people whose calls he answers. I was in luck, he was in the office. We exchanged the usual pleasantries, necessary social grease before the fencing began.

"Ever hear of Voisey Bay?" It was important to build some background before I hit him up for the cash.

"The big nickel mine up in Canada somewhere."

"In Labrador to be exact."

"So?"

"So every ten years this planet uses a volume of nickel equal to the total reserves at Voisey Bay. There's only another three or four years of it left there, and they haven't found a big new deposit in fifteen years."

"I'm already fully invested in exploration technologies, John." His voice was dismissive.

"That's not what I'm talking about."

"I don't want to hear about some warm and fuzzy civic recycling scheme." He sounded testy and I wondered if I'd caught him at a bad time. That would be bad, even disastrous, but there was no backing out now. "There's no centralization there, no money to be made."

"That's not what I'm talking about either. I'm talking about asteroid mining."

"What?" His voice was incredulous.

"We can't get it anywhere else. Not just nickel, but copper, tungsten, titanium: every element you can imagine. It's all up there for the taking. And we're running out down here. This is the opportunity of a lifetime."

"Impossible. Do you know the current cost per pound delivered to orbit?"

I had the figures at my fingertips and ticked them off as I pulled out to pass a semi-trailer. "NASA claims five thousand a pound for the RSV. Of course, that's raw costs. Double it for support costs."

"Exactly. If you had solid gold just floating in low Earth orbit waiting to be scooped up it wouldn't be worth your while to go get it, even with the Reusable Space Vehicle. And that's just low Earth orbit. You want to talk about the asteroids you're talking ten times that cost, round figures. Maybe more." I knew I had him hooked then. When Straughn decides something is impossible its only a matter of time before he makes it happen. He's like Brian that way. How much he was going to make me pay was the critical question.

"This is where you come in, Douglas." I leaned forward in my seat. "Because there *is* solid gold waiting to be scooped up in space. What if I told you I had a way to get to the asteroids cheap."

"How cheap?"

"Six million dollars a launch, another six million in mission costs."

I could almost hear his eyebrows going up. Even if he didn't believe in my space mining pitch, figures like those would own the satellite business, and that's a few billion right there. "How do you plan to do that?"

"I can't discuss the details, the technology is still in development." It was true; I'm sure Holmes hadn't finalized his solution in the hour since I'd left Wild Oaks. I leaned back, relaxed now that I knew I had him sold. "It's revolutionary, I can tell you that much."

"You expect me to buy in to space mining based on an as yet unproven technology—sight unseen."

"That's exactly right."

"You're nuts." He said it, but he was still listening.

"I'm not asking you for money right now. Baker Technologies will bear all the development costs." And own all the patent rights, I didn't add. "I need your commitment to put in the venture capital once we've demonstrated that we have the capability to get there. This is going to take a very aggressive exploitation plan."

"How much are you asking for?"

"A hundred billion dollars."

"That doesn't sound like twelve million dollars a launch."

"Trust me, there's going to be a lot of launches."

He didn't answer right away. I'd surprised him with a figure that big, but Straughn didn't get where he was by being afraid of big numbers. "And what am I buying for that?"

"A hundred-million-ton nickel-iron asteroid hunted down, hauled into Earth orbit, smelted into high-grade stainless steel and delivered to the ground."

He was silent for a minute and I heard keys clicking in the background. Doubtless he was checking the international nickel spot price. "A dollar a kilo for stainless. That's barely cost competitive."

"That's fifty percent below the going rate. Check the price history on nickel. Supply is going down. Demand is going up. By the time we're online with this system these prices will be higher. And the steel just covers the operating costs. The real gravy is in the platinum group metals that come with it. Figure on fifty tons each of platinum, palladium and iridium in the mix, plus five or ten tons of rare earths, and some copper, gold and silver too. Run the numbers and you're looking at total profits of close to fifty billion dollars."

"Over what time frame?"

"It's a ten-year project."

"For fifty-percent return?" He snorted. "I can put my money in bonds and double it in ten years with no risk."

"Bonds that good aren't no risk, and what I'm offering isn't a fifty-percent return. I'm offering fifty *plus* an entire asteroid mining infrastructure installed that will pull in a rock like that every year at first, then two, four, a dozen a year for the indefinite future. World demand for steel is a billion tons a year and growing fast. How would you like to own that market?"

There was a long pause on the other end of the line. He was thinking it over. "The recyclers are planning on providing eighty percent of the market in ten years."

"People are too lazy to recycle. Make steel cheap enough and the recyclers will wither on the vine. And our market control will be unheard of. There aren't any import duties from space, no taxes, no regulations, no possibility of nationalization, no local groups with environmental concerns, nothing. It'll be carte blanche on the biggest Eldorado in human history, and we'll be the only ones with a claim staked."

There was a another long silence on the other end of the line while I waited tensely. "Okay, I'm in. *If* you can prove your technology works. How long till that happens?"

I held the phone away from my mouth and gave a

long sigh of relief. "Six months to know if it's going to work or not, a year to actually make it work."

"That's fast. How far along are you?"

I smiled wide enough that I'm sure he could hear me in New York. "You know I can't tell you that."

"How certain are you it's going to work?" There was doubt in his voice.

"Completely." Well, almost completely.

"That's damn near all the working capital I can break free, you know that?"

"If I'd thought you could give me more I'd have asked for more."

He laughed. "I'm going to have to earmark that money. I need a performance bond to the effect that you'll have a program going in a year."

"How big a bond?" This was the crucial question.

"Twelve percent."

I snorted "Too big. I can get Georgi Stanislaski committed for less than half of that."

"Georgi doesn't stand anything more technical than a corkscrew, but you're welcome to try."

"Six percent."

"The bank will give me six."

"Not on a hundred billion they won't. Eight."

"I'll give you ten."

"Still too high."

"It's high because you need a hundred billion dollars. Who else do you think you're going to get it from?"

"Stanislaski may not understand technology, but he understands opportunity."

"Nine percent. I thought you were certain this was going to work. Why are you worried about the performance bond?"

He had me there, not that I could admit it. "It's

good business practice to make the best of every deal. Nine percent, done and done."

"Have your lawyers call mine and get the details hammered out. I'll call you in a week with the funding plan."

"Always a pleasure, Douglas."

I hung up, satisfied with the morning's work, dodged a slow-moving fuel truck and picked up the pace down the highway. I was only slightly stressed about having to take Straughn's terms pretty much as he dictated them. There were only a handful of people in the world who could swing a hundred-billion-dollar financing deal, and of those the number who would take a flyer on something as wild as asteroid mining I could count on the fingers of one finger—Straughn himself. Georgi Stanislaski was known for taking wild risks, but they had to be risks he understood and as Douglas had pointed out, he was strictly a basic-industry man—petrochemicals, shipping, rail, steel. He never touched anything so frilly as consumer production, which cut out a big chunk of the technology market, and he was unlikely to understand what I was proposing. A nine-billion-dollar performance bond wasn't out of line for what Straughn was delivering, but it represented nearly half of everything I owned. If Brian failed to solve the drive problem I would be hung out to dry. It isn't that I'd wind up impoverished; the eleven billion dollars I had left would still put in me the top ten-millionth of a percent of the world's population so far as wealth went—but I would never recover from the failure. Achieving my goal absolutely required that my net worth continue to rise exponentially, and asteroid mining was not only my ticket to world domination, it was the only ticket I would ever get. I would have rather waited a year, but my own financial structures were in place, and my sources told me that the Seaveni consortium was about to hit Straughn up for absolutely every penny he could swing. They'd be disappointed now. You have to strike when the iron is hot.

Of course Straughn was in the catbird seat. If Brian made the drive work he'd be on the ground floor of the greatest business opportunity in history. If he didn't, he'd make a guaranteed nine percent on a hundred billion dollar investment, risk free. It's hard to get big returns on chunks of cash that large, simply because there are so few places to put so much money at once. By breaking it up, doing a lot of extra work, he could make a couple of more points, but his risk would be higher and it wouldn't be half as easy to realize the returns. The ironic thing about money is—the more you have the easier it is to get more, and the less you actually need.

Now, you may find it surprising that an enterprise so complicated as a complete asteroid mining venture can be started with a visit to a friend and a phone call, and in fact you would be right. I'd spent ten years searching for the way to get my hand around the throat of global commerce and another two years working the numbers to convince myself that aster-oid mining was it. While I was doing that I put five years into making contact with the high-end venture capital club, insinuating myself into their social net-work, setting up the structures I'd need and carefully profiling over two dozen top-of-the-line players before I'd settled on Straughn as my primary patsy. World conquest doesn't happen without a lot of work. You might also think that I've got delusions of grandeur and you'd be right again. At least you can't accuse me of mediocrity. Asteroid mining wasn't just my ticket to absolute global power, it was possibly the only ticket anyone would ever get in the next several generations. Opportunities like this come around only a few times

in a civilization's history—Caesar nearly did it by woo-
ing Cleopatra, but Brutus knifed him before he could
make his empire encompass the known world. Genghis
Khan nearly did it by force, but he died too soon;
Rockefeller himself missed the boat on oil, but communications weren't up to a truly global empire then.
Nuclear weapons and rockets would have done it for
Hitler if he hadn't driven all his best scientists out of
the country before the war, and of course we all know
what happened to Gates. I was gambling everything
now, but the difference between you and me is that
I take calculated risks, and you're afraid to.

Five minutes later I slid the Porsche into my personal space by the Baker Technologies helipad and
went up to my office. I had a dozen messages waiting.
The priority call was from someone at the Securities
and Exchange Commission named Warren Burbridge.
When the government calls its always bad news. I had
Gillian call him back and wondered about it while I
waited for her to buzz that he was on the line.

There are really only four sources of wealth in the
world: agriculture, minerals, energy and people. People
represent labor, and everyone gets the same twenty-
four hours in a day. Sure you can develop a lot of
power if you get enough people working for you, but
people are notoriously fickle; they aren't there because
they like you, they're there because they need to be,
because working for you allows them to fulfill their
own needs. If those needs change, or they get a better
offer, they're gone. Agriculture is a tremendous source
of power, but to control it you have to control the land
that people live on, and because food is so important
the agricultural industry is highly regulated. If you try
to apply food as a source of leverage people quickly
get desperate, and you wind up with civil war. Power
generation and minerals are where the real keys to

wealth lie—if it cannot be grown it must be mined, and modern civilization wouldn't last a week without electricity. Anyone can have a backyard garden, but no one can make their own steel. Before the hydrogen fuel cell and the vortex cell windmill the root of power in the world was oil—at once a mineral and a fuel, it was the ideal product and once upon a time the world's biggest business. Finding it and getting it out of the ground required resources far beyond any individual, and it was available only in certain highly limited areas, easy to control. It was tremendously versatile both as a raw material and as a fuel, and it was fundamentally nonrenewable. Whether burned for power or processed into plastics, the demand was insatiable. Rockefeller could have ruled the world, if he'd developed crude consumption as well as he did production, but the real petroleum economy only developed after he died—and now that era is over.

So my plan is simple, and it works like this. Space is completely beyond the control of any nation on the globe. Those few who even have the capability to get there limit themselves to space because, ultimately, they are focused on the ground. Earth orbit just serves to give them the big picture, for communications, for geosurvey and for navigation. Build the infrastructure up there and you've built yourself a new nation. Base your economy on the provision of metals to Earth's surface cheaper than they can be dug up and sheer economics will drive ground-based mining to extinction. It will take ten years to restart primary production once it stops, reopening mines, rebuilding refineries and extraction plants after they're abandoned—and that's where power comes in to play. Every nation on the planet's surface will depend on me for the raw materials to drive their economies, and given self-sustaining habitats in space, I will be completely beyond the military and economic reach of any Earthbound power. My space mining infrastructure will become the core of a new nation, and it will rule not just the planet but all of Sol System.

And I will rule it. Call me crazy if you like. If I'd met you in college and told you I was going to be worth twenty billion dollars in fifteen years, you'd have called me crazy then, too. So now who's flying the Learjet?

I was smiling at these happy thoughts when the phone chimed. I picked up. "John Watson here."

"Warren Burbridge." The voice was urbane and cultured, controlled, calmly inflected. The voice of a career beaurocrat. "Mr. Watson, I'm calling on behalf of William McCool." I felt something crawling on my spine. William McCool was chairman of the SEC. More importantly, he was firmly in the pocket of Dynacore, who had been vying for access to the split-ring convolver technology for some time now.

"And what can we do for the Security and Exchanges Commission today, Mr. Burbridge?" I already knew, of course, but the call had to play itself out.

"Well, quite frankly we have some concerns about your licensing arrangement with Beijing Semiconductor." Of course they did.

"And these concerns are?" I asked the question with wide-eyed innocence.

"Specifically we feel it's anticompetitive."

I smiled sardonically. "It's an exclusive deal, if that's what you mean."

"That's exactly what we're concerned about. Prior to this you had the technology licensed to a number of firms. We would be more comfortable if you continued that policy." There was a certain smugness to his voice, the certainty of the mailed fist held back as he delivered the velvety smooth demand with careful reasonableness.

I shrugged. The gloves were coming off and he was deluding himself if he thought otherwise. "Those agreements are expired. We've negotiated with several firms. Beijing paid high for the exclusivity deal. They have the Halcion processor in the works, and it relies on split-ring technology. That makes it more advanced than anything else on the market, and they want to protect their edge."

"Exactly. We can reasonably expect that Halcion will be the dominant processor over the next five years, and with this agreement you've signed with them nobody else will be able to build anything remotely similar. They'll have a complete monopoly." He was still trying to be reasonable.

"Shouldn't you be concerned about their monopolistic practices instead of ours then?"

"Beijing Semiconductor is not under the jurisdiction of the SEC, Mr. Watson. You are." There was an edge in his voice now.

"Would you feel better if we negotiated a deal with the Taiwanese Technology Consortium?" I was baiting him now, trying to see how much he'd reveal.

He kept his voice carefully neutral. He was playing on the edge of his authority and wasn't going to let me push him over. "Processor chips are a strategically important market. I think we'd prefer it if an American company remained a player in the field."

"Dynacore, just for instance?" I almost laughed, enjoying myself as I called the tune he'd dance to.

"They are one potential candidate, yes."

"They are the only domestic processor-chip manufacturer left, aren't they?"

"I wouldn't know about that."

Time to stop playing around. I leaned forward,

putting some force behind my words. "Well, you should, Mr. Burbridge, because it's your job to understand the competitive environment we're discussing here, seeing as you're accusing us of anticompetitive practices. Let's not pretend this isn't about what it's about."

The velvet left his voice. "Let me be clear, Mr. Watson. You are exporting a key technology to a foreign power whose interests may not be in line with those of the American government. We are not comfortable with that and we will take whatever action is necessary to correct the problem. I hope that action is limited to this call, but it doesn't have to be."

"I thought the question of the legality of technology exports belonged to the Export Control Commission."

"Don't play games with me." The edge in his voice was getting dangerous.

"Then don't play them with me." I let my own voice get hard. In my position I'm not used to being pushed, and I don't respond well to it. "I recognize that William McCool is going to run for president, and I recognize that Dynacore is one of his major backers. And I am sure the current administration of the SEC, the ECC, the Pentagon and every other branch of our government would rather not see a Chinese or even an Australian corporation holding an exclusive license to the chip technology that's going to run the world in the next five years. However that sad fact is that due to three decades of short-sighted, if not actually blind mismanagement of this nation, the American economy has lost the manufacture of everything from consumer electronics to civil aircraft to Europe and the Pacific Rim. That's not the fault of Baker Technologies. Right now we have a legally binding agreement with Beijing Semiconductor, an agreement I might add that was approved by your department. In case 'legally binding' doesn't make sense down at the SEC, it means I couldn't change that even if I wanted to, so there is absolutely no point in your calling to pressure me to do so. If you'd like to see American technology stay in America then I suggest you call your pals in Congress and suggest they develop a few incentives for American innovators to stay home. I'd like to see a program to fund the commercialization of deep space myself." I leaned back and waited for the reaction.

"I'm sorry you're taking that attitude." He rang off, sounding frustrated, which I found satisfying. I put the phone down and spun around in my office chair, thinking over what to do next. I'd had fun taunting Burbridge, but the SEC was a serious threat. I needed a plan to address it. After a few minutes I called Julie and asked her to come in. Five minutes later she was there.

Julie is my wife, my friend, my partner in crime, a lissome figure with flowing scarlet hair and a razor-sharp mind behind big blue eyes. Her background is engineering, which makes a useful counterbalance to my strictly legalistic view of the world. I quickly outlined the details of my conversation with Burbridge.

"You actually hit him up for innovation incentives?" She laughed. We were one of the major forces behind the global market doctrine of deregulation that made it possible to develop products here and build them overseas where labor was cheap and annoying laws much scarcer.

"Just in case he was recording the conversation for posterity."

"So how serious do you think the threat is?"

"On the one hand, they're way out on a limb. Export controls really aren't their department, and we do have SEC signed off on this deal, as well as the export people and everyone else. The President actively supports increased trade with China, to reduce the chance of war on the Pacific Rim if nothing else. They'll be hard pressed to make it stick."

"And on the other hand?"

"It isn't that we can't beat them." Julie knew all about the asteroid mining plan of course. She knew I was going to ask Brian about the possibility of building the drive I needed. I told her about Straughn and the nine-billion-dollar performance bond I'd just agreed to. She listened attentively, pursed her lips as I finished.

"Bad timing."

"Very bad timing. If McCool does this it won't be on the SEC's authority, because they don't have it. He'll bring in the military, FBI, CIA, whoever he can get to play the National Security angle and have it taken extralegal."

"And we're going to need friends in government to get the approvals to get our ships launched, once we build them."

"Exactly."

She pursed her lips, thinking for a moment. "Call up Dynacore, tell them you'd like to explore some options with them."

"It would buy some time, but not much."

"At least give us time to develop a better strategy."

"We really have nothing to negotiate with. We're contractually bound to Beijing Semiconductor. The SEC is getting heavy-handed for nothing." I drummed my fingers on the desk. The government is used to playing fast and loose with its own rules. It forgets that the rest of us are more constrained.

"So we'll use that as our back-out option. Maybe they'll come to their senses."

"Maybe. There's nothing else we can do." I pondered

some more and remembered my experience driving back from Brian's. Maybe he was making me paranoid, maybe they really were out to get me. After Julie had left I called Mark Stuller, our head of security. Mark is British, ex-Parachute Regiment, ex-SAS, one time bodyguard to the Royal Family, veteran of a dozen or more secret non-wars, nasty little covert clashes that both sides deny ever happened. I set him on the task of finding out if anyone really was following me around, confident that if there was anything to find his team would find it.

The suspicion turned out to be self-fulfilling. My estate is guarded of course, and security at Baker Technologies is tight, but now there really was someone watching me everywhere I went. No matter where I went Stuller's countersurveillance team was there before I was, looking to see who came in after I did, recording license plate numbers, getting a feel for my movements, looking for individuals who were too alert, dressed too heavily, in too much of a hurry or not enough. After a week I was heartily sick of the whole operation, but I let it go on. They swept the estate for wireline taps, wireless taps, frequency hoppers, powerline modulators, burst transmitters, laser links, microwave flood resonators and every other piece of privacy invasion hardware right down for looking for cockroaches with microvocodor chips epoxied to their shells. After hours and in total silence they took my office apart down to the walls, swept it, installed Tempest-rated electromagnetic shielding—a high-priced version of Brian's chicken wire, isolated every line coming in or out and declared it secure. They had a body double take my car on long drives through back country lanes to drag any trackers through prepositioned checkpoints to positively identify them. They did a lot more that

I'm sure I never knew about, and at the end of a month the results were negative.

Well, almost negative. There was the possibility that there had been someone following me in the first couple of days, but that had stopped immediately. There was a small but non-zero chance that whoever it was had picked up the countersurveillance and shut down their operation to avoid being busted. There was a car, a blue Ford. They had traced the registration, found it was a rental, traced the couple who had rented it to Alexandria, Virginia, found nothing unusual in their records but had been unable to find them, which was itself unusual. Stuller had bribed an employee at the rental company to hand over the vehicle's GPS satellite tracking records and found they were simply missing. Unusual again, but nothing was conclusive.

I racked my brain trying to remember the color and description of the vehicle that had driven by me coming back from Brian's, but I couldn't. I left the problem in Stuller's capable hands, authorizing him to use any means necessary to resolve the question, which meant he could break the law if he needed to so long as it never, ever came back to haunt either me or Baker Technologies. Julie and I had to fly the Lear out to Washington for a presidential gala, an opportunity to put in some influence to get a veto on a tax bill that would have cost me a billion dollars a year. I got some face time with the Man after the speeches, and in return for the tacit promise of a five-million-dollar campaign contribution I got the tacit promise of a veto on the bill. Nothing was said directly of course, because everything had to remain deniable. Quid pro quo at this level isn't guaranteed by contracts or even direct deals. It's a gentleman's club, and you stand or fall on your reputation for living up to agreements you never quite make.

While we were talking, my phone buzzed in my pocket annoyingly and I ignored it. POTUS and I had moved on to casual conversation, an excellent opportunity to develop an important lever of power. The issue of Dynacore and William McCool was pressing and rapidly coming to a head—we could only stall them through negotiation for so long, and that time was up. It was going to take some heavy-duty power play to put McCool back on the leash. The phone kept buzzing insistently and I grew concerned. Only a small and select group of people have that number, and all of them knew exactly where I was and what I was doing. If they were calling so persistently it must be something of critical importance. Disaster scenarios flashed through my mind unbidden as POTUS rambled aimlessly on about the situation in the Pacific and the role of Indonesia. Not a particularly smart man, our great leader, but he sure looks good on television.

Fortunately at that moment Julie came up and joined the conversation. I gave her a signal that meant "take over" and gave her a minute to catch his interest—not a hard job for a woman with the presence that she has. When she had him engaged I answered the phone.

It was Brian. "John! I've got it, I've got the launch solution!"

"That's great John—"

"Yah! Like I said, it was a materials problem, so I was thinking about metal foams at first, for strength, but then I realized—"

"Brian I'm with the President—"

"Cool! Tell him to fund more astronomy. There's a real need to understand cosmic rays at high energy. That's something else we have to address is shielding, but I solved that too, but I just mean academically—"

"Brian, I have to go!" Alan Dortmunder, the consumer products magnate, had spotted the opening and was heading to take my place in the conversation.

" . . . there are some incredible breakthroughs just waiting to happen."

I cut him off. "I'll be down tomorrow to see you, okay?" I clicked the phone shut. The President looked up from Julie's megavolt smile and saw Dortmunder.

"Alan! Good to see you." He shook hands with the newcomer. Face time was over. I ground my teeth.

There was no point in getting angry with Holmes of course. He was the way he was and it would be too much to expect him to either remember or care that I was talking with the President when he'd made a discovery he was excited about. He has a good point too—from his perspective he already has more money than he could ever spend, and far more power than he would ever know what to do with. What does he care about politicians? Still, I let Julie fly us home, I was too upset to be trusted at the controls. I wanted McCool and Dynacore flattened from a great height, and I'd missed my opportunity to make that happen by seconds.

Brian had made progress on the launch problem though, and that was important. Concentrated as I had been on the Dynacore situation I hadn't noticed time slipping by. Three months of the six I'd told Straughn the drive development would take had vanished and I hadn't noticed. I had to have a test ship in orbit in nine months or pay a nine-billion-dollar penalty. Viewed in that light, perhaps his call was more important than chitchat with the President.

I drove up to the Wild Oaks plantation the next day. When I pulled in next to the butchered VW van I found Holmes' entire house was covered by a chaotic framework of two-by-fours with chicken wire nailed over it, as though the mess in his lab had somehow overgrown his house. Pandora opened the house's beautiful solid-oak door for me and welcomed me in her sultry way, but I had to open the rickety chicken-wire door through the framework myself. I found Holmes in the kitchen, peering intently at a small video screen and wearing an oversized set of headphones.

"What's with the chicken wire? More big magnets?" I was half afraid he'd say yes.

He shook his head, not taking his eyes off the screen. "No, it's to block electromagnetic radiation. I don't want them listening to me or reading my computer screens, and I couldn't stay in the main lab all the time."

"Them? Who are 'them'?"

Holmes looked around furtively and lowered his voice. "The government! Didn't you hear the warnings on the road?"

I looked at him blankly, wondering if his mind had finally snapped. "You mean the voice in my car? 'Beware—the government is watching you'?"

He nodded. "Did you see the lines?"

"What lines?"

"In the pavement. I wondered if they might be too obvious."

"I have no idea what you're talking about."

"You saw the rig on the back of the van? That's a cutting laser. I record my voice and Pandora converts it into a series of lines, like a washboard pattern with variable spaces between the grooves. I load that pattern into the computer in the van and drive down the road at a set speed. The hydraulics swings the laser back and forth as I drive and it cuts the line pattern into the road. The grooves make the tires of your car vibrate like a record player needle, and you hear my voice." He leaned closer and whispered conspiratorially. "I couldn't tell you last time because I didn't have the shields up then."

I blinked. "Brian, nobody is watching you. I just had Mark Stuller do an exhaustive clearance of my entire life because of that, and he found exactly nothing. Stop doing this stuff before I start thinking you're clinically paranoid. Or before you make *me* clinically paranoid."

"Oh no? Look at this." He showed me the video monitor. A grainy black and white image was jouncing up and down as the camera pursued a couple of people running through a peach orchard that could only be the back acreage of the Grafton plantation.

"Who are they?"

"They're FBI agents."

I ignored that. "Who's chasing them with the camera?"

"Pandora is. That's the camera on the garden bot."

Pandora broke in with her sultry dulcetto. "Brian, I have further remote units positioned to prevent them from escaping."

"Not yet, Pandora." Brian didn't look up from the screen. "We don't want to give away all our capabilities."

I looked aghast as the panicked couple fled through the orchard, trailing picnic supplies. "They're just out to enjoy the peaches and you're scaring them half to death." I felt a sinking feeling. I have always known that someday Brian would need hospitalization. A brain as brilliant as his simply can't be stable.

He shook his head. "They're FBI agents."

"Brian, you're starting to worry me. The FBI does not send people poking around in other people's back gardens. If they were watching the house they'd be doing it from a remote drone or a satellite. You'd be the last person to know." Of course it had to be *now* that his mind snapped, with a hundred-billion-dollar program, the key to my dream of world conquest, riding on his faculties. I could almost hear Fate laughing at me. Maybe if I got Stuller to set up a secure perimeter it would make him feel safe enough to concentrate on his work.

"They had to get their monitoring equipment closer to the house after I set up the screens. I knew that would force their hand."

"They aren't FBI!" I wanted to shake him.

"I've been monitoring their transmissions for weeks now. Their encryption is trivial."

"And they come up on the air and say they're FBI?" I shook my head in disbelief.

He shook his head. "Of course not. They call each other agent. Those two are Agent Black and Agent Macdougall. Macdougall is the woman. Agent Diangelo is waiting for them in the command van."

I had no answer for that. The agents, if that's what they were, were scrambling over the ivy-covered stone wall that surrounds the Grafton property in a blind panic. The garden bot couldn't do anything worse than spray them with weed killer, but of course they didn't know that. Mind you, with the stuff that's in weed killer, that would be bad enough in itself.

Holmes sat up and took off the headphones. "Agent Macdougall is telling them to execute plan Bravo. I think that means they're pulling out."

I blinked and looked at him. He seemed as sane as he had ever been—granted that wasn't always very sane. Still, it was far from the strangest thing I'd seen him do. Focus on business. "You've said got something to show me on the rocket engine?"

"Oh yah, that. Here." He reached over to the kitchen counter and handed me a black rod. It was about two yards long, as thick as a piece of spaghetti and surprisingly light. It seemed rigid despite its slender dimensions, the ends didn't wobble at all when I held it in the middle and shook it.

I looked at it dubiously. "This doesn't look like a rocket engine."

"Well, no. That's a buckytube, a single-molecule hollow fiber of covalently bonded carbon. A whole lot of them really, parallel strands in a cyanate matrix. Actually they aren't hollow because I've packed them with—"

"What does that all mean?"

He smiled. "Bend it."

I tried, but it didn't bend. I put muscle into the effort, then tried bracing it with a foot and pulling. I didn't even feel it flex before I was in danger of cutting my hands. I stopped and looked at it, almost forgetting my need for a revolutionary engine and asteroid mining rights. If it was as strong as it seemed . . . Visions of dollar signs danced in my head.

Brian read my thoughts. "Its strength-to-weight ratio is about a thousand times better than steel."

"Did you say a *thousand*?"

"Yah, well it's a hundred times stronger and weighs about a tenth—"

"How much does it cost?"

"Well, this sample is probably ten thousand dollars a foot, but with volume production I could cut that down to five thousand, maybe four thousand."

The dollar signs vanished. That price tag made it useless for all but the most exotic uses. Advanced space propulsion systems, for example. That thought brought me back to my original purpose. "So what does this have to do with a rocket engine?"

"Well, the problem is all about strength and current density of course."

"Of course." I'm sure the connection was obvious to him.

"Chemical fuels just don't have enough energy per unit mass to make them useable. You need too much fuel to lift fuel out of the gravity well. Diminishing returns set in. So your ship has to be huge to get anywhere, hence expensive."

I saw where he was going and held up a hand. "Nuclear fuels aren't any cheaper, and we can't use them anyway. I'm not even going to talk about the liability issues."

"No no, nuclear fuels are just too dangerous; even without an accident you put a lot of radioactive waste out there. And they aren't any cheaper really. No, the solution is high-field magnetic boosting."

"Explain, please."

Holmes rolled his eyes at my failure to grasp the obvious. "The buckytubes are hollow down the center, so I pack them with C-thirty-six buckyballs doped with potassium. That way it's a one-dimensional high-temperature superconductor."

"Superconductor? I thought they were structural elements." I was used to being out of my depth with Holmes, but now I was actually drowning.

"They're both. We make a tube about twenty kilometers long, run the far end up a mountain or something; we'd have to pick the site carefully so the rate of change of slope isn't too big. So the tube is ringed with superconducting magnets, and your launch vehicle has the same thing down its long axis. Pump all the air out of the tube and turn the magnets on in sequence, changing their polarity as you go—in twenty kilometers you're at escape velocity for cheap."

"How cheap?"

"A dollar or two per kilogram. Maybe less."

"It won't be that cheap if those coils cost a thousand dollars a foot."

"Oh well, the launch tube is just the first part of the program. Once we can get materials into space cheaply we build a factory in geosynchronous orbit." He saw my blank look. "Like communications satellites, twenty-two thousand miles up over the equator, so it just seems to float there. We launch carbon to the factory, spin it into buckytubes and make a beanstalk. That's how you really get into space cheap."

"A beanstalk?"

"A space elevator. It goes from the equator to geosyn orbit, where the factory is, then another twenty-two thousand miles into space after that. You spin it out in both directions at once, and orbital forces keep it under tension and stable. You put elevators on it and you just ride right up into the sky. Its an old concept but no material has been strong enough and light enough to actually build it with, until now."

I looked at him for a long moment to see if he was serious. The scheme seemed too outlandish to possibly work, but I'd learned to trust his most insane-appearing pronouncements. He was serious, but cost was still a problem. "There's a lot of feet in twenty-two thousand—no, forty-four thousand miles of buckytubes at five thousand dollars a foot." I picked up the thin black buckytube rod and tried to flex it again, convincing myself of its reality. "I'm figuring they're going to have to be a lot thicker than this one too."

Holmes waved a hand dismissively. "That's the actual thickness for the leader line. The actual beanstock will be up to a meter across. Five thousand dollars a foot is just making them here on Earth, and in the lab. Gravity messes up the growth process and I have to keep lasering off the ends and starting over. The power costs are tremendous. Grow them in space and they'll be cheaper than nylon. Carbon is basically free."

"How much carbon do we need?"

He stroked his chin, thinking. "The ground-to-orbit leader line is about ten tons. Total cable weight is about a million tons, but you don't have to launch all that to the factory—somewhere along the line you can start sending carbon up the cable so it's cheaper. I haven't quite worked that out yet."

There comes a point when even I can understand. The launch tube puts the factory up, the factory mass produces the buckytubes, which become the beanstalk, which makes the cost of getting to space—somehow launch seemed to be the wrong word for beanstalk climbing—dirt cheap. Plus you could start selling a cheap structural element a thousand times better than steel. Plus a high-temperature superconductor that could carry a hundred times more current than the same size copper wire—it would replace every major power grid on the planet. . . . Plus—plus who knew what else. I had one critical question.

"And these buckytubes—are they new? Can we patent them?"

"Well, not the tubes themselves, they're well known. But until now nobody's made them bigger than a fraction of a centimeter long, and my method for doing that is pretty unique."

"How long are these?"

"Around half a meter, on average. The key was nano-assembly, and as I was saying gravity is a big problem. I could make them longer if . . ."

I wasn't listening anymore. I took out my phone and dialed Julie. Or I tried to. My phone refused to connect, flashing a disconsolate "No Signal" at me.

"It's the shielding." Holmes handed me a landline. "Be careful what you say. They're listening."

I hoped Holmes' sanity lasted at least until he had imparted his breakthrough to someone who could understand it. I dialed again and she picked up. I didn't waste words. "Brian's got something hot down here at Wild Oaks. You need to get Dale Smith and the patent team here right away."

She knew what that meant. "They're on their way. I'll send them in the helicopter."

"We're going to the asteroids. Are you up for doing the project management?"

"Try and stop me."

"You're the best, honey."

"That's why you married me."

I rang off and started pacing. Our patent team is a bunch of brilliant kids who spend their time sitting in Baker Technologies trying to come up with brilliant ideas. Sometimes they do, but that job description exists just to keep them busy until their real job comes up, which is taking what Holmes invents and turning it in to patents and products. There was a lot to do here. This technology and its spinoffs would be bigger than the telephone. Alexander Graham Bell's little baby, you may recall, was the most profitable patent in history. This is why I hold on to patent rights.

The buckytubes were going to give me my ticket to the solar system, but purely by chance the ground-based applications were going to be just as big, if not bigger. I already had Straughn as committed as he could be on the space mining deal. He might be able to pull some more in to finance the rest, but I had a better idea. First I had to be sure of my ground. I talked to Holmes some more about the manufacturing process, what was involved, what was required, how sure he was it would work. He took me into the power systems lab where had a buckytube ring magnet set up, soaking in liquid nitrogen to make it superconduct to store power. He had another ring with an opposing field that floated over the first one. The floating ring was spinning—he explained this was to prevent it from being torqued out of the null, whatever that meant, and he could stack more steel than I could lift on the spinning ring without forcing it into contact with the support disk. Down in the materials lab he had another spaghetti strand supporting two tons of assorted steel slabs on a platform suspended from the ceiling. It could hold more, he explained, but he was worried about the strength of the ceiling supports.

I was convinced enough that I didn't need to see the patent team's reports. I said goodbye to Brian and left him building some gravity-defying mobile with meter sticks while waiting for the patent team. As soon as I got back in the car I told my phone to call Georgi Stanislaski. Buckytube manufacture was going to be huge and I needed to get some serious financing put together immediately. No need to get too cozy with Straughn either. He'd probably give me more, but it's better to share the wealth. Or rather, its better to have as many other people as possible share their wealth with you. Stanislaski answered his phone himself—unusual in my circles, where it's not unheard of for personal secretaries to argue for an hour over which one's Important Person is going to come on the line first. Georgi had heard the rumors about my little adventure in asteroid mining of course, and was all ready to give me the brushoff when he spoke to me. I talked as fast as I drove, and I didn't talk about buckminsterfullerene, twenty-kilometer launch tubes or space manufacturing. I talked about building materials better than steel and high-efficiency power storage and distribution. Asteroid mining was literal pie in the sky to him. Skyscrapers and electrical power grids were subjects he could get his teeth into.

I rang off with an agreement in principle for a twenty-billion-dollar manufacturing effort to commence as soon as the processes were optimized. I didn't tell him the factory had to be in orbit, but by the time that little detail surfaced I was sure Brian would have the launch system under control.

The next three months were frantic. The patent team figured out a way to reduce the manufacturing costs on buckytubes somewhat by fabricating them in a buffered aqueous solution, which turned out to mean in saltwater, using some very special salt and precise temperature controls. How that substituted for zero gravity was beyond me, but it made them cheap enough that our twenty-kilometer launch tube was only going to cost us a million dollars a meter. That's twenty billion dollars, just to put it in perspective for you, twenty percent of my negotiated budget with Straughn before a single payload left the ground. You see now where the deal with Stanislaski came in. Most of that money would go to buy buckytube magnets built on earth, which would go to the manufacturing consortium I was setting up with Stanislaski, so a large chunk of that money would come back to my pocket where I could leverage it back into setting up the system. The details of the arrangement were complex and absorbed a lot of my attention. Meanwhile Julie had better than half of the company's brainpower focused on the development side of things. We compartmentalized everything for security—everyone knew we were building a linear accelerator launch system, a smaller percentage knew it was to feed supplies to an orbital factory, and only a few knew the factory would be building a buckytube beanstalk to space. Nobody at all knew its purpose was to make it possible to mine asteroids, although the rumors abounded. So did other rumors of course, many of which we had started on purpose to cover the deal development with Straughn.

Added to that was the headache of coping with the SEC. Burbridge had stepped up the pressure and the feds were now conducting an investigation, with which we were "voluntarily" cooperating. That means they were generating legal requests at tremendous speed and we were generating legal objections to those requests even faster. Baker Technologies is virtually the sole employer of Megan and Boyd, a law firm you won't have heard of if you're worth less than a billon dollars. Megan and Boyd occupy twenty floors at 350 Fifth Avenue in midtown Manhattan. We pay them to worry about these things so we don't have to, which only removes about half the workload. At the same time we were negotiating, or pretending to, with Dynacore. Around month two Beijing Semiconductor got wind of that and got very upset, wanting to know if we intended to honor our exclusivity deal or not. I had to fly to China in order to smooth their ruffled feathers and explain the situation, and when I got there I found the Chinese government was involved, and also very upset. They leaned on the ambassador, which got the State Department involved, who leaned on the SEC, with the end result that I got a foaming-at-the-mouth call from McCool himself demanding to know who the hell I thought I was. I tried to explain the situation but he didn't listen. Instead he told me that I'd turned a trivial paperwork issue into a vendetta and he swore to bury us. I told him that his man Burbridge had made it clear from the start that it was anything but trivial, at which point he hung up.

Figuring the largely male government group would be sexual putty in Julie's extremely attractive hands I traded her the job of handling the government while

I concentrated on getting the launch system off the ground. It was a much more interesting assignment. Originally we had planned to build our launch facility in Colorado, but because of the issues with the SEC spreading to other branches of the government I'd vetoed that early on and we'd picked a site at Citlaltepetl, a nearly nineteen-thousand-foot extinct volcano near Mexico City. Not only was the regulatory environment better—by which I mean that cash talks even louder in Mexico than it does in Washington, but it was a taller peak than any in Colorado and, being closer to the equator, gave us better launch parameters. Or so Brian told me. If he'd told me it was better to launch from the North Pole I wouldn't have known any better.

I spent a month just flying around, talking to the site managers, getting a feel for the project. In Mexico crews were there busy putting in roads and a base camp at the remote site, and they had already installed the vast pumping array that would evacuate the tube when it was built so the vehicle could be accelerated without air resistance. More crews were stabilizing the mountain's treacherous slopes, and a system was being installed to keep the critical coil alignments intact in the face of the mountain's seismic creep. In Austin the fabrication of the huge fiberconcrete support rings for the launch tube was in progress. Outside San Francisco a two-hundred-million-dollar plant was going up to produce the superconducting buckytube fibers—a plant that would be shut down again in two years, when the orbital facility came online. In Switzerland we'd hired Eurospace to design our high-orbit factory, and they already had mockups complete. It was going to be modular of course, because it was going to become our launch point for mining expeditions and our refining center for the big rocks dragged back home. They didn't know that part, they just knew they had to plan it for expansion.

I don't understand the science, but I do understand progress, and lots of it was being made. When I got back I finally got a chance to sit down and go over the initial design documents and the CAD models with Dale Smith who was running the launch side of things. We chatted for an hour about the various details of the system, but most of my attention was taken up by a three-dimensional model of the cargo vehicle. It was beautiful, a high-technology revival of the early visions of space travel, a needle fuselage on razor-thin, radically swept delta wings. The launch tube couldn't be steered, so the craft would have to use its control surfaces to fly itself onto its specific trajectory in the few seconds it would actually spend in the atmosphere. At some point I realized I hadn't seen any crew facilities in the plans and mentioned that to him.

Dale gave me a funny look. "These are unmanned launch vehicles."

"Sure, but we need a passenger module to get crew up to the orbital factory."

His funny look got funnier. "You're joking, right?" He looked at me and realized I wasn't. "You can't put people in this thing."

"Why not?"

"Because it launches at three hundred and fifty gravities. You'd put a crew in on the ground and you'd have raspberry jam in orbit."

I had a sudden sinking feeling. "It's only that high for a second."

He laughed. "You spend less than a second actually hitting the ground when your parachute doesn't open. A lot of bad things happen fast."

I looked at him in disbelief. "We're building an

orbital factory. How are we supposed to put a crew on the factory?"

"Won't it be automated?"

"No, there's a crew, and anyway we still have to get people to the—" I stopped myself. I'd almost said *asteroids*, but Dale wasn't in on that part of the plan, not yet.

Fortunately he hadn't heard me, he was looking shocked at overlooking the people transport issue. "I figured you were going to get NASA . . ." He saw my expression and stopped. "You didn't tell me . . ."

I was already on my way out the door with the world crashing down around my ears. He was right of course, I hadn't told him. Aside from Julie, Straughn and I, nobody knew the whole plan. I'd specifically told Dale to ignore the rumors about the asteroids, which he was inclined to disbelieve anyway, choosing to believe the less outrageously grandiose space hotel rumor. Most of the rumors we put out were less outlandish than the truth. When you intend to rule the world it's important to keep your plans to yourself.

There was a fax waiting in my inbox. Eurospace had been talking to our people. They wanted to confirm that launch stresses for the factory were three and a half gravities and not three hundred and fifty. They apologized for asking such a silly question, since it was obviously impossible that the stresses could be even thirty-five gravities, but there seemed to be some confusion . . .

I sat down and put my head in my hands. I should have let Julie keep doing the project management and confined myself to legal wrangling with the SEC. Thanks to my own lack of clarity my clever engineers were well on their way toward developing a system that wouldn't do what it needed to do to pay for the tremendous cost of building it. Could we use NASA to get the factory up, and our people? With enough maneuvering we might even get them to chip in for it, but their missions were booked solid for years in advance and trying to get priority through the mass of political red tape involved would be hopeless. We needed tons of gear taken up, and I couldn't allow the schedule to be pushed back whenever some clueless garn wanted a joyride. I locked the door and paced. If I halted construction I'd spook Straughn, and if not Straughn the backers he had behind him—I couldn't risk that. Anyway I needed the launch tube to get the raw carbon into orbit to build the beanstalk—no other system could get that much mass up for anything like the price I needed. I called Eurospace, talked to Jan Hortzellenberg, who with urbane good manners told me that they simply couldn't build a space habitat that would fit in the four-by-eight meter cargo bays of our launch vehicles and withstand three hundred and fifty gravities at launch.

Could Eurospace use their own launch capacity to get the factory and people into geosynchronous orbit? Of course they could, but demand for launch capacity was so high right now—there would only be so many per year they could offer us, and it would seriously delay the project. They had understood we had our own launch capability, was that incorrect?

I hung up and called NASA who were blunt. Neither the RSV or the shuttle were capable of getting to geosynchronous orbit at all by themselves, though they could get a payload there with a booster. When I told them the size of the factory modules we were building they nearly choked and suggested I call the Russians. Dialing with desperation I managed to get someone at the Russian Space Agency before they closed for the day—it was almost evening in Moscow. They were all bureaucratic until I mentioned the amount of money I was willing to spend, at which point they became very interested. I had to hang up, but half an hour later Yuri Glinkov, their director of operations, was on the line, promising me that his huge Energia boosters could do anything I wanted them to do, yes even get an orbital habitat into geosynchronous orbit. He sounded breathless—I suspect they'd dragged him away from the Bolshoi Ballet in their flurry to make a sale—or at least a Bolshoi ballerina.

I breathed out in relief, then wary of being caught again, asked a question. "Would it be possible to send a payload, say, as far as Mars?" I didn't want to give too much away too soon.

"Oh yes, this is not problem for Energia." His voice was big and booming, just as you'd expect a Russian's to be. I pictured a large, shaggy bear of a man.

"How large a payload?"

"As much as you like, maybe ten tons even, with proper mission profile."

That sounded ominously low. "How much could it bring back?"

"For sample return? Many kilograms, very easily."

I hung up. Energia would get my factory up, it wouldn't get me to an asteroid, let alone bring one back. I'd told Brian if he could get me cheap launches I could solve every other problem. I had been thinking financially of course—it never occurred to me that a system that could launch something to the asteroids couldn't bring one back, which just goes to show how much I know about physics.

When everything else fails at Baker Technologies, I call Brian. His number was disconnected. I tried it three times with increasing panic. You have to understand—I can't take over the world without my mad scientist, but with Brian you never know what might happen. He might have decided to go and live in Tibet. I *hoped* he had decided to go and live in Tibet. At least I could track him down and bring him back. He might have simply blown himself up, and that would be the end of that. I nearly sprinted to the parking lot and peeled rubber down the highway. I should have taken the helicopter, but I didn't think of that until I was halfway there.

Brian was out on his lawn in the sunshine, surrounded by a cloud of silver butterflies. Merlin was running around batting at them with his paws, tail twitching furiously. He greeted me as I came up.

"Did you know your phone is disconnected?"

"The FBI was tapping it." He leaned forward and whispered conspiratorially. "I've been feeding them disinformation."

"Disinformation?" One of the butterflies fluttered right past my nose and I realized it wasn't a butterfly at all, it was a tiny flying machine with aluminum-foil wings.

"Straight out of bad monster movies. Death rays, mutated super monsters, you name it." He smiled broadly. "They'll believe anything. It's really quite fun." He leaned forward and whispered again. "I know you want the asteroid thing kept secret."

I decided to ignore his burgeoning paranoia—so long as it didn't affect his ability to produce. We walked under the chicken-wire canopy and inside, followed by the butterflies, which seemed to be programmed to orbit Brian's head. Pandora greeted me and held the door open long enough to let the swarm in too.

"Brian, how am I supposed to get actual people into space with this system?"

"You just send them up the beanstalk." He pushed a key on a computer system set up in the hall and the butterflies all flew up to the top of a bookshelf.

"I mean to get them to the asteroids, and back

again." Merlin mewled plaintively at the loss of his toys, then leapt into my arms for attention.

"Oh that." He waved a hand dismissively. "I worked that all out with Julie a month ago. Didn't she tell you?"

I love Julie with all my heart, which didn't stop me from nearly screaming in frustration at her neglect. She can be as self-absorbed as any technophile—but at least the problem was under control. Relief flooded over me and I slumped down in a chair. "So what's the answer?" Merlin *mrrowled* and I scratched his head absently. He rewarded me with enthusiastic purring.

"I got the idea when you told me that we couldn't use nuclear fuels. It was a challenge." He paused for dramatic effect. "What do you know about carbon-catalyzed fusion?"

I gave him a look. "Enlighten me." I can never tell if he's serious when he asks me that kind of question.

"Its aneutronic." I gave him the look again. "Which means it isn't radioactive, basically. No neutrons."

"Okay."

"It's a hard reaction to make work, which means it needs more temperature and pressure, but all the easier reactions have problems. Deuterium-tritium is the easiest, but it's really radioactively dirty, that's what everyone's been researching for the last generation. Deuterium-helium-three is harder but much cleaner, but helium-three is hard to come by. Hydrogen and lithium-six or boron-eleven work, but they have neutronic subpaths and don't produce much energy anyway. Initially I was going to go for the proton-proton chain, but when I ran the numbers I realized I could really ramp up the pressure with the buckytubes, so I thought—why not go for carbon catalysis? It's much more efficient."

"Makes sense to me." It made no sense to me.

"I mean once I realized how much current I could put through a buckytube array, well, the sky is the limit as far as implosion pressure goes."

"Implosion pressure? I don't get it."

"Magnetic implosion, like the quarter squisher. Fusion reactions need high temperatures and pressures to happen. You've got to squish the atoms together tightly enough and have them moving fast enough that they can bang into each other and stick together. The best way to do that is with a big magnetic field, but big magnets are limited by the strength of their components. The field literally rips them apart. Plus resistive heating generates a lot of heat which tends to melt them. But with superconductor coils there's no heat problem as long as the field doesn't quench the superconductor, and since buckytubes carry a hundred times the current that copper can without quenching we can support fields of a thousand Telsa or more—they're strong enough too. So we just make a big pipeline of magnet coils, feed ionized carbon-twelve and hydrogen in the top, magnetically implode it until it fuses, then valve it out the back through an MHD coil." I looked at him blankly. "Magnetohydrodynamic." I still looked blank. "It generates electricity from the exhaust stream, so the coil provides power to run the system and throttles it at the same time. In back of that we have the reaction chamber, feed in reaction mass, for which we can use water, feed that to a thrust ramp, and bang—you're in orbit for pennies a gram. Once you're in space and have some velocity you cut back on the reaction mass feed and set course for the asteroids. Make it big enough and you've got enough power to de-orbit a big asteroid. You can use the big magnetic fields to shield the crew from deep space radiation and solar flares too." He looked at me. "Or did you already have that part solved?"

"No, no I didn't." I breathed out, deeply relieved. "Listen, Brian—if there's any other technical problem with this whole venture that occurs to you—could you let me know now?" I hadn't been paying attention to Merlin as I listened, and he jumped down and stalked off to find something more interesting to do.

"Oh well, there isn't one really." Brian smiled. "It's all really simple technology. Come see what I've done with these butterflies." He pushed a key and the tiny aluminum creatures flapped into the air again.

I called Stanislaski on the way home to upsell his investment another ten billion—I could see the market for buckytubes was going to be even bigger than I'd anticipated. An hour later I pulled the Porsche around the corner to the Baker Technologies complex, feeling much better. I should have known Brian would have the solution and Julie would have the situation under control and I resolved to get her away from dealing with the government and back into running the technical program—to save me another lecture from my doctor about blood pressure, if nothing else. As soon as I turned into the driveway my equanimity evaporated. Something was wrong, badly wrong. Half a dozen police cruisers were parked at odd angles in front of the building, plus a couple of unmarked cars with temporary lights on their roofs, two white vans and a bunch of nondescript black sedans that screamed Federal Government. The usual lunchtime bustle of people in and out of the building was completely absent, but Julie was waiting on the lawn, close to the road. She waved me down and I stopped for her to get in.

"Drive, just go."

I didn't ask questions, I just popped the Porsche into reverse and slid out the way I'd come in. A pair of patrol cops standing by the main doors watched us leave, but made no move to stop us.

We were back on the street and I instinctively headed for the highway. She kissed me before she spoke, a conjugal reflex no less important because it was automatic. "We have a problem."

"I can see that. What's happening?"

"It's the SEC. They're raiding the corporate accounts office right now, in support of an investigation for noncompetitive business practices. They've served us with a cease trade injunction effective until the matter clears the courts."

"What!" I couldn't believe what I was hearing. "Why didn't you call me?"

"I started calling an hour and a half ago and I've been calling every five minutes since. Your line was busy."

I remembered Brian's shielding and groaned—and of course I'd been on the line to Stanislaski the rest of the time, with call waiting disabled. I hadn't wanted to lose his attention. Half my wealth was committed to Douglas Straughn's performance bond and now just as Brian was getting the drive together we were getting shut down. If I failed to deliver on this deal I'd never get Straughn behind me again—or anyone else in his rarefied world. The SEC couldn't have had worse timing. "What are they going after, exactly?"

"Anything and everything. It's a fishing trip. They have forty investigators going through the files as we speak."

"What's their probable cause?"

"General suspicion of un-American activity."

I looked at her in disbelief. "For God's sake. Un-American went out with McCarthy. They didn't really put that on the search warrant did they?"

"They don't have a warrant, it's a search carried out under the FISA by invoking the ATA anti-terrorist rules, no warrant needed."

"What?" I exploded. FISA is the Foreign Intelligence Surveillance Act and the ATA is the Anti-Terrorist Act, which they had to invoke to allow the SEC to operate under FISA. Both acts give the government tremendous power in dealing with terrorists and spies, and both were so ridiculously inapplicable here I was stunned they'd tried it at all. "How are they making that stick?"

"The guy in charge is Warren Burbridge. Evidently we have with criminal intent signed a deal with Beijing Semiconductor so they could make the Halcion processer. That's close enough to international terrorism for their purposes."

"That was approved by every federal department down to the Post Office. What are they claiming? That we're doing business with Communists? That went out with McCarthy, too."

"That we're selling technology that could potentially be used in weapons to a state potentially hostile to American interests. You and I are both wanted for *interviews*."

"You're joking." I knew she wasn't. The accent she put on "interviews" said it all. If they found us we'd be subject to summary arrest and detention at the government's convenience under the FISA rules, without legal counsel or in fact any outside communication, indefinitely. They weren't even obligated to inform anyone where they'd taken us. It was blatantly gerrymandering the law, but now we were in the position of having to prove they were doing it.

"Maybe he was. I'm not." The was no humor in her voice.

"Did anyone ever suggest to them that restraint of trade and warrantless searches were un-American?" The lawyer in me was fuming at the absolute arrogance involved in such a move.

"Relax, everything that can be done is being done.

Megan and Boyd are on the case and there's nothing we can do about it right now anyway. I just didn't want either of us to be tied up waiting for interviews at their convenience."

"Let's call Stuller and get him digging up some dirt on McCool. This is getting to be hardball."

She nodded and made the call while I drove, which brought up the question of where I was going. Exit thirty was sliding past as she finshed. "Where should we be going?" I asked.

"We're going to have to vanish for a while. I only got out of the building by pretending to be my own secretary having a nervous breakdown because of all the guns."

I raised an eyebrow. "Did you cry?"

"Of course. They were very nice and sent me out for some air."

I had to smile at that. Julie put herself through school in the reserves. She was one of the first women in the country to qualify as a Marine infantry officer and she's forgotten more about firepower than any paper-pushing SEC agent will ever learn.

"You said you had Megan and Boyd involved."

"They're on their way down with armfuls of stays and writs. I celled Rob Farthing from outside and hooked him up as the contact man once they arrive. I think you and I should be unavailable for comment for the next little while."

"Good call." This was more dramatic than most of my interactions with various levels of government, but when you control an empire as large as mine you find yourself almost perpetually under investigation by several departments at once, as well as defending yourself from an unending stream of lawsuits by competitors, customers, private individuals and cranks who think you'll find it cheaper to settle their nuisance suit out of court rather than fight it. "So what do you think is the root of this?"

"McCool is out for our heads, that's the problem."

I nodded. "He has political aspirations, and making himself a reputation as tough on corporations is how he plans to achieve them. He's going to be running for president some day. We should give him some campaign money."

"I think Dynacore already has. This has their fingerprints on it."

Of course she was right. "What are they accusing us of, exactly?"

"Other than trading with evil Communists? Our patent enforcement on the split-ring convolver technology is market restrictive."

"Patents are supposed to be market restrictive. That's what they're for."

"According to the SEC our licensing practices aren't allowing American competitors into the market on an equal footing with those overseas, by which they mean in China. Dynacore is of course the particular competitor whose feet we're stepping on."

I frowned. "They're free to use other technologies if they don't like our license terms." Of course, no other technology compares to the convolver, which was the point.

Julie smirked sardonically. "They're free to cut a deal with McCool, too."

I pursed my lips, considering options. The full impact of what was happening was beginning to sink in. Using the anti-terrorist rules kicked in a whole lot of very serious provisions and gave the government tremendous freedom to act against us. "How bad do you think McCool wants us?"

"Pretty badly."

"I think we should get off the highway before the cameras pick up our licence plate."

She nodded and I pulled past a semi-trailer and then slid over to the exit lane. The beat cops we'd seen at the door had certainly been told to prevent anyone from leaving the building. Once Julie was outside she wasn't their responsibility anymore, and since I'd never gone in I wasn't their responsibility either—though if we'd given them more time to think about it they might have changed their minds. The computers watching the highway cameras wouldn't suffer the same lack of understanding. Their jurisdiction was everywhere, and if they'd been told to look for my license plate, SEC would come knocking wherever we were.

Come to think of it, they could follow us through our phones, and the Porsche's anti-theft satellite tracking system would do an even better job of pinpointing our location. A tall sign by the off-ramp advertised a well-known national truck stop chain, and I pulled in there. In the parking a lot a hefty man was stepping out of five-year-old sedan, gray and nondescript. I slid into the space beside him and got out, leaving my phone in the Porsche.

"Excuse me, I'd like to buy your car."

"Buy my car?" He looked puzzled.

"How much do you want for it."

"It's not really for—"

I held up a hand. "Name a price."

"How will I get home?" He looked perplexed.

"Take a cab. How much do you want?"

The perplexed look vanished, replaced by one of calculation. He was trying to figure out the catch. "Twenty-five thousand." It was easily twice what the car was worth. He wanted to see how serious I was.

"Twenty-five thousand. Done. Do you have a bankchip?"

He looked at me, not quite believing it, then looked at the Porsche. Slowly he drew out his wallet, handed over his bankchip. I tapped it to deposit the twenty-five thousand, then thumbed it. There was a pause while it verified that my thumbprint matched my account number, then beeped. I handed it back to him and he looked at the display rather suspiciously, then handed over his keys.

"Is the registration in it?"

He nodded, still looking at the figures on his bankchip.

"I'll mail you the paperwork."

He looked up. "You don't know my address."

Julie handed him her phone. "We'll call you."

We got in and drove away, leaving him standing there still looking bemused. Back on the highway she turned to look at me. "Now I really feel like a fugitive."

"Relax, you made the right decision." Now that my initial surprise and outrage had worn off I was already plotting countermoves. "We just need a base of operations to fight back from unhampered by the need to answer a bunch of annoying questions. This is just a shock tactic to get us to play ball with Dynacore."

"We can't use a hotel, they'll pinpoint us immediately."

We discussed it as we drove, vanishing from the government's vision is harder than you might think in an age of electronic cash. Buying the car by bankchip was fine—they would trace the transaction and find the man from the parking lot, but he'd be unable to tell them were we went. So long as we left the car before they knew what license plate to get the cameras looking for we'd be fine, but that left open the question of where we'd stay—that transaction would be inextricably linked with where we were. Finally we decided to barter for a room. We drove to a big-box store and while Julie picked up a paper and started looking for accommodation I loaded up the trunk with all the consumer junk I could lay my hands on—holocams, finger phones, personal vid-goggles, beltcomps—expensive baubles that came in small packages. When we left an hour later we had fifty thousand dollars' worth of electronics in the car. Then it was a matter of finding someone who'd take goods instead of cash for rent. We struck out with the first four places, the landlords obviously being concerned that all the goods we were offering were stolen. The fifth one was the charm. Mrs. Marel was a middle-aged matron of uncertain ethnicity who knew an opportunity when she saw it. The rooms certainly weren't up to the standard I'd become accustomed to, but it was reasonably clean, in a reasonably quiet neighbourhood. In exchange for sundry trendy toys she agreed to keep us fed, do the laundry and housekeeping and generally keep the house running while Julie and I did whatever it was we did during the day.

What we did of course was orchestrate our counterattack on William McCool, Dynacore and the SEC. It was harder than you might think, due to the need to keep our location secret with the government looking for us with the basically unrestricted power given them under the anti-terrorist provisions in the Personal Privacy Act. Just calling Megan and Boyd was difficult. There was a phone in the house, but we couldn't use it because any call to our law firm would be monitored, voice-print matched and traced back to us. We couldn't just buy cell phones and use them from the house because those calls would be monitored too, and once they knew the number our location could be triangulated from the phone signal down to the meter. For the first couple of days we drove the car down convoluted routes to pay phones on the street, carefully avoiding intersections with stoplights where the traffic cameras could pick up our licence plate number. After that we decided the purchase had almost certainly been traced and we abandoned the car and went to buy another the same way, only to find our bank accounts had been frozen. All of them. That was a bad sign.

The SEC had our offices completely shut down, a clever move which rendered our organization unable to help us. Megan and Boyd were fantastically busy on our behalf, but were severely hampered by the anti-terrorism measures, which allowed McCool's group to keep everything secret from our legal team. Still, there were a number of other angles we could work and we worked them all. I spent hours at pay phones, calling in political favors and started a congressional investigation into the SEC's investigation, which was sure to throw a few monkey wrenches into their plans, as well as prevent them from getting too loose with their interpretation of the law. Through Megan and Boyd I followed Mark Stuller's progress digging out dirt on McCool. I called the President's private number too, but he was in Australia discussing the Pacific Rim situation. I got on his callback schedule for two weeks later, which probably wouldn't help at all.

At least we didn't have to worry about food. Mrs. Marel took care of that quite cheerfully, as well she might have. She was making about five times the going rate in consumer goods for everything she did for us. She didn't ask any questions either. I'm sure she didn't want to know the answers.

Once we gave up the car our biggest problem was lack of transportation. We couldn't take taxis, we'd be nailed as soon as we thumbed the fare pad. Even getting on a city bus exposed us to security cameras that would recognize us and report us to the hunters. There was no doubt in my mind that our faces were in the databases now, the stakes had gotten too high. McCool was backing Dynacore because he expected Dynacore to back him when the time came to announce his presidential run. It didn't have to become a struggle, but he'd overplayed his hand. That might have paid off if we'd been caught and rendered incommunicado in the raid, but we'd gotten away. In threatening us too badly and forcing us to hit back hard he'd turned us into enemies, and thereby exposed himself to all the pressures we were bringing to bear, which were considerable. It was no longer a matter of doing a favor for his friends in Dynacore, bigger forces were now at play. If he didn't break Baker Technologies we'd break him. He needed to get Julie and me out of circulation to give him the time he needed to finish cobbling his case together and finish the job to vindicate what he'd started. If we managed to beat the rap he would have burned too much political capital to recover and his presidential dreams would be over.

Oh yes, I was certain our faces were in all the watch lists. And our fingerprints, retina prints, gait profiles and favorite brand of breakfast cereal. Megan and Boyd informed us that a million-dollar reward was being offered for information leading to our arrest. That got our faces in the papers, and we were due to be featured on *Crime TV* in a week's time. It was a problem rapidly growing more complex.

The fourth day I got fed up. "Listen, we have to get to New York. Megan and Boyd can look after us once we're there."

"They'd be required to hand us over, that's what the law says."

"The law says a lot of things, and they aren't paid to make things easy for the other side. McCool's legal grounds are shaky at best. They can only make this snatch operation work if they can do it in secret."

"You're the lawyer, but getting to New York is the problem."

"We can't stay here long. If we do we won't even be able to communicate. They've got to know we're in this area by now."

"You're right about that." Julie did some searching on the 'net to learn about the issues involved. They were considerable. We could only walk so far, and there were a very limited number of pay phones within reasonable walking distance. Reusing them was risky—even using them for any great length of time at once was risky, and we were at a minimum narrowing our whereabouts down to a specific geographic area.

Or maybe they weren't even watching for us. I mused on it on the morning of the fourth day. Julie was scanning the news on Mrs. Marel's vidwall.

"We need some options."

She looked up. "Buy a boat, or rent one. Sail to the Caribbean. Maybe the Turks and Caicos Islands, even Cuba—somewhere where there's no extradition. Put a satellite phone on it and we can run the battle from there."

"It'll be hard to get a boat with barter."

"If we stay here we're going to be caught."

"If we go to Cuba we'll seal our fates as Communist sympathizers."

She laughed. "The Cold War is ancient history, we can go where we want."

"Let's try an experiment first." I suggested. "Maybe we can beat the surveillance."

"What?"

"Let's see if we're overreacting here."

She raised an eyebrow. "How so?"

"There must be a way to beat the cameras."

"Sure, put a bag over your head."

"No, something more subtle than that."

"Dark glasses and a fake beard won't work. I know that much. The computers compensate."

"Why don't we look it up and see how they compensate, figure out what will work?"

"By 'we' you mean 'me,' don't you?"

"You're the one with the science degree, I'm just a lawyer." I smiled my best smile at her. "I love you, honey."

She rolled her eyes, but dumped the BBC financial section and the Hong Kong *Times* off the vidwall and started searching. An hour later she had an answer.

"It works like this. A facial fingerprint takes all the features in your face and relates them to each other by distance and angle."

"What features?"

"Edges of your eyebrows, bridge and corners of your nose, corners of your mouth, your chin, distance from pupil to pupil, all that stuff."

"Okay."

"So to beat it you have to change those dimensions. You can't change just one, because it uses statistical matching, you have to change a bunch at once."

"So it can't be beaten without plastic surgery is what you're saying."

"No, I think it can. Faces are broadly similar, so a few small changes would make a big difference."

"What changes?"

"As many as possible. Shave the edges of your eyebrows, put on dark glasses, use actor's putty on the bridge and corner of your nose, and lipstick at the corners of your mouth to make your mouth look bigger. That should mess up the facial-structure metrics pretty badly. For facial shape you'll have to let your jaw go slack. That's not a big change but with the others it should work."

"What about gait recognition?"

"Slouch, mooch along, exaggerate your walk."

I thought it over. "Okay, let's do the experiment."

"You haven't told me what it is yet."

"We find a shopping mall, go in, let the cameras pick us up. Go into the bathroom, make all those changes, come out, go back to the entrance and see if McCool's troops come flying in like the Light Brigade to bust us."

She thought it over. "To what end?"

"They'll be watching Megan and Boyd like hawks, waiting to snap us up. They know we're going to have to go there sooner or later—it's the only real support we've got with everyone at Baker under the SEC's thumb for now. We can't risk going there until we know we can beat the cameras. Their response time at the mall will be a little slower, and it'll be easier to blend with the crowds and vanish if we mess it up."

"Hmmm . . ." She thought more, looked around our cramped quarters distastefully. "All right. Let's make something happen."

We gathered the few supplies necessary and walked down to the nearest shopping mall. It was a hot day, sticky with humidity and I found myself wishing for the climate-controlled interior of my Porsche. The cool air that gushed from the mall doors was like a drink of ice water, but I was acutely aware of the security cameras trained on the entrance. If we were on the watch lists we were busted now, and McCool surely had enough data to know we were in the area. If we were right about the value of the stakes to him he would have rapid-response units standing by. We were about to find out just how rapid.

There were more cameras inside, in mirrored camera balls so we couldn't tell if we were being tracked. We went straight to the first public washroom, split up and went in. The clock was ticking and my hand trembled as I applied the razor to take half an inch off my eyebrows. That took a minute, then another minute to put the putty on my nose. I was sweating and it looked ridiculous, but didn't have time to fix it. I smeared lipstick unevenly on the corners of my mouth, giving myself a lopsided clown smile, put on the sunglasses I'd borrowed from Mrs. Marel and went out again. Time to fix the details later, if McCool's agents found me in the washroom alone my disguise wouldn't matter. Humans aren't so easy to fool as the cameras. Julie was waiting for me outside, looking ridiculous and still recognizably herself. Any human watching the washrooms would have known at once that the slackjawed, oddly made-up pair in dark glasses who shuffled out of the washroom four minutes later were the same ones who went in—known that and further known that something strange was going on. The computers, I hoped, would not be so smart. We had moved outside their "problem space," to steal a phrase I heard Holmes use once.

We shuffled our way up to a food court that overlooked the washroom and waited. We didn't have to wait long. First a security guard arrived, trying too hard to look casual, and checked the washrooms. Before he was done a trio of cops arrived, doing no more than walking quickly so as not to alarm the shoppers, but clearly ready for action. There was a hurried conference outside the washroom, the security guard consulting his datapad and shrugging. The group was joined a minute later by a man and a woman in suits. There was more talking, more shrugging by the security guard, then he spoke into his radio microphone. More talking after the answer, and the group broke up. We stayed where we were for half an hour, time for them to convince themselves that we were gone. One of the cops walked through the food court and my heart pounded, but he went on without noticing us. Too many people there to check them all.

The computers would have saved the video of our motions from the mall entrance to the washroom, they're programmed to do that when they get a facial recognition hit. But since they didn't get a hit when we came out of the washrooms they neglected to track us after that, or record any of the video in the area after we'd left it. Smart, but stupid. I prefer dealing with people.

Julie smiled across the table at me, took my hand. "We got away with it."

"And we know they're serious."

"That's okay. We know how to beat the system, at least for a little while. We can get on a bus to New York, get in to Megan and Boyd. After that we're in control. McCool will wish he'd never heard of Baker Technologies."

"You're right about that."

I took advantage of the mall pay phones to call Brian's private number. It was a risk—they'd surely be monitoring his line too, but I needed to know work was progressing on the buckytubes and the drive.

"Sure, everything is good." He was his normal cheery self, but then his voice dropped with concern. "Where are you guys? Mark Stuller was here setting up security and everyone is looking for you."

I was glad to hear Mark was taking care of business in my absence, making sure the crown jewels were secure. McCool was so far out on a limb going after us that he wouldn't dare go after Brian—but I'm sure someone at Dynacore would be urging him to do it anyway. "I can't tell you where we are, but once we have this legal snarl worked out I'll be up and you can show me live fusion, deal?"

"Sure. We're already laying up the drive tubes and I've got another superconductor storage ring on line."

"Excellent. Tell Dale on the patent team to start looking for a build site for a spaceport." Julie gave me a look, tapped her watch pointedly. "I've got to go, talk to you soon."

We trudged back to the house, plotting strategy on the way. The aim was not only to stop McCool and Dynacore but punish them so badly they never considered trying anything like this again. We went up to our little room, tired and hungry and I reflected on the irony of having twenty billion in net worth and being unable to order takeout Chinese food for lunch. Mrs. Marel had left some peach cobbler out for us and we attacked it.

I was pouring a glass of milk when the door broke in with a crash and a pair of men in black jumpsuits with flak jackets burst in, assault rifles leveled.

"FBI! Search warrant! Get on the floor!" Before I could do it the first agent was already slamming in to me with his weapon, throwing me down, another right behind him got a knee in my back and forced my wrists into handcuffs. I heard Julie curse as boots pounded through the house. More agents poured through the door and spread out, weapons leveled. The four who had taken down Julie and me picked us up and bustled us out the front door. A helicopter *thwopped* down into the tennis court across the road. We were bustled out to it and unceremoniously piled on board. Out in the driveway a convoy of sedans and vans was pulling up and serious, dark-suited men and women were getting out, dragging equipment.

All that for us? What did they expect to find? But then I saw the news van rolling down the street and understanding dawned. The drama was for the news crews, to convince them of the serious danger we represented to life, liberty and the American way. This was going to be a high-profile case, and the SEC had to ram it through hard or they'd lose. This was round one in the public relations fight, and they were already winning. Mrs. Marel was on the lawn, talking excitedly to one of the agents. I caught her eye and read her expression in an instant. She'd turned us in for the money.

My thoughts alternated between anger and despair on the helicopter ride. Another day and we'd have been safe. Our captors put hoods over our heads, a needless and degrading treatment. The helicopter landed and we were herded into a jet. Within minutes the engines turned over and we were airborne. I suspected it was a Learjet, the same model as mine, a suspicion that was confirmed as we took off and the flight computer called out V1 and V2 in the same voice and at the same speeds my own uses. I didn't know if the information would turn out to be important or not, but I made a mental note of it in case it did. My future had suddenly become very uncertain, and the only weapon I had left was my brain.

We were in the air maybe two hours, or maybe three—it was difficult to keep track of time—and when we landed they loaded us into a van. I could tell it was a van from the step up into the back and the slam of the doors when they sat us down. We'd flown a long way. The air was hot and humid. Where were we? Guantanamo Bay? Mexico? Canada? If I was right about the distance we'd flown we could be a lot of places. We were side by side at least, and just that much contact with my wife was reassuring. We were still together, we would beat them yet. The ride from the airport was another hour, maybe. We were taken up a set of steps, into an air-conditioned building, then down more flights of stairs. I tried to keep track of the twists and turns but was quickly disoriented. When they finally removed the hood I was in a bare cell, eight by six, with a bed, a toilet and a sink, nothing else. The heavy metal door had an open slot at the floor and another, covered by a metal slider, at eye level.

I sat on the bed, exhausted, but not for long. Soon they came to get me. I was hooded again, taken up a flight of stairs to a windowless room where I waited, still handcuffed. After about five minutes a heavyset, jowly, balding man came in.

"Mr. Watson. I'm pleased to meet you at last." He didn't sound pleased.

I recognized the voice. "Burbridge." He was carrying a nasty-looking rubber truncheon, which did nothing for my sense of equinamity.

"What happened to your eyebrows?" He tried small talk.

"It's a long story." I kept the answer short and bitter. "I have to say, the SEC has overstepped its authority pretty drastically, don't you think?"

"Not the SEC, Mr. Watson. This branch of the government doesn't have a name." I considered suggesting a name for him, but thought better of it. He smiled a nasty smile. "So suppose you tell me all about your nuclear fusion work."

I was taken aback. "What do you mean?"

"What, did you expect me to ask about Dyna-core? That's an issue beneath my notice. McCool provides us convienient cover, in return for some quiet assistance from time to time. So tell me about the fusion project."

I shrugged, confused as to the purpose of the question. The details were confidential but there was certainly nothing even vaguely illegal about it. "We're trying to build a fusion drive for interplanetary travel."

"Why?"

"To explore the possibility of mining asteroids."

He laughed. "Yes, I heard your conversation with Douglas Straughn. We know all your cover stories." He leaned forward. "It was clever, but it didn't fool anyone. We know that you know we've been watching you. What you didn't know is that we knew you knew." I tried to make sense of that and failed. "Now suppose you tell me what you're really doing?"

"That's what we're really doing."

"Don't play games, Mr. Watson. You really aren't in a position to."

"What else can I tell you?" I was genuinely perplexed now.

"We know what you've been doing. We know about your secret lab in the countryside." He let me look blank for a long minute, then prompted me. "Wild Oaks. The Grafton plantation."

"Holmes' place?" I was incredulous. "That's hardly a secret."

"No, it isn't." He smirked as though he'd put one over on me. "We've had it under surveillance for some time. You almost had us convinced it was innocent. If you hadn't blocked out our electronic intercepts we would have been."

"Blocked out your . . ." I remembered Holmes' chicken wire, and the couple Pandora had chased through the peach orchard. I couldn't believe what I was hearing.

"It made no difference. We know everything important." He spread his arms wide to show how much he knew. "We know you're planning to conquer the world."

"What!?" Genuine shock raced through my system. *Nobody* knows that except Julie. Had he somehow scanned my brain? If he had—why did he need to ask me any questions at all?

"We know everything Mr. Watson." He leaned in closer, smacking his palm with the truncheon. "We know you're researching fusion weapons that don't require fission triggers. We know you're developing magnetically driven directed energy weapons. We know you're developing genetically engineered combat creatures."

"Genetically engineered combat creatures?" I stared at him in stunned amazement, then horrified realization began to seep into my brain. Death rays and mutant monsters. They *had* been listening to Brian, spying on him. And the only part of his technobabble they'd actually been able to understand was the B-movie based disinformation he'd fed them to keep them from finding out about the asteroid plan. He didn't know I intended to rule the world, he only thought he knew because Brian had made up some wild-eyed story along that line.

Burbridge ignored my shock. "We know someone is funneling a lot of money to you through Douglas Straughn to do the work. We just need to know who."

"Listen, you've got it all wrong . . ." If someone tells you a lie that turns out to be the truth is it really a lie? And do you then really know the truth?

"Is it the Chinese or the Russians?"

"It's not a weapon, it's a rocket engine." I could tell he didn't believe me. "You've got to believe me,"

I added, as if it would make a difference. "We're developing it ourselves."

"For asteroid mining?" He gave a contemptuous smirk and without warning smacked me across the face with the rubber truncheon. Pain exploded through my head and I saw stars. When I looked up he had his eyes locked on mine. "Next time choose a cover story that's a little less far-fetched." He leaned close, his gaze locked on to mine. "Now tell me the truth. Is it terrorists?"

I looked back at him, saw the insanity behind his eyes. He really believed what he was saying. I could of course have given him the bigger story—that I planned on building an asteroid mining empire as a necessary prerequisite to world domination. That story would probably play better with his warped psychology, but it really wouldn't advance my cause. I just hoped he wouldn't use the truncheon anymore. It didn't seem like a reasonable hope.

We stared like this for a while, then he turned away." Understand, Mr. Watson, that we have all the time in the world. We're letting your little lab run for now, but we're watching it. Sooner or later we'll get the evidence we need, and you'll be right here when we do."

He left and I breathed out in relief, still shaky from the suddenly violent turn things had taken. After a while a guard came to put my hood back on and take me back to my cell. I was stunned and felt horrible. Throughout the whole experience I had deluded myself into believing it wouldn't—couldn't, last long. There are people the government can harass with impunity, and people it can't. I was—or had believed myself—very firmly in the *can't* category. Even in the midst of evading their pervasive searching I had felt I was only playing business hardball, making sure I kept the upper hand. Burbridge had effectively disabused me of that notion. His agency, whatever it was, was perfectly capable of making Julie and me vanish quite completely. And he was just nuts enough to do exactly that. How he would react when he finally learned that we weren't growing Godzilla in Brian's basement was a question I didn't want to learn the answer to. I needed to get the hell out.

I waited until we were back inside my cell and the guard was taking the hood off again. He was a beefy man, red faced, wearing a blue uniform shirt with no insignia on it, a clip-on radio and microphone, with a nasty-looking baton, a set of cuffs and a spray can of mace on his belt. I smiled my best smile. "What's your name?"

"No talking allowed." He didn't even look at me.

"Do you know who I am?"

"No."

"I'm John Watson, Baker Technologies. They arrested me yesterday in Birmingham, Alabama." I almost added "USA" just in case I was in Panama—how long had the flight been? "Look it up in the papers, they'll have my picture." Time to use all that dramatic press coverage to my advantage.

"So?"

"So I'm one of the top-ten richest men in the world. Look it up, talk to me again tomorrow, there's a million dollars in it for you."

"Oh." He seemed to have cornered the market on monosyllables. The heavy door clanked shut behind him. I smiled. He didn't believe me, but he was going to check anyway.

Dinner that night was some kind of pasty stew, slid through the slot on the bottom of the door. I sat on the bed and thought about Julie. She probably wasn't far away; the cell space didn't seem very large.

I didn't like to think of her being pushed around by Beefy and Burbridge. It wasn't that she couldn't handle herself—I just didn't like to think about it.

In the morning—or at least, I thought it was morning, under the constant artificial light it was impossible to tell, I had another interview with Burbridge. This one was longer and more intense, but the theme was the same. Who was paying us? What weapons were planned? What were the targets? Who were the contacts? Where were the weapons being built? How large were the combat creatures? Over and over we covered the same ground, with Burbridge alternating between ice cold and raging hot, good cop and bad cop in the same porky body. He didn't learn anything, mostly because there was nothing to learn, but from the questions he was asking I gradually came to learn how truly out of contact with reality he and his agency were. As I said, paranoia goes with megalomania, and I am well acquainted with both, but his knew no bounds. He grilled me about biological warheads launched from Mexico, control of citizen's minds through subliminal messages etched into grooves on interstate highways, microrobotic spies, fusion plasma weapons—and yes, an army of mutated salamanders grown to tyrannosaur-like proportions and sent out to terrorize the civilian population. The questions were interspersed with liberal applications of the truncheon. I ground my teeth and wished Brian's imagination hadn't been quite so vivid—and that Burbridge's wasn't either. They had obviously been watching Wild Oaks plantation for quite some time, failed to understand anything they'd seen or heard, and fed it all into some institutional delusion of a resurgent international communist conspiracy. There was no nation, no group they did not suspect of plotting against America—more specifically against their control of America. They had access to millions of pieces of information under the Personal Privacy Act, and they assembled the entire puzzle by hammering those pieces in to place until they had some Daliesque approximation of the conspiracy they needed to continue to justify their own existence. It explained, at least, the bizarre use of FISA rules by the SEC. I had thought Burbridge was just McCool's strongman, but no, McCool was just Burbridge's patsy.

I endured it for hours that grew steadily blurrier, and there was a different guard when the interview ended. I didn't talk to this one. Either the first one had been caught, in which case the second one would have been warned, possibly even bugged, or the first one was still getting his message through, in which case I could only wait.

The next day, the original guard was back, beautiful to my sight in his beefy, red-faced way. He was silent in the cell, but on the way up the stairs for another interview he said, "I read about you in the news."

"Do you want your million dollars?"

He didn't even hesitate. Every man has his price. This specimen I probably could have bought for ten thousand.

"You have to contact the law firm Megan and Boyd in New York, and Mark Stuller in Birmingham, tell them where I am, tell them what this place is. You get your cash when I'm out. Will you do that?"

"Yah, I'll do it." He was practically salivating to do it.

"Good." He took me in for another session of fun and games with Burbridge. This time he presented proof linking me to the Chinese intelligence service, insisting I admit to my complicity. I tried to ignore him and thought about Julie.

Clever prisoners keep track of the days and nights by making some mark in their cell, but I didn't think of that until the second or third day, and after that I was always too glad to simply fall in bed and go to sleep after Burbridge's fanatical questioning. I was tempted to make things up just to add some kind of interest to the endless sessions, or at least to spare myself another head-spinning smack with the truncheon, but I knew I'd live to regret it if I did so I just stuck to the tiny array of facts that were actually true. Yes we were building a fusion drive, no it wasn't a weapon, yes Douglas Straughn was involved, no the Chinese weren't, yes I had talked to the Russians about the use of their boosters, and no, most certainly it was not so I could launch biological weapons at Washington, yes I had a deal going with Georgi Stanislaski, no I wasn't aware he dealt with Azerbaijani rebels, yes I was building a unique launch facility in Mexico, and no, it wasn't for launching biological weapons at Washington either. I had no idea where the obsession with bio-terror came from—Baker Technologies did nothing that even the most paranoid mind could twist into a biological weapon—but Burbridge and his shadowy organization didn't need anything as messy as evidence to feed their fantasies. It was the same thing day after day, and around day six or ten I got fed up and suggested to him that if I were really interested in covering the Capital with bio-engineered Ebola then a secondhand crop duster would be a more effective tool than a surplus Russian rocket booster. He just launched into a tirade about eternal vigilance being the price of American freedom. Probably unwisely I asked him what the price of *my* freedom was going to be. He stared at me coldly for a moment long enough for me to realize that he had yet to put real muscle behind the truncheon. I waited for the inevitable, but he just turned and walked out.

Some long time after that a guard came to take

me back to my cell. I never saw the guard I'd bribed
again. Had he been busted? Had the message gone
through? It was impossible to know. The other guards
worked in a fairly predictable rotation. I didn't dare
approach another one until I found out what happened
to the first. I gradually forgot what he'd even looked
like and began to question whether the exchange
had ever taken place. Isolation does strange things
to the mind.

On the fourteenth or the twentieth or the fiftieth
interrogation Burbridge was going over the Pacific
Rim connection for the hundredth or thousandth or
millionth time when there was a brilliant flash and
the lights went out, all of them. I was getting used to
that, but usually it was because I'd been smacked with
the rubber truncheon again. Have you ever been in
real darkness? At first you think your eyes will adjust,
and then they don't and they start to play tricks on
you. There was only artificial light in this hole, and
with it gone there was nothing, period. I could hear
people blundering around out in the corridor, shouts
and curses and people fruitlessly flipping switches and
yelling about emergency lighting. They needn't have
bothered. I don't know fact number one about electricity, but I know enough to recognize that this was
not a power failure. The lights had flashed because
there was a power surge, one big enough to burn
them all out at once.

On the other hand the emergency lights had been
switched off when the power spiked and they shouldn't
have been affected. They would be running on a completely separate system—which was what they were
for of course, so they would still work no matter what
happened to the main power.

So okay, I didn't know what was going on any
more than anyone else did. I told you I know nothing

about electricity. Maybe there was a point to flipping switches up and down and yelling about emergency power. Whatever the point was though, it didn't seem to be resulting in any light.

That was an opportunity. I got up quietly. Burbridge had gone out to the corridor and was blundering around with the rest of them. I felt for the door, taking small steps to avoid tripping. I got there, found it unlocked. I slipped through, put my hand on the wall and started walking, trying to remember the internal layout of the building. The cells were in the basement—concrete floors, pipes overhead. The interrogation room was up one floor with linoleum flooring and offices, but I'd never seen any windows—possibly there were two basement floors, or maybe more. So when I found stairs, I had to go up. The elevators wouldn't be working of course.

I made my way down the hall, nobody stopped me. It hadn't occurred to them that a prisoner would get so far out of their control. I took a deep breath. If it was daylight upstairs I might find myself in trouble—but I had nothing to lose.

I made it to the stairs, went up one flight, went through the door. That floor was completely dark as well—no windows. I was about to try up another flight when a loud British accent cut through the commotion. "Sherlock, Sherlock, Sherlock."

Mark Stuller! "Sherlock" was the Baker Technologies kidnap code, and all of a sudden I understood the power surge and the failure of the emergency lights. I was being rescued.

"Sherlock!" I called back.

"Stay there! I'll find you." And ten long seconds later he had. A hand on my shoulder. He handed me something. "Here, put these on." Thermal-imaging goggles.

"You got my message?"

"We got part of it. Your messenger wanted half his cash up front before he'd tell us where you were. They must have been watching him—he just vanished before we could set up the exchange."

How had they found us then? It didn't matter at the moment. I fumbled on the night-vision goggles, found the switch, and the world lit up in weird tones of grainy green. A few of the agency's agents were blundering around in the dark, feeling their way up through the corridor, their bodies luminous in the thermal spectrum. Mark had a tight group with him—a woman from his security team and two men. I only knew the woman because I knew her figure, their features where unrecognizable behind their goggles. Unlike the government agents blundering around they were dark on the thermal image—their jumpsuits must have been made of infrared suppressive fabric. They carried backpacks and grenade launchers, headset radios and ammunition bandoliers. Mark keyed his radio. "Base, this is Mobile 1, we have him, extracting now, out." He turned to me. "We're leaving, follow me."

I grabbed him as he turned to go. "Stop! Julie is still here!" I prayed that it was true. I hadn't seen her in—how long had it been?

"Where?"

"I don't know. The cells are downstairs."

He looked at his watch, obviously he was running on a tight schedule. I knew the sour expression that would come across his face, but he was too good a soldier to express any hesitation. "Take us there."

I looked around to get my bearings—everything seemed surreal and different through the thermal goggles, and of course I'd been blindfolded every time I'd been brought there. It was what—fifty paces back down the corridor to the staircase I'd

gone up, and when we got to the bottom there
was a left turn, and another left into the vestibule
before the cell section. I turned and led the small
group down the corridor, found the exit light, no
longer glowing. Through the doors and down the
stairs. At the bottom another door, a vestibule, and
beyond it a heavy steel door with a small barred
window—I remembered that door, the short pause
my captors made while the guard jangled keys to
open it, the heavy *thunk* it made as it closed behind
me on every trip up and down for interrogation.
An armed guard stood by the door, another sat in
a small office protected by heavy bars.

"Who's that?" The first guard was peering helplessly into the darkness. Stuller raised his weapon
and fired before I realized what he was doing. The
weapon's report was a distinctive *bangbang*, painfully loud in the confined space and the muzzle
flash whited out the thermal image for a long two
seconds. Absolute shock gripped me for that endless interval, as I envisioned the guard's body lying
shattered on the floor, making me an accomplice
now to first-degree murder. Before that thought had
even settled in my brain the goggles cleared and I
saw the guard was writhing on the floor, wrapped
in some kind of mesh that enveloped his whole
body. He cursed and struggled, not understanding
what had happened. I didn't understand either but
the results were what counted.

The second guard had drawn his gun at the report
and we all crouched by the stairway door in silence,
hoping he wasn't foolish enough to fire blindly into
the dark. The first one's initial shock and fear gave
way to frustration as he struggled, still not understanding what had happened to him, and he called to his
companion for help. The second guard holstered his

weapon, thank god, and groped his way out of office to help the first. Stuller reloaded and fired again and the second one was caught beside the first.

I remembered the jangling at the door every time I'd been taken through. "We need the keys." I knelt beside the first guard, found them on a ring at his belt. The mesh was sticky and stretchy. Whatever the adhesive was it left no residue on my fingers after I pulled them away, but it stuck the strands of the web together with considerable tenacity wherever they touched. Neither guard was going anywhere until some-one cut them loose. I managed to work the keyring through the mesh, gave a thumbs-up to the rescue party and then fumbled to find the right one for the door. It was more difficult than it should have been in the grainy green light of the thermal goggles. I must have spent no more than a minute playing with the lock, but it seemed like hours. Finally a key slid in and I eased the door open, saw a short corridor set with blank metal doors. More fumbling at the lock of the first door, then it too opened.

Empty.

Thankfully the same key opened all the doors. There was an emaciated-looking man in ragged clothes in the third cell, a young woman looking scared in the seventh. Julie was in the twelfth. I left the other cells unlocked, let their occupants take what advantage they could.

"Julie!"

"John?" Her voice was unbelieving.

"We're getting out of here."

Stuller was already on overtime on his no-doubt clockwork attack plan, but I took a moment to hug her tight. Yes, my goal is wealth beyond the wildest dreams of starved avarice and power to mock the very gods, but Julie is my world, and I would trade all I own for her. You would have done the same, if you had someone like her in your life.

There was no set of thermal goggles for her, so I took her arm and guided her out. Stuller took the lead and we went up the stairs. The stairwell was deserted as we threaded our way through the complex. It turned out to have two sub-basements, but even on the first floor it was clear there wasn't enough light filtering through the windows to see by. The few people present were still milling around, fumbling ineffectively. One woman saw us somehow and immediately shrank back into her office in fear. As we passed I saw what could only be a chemical glowstick in her hands, barely luminescent through the goggles, but it must have flooded the corridor with light. She would have had a clear view of our heavily armed group heading for the exit. The first floor was a standard-issue public building with offices, meeting areas, cubicles with desks and computers, billboards with posters and notices—unreadable blank squares through the thermal goggles. It could have been a hospital, an office building, a police station, anything.

"Get some light for God's sake." A pudgy figure was cursing in the dark—Burbridge. A nasty smile spread over my face—it was too good an opportunity to pass up. Wordlessly I took Stuller's weapon, aimed carefully and fired. The kick bruised my shoulder, but it was worth it to hear Burbridge's yelp of panic as the sticky net wrapped him tight. I gave the gun back to Stuller and we all went over to haul our new trophy away. His screaming grew louder and I took a lot of pleasure in smacking him across the face to shut him up. An eye for an eye, as the Bible says.

In seconds we were in a lobby with another pair of armed guards wrapped in mesh on the floor, surrounded by shattered glass that had once fronted the building. Mark's team had made what the SAS call an explosive entry. The guards had given up struggling and just lay there helplessly. Burbridge was heavy, and we dragged him feet first through the doors and into a darkened parking lot, streetlights off, rain pouring down in buckets. Thunder pealed in the distance. A large commercial van was parked out front, side doors open and engine running, with another of Mark's people behind the wheel. We heaved Burbridge up and piled in, soaked to the skin in our brief exposure to the torrent. The doors slammed shut and we were driving. Even given the time it took to find Julie the entire episode couldn't have taken more than ten minutes from the time the lights went out.

I stripped off the goggles and looked back as we drove away. Our prison had been a nondescript low-rise office complex, glass fronted. The sign at the end of the driveway said simply 2323. As we drove I could vaguely see it was set in a bland commercial strip of similar buildings. All the lights were out, and a few cars were parked haphazardly on the road, hoods up with soaked drivers cursing at unresponsive engines.

"Welcome back." It was a familiar voice.

"Brian!"

"Hi John, Julie!" He was grinning from ear to ear beneath his thermal goggles, like a kid who's pulled off a successful prank.

The urban landscape changed abruptly, from somewhere that could have been any American city to something resembling a war zone. The streetlights here were out because they had been shot out, the only light came from our headlights, on now as they had not been when we left the glass-fronted building. Burned cars were shoved up on rubble-strewn sidewalks in front of the burned-out ruins of houses, empty windows staring like skulls' eyesockets. We passed entire blocks that were simply rubble. I caught a glimpse of a shadowy figure in a doorway, but it was gone before I could turn to get a closer look. Other than that, we were the only things moving in the downpour.

"Brian, where are we?"

"Washington, D.C. Didn't you know?"

I looked out at a side of the capital I'd never seen before, not quite believing him, but minutes later we were pulling on to a highway on-ramp and a sign for Interstate 295 and the Beltway flashed past. Police sirens wailed in the distance, giving me a quick shot of adrenaline, but it was quickly clear they weren't pursuing us. The highway lights were on, and I could see the glow of the vast city beyond through the downpour.

That reminded me of the power surge that had made the rescue possible. "What did you do to the power?"

He smiled and pointed to the back of the van. It was crammed with compressed-gas cylinders, ranks of batteries and capacitors, instruments and cables and a large black ring with frost caked onto it. The apparatus was enclosed in the now familiar framework of chicken wire.

"Behold the carbon-cycle fusion drive, mark one."

"You're kidding me."

"Well, really it's only the buckytube superconducting storage ring, the rest of the drive is back at the lab. There was a big field coil on the top of the van, but its gone now. We dumped a few megawatt hours into the ring, then when we got here we pumped it all through the coil. Blew out everything electrical in a four-block radius. It worked perfectly." He was positively gleeful. "We had to shield all our gear, of course. The van engine was the hardest—"

"How did you know where we were?"

Stuller turned around in his seat. "Once I learned from your contact that you'd been snatched we agreed to pay him half a million up front. Of course I never heard from him again—I can only presume his employers were monitoring his phone. Once I knew you'd been taken I knew that must have been the helicopter incident in the news, right before you stopped calling Megan and Boyd. So I called Brian and we got to work on it."

Brian nodded. "The helicopters made it easy. I just got access to the air traffic control data. That let us track the helicopters to the Huntsville airport. Of course the first aircraft to leave Huntsville after you arrived was a government jet bound for Washington—that *had* to be you. They had a vehicle waiting at the airport for you, and it drove right up to the plane, so we tracked that, which lead us to this building. If they'd delayed in transporting you at any point it would have been harder. They were too efficient."

"What took you so long?"

Stuller paused, composing his words before he spoke. "I really don't know who it is who works in that building. We can assume they're the government; nobody else would have an operation like this, especially in Washington." He paused. "What branch of the government I've been unable to find out. This building doesn't seem to be owned by anyone, it doesn't seem to have been built by anyone, and nobody knows what goes on inside. However they do have quite extensive security, which made it hard to get close enough to find anything out at all. It took a while to learn enough to get the plan together, and then we had to wait for the moon and weather to cooperate. We needed total darkness to have a chance of getting you out."

"And I had to finish building the coil." Brian was still feeling proud of his baby.

"Do you realize we're fugitives now?" Julie's voice had a quaver in it that I didn't like. "Whatever trumped-up case they had against us before, they've got a real one now. Fleeing custody, for God's sake, we'll have to leave the country." I drew her close and held her.

Brian looked at her, shock on his face. He hadn't considered the legal implications. "I thought you guys would straighten that all out once you were free. That's what you're good at isn't it?"

Stuller looked back at Burbridge, unceremoniously dumped on the floor. "What about him?"

The idea that had flashed into my brain when I saw my tormentor in the hallway came back to me. "Just wait. I've got plans for him." I let a little maniacal edge creep into my voice as I said it, and was gratified to see him flinch.

Stuller had a Swiss Army knife on him, and I borrowed it and told the driver to find a quiet corner. I unfolded the spike attachment, and when the van was stopped I leaned over Burbridge with the knife, holding it low so he couldn't see it. I was surprised to find myself reluctant to stab him in cold blood, despite the fact that he had abused me violently and repeatedly. I reminded myself of the demands of power.

He was trembling. "For God's sake let me go—I'll make sure the charges vanish, just don't kill me."

I laughed, and this time the maniacal edge was real—the endless abuse he'd visited on me surging out in something colder than rage. You might think I'm insane to want to rule the world and you'd be right—and sometimes that madness finds its way to the top. "I don't like the way you play the game, Burbridge." I forced my knee into his groin hard enough to be painful, not so hard that it couldn't get a lot worse if I wanted it to. He held rigidly still, which was exactly the response I wanted from him. "I don't like the way you play at all, so I'm going to change the rules."

I drove the point of the spike deep into his bicep. He screamed in pain and struggled helplessly in the net—that stopped when I forced my knee forward hard enough to refocus his attention. I left the point in his arm for a long thirty seconds, then yanked it out. I leaned over and grabbed him by the throat.

"Now you listen to me, you warped son of a bitch." I was literally foaming at the mouth and I had to fight to keep my hand from choking his life out. "What I've just injected in you is the most sophisticated nerve toxin our bioengineering has managed to produce. It binds permanently to the neurons in your brain and it's killing them, right now, slowly. You need the antidote administered every month if you don't want your mind destroyed piece by piece." I let go of his throat and looked at his features, now contorted in fear. "If I'm in a good mood I'll send it to you." I jerked my head at the driver, who pushed the button to slide the door open. "Maybe you should make sure I'm always in a good mood." Without waiting for a reply I shoved him out the door and onto the pavement, pleased to see him land in a puddle.

We drove off and I breathed out, the insanity was gone as quickly as it had come, leaving me shaking with the intensity of the moment. Julie put her hand on my shoulder. There was silence in the van. A nasty little trick, but it had to be done—now we'd find out if it worked. The frightening thing was how much I'd enjoyed it.

The next morning found me feeling much better, my normal world-conquering self restored. I was enjoying a bubble bath with Julie in a luxury suite in the Watergate Hotel. Her story was much the same as mine, right down to bribing a guard to get the word out to Baker Technologies—another one who'd never been heard from again. She had a few bruises from the rubber truncheon too, but nothing that wouldn't heal. After the bath I picked up the phone and dialed the President's private number. POTUS is used to being addressed with respect, but I wasn't in the mood to mince words. Since I'd given him enough money to buy California's vote I had no reason to either. The conversation was sharp and to the point. Was he aware of an anonymous government organization acting in the name of national security? Of course he couldn't tell me that. Was he aware that this organization was using the SEC as cover to conduct covert investigations of American corporations? He couldn't address that either. Did he know they were abusing the rules of FISA and ATA to kidnap private citizens with insane charges? No? Was he aware that in addition they'd nearly done irreparable damage to the nation's commercial relationships just as he was trying to stabilize the situation in the Pacific Rim? No? Did he have any clue how effective nine billion dollars could be in support of a campaign to ruin his presidency and destroy his party before the next election? He understood that part quite clearly.

The events that followed were completely inevitable. The resignation of William McCool from the SEC was a page-twelve item that few noticed and everyone immediately forgot. The glass-fronted office building in Washington is still there, but it now has a sign by the driveway. It's the new home of the Department of Regional Incentive Targets, a vague and bureaucratic organization with a vague and bureaucratic purpose. I'd like to think the nameless agency that occupied it is gone, but of course I know better. The repeal of the Personal Privacy Act was welcomed by liberals and conservatives alike. From my point of view the most important result was the introduction of the Deep Space Commercialization Initiative. It was a surprise from an administration that had strongly favored a purely military national space program, but the papers were full of the spinoff benefits of funneling fifty billion dollars to firms looking to commercialize space beyond earth orbit. Oddly they never mentioned that there was only one firm in the whole country looking to do that, although after the program was announced a dozen quick startup ventures rushed to get on the bandwagon. The government generously distributed several million dollars of that money to them, which I thought was an eminently fair division of resources.

As for Baker Technologies, our launch program proceeded as fast as we could build it. Any red tape our effort hit dissolved effortlessly at a call to a pudgy man at in some anonymous office in Washington—and every month I faithfully mail him a tiny vial containing saline and some bizarre but harmless extract of primroses that Brian assures me will defy chemical analysis for years. And it was four years later to the day that I watched the carbon-cycle drive ship *Freedom* make its first manned test flight from our facility in the Mexican desert. In another year it would be on its way to the asteroids, following more than a hundred fast-transit probes launched over the previous two years by the Citlaltepetl launch system. Its rings marched up the mountain in the background as the ship rose past the peak, ready to pump raw materials up to the buckytube factory in the sky *Freedom* and her sister ships were going to let us build. The engineers thought it would take five years to get the beanstalk up and running, after which the Citlaltepetl system could be devoted entirely to launching probes—not just to find mineable asteroids but to explore Mars and its moons as potential colonies, to Jupiter, and to Saturn. Humanity's future is in space, and I am going to rule all of Sol System.

And I was supposed to be thinking about the wealth that was going to come tumbling out of the sky to make that dream real—yes, wealth beyond the wildest dreams of avarice. Nickel and iron, gold, silver and platinum, smelted in solar furnaces a kilometer across. I had my claim staked in the last great bonanza, and I was going to own the world. Well, I won't tell you I *wasn't* thinking about that. I'll admit there was a tear in my eye as I watched the ship streak skyward, but it was just a reaction to the dry desert wind. Nobody saw it, and if anyone had dared to suggest it was the sheer emotion of watching mankind finally reach out to claim the stars I would have called them a liar. I'm a lawyer. We call people liars all the time when we know it isn't true.

I pulled Julie tight to my side as the pillar of incandescent steam rose into the darkening sky and the ship faded to a tiny spark, lost among stars now beginning to twinkle. Beside us Brian looked down from the place where the ship had been. There was a long silence, then he pulled a little black box out of his pocket.

"Hey!" he said. "You guys have got to see this . . ."

The Science in the Story

Paul Chafe

Counting to 1023 on 10 Fingers

Brian's parlor trick is easy if you put in five minutes figuring it out. To start we'll learn to count to 255 on eight fingers. This leaves the thumbs out of the equation and is actually useful for doing hexadecimal math for computer work. The trick is to count in binary. This way each finger is a binary digit, 1 or 0 (a bit in computer terms). Your fingers represent these digits in number columns as follows:

128	64	32	16	8	4	2	1
index	middle	ring	pinky	pinky	ring	middle	index
Left Hand				Right Hand			

To represent a number, raise the fingers that add up to that number. For 5 you would raise the ring and index fingers of your right hand (4 + 1 = 5). For

100 you would raise the middle and ring fingers on your left hand and the ring finger on your right hand (64 + 32 + 4 = 100).

To count in binary, use the following three rules every time you want to increase the count by one.

1) Start with the 1's finger.
2) If a finger is raised, lower it and move to the next finger.
3) If a finger is lowered, raise it and stop.

So we start with all our fingers down and look at the right index finger—the 1's finger. It's lowered, so we follow rule 3, raise it and stop. Incredibly, we've counted to one. To count higher, we start again with the index finger. This time it's raised, so we lower it and move to the middle finger. It's lowered, so we raise it and stop. Be sure you're not facing anyone when you do this, as your gesture may be misinterpreted. This finger is worth two by itself. Leave the middle finger up, and go back to the first finger for the next count. It's lowered, so we raise it and stop, and we're left with both the 2's finger and the 1's finger upraised, for a total of three. The next go-round lowers both these fingers and raises the 4's finger, and so on. When all four fingers of the right hand are raised (total 15) the next cycle lowers them all and takes us to the pinky of the left hand (worth 16). Conveniently this allows each hand to represent one hexadecimal digit (a nybble). Both hands together represent a byte. The mathematically motivated will quickly figure out how to take ones and twos complements, subtract, multiply and divide, and add in the thumbs to get a count up to 1023.

Squishing Quarters

The journey from the electromagnets in your door-bell to nuclear fusion isn't quite so long as you'd think, and Brian's quarter squisher is an interesting waysta-tion on the trip. The process of high-velocity magnetic metal-forming is actually an old and well-developed technology, although it is a fairly specialized one. The basic theory is simple. A metal disk or ring is placed inside a coil of wire, and a huge current is dumped through the coil from a big capacitor bank. The coil forms a magnetic field, and by induction induces a current in the edge of the metal disk. This secondary current generates its own magnetic field, which by Lentz' law must oppose the field which generated it. The opposing fields generate a reaction force between the disk and the coil, the disk is compressed inward and the coil expands outward. Make the currents large enough and this reaction force is enough to overcome the compressive strength of the metal. With high fields the collapse is very fast and symmetrical and excellent seals and cold welds can be created. This technique is used to close the sealing rings on Boeing 777 landing-gear pistons, just for example.

As such magneforming is a clever but specialized industrial process, not really any more interesting than plasma arc welding or X-ray part inspection. However there are a few experimental enthusiasts who use huge capacitor banks and discharge coils to collapse quarters (and other coins), as well as perform other dramatic and potentially dangerous high-energy experiments of dubious utility. At the power levels available in home-brew setups the coin is usually just reduced in diameter and increased in thickness (the coil, which experiences an outward reaction force as strong as the inward force experienced by the coin, is usually blown into pieces). However, with higher powers and some clever control of the field geometry there is no reason they couldn't be collapsed into spheres. If we imagine even higher-field devices the possibilities become more interesting—magnetic confinement fusion uses a ring of magnets to confine a plasma, and magnetic target confinement fusion actually implodes a beer-can-sized container full of fusion fuel to compress it as well. Both are active areas of fusion-power research today. The fusion drive described in the story uses a similar technique, with a conductive disk of plasmized carbon and hydrogen standing in for the coin. If we are willing to sacrifice the coil (and perhaps the rest of the setup) in the effort then the ultimate limit to the compressive forces generated by this arrangement is governed only by the rise time of the current dumped through the coil and the length of time the coil manages to conduct that current before it fails. One-shot systems aren't practical for a fusion drive, but given strong enough materials and high enough fields magnetically driven implosion of fusion plasmas for power and thrust generation are a possibility.

Considering one-shot systems again, explosively driven field generators are under development as "soft" weapons to knock out electronic and electrical systems via electromagnetic pulse—as was done in the story with the fusion drive's power-storage ring. Such explosively driven systems are capable of producing tremendous fields and the use of these goes beyond soft weapons to serious fundamental research. Of course these fields could also produce tremendous, if brief, magnetic compressions. In fusion research this field overlaps with other forms of implosion, like those used to detonate nuclear weapons, which produce temperatures and pressures akin to the interior of a star. Given research done out of Earth's orbit with really large implosions we can imagine a whole new field of research dealing with materials compressed, at least briefly, to unimaginable densities—maybe white-dwarf or even neutron-star densities. The energy required to produce compressions like this is tremendous, but if the amount of material compressed is small enough it may not be impossible (whether this is practical or the best way to do this is an entirely separate question). It is appealing to consider creating a tiny, tame black hole through implosion, which would be an experimental tool of incalculable value in extending our understanding of space and time. Unlike a sample compressed to white-dwarf or neutron-star densities, which would violently decompress as soon as the compressing force was removed, material compressed to black-hole densities would be held in that state by its own gravitational field. However, all black holes evaporate via Hawking radiation, a quantum mechanical effect, and the lower the mass of the hole the faster it evaporates. The large black holes formed in supernovae evaporate so slowly as to be about as permanent a feature of the universe as can be imagined, but any mass that humans might conceivably contrive to compress into a black hole would certainly evaporate the instant it was formed—but we might well learn more about the structure of the universe in that instant than we have in all of previous recorded history.

Pervasive Surveillance

George Orwell predicted the totalitarian surveillance state in the prophetic *1984*, which depicted a government perpetually at war to generate the social conditions necessary to impose its restrictions on every aspect of domestic personal life. The Orwellian surveillance state was a reality for those who lived in Nazi Germany and the Soviet Union, where the Gestapo and the KGB enjoyed complete freedom to wiretap and bug private citizens as well as cause the disappearance of those who opposed the regime, but it was postwar East Germany that developed the most intrusive (if not the most brutal) police state in history. Before the fall of the Berlin Wall the Stasi (Ministerium für Staatssicherheit, or Ministry for State Security) directly employed nearly one in fifty East Germans as either officers or paid informants, and some estimate that their unofficial (unpaid) informant network may have involved over ten percent of the population. Friends, colleagues, husbands and wives, parents and children spied on each other and reported to the secret police. The repression of dissent and omnipresent fear that living in such a surveillance society engenders is well documented and needs no repeating here. However, it is important to note that the East German situation is probably as intrusive as it is possible for a police state to become. Surveillance requires manpower to process the data gathered, and the problem becomes one of *quis custodiet ipsos custodes?*—who shall watch the watchers? There is an upper limit to the amount of watching that can be done before the state starts to bog down under the demands of the surveillance regime. It is also important to note that even the almost complete pervasion of East German society by the Stasi was not enough to prevent the collapse of the East German government when the Berlin Wall fell. The historical record shows that repressive regimes inevitably engender their own destruction, a lesson seemingly lost on governments in general, which seem to have an almost automatic reflex to extend their control over their populations.

In the Western world surveillance technology has progressed a long way from the days when an eavesdropper was someone who literally hung from the eaves of a building in order to overhear the private conversations going on inside. We have grown accustomed to the constant overwatch of surveillance cameras, in banks, in shopping malls, and convienience stores, in government buildings, office buildings and apartment buildings and airports, on highways, at intersections and in parking lots. East Germany was not wealthy enough to afford this largesse of video cameras (which have only become relatively cheap in the last ten years anyway), but even if it had been it is doubtful this would have changed things much. *Quis custodiet ipsos custodes* holds as well for video surveillance as for informers—it is not enough to simply gather the information, it must be processed, and it is here that the bottleneck occurs in any surveillance system, or in fact in any intelligence system. Because of this basic fact most of the cameras that watch us go through our daily lives just flash our image in front of bored security guards or store it on grainy videotape to be overwritten the next day. Only if we are unfortunate enough to be involved in some sort of incident (or be caught doing something embarrassing) will the evidence see the light of day—hopefully just on a TV reality show but potentially in a court of law.

This reassuring limit on the surveillance state changes when the need for a human watcher is eliminated. Computer image-processing techniques now allow a person's facial fingerprint to be stored in a database. An unattended video camera can then scan a crowd and the computer can pinpoint individuals whose faces appear in the database as they appear in the scene. Depending on the details of the system other cameras can then be brought to bear, tracking the target through the crowd. Systems like this are already in use in London, England, and Miami, Florida, at the Superbowl and other large public events, and soon they will be widespread. More advanced systems are able to identify specific activities and categorize them as suspicious or not. As the price and size of both computing and video equipment continues to fall it is perhaps inevitable that computer automated surveillance will become even more ubiquitous than human monitored surveillance is today.

Of course automated video surveillance is only the most obvious of a growing host of mass tracking technologies that allow a tremendously detailed picture of an individual's life to be built up. Every single one of the technologies detailed in the story exists in working form today and the government's Total Information Awareness program intends to pull all the threads together to build the big picture. Luxury cars and rental fleets now routinely have satellite tracking systems installed in them. The purpose is to prevent theft (and speeding), but the system can also be used to track the car's legitimate owner at will. Telephone companies have the not-well-publicized ability to individually triangulate and track any switched-on cell phone, even when it isn't being used for a call, and when a call is made the location it was made from is recorded along with the rest of the call billing information. Soon biometric chips scanning finger or retina prints will control access to buildings, vehicles and even personal computers and cell phones. This will ensure that only legitimate users have this access—but also provide detailed tracking information as to an individual's whereabouts. Proposed legislation would change the Internet email system to positively verify the identity of every person using an email address. The espoused purpose is to eliminate spam, but the system would also effectively destroy electronic anonymity, allowing every email to be tracked to a specific individual. Perhaps the most effective high-technology tracking device is the simple instabank card. With direct electronic funds transfer rapidly replacing cash, every purchase an individual makes is logged into the bank's (and the seller's) computer system. When cash becomes an anachronism every transaction will be traceable.

It is likely that most of this surveillance will not be done by federal government agencies but by private corporations and, to a lesser extent, by local and state police agencies. However, the search targets in the databases will almost certainly come from records held by the federal government, and various laws (notably the USA Patriot Act, the anti-terrorism bill passed in the wake of September 11th) allows the government almost unlimited access to private data in corporate databases, on demand and without a subpoena. This confluence of government and corporate control is a disturbing development because each has different areas of power that reinforce each other. The legal never-neverland that John and Julie found themselves caught in also exists today, thanks to the Foreign Intelligence Surveillance Act (FISA) and the Patriot Act. Innocent individuals who have been unfortunate enough to fit government profiles (by, for example, buying one-way train tickets with cash and looking Arabic) have been arrested and held incommunicado in solitary confinement for months.

Due process of law demands certain stringent standards of proof, but addition to a government watch list requires no proof at all—there is no accusastion of crime involved, merely generalized suspicion. Private companies are under no obligation to provide service to any given individual. Of course private companies are also under no obligation to pay attention to government watch lists, but any company which does so would undertake a tremendous liability risk if something went wrong, and we can expect that most companies will use them for this reason if for no other, denying service to those the government deems suspect. Experience with government no-fly lists distributed to airlines after September 11th shows that these lists contain large numbers of law-abiding citizens, from gun control opponents to civil rights activists, whose only crime seems to be standing in opposition to federal government policy (as yet no bona fide terrorists have been arrested as a result of the no-fly program). When automated video surveillance becomes widespread individuals on government watch lists may find themselves denied entry to stores and malls, refused banking services and public transportation, perhaps even denied entrance to their place of work (if their employer rents space in an office building owned by another company). Such individuals would be effectively expunged from everyday life, with no recourse whatsoever under current law.

In the West we enjoy a strong tradition of democracy and hold individual rights and freedoms as sacrosanct, and the right to personal privacy is foremost among them. It is tempting to assume that we will always enjoy these freedoms, but we cannot take them for granted. It is important to remember that Adolf Hitler was democratically elected and used a series of self-generated "emergencies" (most notably the burning of the Weimar German parliament, the Reichstag) to extend his power until he reigned as dictator. The excesses of Joe McCarthy, Herbert Hoover, the Iran-Contra conspiracy and the Clinton FBI file scandal show that our own systems are not immune to manipulation by those who might use them abusively.

It is important to address the issues of both terrorism and more conventional crime, but it is also important to keep them in perspective. September 11th was a horrendous attack, but it killed fewer people than die in a typical month of car accidents on American highways or in a week due to tobacco smoke diseases in American hospitals. Despite repeated alerts there has not been a terrorist attack since then, presumably despite the best efforts of the terrorists. (The anthrax attacks that followed September 11th were traced to an American bioweapons facility and the investigation is now focusing on individual government scientists employed there.)

There is always a trade-off to be made between collective security and personal freedom, but the equation is not simple and less freedom does not automatically lead to more security. Both Nazi Germany and Stalinist Russia had very low crime rates and no terrorism whatsoever, but this did not contribute to the collective security of their citizens. In January 2003 the proposed Domestic Security Enhancement Act was leaked from the Department of Justice (who at the time were denying that any such legislation was under consideration). Commonly known as Patriot II, the DSE act introduces measures which give the government the effectively unlimited right to spy on, arrest and detain indefinitely and in secret any person suspected of terrorism—but then goes on to broaden the definition of terrorism to include the commission of any crime, or even unknowingly assisting in the commission of any crime. Significantly, Patriot II would allow the government to strip the citizenship of any such person, leaving them vulnerable to the draconian provisions already applicable to non-citizens suspected of terrorism in the already passed Patriot I, including unlimited detention without charge, secret trial by military tribunal, and secret execution. These are the ground rules of a totalitarian state. Combined with the advent of pervasive surveillance technology these measures would give the government powers of control that Stalin and Hitler could only dream of. Power flows from the muzzle of a gun. Freedom flows from the refusal of a people to allow their rulers too much power.

The Economics of Space Mining

In fifty years space flight has moved from a starry-eyed dream to a multibillion-dollar industry with hundreds of geosurvey and communications satellites now circling the globe. However, these profit-based efforts are all ultimately based on providing services to the earth's surface, exploiting the big picture that only space can provide. To date interplanetary travel has remained the domain of scientific research, which has to meet less stringent economic tests than purely commercial enterprises. Making the jump to the commercial exploitation of the solar system depends on the economic viability of the venture, and the numbers are daunting.

As an example, Boeing charges $19,000 per kilogram for a payload delivered to orbit on its Delta IV booster, which makes anything at all delivered to orbit literally worth its weight in solid platinum (spot price the day I wrote this: $20,500 per kilogram). Boeing intends to make money putting up satellites so we can assume these figures represent the real costs of launch. Take mission costs into account and the reality is stark. If there were pure platinum just floating around in low Earth orbit, it simply wouldn't be worth our while to go collect it—at least not with Boeing.

The heavily subsidised Space Shuttle doesn't make money for the government but taking advantage of government largesse is a routine business practice. In addition the Shuttle can put a 22,000-kilo payload on the runway from orbit—something the Delta IV can't do. At NASA's current figure of $300,000,000 per launch that gives us a transportation cost of $13,600 per kilogram. Now it's worth flying to fill the cargo hold with platinum—at least until Congress catches on that we're milking the taxpayer, but pure gold (at just over $10,000 per kilo) is still a losing proposition, and this is just low Earth orbit. Contrast this with the transportation cost of $5 per *metric ton* required to ship iron ore from mines in the Canadian arctic and Brazil to the ore terminals in Rotterdam and the economic obstacles facing an asteroid-mining venture are made very clear.

This doesn't necessarily slam the door on space *manufacturing*, because some products can have tremendous value packed into very little mass. My tenth-of-a-gram contact lenses are a hundred dollars each, making them worth a cool million dollars a kilo. This cost has nothing to with the price of plastic, a little to do with the computer-controlled lathe that custom cuts them to fit my eyes, and everything to do with the skill of my optometrist and the tremendous research and development effort that went into proving them safe and effective. Microchips (just the thin thumbnail of silicon, not the bulky black pin-package you plug into your computer) can be worth tens of millions per kilo, and some drugs can be worth billions.

The orbital manufacture of products like this is worth pursuing, although there may be very few that absolutely require zero gravity or limitless hard vacuum to manufacture. However space *mining* seems to be out of the running before we get started because no

raw material is even close to valuable enough. Space
mining means going to the asteroids, and even assuming a tenfold price reduction for a ticket to low Earth
orbit, getting out to the asteroids is going to cost more.
Mars Global Surveyor cost $85,000 a kilo to launch to
the red planet, plus another $200,000 a kilo for the
hardware and support, and Mars Observer was five
times more than this—and it was lost due to error.
These are just observation missions—the equivalent
to prospecting in a space mining operation. Getting
launch costs way down is only part of the equation,
we also have to radically slice mission costs. This
has some promise—a lot of that $200,000 a kilo is
due to the fact that space probes are one-of-a-kind
creations of tremendous sophistication, and making a
simpler probe can save a lot of money. The Japanese
Muses-C asteroid sample-and-return probe (which *is*
asteroid prospecting) cost just $33,000 per kilogram,
plus mission costs. However, the unavoidable fact is,
high technology costs a lot of money. NASA tried to
escape this equation with its Faster-Better-Cheaper
program and wound up with a string of spectacular
failures (only one in three Mars missions has been
successful). This isn't only true in space. The B2
bomber is worth (or costs, which is not quite the
same thing) its 153 tons in solid platinum and it's
never going to orbit.

With these figures in mind the hundred-billion-dollar
figure mentioned in the story for a running asteroid-
mining infrastructure is probably very conservative. The
International Space Station is a thirty-five-billion-dollar
effort and represents only a faltering first step in the
direction of the infrastructure required. However, the
size of the investment required is not an insurmount-
able obstacle. Regardless of the capital costs involved
the key measure of any investment is its ability to turn

a profit, which ultimately hinges on supply and demand. It is this economic reality which is likely to prevent asteroid mining from getting off the ground.

In the story I make the assumption that metals will become increasingly scarce and therefore expensive in the future as supplies are mined out, but current trends do not support that assumption. Despite tremendous increases in demand, industrially useful metals have gotten steadily cheaper and more readily available throughout all of history and this curve has accelerated drastically in our century. A factor which Watson overlooks in his enthusiasm for asteroid mining is that if buckytube composites can be made cheap enough to make a space elevator possible they will entirely replace steel as a structural material. The trend of replacing metals with composites is already well established in the aerospace and automotive industries, and fiberglass is now being used instead of steel in reinforced concrete structures.

Even without this trend we won't be running out of metals any time soon. Refining has become much more efficient, mines can now reach miles down into the earth's crust and out under the oceans, and improvements in prospecting techniques have meant proven and untapped reserves are larger now than they have ever been. Earth's mineral resources are vast and we have barely begun to flirt with seafloor mining. Although this is certainly an expensive high-technology venture, it would still be cheaper than asteroid mining and it quadruples the area available for exploration. Furthermore, metals are an infinitely recycleable resource, and even much of what is "thrown away" can be recovered. Any urban landfill amounts to a high-grade ore deposit in terms of metal content per tonne and some companies are beginning to explore "secondary mining" of landfills as a serious option. There is already a small but thriving industry which raises sunken Second World War warships for the steel in their armor plating, valued for certain scientific applications because it is free of the trace radioactive contamination that has filled the world since Hiroshima. Unlike a space-mining operation, recycling programs are cheap, low risk and require no technological breakthroughs.

Buckytubes

Holmes' key enabling technology, buckytubes, is here today, although it's currently confined to the lab. Carbon materials are the strongest in nature, both because of the tremendous strength of the carbon-carbon covalent bond and because carbon likes to arrange itself in triangles and hexagons, which are the stablest geometric structures possible. Diamond (tetrahedronal) and graphite (hexagonal) are the most familiar forms and both are repeating crystal lattices of arbitrary size. The edges of the crystal lattice have dangling bonds (like the edge of a cut piece of chicken wire), which are usually taken up by hydrogen atoms. The discovery of C_{60} by Kroto and Smalley—named Buckminsterfullerene for its structural resemblance to the geodesic dome invented by Buckminster Fuller—has triggered a revolution in carbon chemistry. Unlike the infinitely repeating lattices of diamond and graphite, each molecule of C_{60} is complete unto itself, twelve pentagons, each surrounded by five hexagons, with carbon atoms at the vertices—an atomic-scale soccerball, commonly called a buckyball. C_{60} is tremendously stable both chemically and physically and boasts a host of superlative characteristics. Because of its icosahedral structure it is the roundest molecule possible. Fully fluorinated as $C_{60}F_{60}$ it is the most stable molecule known to exist and may be the most stable molecule which *can* exist. Compressible by up to seventy percent without breaking down, it is the most resilient molecule, and in this state it is twice as hard as diamond. Because of this it is capable of withstanding impacts of 15,000 mph unscathed. Buckyballs are normally insulators, but doped with potassium they become superconductors. Fullerenes in general are variations on the carbon geodesic theme, always with twelve pentagons but with more or fewer hexagons in the mix. A buckytube is simply a buckyball with a long, winding spiral of hexagons between two half-buckyball end caps. Because of the strength of the bonds and the rigidity of the hexagonal structure, buckytubes are the stiffest structures ever made. There is no theoretical limit on the length of a buckytube, although current techniques produce samples only a few microns long. When you consider that carbon-carbon composites made with graphite already demonstrate strength-to-weight ratios ten or more times better than steel, the structural potential of buckytubes becomes clear. Buckytube composites can reasonably be expected to have a strength-to-weight ratio a thousand times better than steel.

In addition to their physical properties buckytubes display interesting electrical properties. By varying the pitch of the spiral, buckytubes can be made as semiconductors or as conductors as good as copper. Doping them with compounds like tantalum carbide makes them into submicron-sized superconducting wires, and packing them with potassium-doped buckyballs achieves the same effect, and if the buckytube is sized properly to fit the buckyball such packing would probably also serve to increase their already phenomenal stiffness and boost their compressive strength as well. There is some indication that it may be possible to build packed buckytubes like this that superconduct above the temperature of liquid nitrogen—the point at which superconductors can move from an expensive, specialized laboratory item to a low-cost industrial item. Further, it seems that their high-current carrying capacity may be preserved in the superconducting state.

Fullerenes clearly have tremendous potential, but commercial realization of those potentials involves overcoming a number of hurdles, one of the major ones being that the mass production of fullerenes is not simple. High-purity samples of high-quality buckytubes go for $14,000 a kilogram and up. If zero gravity turned out to be the key to mass production, buckytube composites would be worth building in orbit even with today's launch costs, although the demand would not be very high at that price.

Carbon nanotubes make possible a tremendous range of new technologies. The ground-to-space "beanstalk" space-elevator system and the electromagnetic launcher discussed in the story are two of the most dramatic examples, but, like fiberglass and graphite epoxy composites, they would find their way into everything from aircraft to sports equipment. If it does turn out to be possible to make them into cheap high-temperature superconductors they will have an impact on civilization akin to the introduction of plastic. Their primary use will be in superconducting power grids, power-storage rings, but the most exciting possibility then becomes high-field superconducting magnets, usable not only in fusion drives and fusion reactors, but maglev trains, high-efficiency generators and motors and a host of other applications.

Electromagnetic Space Launchers

The concept of the mass driver has been around for a long time. The idea is simple—put a magnetic projectile into a long tube made of consecutive rings of magnetic coils, and switch the coils so that magnetic forces accelerate the projectile down the tube. Make the tube long enough and the field strengths high enough and you can launch something right into space. To date coil guns have been limited to the laboratory although, as with the quarter squisher, there is a core group of enthusiasts who build working models with impressive and occasionally dangerous performance. A full-scale mass driver for space launch would be a tremendous piece of machinery—the launch tube would have to be many kilometers long and the coils would require the rapid and precise switching of vast amounts of electrical power. In the story (and in most systems given serious study) the launch tube runs up a mountain. This is not necessary to get the launch vehicle into space—a perfectly horizontal trajectory would work just as well, given a muzzle velocity equal to escape velocity plus a bit, but serves to reduce the amount of atmosphere it has to punch through. This is important because atmospheric heating at speeds of eleven or more kilometers per second is considerable. An ablative heat shield on the launch vehicle is a given, and it may be desirable to put a vacuum in the launch tube to both save energy and reduce heat loads in the thickest part of the atmosphere. The vacuum would be maintained by a thin, frangible membrane over the far end of the tube, which the vehicle would simply shatter on its way through.

However, running the tube up a mountainside

might not be the best solution. This is more difficult
to build than a horizontal launcher from a construction standpoint, and also requires that energy be
put into turning the launch vehicle and its carrier
as they travel down the tube. In addition a primary
drawback of a mass driver is that it can only insert
launch vehicles into a limited subset of all possible
orbits because it is inherently unsteerable—and the
orbits it can launch have a perigee at the altitude of
the launch point, which is probably lower than we'd
like. Using aerodynamic surfaces on the launch vehicle
increases the range of possible orbits considerably, and
a horizontal launch would give the vehicle more time
in the atmosphere to effect course changes. Engines
on the launch vehicle would also be necessary to effect
orbit changes (at a mininum to brake for re-entry)
but they wouldn't have to be large.

One of the beauties of the mass driver is its
very high efficiency. Almost all the power put into
the coils can be recovered, save that actually transferred to the launch vehicle. Launch costs for a
mass driver would be quite low, tens of dollars per
kilogram launched right out of earth orbit, but the
accelerations are tremendous—the details depend on
the launch parameters, but three hundred and fifty
gravities is not an unreasonable figure. Bulk cargoes
wouldn't be a problem, but mechanical and electronic
systems would have to be specifically designed to take
the load. Humans simply couldn't take the trip, but
there is another way. . . .

The Skyhook

The Soviet scientist Y.N. Artsutanov first advanced
the concept of a cable suspended from orbit in 1960,

and it has been seriously studied since. Commonly called a beanstalk (after the fairytale plant that let Jack climb to the clouds) it is, in theory, very simple. A cable stretches from the ground right up to the sky, kept under tension by the centripetal acceleration of a counterweight at its far end, defying gravity just the way a child's ball whirled at the end of a string does. The snag is getting the ball high enough for the whirling of earth's rotation to be strong enough to overcome its gravity—and this height is geosynchronous Earth orbit, 22,000 miles up. This is where the center of mass of the system has to orbit, so we can either put a lot of mass, like an asteroid, a little above the 22,000-mile mark, or simply spin more cable out into space above this point. This second option is attractive, since we can then take payloads even higher if we want to, and use the slingshot effect to launch them for destinations around the solar system. The cable has to be able to support a transport vehicle, its associated hardware, and of course its own weight. A cable capable of supporting twenty tons, the shuttle's payload, is no earth-shattering achievement, and any cable can be made to support its own weight simply by tapering it—the bottom of the cable supports hardly any weight at all and so can be very thin, the top of the cable supports the entire thing and must be thicker. By choosing an appropriate degree of taper any tensile material can support any length of itself, and with a little more effort can support some additional weight, like the tracks and so on of the transport vehicle. From a theoretical perspective the beanstalk is completely possible.

Looking a little deeper, the hook in the skyhook is contained in the phrase "an appropriate degree of taper." The stronger the material the less it needs to be tapered, but if we consider carbon-fiber epoxy resin composites, the strongest material we can currently build things with, the appropriate taper (about two and a half thousandths of a degree) for a cable just a millimeter in diameter at the ground produces a cable two kilometers in diameter at geosynchronous Earth orbit and massing sixty trillion metric tons. This is clearly impractical. However, if we consider a cable made of carbon nanotubes at a strength-to-weight ratio a thousand times better than steel, then a self-supporting cable would be just over a tenth of a millimeter at ground level and just over a quarter millimetre in orbit, and weigh in at around ten metric tons. This could be spooled up and flown in the shuttle's cargo bay (the shuttle can't reach geosynchronous orbit of course, so the spool would need its own booster as well). This is a much more practical solution.

In the story I make the assumption that cheap nanotube manufacture requires zero gravity, and so we have to build a large and expensive electromagnetic launch system to get the raw carbon up to a factory in geosynchronous Earth orbit. On the more reasonable assumption that, if we can mass produce nanotubes at all we can do it just fine on the ground, then turning the initial thin "leader line" into a robust elevator cable isn't too hard. NASA suggests small, automated bobbins, powered by ground-based lasers, climbing the cable from the ground up, adding strands as they go until a cable strong enough to support serious payloads is complete. These bobbins are kept busy after this, searching out damage caused by micrometeors and space debris and repairing it. Some estimates put the cost of installing such a system (given cheap manufacture of buckytubes) as low as five billion dollars over ten years.

Interestingly enough, at a given strength-to-density ratio it actually takes less material to build a tower into space than it does to hang a cable from orbit. Cables get more press partly because they're a neater concept, but mostly because we can get far more strength out of the best materials in tension than we can in compression. The tallest building in the world, Toronto's CN tower, is over half a kilometer high using ordinary concrete, which is nowhere near even the practical limit. The theoretical maximum height for a steel tower is five kilometers, for aluminum it's fifteen kilometers. As with the cable we can get better results by tapering the structure, and by pressurizing the structural members we can effectively swap tensile strength for compressive strength. These techniques, using high-strength polyaramid composites as the material of choice, would allow a tower three *thousand* kilometers high. Using this as the base structure for a tensile cable that went the rest of the way to geosynchronous orbit would reduce the cable's mass one hundred and fifty times.

However we build a skyhook, once it is complete the raw energy costs of transport (it could hardly be called launch) to geosynchronous orbit would be around $1.50 a kilogram, and the landed cost for a product returned from orbit would be only marginally higher. This radically changes the economics of space industry, and any slight advantage to be gained from space manufacturing would be well worth it, even for basic industrial processes. As an example, it takes about the same amount of energy to refine a kilogram of alumimum from bauxite (aluminum ore) as it does to beanstalk a kilogram to orbit. The energy available in an orbital solar furnace is basically free, so it would be almost cost effective to ship raw ore from Earth to orbit for smelting (not quite though, because we have to process about two kilos of bauxite for every one kilo of aluminum we get back). A product made using zero G, vast amounts of solar power or limitless vacuum doesn't have to get too much more sophisticated than aluminum ingots to be worth making in space—once a beanstalk is up and running.

In addition to allowing cheap access to orbit, the beanstalk can be used to launch spacecraft for destinations around the solar system. Energy has to be used to raise a mass up the cable to geosynchronous orbit—but less and less as we get higher. At geosynchronous orbit a mass is effectively weightless. If we give it a little push downward it will fall to Earth. If we give it a little push *upward* it will fall into space. If the cable extends out to the point where its rotational velocity exceeds Earth's escape velocity then the mass can be launched on an orbit to anywhere in the solar system we like—with the proviso that we will have to expend some energy to change the plane of its orbit to intersect useful destinations like planets and asteroids. This isn't too arduous a demand, because except for space probes, we want what we've launched to come back, and we want to be able to maneuver and do useful things while we're out there too, so we require some sort of engine anyway. Read on.

The Carbon-Catalyzed Fusion Drive

Mass drivers can get materials into space and beanstalks can get people into orbit, but to move around the solar system a drive of some kind is necessary. Fusion drives are a staple of science fiction for the simple reason that chemical fuels simply lack the energy content required to make an interplanetary, let alone interstellar, civilization possible. However, the reality is that controlled fusion has proven a tremendously difficult genie to get out of its bottle even for simple power generation, an easier problem to solve than a space drive. The first serious attempt at developing a fusion drive was Project Orion, which envisioned propelling a ship through the simple mechanism of kicking a nuclear bomb out the back and detonating it, repeating as necessary. This is hardly a graceful technique, but despite its seeming insanity it is not, a priori, unworkable. Calculation and experiment showed that a large "pusher plate" close to a nuclear explosion would experience a considerable acceleration—hardly surprising. More surprising is the fact that, given a thin protective layer of ablatable graphite, both the plate and a spacecraft on the other side of it could survive the detonation unscathed, could travel in a reasonably predictable direction and that a not-impossibly-large system of shock absorbers could make the ride survivable by people. Project Orion envisioned putting payloads measuring thousands of tons into orbit and saw a manned trip to Mars by 1965 and a trip to Saturn by 1970. However a bomb-powered spacecraft would inevitably generate a tremendous amount of radioactive fallout, and the accident risk involved with a ship carrying several thousand nuclear "pulse units" into orbit needs no elaboration. After the investment of several million dollars the project was shelved with the surface test-ban treaty. More advanced concepts have been put forward, including the British Interplanetary Society's project Daedelus which proposed laser-imploded microfusion capsules as the drive source. NASA's Variable Specific Impulse Magnetoplasma Rocket (VASIMR) plasma drive uses many of the techniques relevant to a fusion drive and the Gas Dynamic Mirror (GDM) project (currently shelved to pay for shuttle refurbishment) was aimed at creating a true fusion drive. A primary stumbling block to the

GDM drive is the availability of sufficiently strong magnetic fields. Beyond this problems to be solved are not small, given that even fusion power production still has large technological hurdles to clear. Fission power plants are now a fifty-year-old technology, but fission rockets require too much shielding and operate at too low a temperature to be practical, even ignoring the specter of accident and widespread radiological contamination. The same concerns have left atomic cars and airplanes on 1950s drawing boards. Fission fuel contains millions of times more energy, kilo for kilo, than chemical fuel, but the realities of harnessing it confine its use to large power plants.

Fusion happens whenever atomic nuclei get close enough together that the short range but powerful attraction of the strong nuclear force can overcome the weaker but longer-ranged electrostatic repulsion of the positive protons in the nucleus. Fused nuclei are more stable together than apart, and the stability difference shows up as energy that can then be put to work. The key variables are temperature and pressure—the nuclei have to be moving fast and be close enough together to make them fuse, and it takes a lot of both. Fusion bombs use no less a force than a fission bomb to heat and compress their fuel, but power generation and space drives (Project Orion excepted) require less violent methods. Adding to the headaches, the easiest fusion reaction to ignite is the deuterium-tritium reaction, and this gives off a lot of neutrons which require a lot of shielding, and which generate a tremendous waste disposal problem by slowly rendering the reactor itself radioactive. In addition tritium, also radioactive, must be made in a nuclear reactor at tremendous expense, generating more waste in the process (tritium is roughly eighty times the cost of plutonium, weight for weight). Current reactor concepts cleverly use the neutron flux from the fusion reactor itself to make more tritium, solving some of the neutron contamination problem at the same time, but it would be nice if we could tap into fusion power without having to deal with radioactive waste at all, and preferably without using exotic and expensive isotopes either.

The primary fusion pathways in the sun (the proton-proton chain, which burns normal light hydrogen and the carbon-nitrogen-oxygen catalysis cycle, or CNO cycle, which burns light hydrogen using carbon –12 as a catalyst) are aneutronic—fortunately for us, as any large-scale neutron flux from the sun would certainly bake our planet sterile. The sun uses nothing more than gravity to produce a stable, long-lived, high-flux fusion output without too many nasty side effects. In a star temperatures of ten million degrees and densities of 100 gm/cm^3 are required for the p-p chain and sixteen million degrees and densities of over 150 gm/cm^3 for the CNO cycle.

For the sun, which is held together by gravity and isn't going anywhere in a hurry, temperature and pressure are the end of the story, but for an artificial fusion reactor a third critical variable enters the picture—confinement time. This is the length of time the system can hold the fusing plasma together against the expansion caused by the fusion energy. This expansion lowers the pressure and temperature and eventually stops the reaction. In order for fusion to occur efficiently at a given temperature the plasma particles have to be held together long enough for a significant number of fusion events to occur. Lawson's criterion, the product of particle density and confinement time, serves as a figure of merit for fusion reactors, and successive generations of research machines have striven to come ever closer to the magic point of breakeven, where the reactor produces as much power as it consumes, and ignition, where the plasma burn becomes self-sustaining, requiring no further energy input from outside. (The third magic point, profitability, the point where a fusion reactor produces power for something like a nickel per kilowatt hour, is nowhere on the horizon.) The oldest and best-explored fusion scheme, the toroidal magnetic tokamak, uses low pressures (a few atmospheres), long confinement times (a few seconds to half an hour) and temperatures of hundreds of millions of degrees to achieve fusion. The more recent inertial confinement fusion approach uses intersecting laser beams to compress a tiny fuel pellet to pressures more than ten million times higher. Fusion occurs so quickly in this regime that the fuel pellet's own inertia holds it together for the nanoseconds necessary for the reaction to complete. A third fairly recent development is magnetic target fusion, which magnetically implodes a thin-walled aluminum cylinder to achieve a fusion regime intermediate between these two. MTF achieves, for a few microseconds, magnetic field strengths of 500 Tesla.

Given that all of these techniques are barely capable of generating fusion with deuterium-tritium it may seem needlessly ambitious to plan a drive around the CNO cycle. Even granted that we want aneutronic fusion, the proton-proton chain is available at much lower pressures and temperatures. However, the CNO cycle's reaction rate goes up no less than 350 percent for every 10 percent increase in temperature, rising as the *sixteenth* power of temperature, compared to the proton-proton chain's reaction rate which goes up as the fourth power of temperature. This means that, given the ability to reach this extreme regime, it should be possible to reach a point where the CNO cycle will become very efficient.

The trick of course is reaching the CNO operating point at all, and whether this is possible is an open question—even buckytube supermagnets might not do the job. However if they do, the system might work like this.

Imagine a hollow tube ringed with magnetic coils. A small stream of hydrogen and carbon plasma is fed in at one end, and a current is run through it to generate its own magnetic field. A magnetic wave is sent down the tube by successively energizing rings of magnets. This wave accelerates the ionized gases down the tube, and if the wave amplitude is made to increase down the tube while the wavelength decreases, the gases will also be compressed and heated as they travel. At some point, possibly with further energy inputs, the plasma begins to fuse. This tremendously increases its energy content—temperature and pressure soar and it begins to expand, still fusing. Forward and outward expansion are limited by the incoming magnetic wave, still increasing in amplitude, and the reaction forces of fusion particles moving against this wave provide thrust for the ship. Wave amplitude decreases and wavelength increases past the fusion point, allowing the plasma to expand and stop fusing in that direction, focusing it into a coherent jet. Finally the plasma exits the rear of the tube through another magnetic field which uses the stream of charged particles to generate electrical power to run the system. Behind the tube is a reaction chamber into which water can be sprayed to trade exhaust velocity for thrust for planetary launch. Once in orbit we turn off the water and use the jet by itself to accelerate.

Exploring the detailed physics of this system is far beyond the scope of this discussion. In a story it's easy to gloss over details like plasma disruption and wall interactions, but these are critical problems for real-world reactors. This may be the drive of the future; it may, like Project Orion and the atomic airplane, be possible but impractical; or it may be simply impossible. Assuming it *is* possible then the magnetic wave system means the thrust would be continuous and very controllable. This is the fusion equivalent of a jet engine with constant, or nearly constant, combustion, as opposed to a pulsed fusion drive (Project Orion being the extreme example) which, like a piston engine, produces power in discrete bursts. This steady, throttled power is exactly what we're looking for, and this drive is easily adaptable to the fusion ramjet concept which gathers its fuel from the interstellar medium as it travels. It should be noted though that the fusion ramjet requires solving even larger problems than a "simple" fusion drive, including the generation and control of a magnetic funnel about the size of Jupiter. Even buckytube supermagnets are probably inadequate to this task, but a field too small to serve as an interstellar fuel scoop could still serve well as an unconfined magnetic particle shield. As discussed above, some sort of particle shield is absolutely essential for manned interplanetary flight, with or without a fusion drive system, and supermagnets like this are a primary enabling technology. Solving the shield problem like this would open up the solar system to large-scale exploration and completely revolutionize the commercialization of space. Even if we don't want to colonize Mars or set up an asteroid-mining industry the scientific benefits alone would be incalculable.

A Deep-Space Radiation Shield

The single largest obstacle to manned interplanetary space flight is not efficient drives or long-term life support, it is the radiation that floods interplanetary space. This comes in two major varieties—the relatively soft protons and electrons streaming out from the sun (the solar wind), and the very hard interstellar cosmic rays, some of which have the impact of a major league fastball packed into a single heavy nucleus. Earth's magnetic field and atmosphere protect us from most of this radiation and in low earth orbit the doses are tolerable. Once you get beyond the Van Allen belts the situation changes drastically. The Apollo flights were possible only because they were short enough that the radiation risk was considered acceptable. Any long-duration flight, such as one to Mars or the asteroids, would be out of the question without shielding. There are five basic possibilities for shielding a spacecraft—mass, plasma volumes, electrostatic fields, confined magnetic fields and unconfined magnetic fields. None of these are perfect solutions, particularly against the heavy ion component of the cosmic ray background, however, the one with the most promise is unconfined magnetic shielding—this is what works for the Earth, after all. The Earth's magnetic field is tenuous here on the surface, but the dynamo that drives it is the entire iron inner core of the planet and the total energy in the field is tremendous. The 1000 Tesla field mentioned in the story is about twenty times the strongest constant field yet produced on Earth (about 45T, at the National High Magnetic Field research facility at Florida State University). Given the material properties of the buckytube components used in the story, this is a conservative estimate, and 5000T might not be out of the question. A 1000T field is starting to get within reach of the required field strength for a reasonable shield, although much depends on the details of the design and on the characteristics of the cosmic radiation profile, both of which are sketchily

understood right now. One interesting side effect of
a magnetic radiation shield is that it would capture
particles from the solar wind and produce its own
miniature version of Earth's Van Allen belts. The drag
caused by this capture would exert a small but steady
force on the bubble which would over time produce
tremendous velocities, and magnetic sails like this have
been considered along with light sails as a potential
interplanetary drive mechanism. There are important
differences though—a light sail uses photon pressure
from the sun acting on a huge reflective sheet and
can be positioned to "tack" a spacecraft up or down
in the sun's gravity well. A magnetic sail of this type
would only be able to accelerate away from the sun,
like a surfer riding a wave in to shore. A ship which
used a magnetic shield and a light sail would be able
to accelerate rapidly out from Earth but would still
be able to make it back down the gravity well on the
return leg of the mission. This raises the rather beautiful image of space captains laying courses balancing
the solar wind and photon pressure just as clipper
captains balanced trade winds and ocean currents.

This story of a girl and her racoon is an excerpted episode from a new novel, Beyond Infinity. *Greg was one of the earliest supporters of the "swoosh" concept for this anthology, and I thank him for his enthusiasm. In* From Dawn to Decadence *Jaques Barzun wrote: "The great advantage for science of an aimless universe is that it frees the imagination." Greg has spent his professional career as a physicist looking to explain the universe, and it clearly has done nothing to impair his imagination. Rather the reverse, as Barzun implies. Prepare your mind to spread its wings and fly along with Greg as he takes us on a tour of the future. And watch for another new story by Greg in the next Cosmic Tales anthology:* Adventures in Far Futures.

BLOOD'S A ROVER

Gregory Benford

Clay lies still, but blood's a rover;
Breath's a ware that will not keep.
Up, lad: when the journey's over
There'll be time enough to sleep.

—A.E. Housman

Dawn and Searcher had been on the run for days. Hart days.

Before that, an enemy had killed all Dawn's tribe—

365

her Meta, as the lingo had it—and driven Dawn into the forests of old Earth. But Searcher stayed with Dawn, scampering along as well as an augmented racoon could.

They had made steady progress climbing the flanks of the saw-toothed mountain range, and now the terrain and rich fauna resembled the territory where Dawn had grown up. She searched the distant ridgelines for hints of lookouts. Hers was not the only tribe of Original humans, and someone else might have escaped. She asked Searcher to tune its nose to human tangs, but no traces stirred the fitful breezes.

Twice they sought cover when flying foxes glided over, their ballooned arm-wings shining against the sky. By this time surely the Supras—advanced humans, superintendents really, but not the enemy who had smashed Dawn's people like a fist from the sky—would have sent their birds to reconnoiter, but in the blank blue bowl above neither her nor Searcher's even sharper vision could make out any of the ponderous, wide-winged silhouettes.

They watched a vast covey of the diaphanous silvery foxes bank and swoop down the valley currents. Distant rumblings came, as though the mountains above them rubbed against a coarse sky. The foxes reacted, drawing in their formation like silver leaves assembling into a ghostly tree.

Blue striations frenzied the air. Clouds dissipated in a cyclonic churn.

Dawn began, "What—"

Sheets of boiling yellow light shot overhead. A wall of hard sound followed, knocking Dawn against Searcher. She found herself facedown among piney needles without any memory of getting there.

All around them the forest lay crushed, as though an enormous thing had trampled it in haste. Deep booms faded slowly in the sky. An eerie silence settled. Dawn got up and inspected the wrenched trees, gagging at fumes from a split stinkbush. Nearby two flying foxes lay side by side, as though mated in death. Their glassy eyes were still open and jerked erratically in their narrow, bony heads.

"Their brains still struggle," Searcher said. "But in vain."

"What *was* that?"

"Like the assault before on your people, yes." Searcher lifted a snapped wing. "The foxes took the brunt of it for us."

"Poor things . . ." Her voice trailed off as the animals' bright eyes slowed, dimmed, then closed. "They died of electrodynamic overload, I guess."

"Our pursuer does not know precisely where we are, so it sends generous slabs of electrical energy to do its work."

Searcher gently lifted the two foxes and made a slow, grave gesture, as if offering them to the sky. A long moment passed. When Searcher lowered its claws Dawn could not see the foxes and they were not on the ground or anywhere nearby. Searcher said crisply, "I judge we should shelter for a while."

They climbed swiftly up the rough rise to a large stand of the tallest trees Dawn had ever seen. Long, fingerlike branches reached far up into the air, hooking over at the very end, as if blown by a wind on high. Yet there was no breeze at all here. She felt exposed by moving to higher ground, closer to the sky that spat death. From here she could see distant banks of purple clouds that roiled with spokes of virulent light. Filaments of orange arced down along long curves.

"Following the magnetic field of Earth," Searcher said when she pointed them out. "Probing."

Dawn saw why the Supras had sent no searching

birds. Far away quick darts of blue and orange
appeared. "The Talent," she said. Searcher looked
quizzically at her. "I can feel . . . emotion." She
remembered Searcher once remarked, *You do not
have emotions, emotions possess you.* "The Supras
are fighting . . . worried . . . afraid."

"The being above keeps them busy while it
searches."

They moved on quickly. Dawn had always been a
good runner, but Searcher got ahead without showing
signs of effort. When she caught up it had stopped
beside a big, gnarled tree and was sniffing around the
roots. Searcher took its time, moving cautiously, and
Dawn knew enough by now to let it have its way.

So she stuck to what she knew, as they moved
quickly through the shrouding forests, hiding from
the flitting ships above. They passed by colonies of
plants that had a social life, communicating through
pollen-sprays their needs and distresses. Dawn could
read these from childhood on, and was pleased to
find that Searcher asked for instruction. Some of
these signals her Meta had adjusted, and seen
propagated around the globe by genetic invader-seed.
These were the long crafts her Meta had cherished.
They were part of a philosophy the Originals had
brought to the world, and with Supra help, had
been applying to this latest of many revivals old
Earth had seen. In the millennia since the Techno
Age, much had been lost.

Dawn knew these lessons deeply. The chant of her
Meta had ingrained them:

> *Fast learns, slow remembers. The quick,
> small things instruct the slow and big by
> bringing change. The big and slow controls
> by constraint and constancy. Fast gets all*

the attention, slow has all the power. A
robust system needs both.

They had recited it every day at breakfast. She yearned for those lost days.

Both she and Searcher sensed an ominous tone flavoring the air. "Time to move on," Dawn said.

"I agree. We have a meeting."

"With whom?"

"With what—but you shall see." Searcher eyed the sky. "Abominations are up there—the Malign." Searcher stopped, opened the side of a large tree. The horny bark peeled back in curls and light seeped from within.

This was no surprise to Dawn, whose people had often sheltered in the many trees 'teched for just such use. She squeezed through the narrow slit and soon the bark closed upon them, crackling, leaving only a wan phosphorescent glow from the walls to guide them. The tree was hollow. All trees were dead inside, anyway, just big cylinders of cellulose with living skins. Someone long ago had engineered this form that built an interior from the compacted dead matter.

She looked up. In this variation there were vertical compartments connected by ramps. U-shaped growths grew all along the walls. Some creature had nearly filled the compartments with large containers, grainy packages of rough fiber.

"Storage," was all Searcher would say in answer to her questions. "Come."

Using the U-growths they climbed up through ten compartments. All were crowded with stacks of oblong, crusty containers. Sweating, Dawn hoisted herself up into a large vault, completely empty, with a wide transparent wall. Dawn thumped the window-wall and the heavy, waxy stuff gave with a soft resistance.

She watched the still trees outside, stately cylinders pointing up into a sky that flickered with traceries of quick luminescence.

The Supras were still searching. Something else, too. A bright flare of momentary combat spoke of a conflict she had seen too much of already. She turned away, glad to be in a shelter.

This place might be safer; she let herself relax slightly. As a girl she had camped among trees something like this. They had eaten—

They were all dead.

The impact of this stunned her. She froze. And then slowly she recalled what her dear lost Mom had always said. *Head's too full? Use your hands.*

She took out a knife and gouged the wall. A piece came off with some work. As a girl, she had eaten this way. She took a tentative bite. It tasted surprisingly good. She ate a while and Searcher took some. Patches on the walls, ceiling and floor were sticky, without apparent scheme. The compartment smelled of resin and damp wood.

She chanced to glance out the big window as she chewed and that was why she saw it coming.

Something like a stick poked down through high clouds, swelling as it approached. Perspective told her that it was enormously long. Coming straight down. Its ribbed sinews were knobbed like the vertebrae of a huge spine. Groans and splitting cracks boomed down so loudly that she could hear them here, inside. Curving as it plunged, the great round stalk speared through the sky like an accusing finger. Her jaw dropped. As she watched, frozen, the very end of it curved further, like a finger beckoning upward.

"Time to lie down," Searcher said mildly.

A sonic boom slammed through the forest. The window-wall rattled. She hastily flattened herself on the resilient green floor of the compartment and gazed up through the big window.

"It's falling on us!" she cried.

Searcher grinned, right beside her. "Its feat is to forever fall and forever recover."

"It'll smash these!"

"Lie still."

Something immense, whirling through the air. It rushed toward them. Graphite-dark cords wound across the deep mahogany of the huge, trunklike thing.

A high, supersonic shriek rose. Fingers of ropy vine unfolded from its tip as it plunged straight downward. The vines flung themselves toward the treetops. Some snagged in the branches there.

"Grapplers," Searcher said over the shrilling howl.

A hard thump ran through their tree.

She just had time to see the thick vines snatch at the branches of neighboring trees, grip, and tighten.

The broad brown nub hung in air for a long moment. As if, she thought, it was contemplating the green skin of the planet below it and selecting what it liked. It drifted eastward for one heartbeat. Then snatched upward.

Heavy acceleration pressed her into the soft floor. They were yanked aloft. Popping strain flooded their compartment with creaks and snaps and low groans.

Out the window she could see a nearby tree speed ahead. Its roots had curled beneath it, dropping tumbling brown clods behind. The forest dropped away. Other trees dangled from vine grips beside theirs. On one, the uppermost branches sheared off where several thick vines had clutched together. Unable to take the acceleration, it dropped away to crash into the forest below.

She could only lie mutely, struggling to breathe. A

flock of tree trunks rose beside them, drawn up to the great beckoning finger. The stalk now retracted up into the sky with gathering speed. It swept them eastward. Their tree lashed in air turbulence. She saw the other trees outside, flapping. As if shaking themselves free of the grip of gravity, and of dirt.

She watched, flooded with fear. Hopeless to try to get up—and what would be the point? They were helpless.

Searcher was enjoying the ride, its tongue lolling, eyes alight. She grimaced. Did *nothing* bother the beast?

Their tree groaned in long bass notes. She watched the nearby trees to see what was happening. The sight of one falling away had not given her great confidence.

Against the steadily increasing tension the ribbed and polished vines managed to retract. They drew their cargo trees up, turbulence diminishing as they all rose into the upper atmosphere. The trees nuzzled into a snug fitting at the base of the blunt, curving rod.

"What . . . is . . . it . . . ?" Even grunting out a word at a time was hard against the punishing acceleration.

"Pinwheel," Searcher said. "The center . . . rides high in space . . . and it spins as it orbits. The ends rotate . . . down . . . through the air . . . and kiss the Earth."

Searcher's calm, melodious voice helped stave off her rising panic. They were tilting as they rose. Cloud banks rushed at them, shrouded the nearby trunks in ghostly white—and shredded away as they shot higher. She glimpsed the underside of the Pinwheel itself, where corded bunches of wiry strands held the vines in place.

"What . . . is . . ."

"We spin . . . against Earth's pull. But will slip free."

She sent a query to her inboards, and instantly they gave her an image.

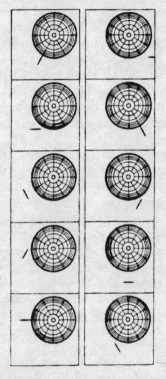

She was looking down on the planet from a pole. An enormous rotating stick orbited it. This rod slowly dipped down into the planet's air, one tip touching the surface at the same moment that the other end was farthest out in space. It was in orbit, but reached down to the surface six times as it circled. At each touchdown, the stick's tip moved backward at a speed equal to the whole shaft's orbital velocity.

Briefly, its ground-track velocity was zero. As it touched down, it could lift the trees with its vines, making a pickup. And move, in a few moments, cargo from one part of the globe to another.

The scale was dizzying. She had thought little about anything beyond the envelope of Earth's air; forest folk lived in the local. The sole Supra craft she had ridden in seemed capable of going into space, and she had supposed that was all there was. But this . . .

This vast thing was far longer than the depth of Earth's air itself. And they were fastened to one end of it, soaring along on an arc that would take them into space.

Still, she could barely conceive of the scale. This creation was like a small, slender world unto itself. Rolling bass wrenchings strummed through the walls and floor. Her heart thudded painfully and wind whistled in her ears. Pressures adjusting.

She could see outside that the strain of withstanding the steadily rising acceleration warped the vines. They stretched and twisted in their own agony, but held the long, tubular trees tight to the underside. Shrubs and brush festooned the nub. The Pinwheel stretched up into blue-black vistas as the air thinned around them. Hopeless, she realized, to try to see the end of it.

The wind in their compartment wailed and she sucked in air, fearing a leak. Searcher patted her outstretched hand. It lazed, eyes closed as though asleep. This startled her and a long moment passed before she guessed that Searcher had done this before, that this was not some colossal accident they had blundered into.

As if in reply Searcher licked its lips, exposing black gums and pointed yellow teeth.

Her ears popped. She looked outward again, beyond

the nearby slow buffeting of tree trunks. "Upward" was now tilted away from the darkening bowl of sky. But their acceleration still lay along the chestnut-brown length of the Pinwheel, as they rotated with it. Black shrubs dotted the great stretched expanse of the length that dwindled away, gray laminations making the perspective even starker. Cross-struts of cedar-red tied the long strips into an interlocking network that twisted visibly in the howling gale that tore along it. The Pinwheel was flexible, bowing like a tree in a hurricane.

They smacked into the nearest tree and a big, sharp branch almost punched through the window. But in the buffeting wind their tree wrenched aside and the impact slammed against another part of the wall. Could the window hold against such impacts? She did not want to find out.

Her ears popped again and her breath came raggedly. Along the Pinwheel's length great strips of lighter wood rose, with walnut-colored edges.The great shaft canted, sculpting the wind—and the roaring gale subsided, the twisting and wrenching lessened. Pops and creaks still rang out but she felt a subtle loosening in the coupled structure. It was flying itself.

The last thin haze of atmosphere faded into star-sprinkled black. The floor vibrated. She felt that an invisible, implacable enemy sat on her chest and would forever, talking to her in a language of wrenching low bass notes. Cold thin air stung her nostrils. She almost panicked, but found that there was enough if she labored to fill her lungs.

As she panted the ample curve of the planet rose serenely at the base of the window. Its smooth ivory cloud decks seemed near enough to touch . . . but she could not raise her arms.

Along the tapering length of the Pinwheel, slow,

lazy undulations came marching. They rushed toward her, growing in height. When the first arrived it gave the nub a hard snap and the trees thrashed on their vine-tethers. Turbulence, she guessed, summed into these waves, which dissipated in the whipcrack at its ends. Tree trunks thumped and battered but their pressure held.

Searcher licked its lips again without opening its eyes.

They revolved higher. Now she could see the complete expanse of the Pinwheel. It curved slightly, tapering away, like an infinite highway unconcerned with the impossibility of surmounting the will of planets. Vines wrapped along it and near the middle a green forest flourished.

They were arcing up over the planet. The far end was a needle-thin line. As she watched, its point plunged into the atmosphere. Undulations from this shock raced back toward her. When these reached her the buffetings were mild, for the trees were now tied snugly against the underside of the Pinwheel's nub end.

Deep, solemn notes beat through the walls. The entire Pinwheel was like a huge instrument strummed by wind and gravity, the waves singing a strange song that sounded through her bones.

The Pinwheel was now framed against the whole expanse of Earth. Dawn still felt strong acceleration into the compartment's floor, but it was lesser now as gravity countered the centrifugal whirl. Their air, too, thickened as the tree's walls exuded a sweet-scented, moist vapor.

The spectacle of her whole world, spread out in silent majesty, struck her. They were nearing the top of their ascent, the Pinwheel pointing vertically, as if to bury itself in the heart of the planet.

She wondered what would happen to them next. If

they stayed here, their trees would be dropped onto the surface partway around the world. Was that why Searcher had met this whirling machine?

The Pinwheel throbbed. She had felt its many adjustments and percussive changes as it struggled against both elements, air and vacuum, so this latest long undulation seemed unremarkable. Only a short while ago she had thought that the ravenous green, eating at the pale deserts, waged an epic struggle. Now she rode an unending whirl of immeasurably greater difficulty.

The kinetic whirligig of all these events dizzied her. The last few days had stripped away her comfortable preconceptions, leaving her open to naked wonder. She was beyond fear now, in a curious calm. Ideas floated through her mind like silent fireworks. She looked down and in a glance knew that the Earth and the Pinwheel were two similar systems, brothers of vastly different scales.

The Pinwheel was like a tree, she guessed. Quite certainly alive and yet also a dead spire, cellulose used and discarded by the ancestors of the living cells that made its bark.

"How can this thing be so strong?" she whispered.

"It is made of tiny carbon fibers," Searcher said. "They regrow daily, and can take more strain than any material."

"I thought diamond was strongest."

"It, too, is carbon—but not living, and so evolution has not worked upon it."

She gazed down at the shimmering Earth. It, too, was a thin skin of verdant life atop a huge bulk of rocks. But far down in the magma were elements of the ancestral hordes which had come before. She felt the slide and smack of whole continents as they rode on a slippery base of limestone, layers built up from an infinitude of seashell carcasses. All living systems, in the large, were a skin wrapped around the dead.

"Time to go," Searcher said, getting up awkwardly. Even its strength was barely equal to the centrifugal thrust.

"What! You're not leaving?"

"We both are."

A loud bang. Dawn felt herself falling. She kicked out in her fright. This only served to propel her into the ceiling. She struck and painfully rebounded. Flailing, she hit another wall, and another. Her instincts kept telling herself she was falling, despite the evidence of her eyes—and then some ancient subsystem of her brain cut in, and she automatically quieted. She was not truly falling, except in a sense used by physicists. She was merely weightless, bouncing about the compartment before Searcher's amused yawn.

"What happened?" she called, grabbing a protruding handle and stopping herself.

"We are free, for a bit."

"Why?"

"See ahead."

Their vines had slipped off, retracting back to the nub. Freed, their tree shot away from the Pinwheel. They sped out on a tangent to its circle of revolution. Already the nub was a shrinking spot on the huge, curved tree that hung between air and space. She had an impression of the Pinwheel dipping its mouth into the rich swamp of Earth's air, drinking its fill alternately from one side of itself and then the other. But what kept it going, against the constant drag of those fierce winds?

She was sure it had some enormous skill to solve that problem, but there was no sign what that might be. She looked out, along the curve of Earth. Ahead was a dark-brown splotch on the star-littered blackness.

"A friend," Searcher said. "There."

They soared away from the release point with surprising speed. The Pinwheel whirled away, its grandiose gyre casting long shadows along its woody length.

She could see it better now. Despite the winds it suffered, bushes clung to its flanks. The upper end, which they had just left, now rotated down toward the coming twilight. Its midpoint was thickest and oval, following a circular orbit a third of Earth's radius above the surface. At its furthest extension, groaning and popping with the strain, the great log had reached a distance two-thirds of the Earth's radius, poking well out into the cold of space.

"We're going fast," Dawn said.

Searcher yawned. "Enough to take trees to other planets, yes."

"That's where we're—?"

"No, that is not our destination."

She knew better now than to press Searcher for its plans. When Dawn had asked for help escaping the Supras, the procyon had been following some agenda, and part of it was nondisclosure. Maybe it didn't like to give away its moves and then have them fail; everybody had pride.

Or maybe it didn't want to scare her. Or scare her off. The Pinwheel—who would sign up to ride that? Not Dawn, no. Or anybody she knew.

So far, Searcher's mysterious aims had aligned with Dawn's. Plainly something enormous was happening, and neither Supras nor Searcher would explain in bite-sized words exactly what was up. So be it.

But Dawn remembered Searcher's answer when she

had asked about other Originals. "They are gone."
Gone from Earth, maybe, but not gone as in extinct.
So there might be Originals up in the sky somewhere.
Not her Meta, but kin.

And just maybe . . . her father.

They shot ahead of the nub, watching it turn
downward with stately resolution, as though gravely
bowing to necessity by returning to the planet which
held it in bondage.

She could not take her eyes from the grandiosity of
the Pinwheel. Its lot was to be forever the mediator
between two great oceans. Others could sail the skies
in serenity, in air or in space. The Pinwheel knew
both the ceaseless tumult of the air and the biting
cold of vacuum. She wondered if many life forms had
dwelled at the border of the ancient oceans of Earth,
where waves crunched against shore. Some had to,
mediating between worlds—and must have paid the
price, beset by storm and predator.

Dawn watched silently, clinging to one of the
sticky patches on the compartment's walls. There
was a solemn majesty to the Pinwheel, a remorseless resignation to the dip of its leading arm into the
battering winds. She saw the snug pocket where they
had been moored show a flare of ivory light—plasma
conjured up by the shock of re-entry, she guessed.
Yet the great arm plunged on, momentum's captive,
for its next touchdown.

She saw why it had momentarily hung steady over
the forest; at bottom, the rotation nearly canceled the
orbital velocity. The backward sweep of the Pinwheel's
arm was opposite to the orbital velocity. That subtrac-
tion happened just as the tip reached bottom, hanging over the treetops. Craft on such a scale bespoke
enormous control, and she asked in a whisper, "Is
it . . . intelligent?"

"Of course," Searcher said. "And quite old."

"Forever moving, forever going nowhere." She noticed that she was whispering, as if it might overhear. "What thoughts, what dreams it must have."

"It is a different form of intelligence from you—neither greater nor lesser."

"Somebody planned that thing."

"Some body? Yes, the body plans—not the mind."

"Huh? No, I mean—"

"In far antiquity there were beasts designed to forage for iceteroids among the cold spaces beyond the planets—ooof! They knew enough of genecraft to modify themselves—ah! Perhaps they met other life-forms which came from other stars—I do not know—uh! I doubt that it matters. Time's hand shaped some such creatures into this—oof!—and then came the Quickening." Searcher seldom spoke so long, and it had managed this time to punctuate each sentence with a bounce from the walls. Which it enjoyed immensely.

"Creatures that gobbled ice?"

Searcher settled onto a sticky patch on the wall, held on with two legs, and fanned its remaining legs and arms into the air. "They were sent to seek such, then spiral it into the inner worlds."

"Water for Earth?"

"By that time the bots had decreed a dry planet, as I recall. The outer iceteroid halo was employed elsewhere."

"Why not use spaceships?"

"Of metal? They do not reproduce."

Dawn blinked. "These things would give birth, out there in the cold?"

"Slowly, yes."

"How'd they make the Pinwheel? It's sure not an ice-eater, I can tell that much."

"Time is deep. Circumstance has worked on it. More so than upon your kind."

"Is it smarter?"

"You humans return to that subject always. Different, not greater or lesser."

Embarrassed without quite knowing why, Dawn said, "I figured it must be smarter than me, to do all that."

"It flies like a bird, without bother. And thinks long, as befits a thing from the great slow spaces."

"How does it fly? The wind alone—" The question spoken, she saw the answer. As the other arm of Pinwheel rose to the top of its circular arc, she could make out thin plumes of white spurting behind it. She had seen Supra craft do that, leaving a line of cloud in their wake. Jets, probably of water plucked from the air.

"Consider it a large tree that flies," Searcher said.

"Huh? Trees have roots."

"Trees walk, why not fly? We are guests now inside a smaller flying tree."

"Ummm. What's it eat?"

"Some from air, some—" Searcher gestured ahead, along their trajectory. They shot above and away from the spinning, curved colossus. And Dawn saw a thin haze now hanging against the black of space, dimmer than stars but more plentiful. There was a halo around the world, like fireflies drawn to the planet's immense ripe glow. Beyond the nightline the gossamer halo hung like a wreath above Earth's shadow.

One mote grew as they sped near it. It swelled into a complex structure of struts and half-swollen balloons. It had sinews like knotty walnut. Fleshy vines webbed its intersections. Dawn tried to imagine the Pinwheel digesting this oddity and decided she would have to see it to believe.

But this minor issue faded as she peered ahead. Other trees like theirs lay fore and aft, some spinning slightly, others tumbling. But all were headed toward a thing that reminded her of a pineapple, prickly with spikes but bristling with slow-waving fur. Around this slowly revolving thing a haze of pale motes clustered.

"All that . . . alive?"

"In a way. Are bots alive?"

"No, of course—are those bots?"

"Not of metal, no. And they do mate. But even bots can make copies of themselves."

Dawn said with exasperation, "You know what I mean when something's alive."

"I am deficient in that."

"Well, if you don't know, I can't tell you." Sometimes Searcher was deliberately opaque.

"Good."

"What?"

"Talk is a trick for taking the mystery out of the world."

Dawn did not know what to say and decided to let sleeping mysteries lie. Their tree convoy was approaching the fog-glow swathing the pineapple.

Gravity imposes flat floors, straight walls, rectangular rigidities. Weightlessness allows the ample symmetries of the cylinder and sphere. In the swarm of objects, large and small, Dawn saw an expressive freedom of effortless new geometries. Necessity dictates form, she knew. Myriad spokes and limbs jutted from the many shells and rough skins, but she could not imagine their uses.

She watched an orange sphere extend a thin stalk

into a nearby array of pale green cylinders. It began to spin about the stalk. This gave it stability so that the stalk punched surely through the thin walls of its . . . its prey, Dawn realized. She wondered how the sphere spun itself up, and suspected that internal fluids had to counterrotate. But was this an attack? The array of rubbery green columns did not behave like a victim. Instead, it gathered around the sphere. Slow stems embraced and pulses worked along their crusted brown lengths. Dawn wondered if she was watching an exchange, the cylinders throbbing energetically to negotiate a biochemical transaction. Sex among the geometries?

Swiftly their flotilla of trees cut through the insect-like haze of life, passing near myriad forms that sometimes veered to avoid them. Some, though, tried to catch them. These had angular shapes, needle-nosed and surprisingly quick. But the trees still plunged on, outstripping pursuit, directly into the barnacled pineapple. She braced for an impact.

But she saw now that only parts of the huge thing were solid. Large caps at the ends looked firm enough, but the main body revealed more and more detail as they approached. Sunlight glinted from multifaceted specks. Dawn realized that these were a multitude of spindly growths projecting out from a central axis. She could see the axis buried deep in the profusion of stalks and webbing, like a bulbous brown root.

She stopped thinking of it as a pineapple and substituted "prickly pear," a plant she had seen. As they came in above the lime-green crown at one end of the "pear" a wave passed across it. The sudden flash made her blink and shield her eyes. Many facets sent the harsh sunlight back in jeweled bands of color. Her iris corrected swiftly to let her see through the glare. The wave had stopped neatly halfway across the cap,

one side still green, the other a chrome-bright sheen.
The piercing shine reminded her of how hard sunlight
was, unfiltered by air.

"It swims," Searcher said.

"Where?"

"Or better to say, it paces its cage."

"I . . ." Dawn began, then remembered Searcher's
remark about words robbing mystery. She saw that
the shiny half would reflect sunlight, giving the prickly
pear a small push from that side. As it rotated, the
wave of color-change swept around the dome, keeping
the thrust always in the same direction.

"Hold to the wall," Searcher said quickly.

"Who, what's—oh."

The spectacle had distracted her from their
approach. She had unconsciously expected the
trees to slow. Now the fibrous wealth of stalks
sticking out from the axis grew alarmingly fast.
They were headed into a clotted region of inter-
laced strands.

In the absolute clarity of space she saw smaller
and smaller features, many not attached to the prickly
pear at all, but hovering like feasting insects. She
realized only then the true scale of the complexity
they sped toward. The prickly pear was as large as
a mountain. Their tree was a matchstick plunging
headfirst into it.

The lead tree struck a broad tan web. It stretched
this membrane and then rebounded—but did not
bounce off. Instead, the huge catcher's mitt damped
the bounce into rippling waves. Then a second tree
struck near the web's edge, sending more circular
waves racing away. A third, a fourth—then it was
their turn.

Searcher said nothing. A sudden, sickening tug
reminded her of acceleration's liabilities—then reversed,

sending her stomach aflutter. The lurching lasted for long sloshing moments and then they were at rest. Out the window she could see other trees embed themselves in the web, felt their impacts make the net bob erratically.

When the tossing had damped away she said shakily, "Rough . . . landing."

"The price of passage. The Pinwheel pays its momentum debt this way," Searcher said, detaching itself from the stick-pad.

"Debt? For what?"

"For the momentum it in turn receives back, as it takes on passengers."

Dawn blinked. "People go down in the Pinwheel, too?"

"And cargo. The flow runs both ways."

"Well, sure, but—" She still could not imagine that anyone would brave the descent through the atmosphere, ending up hanging by the tail of the great space-tree as it hesitated, straining, above the ground. How did they jump off? Dawn felt herself getting overwhelmed by complexities—and quiet fear. She focused on the present. "Look, who's this momentum debt paid to?"

"Our host."

"What is this?"

"A Jonah."

"What's that mean?"

"A truly ancient term."

Dawn frowned as she felt long, slow pulses surge through the walls of their tree. "Say, what's a Jonah do?"

"It desires to swallow us."

"Swallow us?—and we want that?"

"We could return to Earth and face the things in the sky."

"Um, return on the Pinwheel? No." Her nerves were not up for that.

Creatures were already busy in the compartments. Many-legged, scarcely more than anthologies of ebony sticks and ropy muscle strung together by gray gristle, they poked and shoved the bulky cargo adroitly, forming into long processions.

Though they were quick and able, Dawn sensed that these were in a true sense not single individuals. They no more had lives of their own than did a cast-off cell marooned from her own skin.

She and Searcher followed the flow of cargo out the main port, the entrance they had used in the forest only two hours before. Swimming in zero-g was fun, though she had quick moments of disoriented panic she managed to cover. They floated out into a confusing melange of clacking spiderlike workers, oblong packages, and forking tubular passages that led away into green profusion.

Dawn was surprised at how quickly she had adjusted to the strangeness of zero gravity. Like many abilities which seemed natural once they are learned, like the complex trick of walking itself, weightlessness reflexes had been hard-wired into her kind. Had she paused a moment to reflect, this would have been yet another reminder that she could not possibly represent the planet-bound earliest humans.

But she did not reflect. She launched herself through the moist air of the great noisy, moist shafts, rebounding with eager zest from the rubbery walls. The spiders ignored her. Several jostled her in their mechanical haste to carry away what appeared to be a kind of inverted tree. Its outside was hard bark, forming a hollow, thick-walled container open at top and bottom. Inside sprouted fine gray branches, meeting at the center in large, pendulous blue fruit.

She hungrily reached for one, only to have a spider knock her away with a vicious kick. Searcher, though, lazily picked two of the fruit and the spiders back-pedaled in air to avoid it. She wondered what musk or gestures Searcher had used; the beast seemed scarcely awake, much less concerned.

They ate, ruby juice hanging in droplets in the humid air. Canyons rimmed in shimmering light beckoned in all directions. Dawn tugged on a nearby transparent tube as big as she was, through which an amber fluid gurgled. From this anchorage she could hold steady and orient herself in the confusing welter of brown spokes, green foliage, metallic-gray shafts and knobby damp protrusions.

Their tree-ship hung in the embrace of filmy leaves. From the hard vacuum of space the tree had apparently been propelled through a translucent passage. Through a membrane Dawn could see a slow pusher-plate already retracting back toward the catcher's mitt that had stopped them. Small animals scampered along knotted cables and flaking vines, chirruping, squealing, venting visible yellow farts. Everywhere was animation, purpose, hurry. Momentum.

"Come, please," Searcher said. It cast off smoothly and Dawn followed down a wide-mouthed, olive-green tube. She was surprised to find that she could see through its walls.

Sunlight filtered through an enchanted canopy. Clouds formed from mere wisps, made droplets, and eager cone-shaped emerald leaves sucked them in. She was kept busy watching the slow-motion but perpetual rhythm of this place until Searcher darted away, out of the tube. She followed hand over hand into a vast volume dominated by a hollow half-sphere of green moss. The other hemisphere, she saw, was transparent. It let in a bar of hot yellow sunlight that must have been reflected and refracted far down into the living maze around them.

Searcher headed straight for the mossy bowl and dug claws into a low plant. Dawn awkwardly bounced off the resilient moss, snatched at a spindly tree, and finally got a hold. Searcher was eating crimson bulbs that grew profusely in grape-like bunches. Dawn reached for some—and the bulbs hissed angrily as she plucked one loose. All bluster—the plant did nothing more as she bit in. She liked the rich, grainy taste.

But her irritation grew as her hunger dwindled. Searcher seemed about to go to sleep when she said, "You brought us here on purpose, didn't you?"

"Surely." Searcher lazily blinked, tongue lolling.

Angered by this display of unconcern, Dawn shouted, "I wanted to find my people!"

"They are gone."

"And you said I could find people like me if I followed you."

"So I believe."

"But—but—" Dawn wanted to express her dismay at being snatched away from everything she knew, but pride forced her to say, "Something in the sky wants to kill me, right? So to get away we go into the sky? Nonsense!"

"You are unsettled." Searcher folded its hands across its belly in a gesture that somehow conveyed contrition. "Still, we must flee as far and as fast as we can."

"Me, sure. But why you?" She jutted out her chin, thinking, *I can fend for myself*, and knew immediately that she was lying. Adolescent bravado was not going to work here.

"You would be helpless without me."

Dawn's mouth twisted, irritation and self-mockery mingling. "Guess so, up here. In the woods we'd be even."

"Perhaps. But against the entities who live in higher dimensions, we are equally powerless."

Dawn shook her head. "We pinned that one, right after we got back from the Tubeworld."

"I believe they are from the other 'brane,' as humans term it. They wish to intervene in our struggle, clearly, but have trouble manifesting here. I think they will learn quickly and we will lose whatever small advantage we had."

"Intervene why?"

"To affect the pinch-point—you."

"Because I'm Original? There may be others."

Searcher smiled. "Out here? Not with certainty. No one keeps an inventory anywhere, except the Supras of course."

"And if I don't make it to this big party somebody's planning, what happens?"

"We all die, I imagine."

Dawn blinked. "The Malign? It'll—"

"Lay waste to the system solar, and much else."

"Me? I . . . wish I . . ." She let it trail off, not knowing how to finish. She had almost said, *had my Meta.*

Searcher said nothing and Dawn realized it was being diplomatic. In truth, despite all Dawn's woodsy experience and skills, Searcher had moved through mixed terrains with an unconscious assurance and craft she envied. "Where do we go, then?"

"For now, Earth's moon."

"The . . ." She had assumed they were arcing above the Earth but would return to it along some distant trajectory. Searcher had said they weren't going to the planets, after all. She knew the Supras went to other worlds, too, but she had never heard of her own kind doing so. So— ". . . For what?"

"We must move outward and be careful."

Searcher leaned back and arranged itself, all six

muscular limbs folded in a comfortable cross-legged posture. It began to speak, softly and melodiously, of times so distant that the very names of their eras had passed away. The great heavy-pelted beast told her of how humanity had met greater intelligences in the vault of stars, and had fallen back, recoiling at the blow to its deepest pride. They had tried to create a higher mentality, and their failure was as vast as their intention.

And had made a thing that was said to be as much beyond ordinary intellects as a woman was beyond the bacteria that flourished in her gut—and the comparison was deliberate in both magnitude and status.

This strange mind, the Malign, was embodied without need of inscribing patterns on matter. And it had proved malignant beyond measure, returning at times to prey upon its creators.

Communications showed that the Malign had formulated a Theory of Everything of infinite, supple nuance.

Against it humanity had made a guard, the Multifold. Both dwelled in the depths of far space.

Searcher sighed. "There is more, but I cannot bear to say it."

"So we've got to help this Multifold against the Malign?"

"We are doomed to live in a drama created long ago."

"Why me?"

Searcher sighed. "Because the Originals know codes that the Multifold can use to unlock its own powers. To give it any chance whatever of defeating the Malign."

"I don't know any codes."

"You do not know what you know."

Dawn was subdued for most of the voyage to the moon. She had known a bit of Searcher's story, for fragments of it formed a tribal fable.

But the Malign was older now than the mountains she had roved, a gauzy myth told by the Supras. They spoke, too, of the Multifold, but that equally tenuous entity was said to be strung like a veil among the crush of stars and radiant clouds.

The moon swam green and opulent as they looped outward. Jonah's slight spin gave an obliging purchase to the outer segments of the great vessel, and Dawn ventured with Searcher through verdant labyrinths to watch their approach. They spoke little. Dawn sensed a momentum to their passage, a drama being played out beyond her understanding. And Searcher would say nothing more of this, for now.

The lunar landscape was a jagged creation of sharp mountains and colossal waterfalls. At the edge of the dusk line, valleys sank into shadows lit by reflected yellow from high peaks. Thick clouds, far higher than any on Earth because of the lesser gravity, glowed like live coals. Raw peaks cleaved the flowing cloud decks, leaving a wake like that of a giant ship. From these flashed lightning, like the blooming buds of blue roses.

These stark contrasts had been shaped by a bombardment of light elements, hauled sunward in comets. To kindle this, a rain had fallen for a thousand years in droplets the size of a human hand. Atop the lunar air sat a translucent film a few molecules thick, holding in a thick blanket of air. The film had permanent holes allowing spacecraft and spaceborne life access, the whole arrangement kept buoyant by steady replenishment from belching volcanoes. This trap offset the moon's feebler gravitational grasp so well that it lost

less of its air than did the Earth. Intact, the moon
swam like a single cell in the sun's warmth.

The fat, beckoning crescent moon hung almost
directly sunward and so was nearly drowned in shadow
until Jonah began to curve toward its far side. For
this passing moment the sun, moon and Earth were
aligned in geometric perfection, before plunging back
along their complicated courses. Dawn watched this
moment of uncanny, simple equilibrium and felt, as
she had not in a long while, the paradox that balance
and stillness lay at the heart of all change.

Her Mom had taught that, using examples as humble
as a bird's flight on rising warm winds. Dawn had
never imagined that the lesson could play out on such
immense scale, in silent majesty.

"See," Searcher said. "Storms."

Dawn looked down into the murk and whirl of the
bottled lunar air. But the disturbance lay above that
sharp division. In the blackness over both poles there
snaked slow filaments of blushing orange.

"Damn." Dawn whispered, as though the helical
strands could hear. "Is that . . . ?"

"The Malign? I suspect so."

"You've seen it before?"

"No. But whatever it is, I think it probes for us.
I had thought the Malign would forage elsewhere
first."

Searcher did not explain further. It pointed with
its ears at what seemed to Dawn to be empty space
around Earth. Searcher described how the Earth's
magnetic domain was compressed by the wind from
the sun, and streams out in the wake. Dawn blinked
her eyes up into ultraviolet and caught the delicate
shimmer of a huge volume around the planet. She
witnessed a province she had never suspected, the
realm dominated by the planet's sturdy magnetic fields.

They made a gossamer ball, crumpled in on the sun side, stretched and slimmed by the wind from the sun into a tapering tail.

Arcades of momentary fretwork grew and died in the rubbery architecture of this magnetosphere, roving violences. Suddenly she knew that these, too, were the footprints of the Malign. That had been Searcher's point. A sullen dread she had been resisting fell upon her like a black weight. "It's searching there, too."

"It relishes the bands of magnetic field," Searcher said somberly. "I hoped it would seek us only in that realm."

"But it has spread here, too."

"It is vast in a way that seems beyond description."

"Huh? How?"

"There is mathematics our sort cannot comprehend."

"Hell, there's *arithmetic* I had trouble with."

Though she chuckled, Dawn felt a cold shudder. Immense forces lumbered through these colossal spaces, and she was a woman born to pad the quiet paths of sheltered forests, to prune and plant and catch the savor of the sighing wind. These chilly reaches were not her place.

She stiffened her spine and asked, "It's able to punch through the air blanket?"

Searcher simply poked one ear at the lunar south pole. She shifted down into the infrared and saw faint plumes geyser below the hard curve of the atmosphere. Orange sparks worked there.

Dawn felt her pulse quicken. "Damn-all! It's already breached the air layer." She bit her lip and nearly lost her hold on a branch.

"And it can hunt and prey at will, once inside. It follows the lunar magnetic-field lines where it wishes."

Searcher cast off without warning, kicked against an enormous orchid, and shot down a connecting tube.

"Hey, wait!"

She caught up in an ellipsoidal vault, where an army of the clacking black spiders was assembling ranks of oval containers. In the dizzying activity she could barely keep up with Searcher. Larger animals shot by her, some big enough to swat her with a single flipper or snap her in two with a beak, moving in a blur—but all ignored her. A fever pitch resounded through the noisy mob.

Searcher had stopped, though, and was sunning itself just beneath the upper dome.

"What can we do? Ride back to Earth?"

Dawn bit her lip. "I don't want to go back to the Supras with an apology in my mouth."

"I agree." Searcher grinned. "My friend, I sense your foreboding. It is needless. Our deaths need no previews."

"Thanks for the dollop of optimism."

"Um. I had thought to catch the vessel now approaching."

She saw through the dome a smaller version of their Jonah, arcing up from one of the portal holes in the lunar air layer. Searcher had said that the Jonah was one of the indentured of its species, caged in an endless cycle between Earth and moon. The smaller Jonah dipped into the lunar air, enjoying some tiny freedom. She felt a trace of pity for such living vessels, but then she saw something which banished minor troubles. A great mass came into view, closing with them from a higher orbit.

"What's—"

"We approach a momentary mating."

"Mating? They actually . . . in flight?"

"They are always in flight.

"But . . . that thing, it's so huge."

Searcher had found some small wriggling creature. It paused to bite it in half, chewed with an assessing look, and swallowed. Dawn remembered the Semisent. Searcher tossed the rest of the carcass away and said, "It is a Leviathan. The small Jonahs are its half-grown spawn. As it swoops closest to the sun, desires well in it, as they have for ages past. We shall simply take advantage of the joy of merging."

"So we're part of a sex act?"

"An honor, yes."

As the great bulk glided effortlessly toward them she surveyed its mottled blue-green skin, the tangled jungles it held to the sun's eternal nourishing blare.

Dawn could not help but smile. "I think I prefer my lust in smaller doses."

Grand beings communicate through emissaries. Slow, ponderous oscillations began to course through the Jonah. Dawn saw a watery bubble pop into space from the Jonah's leathery skin nearby. It wobbled, seeking definition, and made itself into an ellipsoid.

"Hurry," Searcher said. "Departure."

Searcher adroitly tugged her along through green labyrinths. When they came to the flared mouth of what seemed to be a giant hollow root, it shoved her ahead. She tumbled head over heels and smacked into a spongy resilient pad. Velvet-fine hairs oozing white sap stuck to her. A sharp, meaty flavor clung in her nose. She felt light-headed and realized that the air was thick with a vapor that formed and dissolved and met again in billowing, translucent sheets. Searcher slapped away a rubbery blob as big as a man but seemed unconcerned. A shrill hissing began.

They were drifting down the bore of a narrowing

tube. The walls glowed pearly and warm and she felt the cloying sap cloaking her feet and back.

Searcher snagged a shimmering plate and launched it like an ancient discus toward her. The disk unfurled into a strand and Searcher jerked on it at the right instant so that it spun around her. The sticky stuff wrapped about her twice, whiplash fast, then twisted away. Searcher caught it on the comearound, pivoted and slapped the end against a prickly strand. Dawn was tightly bound. They gathered speed in a swirl of refracting light. Dawn held her breath, frightened by the rising hiss around them.

"What—" she began, but a soft cool ball of sap caught against her mouth when she breathed in. She blew it away and felt Searcher next to her as the wall glow ebbed. The ribbed tube ahead flexed, bulged with a hollow groan—and they shot through into the hard glare of space itself.

The Jonah had blown a rubbery bubble. A sap envelope enclosed them, quickly plumping into a perfect sphere.

"Our Jonah is making love to the Leviathan," Searcher said, holding her firmly.

"We're seeds?"

"So we have misled it, yes."

"What happens when something tries to hatch us?"

"We politely disregard the invitation."

Such graciousness seemed doubtful. They were closing with a broad speckled underbelly, the Jonah already dwindling behind. The speckles were clusters of ruby-dark froth. The Leviathan was at least ten times the size of the Jonah, giving the sex act an air of elephantine comedy. As they approached she felt fresh fear; this creature was the size of a small mountain range.

This time they donated momentum to their new host through a web of bubbles that seemed to pop and re-form as they plunged through, each impact buffeting them. Dawn bounced off the elastic walls of their own seed-sphere. Searcher seemed to absorb them and barely move.

When they came to rest a large needle expertly jabbed at their bubble. Ruby light from the walls gave a hellish, threatening cast to the approaching spiky point. The needle entered, Dawn braced herself—but the bubble did not pop. The needle snout seemed to sniff around. The point moved powerfully and was quite capable, Dawn saw, of skewering them both. She backed away from it—and Searcher raised a leg and urinated directly onto it. "No, thank you," Searcher said.

The needle jerked back and fled. Then their bubble popped, releasing them.

Again Searcher led her through a dizzy maze of verdant growths, following clues she could not see. "Where're we going?"

"To find the Captain."

"Somebody guides this?"

"Doesn't your body guide you?"

"Well, I sure thought I was in charge."

"Then please adjust your digestion so that you never fart again."

"Is that a complaint? I'll work on it. Where's this Leviathan going?"

"To the outer worlds."

"You think we're safe here for now?"

"We are safe nowhere. But here we hide in numbers."

Dawn dodged a wriggling slick-skinned teardrop that had sprouted teeth. "You figure the Malign can't be sure where I am? It tracked me pretty well so far."

"Here there are many more complex forms than you. They may smother your traces."

"What about this Talent of mine? Can't this Mind pick up my, well, my Talent-smell?"

Searcher's mouth twisted judicially. "That is possible."

Dawn had been following Searcher closely, scrambling to keep up as they bounced from rubbery walls and glided down twisted passageways, deeper into the Leviathan. Searcher's remark made her stop for a moment, gasping in the sweet, cloying air.

Dawn wanted to bellow out her frustration at the speed and confusion of events, but she knew by now that Searcher would only give her its savage, black-lipped grin. Searcher slowed and veered into crowded layers of great broad leaves. These seemed to attach to branches, but the scale was so large Dawn could not see where the gradually thickening, dark brown wood ended. Among the leaves scampered and leaped many small creatures.

She found that without her noticing any transition somehow this zone had gained a slight gravity. She fell from one leaf to another, slid down to a third, and landed on a catlike creature. It squashed like a pillow. Then with a shudder it died in her hands, provoking a pang of guilt. The cat had wings and sleek orange fur. Her heart ached at the beauty of it.

Searcher came ambling along a thin branch, saw the bird-cat, and gruffed approval. "You are learning." With a few movements of its razor-claws it had skinned the cat and plucked off gobbets of meat. Dawn bit her lip, concentrated on the dripping leaves and moved on.

The goal of finding the Captain faded as she grew hungry. Searcher snatched at tubular insects and crunched them with relish, but Dawn wasn't up to that . . . yet. It slowly dawned on Dawn that this immense inner territory was not some comfortable green lounge for passengers. It was a world, intact and with its own purposes.

Passengers were in no way special. They had to compete for advantages and food. This point came clear when they chanced upon a large ribbed beast lying partly dismembered on a branch. Searcher stopped, pensively studying the savaged hulk. Dawn saw that the fur markings, snout and wide teeth resembled Searcher's.

"Your, uh, kind?"

"We had common origins."

Dawn could not read anything resembling sadness in Searcher's face. "How many of you are there?"

"Not enough. Though the numbers mean nothing."

"You knew this one?"

Searcher gazed at the mess pensively. "Ummmm . . . yes. I mingled genetic information with it."

"Oh! I'm sorry, I . . ."

Searcher kicked at the carcass, which was now attracting a cloud of scavenger mites. "It was an enemy."

"After you, ah, 'mingled'? I mean . . ."

"Before and after."

"But then why did you—I mean, usually we don't . . ."

Searcher gave Dawn a glance which combined a fierce scowl with a tongue-lolling grin. "Whereas we never think of one thing at a time."

"Even during sex?" Dawn laughed. "Do you have children?"

"Two litters, which I bore with joy."

"Searcher! You're female? I never imagined!"

"Not female as you are."

Dawn's mind whirled around this new, fulcrum fact. Searcher had been looking after her, *like a mother*. At once came rushing in the memories of her own Mom, the warm force of her, mother and Meta. Somehow, she saw, Searcher had known this, how to make contact with Dawn at a level below conscious understanding. Otherwise, Dawn would never have gone along on this strange odyssey, no destination known. What else was going on beyond the powers of her observation?

She groped for words, "Well, uh, you're certainly not male if you bear litters."

"The choice is not always binary. Simple sex like yours was a passing adaptation."

Dawn chuckled. "Searcher, sounds like you're missing a lot of fun."

"You have no idea." Searcher grinned. "Literally."

"It'll take a while to think of you as a she."

"As it was for me with you. Humans are noted as sexual connoisseurs, and Originals especially so."

Dawn blinked. "My . . ."

"With enlarged organs as a result of evolutionary selection."

"Ummm. I'll take that as a compliment."

Out of nowhere she made another connection. "That Semisent—you were acting like a mother. Protecting me."

"I suppose there is some truth in that."

A faint scurrying distracted Dawn. She pushed aside a huge fern bough and saw a human shape moving away from them. "Hey!" she called. The prospect of company lifted her heart; the last few days had made her miss terribly the comforts of simple humanity.

The silhouette looked back and quickly turned away.

"Hey, stop! I'm friendly."

But the profile blended like liquid into the shifting greens and browns and was gone. Dawn ran after it.

After blundering along limbs and down trunks she stopped, listening, and heard nothing more than a sigh of breezes and the cooing calls of unknown birds.

Searcher had followed her. "You wished to mate?"

"Huh? No, no, we're not *always* thinking about that. Is that what you think? I just wanted to talk to him."

Searcher said, "You will find no one. And you were sure it was male."

She dipped her head in salute. "I apologize for thinking you weren't female."

"You humans do not enjoy the advantage of extra appendages beyond two, so you make binary choices."

"But who *was* that?" She swung on a limb, spun completely around it in the light gravity of this place, and laughed with the joy of it. "Say, that wasn't an illusion, was it? Like those who killed my tribe and that Rin said were just images?"

"No, that was the Captain."

Dawn felt a surge of pride. Humans ran this huge thing. "So this Captain is some other kind? Supra?"

"No. I do not think you truly wish to explore such matters. They are immaterial—"

"Look, I'm alone. If I can find any kind of human, I will."

Searcher tilted its massive head back, raising and lowering its brow ridges in a way that Dawn found vaguely unsettling. "We have other pursuits."

"If you won't help me, I'll find the Captain myself."

They worked their way upward against the slight centripetal gravity and finally stood on a broad slope made only of great leaves. Sunlight streamed fierce and golden from an open sky that framed the shrinking moon. Dawn knew that when the Earth had come alive, over five billion years ago, it had begun wrapping itself in a membrane it made of tailored air and water, for the general purpose of editing the sun.

Buried deep in Earth's forest, she had never bothered to think of other planets, but now she saw that the moon too had learned this skill from Earth. She was beginning to think of worlds as self-aware, larger entities with their own agendas. There was something fresh and vibrant about the filmed moon, and she guessed that it had not shared the long withering imposed by the Supras' bots. Where once maria had meant the dark blotches of volcanic flows, now true dappled seas lapped at rugged mountains with snow-dappled peaks. And once again, Earth's spreading voracious green could mimic its junior companion in exuberant disequilibrium.

"See there?" Searcher pointed, as if reading her thoughts.

She shielded her eyes against the sun's glare and looked that way. A barely visible circular film floated inward from Earth, glowing with refracted energy.

"It was put into place long ago, to deflect a fraction of the sun's glare from our world," Searcher said admiringly. "It solved the problem of warming for you Originals."

"Our kind made that?" She was feeling more proud of humans than ever.

"It is less thick than your skin. Of course it worked only for a while." Searcher brushed her hands together, as if dismissing such obvious measures. "Over there—" another pointed claw "—is a later solution."

Dawn made out a swiftly moving mote. She judged angles and guessed that it came arcing in from the outer depths of the solar system, for it was moving fast with its infall velocity. The tiny twinkle of tumbling light was passing close in to the leading edge of Earth, breathtakingly close but also furiously fast. Suddenly she saw the point—to tug the planet outward with this fleeting kiss, seducing it with gravity into a small step outward. To flee the sun's growing wrath.

She was even more impressed. "And it keeps working . . ."

"With the fine tuning of those we can hope to meet, later."

"People?"

"You mean humans? No, these crafters work in space itself."

"All this to make the Earth work a little longer?"

"Editing the sun is not enough." Searcher bent and pressed an ear against a purple stalk. She nibbled at the young shoots breaking through the slick bark but also seemed to be listening. Then she sat up alertly. "The Captain says that we are bound for Venus."

Ignoring how the procyon knew this, she asked, "What's that?"

"The planet next out from Earth. Second from the sun."

"Um. Can we live there?"

"I expect the question will be whether we can avoid death there."

With that Searcher fell asleep, as abruptly as ever. Dawn, wary of the tangled jungle, did not venture away. She watched the Earth and moon shrink, twin planets brimming against the timeless blaze of the galaxy.

She knew instinctively that the moon was not merely a sheltered greenhouse maintained by constant outside management. Who would tend it, after all? For long eons humankind had been locked into its desert fastnesses. No, the ripeness came from organisms endlessly adapting. To imagine otherwise—as ancient humans had—was to see the world as a game with fixed rules, like human sports, strict and static. Yet even planets had to yield to the press of suns.

She had learned much in the Library, but seeing this silent grandeur made the points far better. The sun had burned hydrogen for nearly five billion years before Earth evolved a species which could understand that simple fact, and its implications. Unlike campfires, solar furnaces blaze brighter as their ash gathers.

Earthlife had escaped this dead hand of physics . . . for a while. Long before humans emerged, a blanket of carbon dioxide had helped warm the Earth. As the sun grew hotter, though, life thinned that blanket to keep a comfortable clime.

But carbon dioxide was also the medium through which the rich energy of the sun's fusing hydrogen became transmuted into living matter. Thinning the carbon dioxide blanket threatened that essential reaction. So a jot of time after the evolution of humans—a mere hundred million years—the air had such skimpy carbon dioxide that this imperiled all the plant kingdom.

At that point the biota of Earth could have radically adjusted their chemical rhythms. Other planets had passed through this knothole before and survived. But the intelligences which thronged that era, including the forerunners of Searcher, had intervened.

Moving the Earth farther from the solar furnace would offset the steady banking of the inner fires. So came the era known as the Reworking. It led to the great maneuvers which rearranged the planets, opening them to fresh uses. All this lay buried in Sonomulia's dusty records and crossed Dawn's thoughts only as a filigree of myth.

The much-embellished stories her tribe had told around campfires taught such things through parable and grandiose yarns. Her kind were not studious in the strict sense of the term, but their forest crafts had needed an underpinning of sage myth, the "feel" of why and how biospheres were knit and fed. Some lore was even hard-wired in Dawn at the level of instinctive comprehension. She knew this, too, and was deeply grateful that she would never know which of her ideas came from those depths.

So the cloud-wreathed beauty of the twin worlds made her breath catch, her heart race with a love which was perhaps the hallmark of true intelligence. As Searcher slept she watched specks climb above the sharp-edged air of Luna to meet other dabs in a slow, grand gavotte. Another Jonah approached from Earth. Motes converged on it from eccentric orbits about the moon.

She adjusted her eyes to pick out the seeping infra-red glow that spoke of internal warmth, and saw a greater cloud, a snapshot of teeming bee-swarm wealth. Streamers swung between Earth and moon, endless transactions of species. A thinner rivulet broke away from the figure-eight orbits that linked the twins. It trickled inward and Dawn—holding a hand against the sun's glare, shutting down her infrared vision entirely—saw that it looped toward a thick swarm that clustered about the sun itself.

She felt then both awe—that reverent fear of immensity—and a hollow loneliness. She wished her clan could see this, wished that there were other minds of her cut and shape to share this spectacle.

Her attention was so riveted on the unfolding sky that she did not hear the stealthy approach of scraping paws. But she did catch the jostle as something launched itself in the weak gravity.

The shape came at her from behind. She got only a snatched instant to see it, a thing of sleek-jacketed black and flagrant reds. It was hinged like a bat at the wings and slung with ball-bearing agility in its swiveling, three-legged attack.

Claws snatched at the air where Dawn had been. She had ducked and shot sideways, rebounding from a barnacled branch. In a heartbeat she decided. Instead of fleeing into unknown leafy wilderness, where a pack of the attackers might well be waiting, she launched herself back into the silent sleek thing.

This it had not expected. It had just seen the sleeping Searcher and was trying to decide if this new development was a threat or an unexpected banquet.

Dawn hit it amidships. A leg snapped; weightlessness makes for flimsy construction. She had flicked two of her fingers into needles, usually used for the fine treatment of ailing creatures. They plunged into the flared red ears of the attacker, puncturing the enlarged eardrums which were its principal sensory organ. The creature jerked, yowled—and departed, a squawking blur of pain and anger.

Dawn landed on a wide branch, hands ready. She trembled with a mixture of eagerness and fear which a billion years of selection had still retained as fundamental to the human constitution. The foliage replied to her intent wariness with silent indifference. Silence.

Searcher awoke, stretching and yawning. "More food?"

They sighted the Supra ship their third day out. It came flaring into view from Earthside, as Dawn now thought of the aft layers of the Leviathan.

She and Searcher spent much of their time aft. They enjoyed the view of the steadily shrinking, cloud-shrouded moon as they rested among a tangle of enormous fragrant flowerpods. Searcher spotted the bright speck first. Near the moon a yellow star grew swiftly. It became a sleek, silver ship balancing on a thin torch flame.

This had just registered with Dawn when Searcher jerked her back behind an overarching stamen, whispering, "Do not move."

The slim craft darted around the Leviathan as though it were sniffing. Its nose turned and swiveled despite being glossy metal. The torch ebbed and fine jets sent it zooming beyond view along the long coarse bulk of the Leviathan.

In her mind Dawn felt a shadowy presence, like a sound just beyond recognition. A murmur of Talent-talk. The Supra ship returned, prowling close enough to the prickly growths to risk colliding with upper stems.

Searcher put both of her large, padded hands on Dawn's face. Searcher had done this before, to soothe Dawn when her anxieties refused to let her sleep. Now the pressure of those rough red palms sent a calming thread through her.

She knew what the touch implied: let her mind go blank, so her Talent would transmit as little as possible. Any Supra aboard the ship could pick up her thoughts, but only if they were focused clearly into perceptible messages. Or so Dawn hoped. After all, she knew little of this.

The ship held absolutely still for a long while, as if deciding whether to venture inside. The cloud of spaceborne life that surrounded the Leviathan had drawn away from the ship, perhaps fearing its rockets. Its exact cylindrical symmetries and severe gleam seemed strange and malevolent among the drifting swarms—hard and enclosed, giving nothing away. Suddenly the yellow blowtorch ignited again, sending the life-forms skittering in all directions. The ship vanished in moments, heading out from the sun.

"They must've guessed I was running this way," Dawn said.

Searcher took her paws away. "They try every fleeting possibility."

Searcher still seemed concerned, though Dawn was seldom sure what meanings attached to her quick frowns, fur-ripplings and teeth displays. "I felt something . . ."

"They sought your thought-smell."

"Didn't know I had one."

"It is distinctive."

"You can smell it?"

"In your species many memories are lodged near the brain's receptors for smell. Scents then evoke memories. Remember where you were as a child and first caught the wonderful bouquet of approaching rain?"

"Oh, yes. I was under a tree—"

"I do not share this property, but I've heard of it."

"That's sad. So?" Sometimes Searcher's roundabout manner irked her. She was not sure whether the procyon was suggesting much by saying little, or simply amusing herself. Maybe both.

"A Supra can remember the savor of your thinking. This act of recollection calls up your Talent, makes it stronger."

"Just by remembering, they make me transmit better?"

"Something like that."

Dawn could not match this idea with the odd, scratchy presence she had felt. "Well, they're gone now."

"They may return."

"You've got the Talent, don't you?"

Searcher grinned. "If you cannot tell, then I suppose I do not."

"Well, yeah, I sure can't pick up anything from you. But—"

"Let us move away from here. The ship could try again."

They left the flower zone where they had foraged for a day, supping on thick nectar. Dawn did not register a transition but somehow they came into a region with little centripetal gravity. This place did not have as simple an inner geometry as the Jonah's. Internal portions of Leviathan spun on unseen axes, and streams flowed along sloping hillsides that seemed to the eye uphill. The local gravity was never more than a subtle touch, but it gave shape and order to the rampant vegetation.

They came into a vast chamber with teeming platforms, passageways, tunnels, balustrades, antechambers, all thronged with small animals moving on intent paths. It was a central station for a system of tubes that seemed to sprout everywhere, even high up the walls. The moist air above was crisscrossed by great shafts of filtered sunlight rising from sources near the floor, up to a distant arched ceiling.

She could see no obvious biological point to this, nor to the transparent membrane brimmed with a view of the starscape outside. In the middle, the galactic center glowed brilliantly. The sun had migrated inward from its original orbit, due to swing-bys with other suns. Dawn knew this from far history, but could not imagine how it was done, or why.

Yet all the moist, busy grandeur of this place did not intimidate her; it was even inviting. The scurrying animals were intelligent, in their way, going about swift tasks without giving her more than a glance. Humans were apparently uninteresting, maybe not even unusual. She doubted that many Supras used Leviathans to journey, given their swift ships.

She did not dwell on the Supra pursuit. As the momentum of events carried her farther from her lands she had resolved to plunge forward rather than endlessly fret. Perhaps she could find Ur-humans somewhere out here, as Searcher had said.

It had taken a few restless nights to truly feel this, but now it held firm in her. She remembered the bright-eyed girl who had breathlessly sought the company of Supras, especially the men. That girl seemed very far away now. Yet she lay fewer than ten megaseconds in the past, her inboards told her.

Her hunting skills reawakened as she followed Searcher in her foraging, unhurried but quick. They trekked through the light gravity of this inner vault, eating berries that swung from palmy trees. These were not mere passive trees, though; the berries were a lure. The sharp fronds could slice off an arm. Searcher showed her how to confuse the tree's ropy reflexes long enough to snatch a handful of berries.

There were even lakes. They hiked for two days along a broad beach, Searcher catching the yellow fish that thronged the shore. Through clouds Dawn could see the lake curling over their heads, far away, describing the vast curve of a rotating cylinder.

"Why do we keep moving so much?" Dawn asked when Searcher marched on resolutely, despite gathering gloom. Blades of sunlight ebbed and flowed in the huge cylindrical vault like tides of light.

"We hide among life. Life moves."

"You figure the Supras're still looking for me?"

"They have gone. They continue outward."

"Great. Let's go back to Leviathan's skin, then. I liked the view."

Actually she wanted to search for the Captain. She

had glimpsed humans near the transparent blisters and each time they had seemed to evaporate into the humid jungle before she could pursue.

Searcher did not comment on her desire to find humans and would not help track them, though she suspected the procyon could sense the smallest animals which swung or padded through the layers of green. For three days they worked their way along the lake, stopping only to swim and, when the wind rose, to body surf. This zone of Leviathan was spinning, driving curious spiral waves in the lake that worked up and down the shore.

Two more days, by Dawn's inner clock, brought them to the skin. Again Dawn could not sense when they left the region of spin-gravity. Fogs had hampered their way, blowing into the Leviathan's recesses. They blew through wide shafts that admitted to the interior great blades of reflected sunlight.

Searcher taught her a favorite game. They perched in one of the translucent bubbles in Leviathan's outer reaches, waiting. In the utter vacuum outside, a mere finger's width away, strange forms glided and worked. Shelled silvery things like abalone attached themselves to Leviathan's skin. From there, a steady perch, they could snag wandering prey.

But sometimes they mistakenly triggered a Leviathan reflex. In a convulsive gulp, the slick skin double-folded inward. Abruptly the predator became prey, in a gassy world it had never known. Disoriented, it would flail about.

When one slipped inside, Searcher would snatch it, crack it open between her hard-soled feet, and gulp the shell's inhabitant with lip-smacking relish.

"Yes!" Searcher cried. Dawn applauded and turned down any offered tidbits.

Long, black creatures crawled over Leviathan,

grazing on the photosynthetic mats that grew everywhere. Dawn could see these dark algae mottling the
carbuncled skin, occasionally puffing out spores. The
grazers slurped up the brown sun-worshipping goo of
mat-life and moved on, the cattle of the skies.

Searcher tried to entice one close to the translucent
layer, whirling and grimacing to attract its attention.
The vacuum cow turned its slitted dark eyes toward
this display. Bovine curiosity brought it closer.

Searcher grabbed for it, stretching the tough, waxy
wall with her paw-hands and feet. Grunting, she managed to hang on to the grazer through the thin skin.
Searcher was strong enough to pluck the struggling
cow inward against the atmospheric pressure pushing
the envelope out. For a moment Dawn thought the
growling Searcher would manage to drag the grazer
far enough in, despite all logic, to trigger the folding instability and pluck it through. Smelling victory,
Searcher yelped with tenor joy. But then the vacuum
cow spurted steam, wriggled and jetted away.

Searcher gnashed her teeth. "Devilish things."

"Yeah, looked appetizing."

"They are a great delicacy. I have been trying to
taste one for a very long time."

"Pretty resistant, though. How long?"

"Three centuries."

It took a while for Searcher to stop laughing at
the expression on Dawn's face. Before Dawn could
recover she glanced to the side—and was startled to
find standing there a human form. But only a form,
for this was like nothing she had ever seen.

The face worked with expression—frowns and smiles
and wild flaring eyes, all fidgeting and dissolving. The
thing seemed demented. Then she saw that she had
been imposing her own need to find a facial expression, to impose order. In fact the skittering storms

rippled and fought all through the body. Colors and shapes were but passing approximations.

The form took a tentative step toward Dawn. She bit her lip. Could not breathe.

The body jiggled and warped like a bad image projected on a wobbly screen. But this was no illusion. Its lumpy foot brushed aside a stem as it took another step. The fidgeting skin seemed like a mulatto wash that blurred and shifted as the body moved.

She realized that she could see through the thing. Plants behind it appeared as flickering images. She heard a slight thrumming as it raised an arm with one unnaturally smooth motion—a swoop, not the hinged pull of muscles at the pivots of shoulder and elbow.

"Aurronugh," it said, a sound like stones rattling in a jug.

Dawn still could not breathe. She was frozen.

"It is imitating you, as it did before," Searcher said.

A gasp. "What—what is it?"

"You wanted to meet it. The Captain."

"But—it's—"

"Not all of the Captain, of course."

"What does he—does it—want?"

"I do not know. Often it manifests itself in the form of a new passenger, as a kind of politeness. To learn something it cannot otherwise know."

The shape said, "Yooou waaanteed by maaaany."

Dawn took a deep breath and made herself say, "Yes. Many want to find me."

"Yooou musssst lee—vah."

"I, I can't leave. And why should I?"

"Daaaanger. To meeee."

"You? What are you?"

The shape stretched its arms up to encompass all the surrounding growth. Its arms ended in stumps,

though momentarily a stubby finger or two would
sprout at the ends, flutter, and then ease back into
the constant flow of the body.

"Everything? You're everything?" Dawn asked.

"Wooorld."

Searcher said, "It is the Leviathan. Composite
intelligence. This directs its many parts and lesser
minds."

Dawn gaped. "Every part of it adds to its intelligence?"

"Rin thought the phylum Myriasoma was extinct,"
Searcher said. "He would be happy to see that he
was wrong yet again."

Dawn smiled despite her tingling fear. "Supras don't
like news like that."

As she watched, the Captain's legs dissolved into
a swarm of bits. Each was the size of a thumb and
swam in the air with stubby wings. The Captain
was an assembly that moved incessantly, each flyer
brushing the other but capable of flitting away at any
moment. The individual members looked like a bizarre
mixture of bird and insect. Each had four eyes, two
on opposite sides of their cylindrical bodies and one
each at top and bottom. Hovering. Each thinking, in
its own tiny way.

Dawn heard the Captain then in her mind. The
thrumming whisper of wings she had heard was echoed
by a soft flurry of thoughts in her mind.

You are a danger to me.

"You? The ship?"

I am The World.

And so it must seem to this thing, she realized. It
governed the entwined complexity of the Leviathan
and at some level must *be* the Leviathan, its dispersed
mind instead of merely its brain. Yet each moment
a flying thumb shot away on some buzzing mission

and others flew in, to merge with the standing, rippling cloud.

Beneath its clear message she felt the darting of quicksilver thought. She sensed this as a thrumming echo of the infinitude of transactions the Leviathan must make to keep so vast an enterprise going. It was as though she could listen to the individual negotiations between her own blood cells and the walls of her veins, the acids of her stomach, the sour biles of her liver.

Dawn thought precisely, slowly, *How can you be self-aware? You change all the time.*

The shape let its right arm fall off, scattering into fluttering clumps that then departed on new tasks. *I do not need to feel myself intact, as you do.*

"So how do I know who's talking?" Dawn countered aloud.

The Captain answered, *I speak for the moment. A little while later I shall speak for that time. Only the I will change, not the me.*

Dawn glanced at Searcher, who watched with bemused interest. Maybe in three centuries it all got dated. She thought, *Will that be the same you?*

How could you tell? Or I? I always find that your kind of intelligence is obsessed with knowing what you are.

Dawn smiled. *Seems a reasonable question.*

The thing shook. *Not reasonable. Reason cannot tell you deep things.*

What can, then?

Those come through the body. Always the body.

Dawn watched as the shape gradually, with pops and sighs and slow moans, decomposed into an oblong cloud of the thumb-things. It had made its polite gesture and now relaxed into a wobbly sphere, perhaps to bring its individual elements closer while lowering its surface area.

Are you afraid of me? she asked impishly.

My parts know fear. Hunger and desire, as well. They are a species, like you. I am another kind of being, able to elude attack by dispersing. I do not know fear for myself but I do know caution. I cannot die but I can be hurt.

Dawn thought of the honeybees she had tended in the forest—satisfying, sweaty labor that now seemed to have happened a very long time ago. Bees had fewer than ten thousand neurons, she knew, yet did complex tasks. How much more intelligent would be a single arm of this cloud-Captain, when its thumb-things united to merge their minds?

Not hurt by anybody like me, I assume?

The swarm churned. *Yes. I am not vulnerable to destruction of special parts, as are you. Merely by taking away your head, for example, I could leach life from you, rob you of all you know. But each part of me contains some of my intelligence and feels what a part of the world feels.*

Dawn felt suddenly the strangeness of this thing. Hanging before her, bulging and working with sluggish energy, its misshapen head turned at impossible angles as it seemed to ponder the Leviathan's intricacies. Another phylum? No, something more—another kingdom of life, a development beyond beings like her, forever separated into inevitable loneliness.

In a way she envied it. Each thumb-flyer knew the press of competition, of hunger and longing, but the composite could rise above that raw turbulence, into realms she could not even guess. She glanced at Searcher again and saw that her expression was not truly of indifference, but of reverence.

Searcher had not wanted her to seek the Captain because it was, even for Searcher, a holy being. Beyond even three centuries of learning.

I speak to you now because the world cannot tolerate you, the Captain sent.

"How come you ran away before?" Dawn asked.

I needed time to speak to my brothers.

Other Leviathans? As she framed the thought the Captain's answer came lightning-fast: *Other worlds.*

Is there something beyond Leviathans? Something—Dawn had never literally had a thought interrupted in her own mind. Running right over her own sentence-forming, the Captain imposed, *I now grasp many recent events. Your connection with them. There is an entity called the Malign and it reaches for you.*

I know.

Then know this—

In a flooded single moment a torrent of sensations, ideas and conclusions forked through her. She had for an instant the waterfall perception of what the mind before her was truly like. The layers of its logic were translucent, like a building of softly lit glass. Every fact shone up through floors of stacked detail, breaking through to illuminate the denser lattice-lacing of concepts on a higher level. And that piercing light in turn refracted through the web of mind, shedding its fitful glow on assumptions lying buried in a shadowy web beneath.

She staggered with the impact, trying to wrench away.

A realization came, a thin reed tossing on the crackling surge that swamped her. She sagged with the weight of what the Captain had given her, stunned. She was dimly conscious of Searcher leaping forward to cradle her. Then the air clouded with ebony striations and she felt herself dwindling, falling beneath a towering, dark weight.

❖   ❖   ❖

"You can speak?" Searcher asked, her tilted chin and rippling amber fur patterns showing concern.

"I, I think so." Dawn had slept for many hours, awakening with only a groggy sense of herself. When she revived, Searcher had brought her a banquet of berries and fruits and thick, meaty leaves like slices of spongy bread. Now she tried to explain what she had sensed in the brief collision of minds. The Captain sent information faster and at greater depth than Dawn could handle.

"It was . . . thought without any human filter."

"Um. I get that all the time."

"No, I meant *really* strange, not like you."

Searcher grinned. "You truly have no idea, my dear human."

"No, I mean, it was—like being licked with a rasping wet tongue that *wouldn't quit!*" Her voice had gotten away from her at the end, letting out the brittle, heart-stopping fear she had felt.

Searcher looked unimpressed. "Humans are not good at diving into the pools of others' minds."

"Especially Originals?"

"I was not going to mention . . ."

"Okay, and I'm not an Original anyway, right?" She held up her fingers and extruded two bony tools. "These don't look like anything that got worked out on the plains of Afrik."

"These fingers are tekky, not evolved. I'll bet the Captain's a product of engineering, too."

This even little children learned. That rapid selection pressure operated on what already existed. It added capability to minds rather than snipping away parts which worked imperfectly. The human brain was always retrofitted, and showed its origins in its cumbersome, layered workings. The Captain had arisen from some engineering she could not imagine.

Searcher shrugged. "Perhaps the Supras know."

"They know so much, let them fight the Malign. I want out of it."

"There is no way out."

"Well, moving further from the sun sure doesn't seem so smart. That's where the Malign is accumulating itself."

Searcher studied the stars, bright holes punched in the pervading night. "Your Talent made you too easy to find on Earth. Here you blend into the many mind-voices."

"I can hear one voice in my head," Dawn said suddenly. "Supras. They're alongside."

The Supras boarded the Leviathan after protracted negotiation. The Captain appeared before Searcher and Dawn, humming and darting madly, alarmed for some reason Dawn could not understand. She had to reassure the Captain three times that she was indeed the primitive human form the Supras sought.

Only then did the Captain let the Supras board. It was some time before one Dawn had known before, a tall man called Rin appeared alone, thrashing his way through the luxuriant greenery. He was tired and disheveled, his usually immaculate one-piece suit stained and dirty.

Rin waved his hand dismissively. "We must talk."

"You've been after me?" Dawn asked.

Rin said to Searcher, "You promised you would help keep her safe."

Searcher yawned. "I did."

"But you did *not* have permission to take her away from us. And certainly not to escape into the system solar."

Dawn had expected anger, not this air of precise displeasure. Both he and Searcher glanced at her, as if she was the most likely to explode. Not so, she realized suddenly. She was not surprised that Searcher had struck some kind of deal with them back on Earth. Their escape had gone far better than it should have.

Searcher said, "I did not need permission."

"I should think—"

"After all, who could give it?" Searcher asked lazily.

"She is of our kind. That gives us species rights."

"You are Homo Technologicus. She is Ur-human, several species removed from you."

Rin pursed his lips. "Still, we are more nearly related than you."

"Are you so sure?" Searcher grinned devilishly. "I span the genetic heritage of many earlier forms."

"I am quite confident that if I read your helix I could easily find many more differences in—"

"Listen, you two," Dawn broke in. "I wanted to get away—Searcher was just along for company."

Rin blinked, looked at her for a long moment and then said calmly, "At least you are safe and have made the journey to where we need you."

"You intended to bring me here yourself?" Dawn asked.

Rin's mouth played with amused shapes. "Yes, in a ship. Comfortably."

Dawn's temper flared despite her efforts to maintain the easy calm of a Supra. "What? I could have zipped out here in a ship?"

"Well, yes." Rin seemed surprised at her question.

She whirled to confront Searcher. "You made me go through all this?"

Searcher worked her mouth awkwardly. "I perceived that as the correct course."

"My God! It was damned dangerous. And you didn't even consult me!"

"You did not know enough to judge," Searcher said uncertainly.

"I'll decide that!"

Searcher backed away. "Perhaps I erred."

"*Perhaps?* You—"

"Do not be hasty," Rin said mildly. "This animal is clever, and in this case it showed foresight. It was lucky for you that I did not convey you outward by our planned route. We thought it intact. Yet several craft carrying needed Ur-human passengers were destroyed after leaving Earth, and you could well have been among them."

"What?" Dawn's flare of anger guttered out. "My people?" Dawn was so excited she lost her grip on a vine and had to catch herself.

"Not exactly. We grew them from your helix."

"You mean they're—they're me?"

"Some, yes. Others we varied slightly, to get the proper mix of abilities. We shall use them, like amplifiers—of you."

Dawn shook her head, trying to clear it. "I can't possibly amount to much in all this."

"So I would have said as well, once." Rin had settled on a branch and even in the low spin-gravity the lines in his face sagged. "But you do matter. You Ur-humans had a hand, along with more advanced human forms and alien races, in contributing to both these entities."

"Us? Originals? Impossible."

Rin looked rueful. "I admit it seems extremely unlikely. Yet the deep records of the Library are clear, if read closely."

"Well, even if we helped make the Multifold, what's that matter now? I don't know anything about it."

Rin looked at Searcher, but the big creature seemed unconcerned. Dawn got the feeling that all this was running more or less as Searcher expected, and she was never one to trouble herself with assisting the inevitable.

Rin spread his hands. "Deep in the Multifold lies a set of assumptions, of worldview. They depend on the kinesthetic senses of Ur-humans, upon your perceptual space."

Dawn bit into a piece of ruby fruit. "Um. What's that?"

Rin looked at her solemnly. "What matters is that we cannot duplicate such things."

"Come *on*," Dawn said. "I know I'm dumber than anyone here, but that doesn't mean you can—"

Rin said, "We find communicating with the Multifold exceedingly difficult. We have struggled for centuries to no avail."

"Centuries?" So this was not a new problem, Dawn realized. "I thought you people could do anything."

"We cannot transcend our worldview, any more than you can."

"Look," Dawn said, "how do you talk to the Multifold?"

"Badly. To reach it we must step through the thicket of the Ur-human mind-set."

"Thicket?" Dawn asked.

Rin shifted uncomfortably. "A swamp is perhaps a better term. A morass ingrained in the Multifold's being."

"It has some of us, dirty old Originals, in it?" Dawn laughed and felt a spurt of elation. This was at least some mark her kind had left in the great ruined architecture of time.

"Look, I have to think about all this." Dawn reverted to speech in self-defense.

Rin said, "There is no time for the kind of thinking you do. The moment is upon us."

Dawn turned to Searcher. "What should I do?"

Searcher held up a cautionary paw. "It is true, as the Supras say, that your innate abilities are much needed."

"No, I didn't mean help with their fight. I want you to—well, tell them they're *wrong*. That they're treating my people like, like animals."

"I am an animal. They do not treat me as you."

"You're not an animal!"

"I am not remotely human."

"But you're, you're . . ."

Searcher gave her a wolfish grin. "I am like you when I need to be. But that is to accomplish an end."

"What end?" Dawn asked, her confusion deepening.

"To bring you here at this time. You are essential to the struggle. And eventually to unite you with Ur-humans, as I promised—eventually." She glanced at Rin. "I knew the Supras would probably fail to do so."

Across Rin's face flitted an expression Dawn could not read, but the nearest equivalent was a mixture of irritation and surprised respect.

Rin said warily to Searcher, "It would have been simple to bring you here, had the Malign not managed to learn how to enter our ships. And you could not have known it would understand that so quickly, correct? Much less that it could find the Ur-humans among all the ships we have."

"I could not?" Searcher grinned. "You presume much." Searcher turned to Dawn. "We must all fight now. That is what I have not told you—that none of us truly had any choice."

❖   ❖   ❖

Dawn laughed, but at the back of her mind a growing tenor cry demanded attention. "Say, something's . . ."

Searcher nodded. "Yes."

She felt the Supras now in many cascading voices. They formed tight links, some in their ships, some in this Leviathan, others dispersed among Jonahs and Leviathans and the churning life-mats of the Jove system. A long, soaring chorus. Yet anxious, trembling.

They all sensed it. Something coming.

"How quickly does it approach?" Rin asked urgently. The earlier mood was broken, his doubts momentarily dispelled. Now he was all cool efficiency.

"I can't tell." Dawn frowned. "There are refractions . . . Is it possible that the Malign can move even faster than light?"

"That is but one of its achievements," Rin said, concern creasing his forehead. "We humans attained that long ago, but only for small volumes in warped geometries—for tunnels, for ships. The Malign was limited, as are the magnetic beings."

"But it broke out . . . using what?" Dawn pressed. "Its Final Theory?"

Rin nodded. "Somehow, yes. Until then, a single great fact—that the speed of light was a true limit—ordained that the linking of the natural magnetic minds proceeded slowly, all across the galaxy. Nothing large can move faster than light. Or so we thought. The Malign found a way. Somehow."

"That's how the Malign finally got out of the galactic center, isn't it?" Dawn asked. She caught thin shouts of alarm in her mind.

"It used the quantum vacuum," Rin said. His cheeks hollowed again with a cast of relief. He found it comforting, Dawn guessed, to be secure in his knowledge.

Rin leaned forward, his eyes soft as he peered into the dying firelight. "On average, empty space has zero energy. But by enclosing a volume with a sphere of conducting plasma, the Malign prevented the creation of waves with wavelengths larger than that volume. These missing waves gave the vacuum a net negative energy, and allowed formation of a wormhole in space-time. All such processes are ruled by probabilities requiring great calculation. Yet through that hole the Malign slithered."

"To our solar system," Dawn concluded.

"Never before has a magnetic mind done this," Rin said. "It escaped from the prison of time—a feat on such a scale that even the Singular did not anticipate."

Searcher whispered, "Coincidence, Rin?" This was the first time Dawn had ever heard Searcher use the name. There was a tinge of pity in the beast's voice, or what she took for that.

Rin's head jerked up. He flicked a suspicious glance at Searcher. "The thought occurred to us, too. Why should the Malign emerge now?"

"Just as you're getting free of Earth again?" Dawn asked.

"Exactly," Rin said. "So we studied all the physical evidence. Observed the path of damage the Malign has wrecked as it left the galactic center." He hesitated. "And made a guess."

Searcher said, "You found something and your discovery had unforseen effects."

Rin's eyes shifted away from the waning fire, as though he sought refuge in the gloom surrounding them. "So you guessed. Yes, I found the Multifold."

Dawn whispered, "And . . . ?"

Rin's voice came to them in the twilight glow as a slow, solemn dirge. "The exuberance of the Multifold was so great at being discovered! That sent enormous magnetosonic twists echoing through the whorls of an entire galactic arm. These reached the Malign in its cage. To see ancient foes reuniting again sent it into a rage, a malevolence so strong that it exerted itself supremely. And forced its exit."

They sat silently for a long moment. Dawn looked up and out, in search of some consolation. The inky recesses of the Leviathan were unrelieved by the distant promise of stars.

Rin said hollowly, "If I hadn't been so curious. Hadn't searched the Library's records, the plots of magnetic fields throughout the galaxy. Hadn't sent the signals . . ."

Dawn said finally, "You didn't know. Curiousity is built into us humans. And all the lore of the Library of Life did not warn you."

He smiled mirthlessly. "But I did it. All the same."

Dawn said, "That Singular of yours might have troubled their mighty selves to make a jail that held."

Rin shook his head. "There is none better in this space-time."

"Well, damn it, at least they shouldn't have just left it as a problem to be solved by us."

Searcher lifted her sniffing snout, seeming to listen to something far away. She said, "Shoulds and mights are of no consequence. The problem has arrived."

Dawn felt a light, keening note sound through her thoughts. She blinked. It was a hunting call, she knew immediately—a flavor that eons had not erased, as though from some quick bird swooping down through velvet air, eyes intent on scampering prey below.

She glanced back at the smoldering glow of the galactic center. Against it were black shapes, angular and swift, growing. Not metal, like Supra ships, but green and brown and gray. "Call the Captain!"

"I have," Searcher said.

As Dawn watched the approaching sleek creatures she saw that they were larger than the usual space-borne life she had known. It was far too late to avoid them, even if Leviathan could have readily turned its great bulk.

Skysharks, Dawn thought, the word leaping up from her buried inboard vocabulary. The term fit, though she did not know its origin. They were elegantly molded for speed, with jets for venting gases. Solar sails gave added thrust, but the lead skyshark had reeled in its sails as it approached, retracting the silvery sheets into pouches in its side. Cupped parabolas fore and aft showed that it had evolved radar senses. These, too, collapsed moments before contact, saving themselves from the fray.

Dawn gasped as they dove straight in. The first of them came lancing into the Leviathan without attempting to brake. It slammed into the skin aft of the blister that held Searcher and Dawn. They could see it gouge a great hole in the puckered hide.

Shrieks came through the foliage. Dawn's ears popped. Outside, the sleek skysharks banked and fought small defenders. A great head bit deep into a small opponent. Muscular, powerful jaws worked. Throats swallowed. Dawn watched the first few plow headlong into the mottled hide of the Leviathan and wondered why they would risk such damage merely for food. But then her ears popped again and a *whoosh* rushed through the air.

"They're breaking the seals!"

"Yes," Searcher said calmly, "such is their strategy."

"But they'll kill everything aboard."

"Not all, no. They penetrate inward a few layers. This lets the outrushing air bring to them the smaller animals."

Dawn watched a skyshark back away from the jagged wound it had made. A wind blew the backdrop of stars around, the only evidence of escaping air. Then flecks and motes came from the wound, a geyser of helpless wriggling prey. The skyshark caught each with its quick, wide mouth, seeming to inhale them.

Dawn had to remind herself that these gliding shapes with their cool, soundless, artful movements were actually carrying out a savage attack, remorseless and efficient. Weightless vacuum gave even death a quality of silent grace. Yet the beauty of threat shone through, a quality shared alike by the grizzly, falcon and rattler. Her ears popped again. "If we lose all our air—"

"We should not," Searcher said, though plainly she was worried, her coat running with swarthy spirals. "Membranes close to limit the loss."

"Good," Dawn said uncertainly. But as she spoke a wind rose, sucking dry leaves into a cyclone about them.

"That should not happen," Searcher said stiffly. "Look."

Outside two skysharks were wriggling into older gouges. Waves rippled along their sleek torsos. Air had ceased to stream from them, so the beasts could enter easily. Others withdrew from the rents they had torn after only a few vicious bites. They jetted along the broad sweep of skin, seeking other weak points. In their tails were nozzled and gimbaled chambers. She saw a bright flame pucker and flare. Her inboards told her this was hydrogen peroxide and catalase, combining in shaped rear chambers. Puffs and streamers pushed the muscular bodies adroitly along the rumpled brown hide. It was a mad harvest. From the gaping gashes where skysharks had entered came fresh puffs of air. Some carried animals tumbling in the thinning gale, and skysharks snapped these up eagerly.

"The sharks that went inside—they must be tearing up those membranes," Dawn shouted against the rising shriek. "Sucks out the protected areas."

Searcher braced herself against the gathering winds. "A modified tactic. Even if those inside perish, their fellows benefit from the added game. Good for the species overall, despite the sacrifice of a few."

"Not much consolation." Already it was getting harder to suck in a breath.

"I am becoming concerned, yes."

Searcher's calm exasperated. "Yeah, but what'll we *do*?"

"Come."

Searcher launched herself away, paws spread wide. Dawn followed. The air was alive with crosscurrents that plucked at her. Between bounces off trunks and bowers, Searcher curled up into a ball to minimize the pull of the howling gale. Dawn copied this, narrowing her eyes against the rain of leaves and bark and twigs that raked her.

Searcher led her along a zigzag path. They bounced from bower to vine, just beneath the Leviathan's skin. Over the whirling winds she heard the yelps and cries of animals. Nearby a yowling catlike creature lost its grip on a tubular root and pinwheeled away. A triangular mat with legs caromed off Searcher and ricocheted from Dawn, spitting, before whirling into the madhouse mist.

They came twirling toward a system that looked like a blue-green heart, with veins and arteries stretching away in all directions. Fluids gushed here, fraying away into the thinning air. The wind moaned and gathered itself here with a promise of worse to come. The open wounds behind them were probably tearing further, she guessed, evacuating more and more of the Leviathan. For the first time it occurred to Dawn that even this colossal creature could perhaps die, its fluids and air bled into space.

She hurried after Searcher. A gray cloud streamed by them, shredding, headed toward the sighing breezes. Dawn recognized them—a flight of the thumb-sized flyers that had made up the Captain, now streaming to defend its ship. There might even be more than one Captain, she realized, or an entire crew of the anthology-beings. Or perhaps the distinction of individual entities was meaningless.

Ahead was a zone of gauzy, translucent surfaces lit by phosphorescent streaks. Searcher grabbed a sheet of the waxy stuff, sinking in her claws. The flapping sheet seemed to be a great membrane for catching pollen. Even in the chaos of drifting debris Dawn could see that this was part of an enormous plant. They were at the tip of a great pistil. Searcher was wrenching off a slab of its sticky walls, clawing energetically. Above this was a broad transparent dome which brought sunlight streaming into the leathery bud of the plant. Its inner bulb had mirrored surfaces that reflected the intense sunlight into bright blades, sending illumination deep into the inner recesses of the Leviathan.

She took this in at a glance. Then Searcher yanked her into position on the bulb wall, where her feet caught in sticky goo. The wind lashed at her, but the goo held. Searcher barked orders and Dawn followed them. They fashioned the tough sheet into a pyramidal shape. Searcher stuck the edges together with the wall adhesive. She turned down the last side, leaving them inside the pyramid.

Dawn got her bearings. They were drifting toward

the transparent ceiling, moving on an eddy of the shrieking, building winds. Their pyramid smacked against the outer skin of the Leviathan.

Searcher crouched at an apex of the pyramid. She touched the ceiling and quickly twisted the wall. "Here—help—"

Dawn grabbed a waxy fold and torqued it opposite to Searcher. The Leviathan's hide puckered and parted—and *pop!*—they passed through, into naked space. The pyramid drifted in the slight breeze of escaping gas from the pucker, which was closing like a quick smile behind them.

"We're out!" Dawn cried, delighted.

"This will last for only a while," Searcher said.

"Till we run out of air?" Dawn said.

"If that long."

The advantage of living construction material was that it grew together, if encouraged by an adhesive, becoming tighter than any manufactured seal. One side of their pyramid was so thin Dawn could see out through it, yet the film held pressure. Nature loved the smooth and seamless. She and Searcher helped it along with spit—Searcher had a lot of faith in her own fluids—and some muscle work. Soon their pyramid held firm and snug.

They drifted away from Leviathan. Dawn hoped the skysharks would ignore them, and indeed the predators were nuzzling greedily at the raw wounds amidships. Around Leviathan swam debris. Into this cloud came spaceborne life of every description. Some were smaller predators who scavenged on whatever the skysharks left. Others spread great gossamer sheets, eager to catch the air that poured forth from the Leviathan's wounds. Small creatures billowed into great gas bags, fat with rare wealth. Limpets crawled eagerly along the crusty hide toward the rents. When they arrived they caught streamers of fluid that spouted irregularly into the vacuum.

This was a riotous harvest for some. Dawn could see joy in the excited darting of thin-shelled beetles who snatched at the tumbling fragments of once-glorious ferns. The wounds created fountains from the Leviathan skin. These geysers shot motley clouds of plant and animal life into a gathering crowd of eager consumers, their appetites quickened by the bounty of gushing air.

"Hope they don't fancy our taste," Dawn said.

Her mouth was dry and she had long since passed the point of fear. Now she simply watched. Gargantuan forces had a way of rendering her pensive, reflective. This trait had been more effective in the survival of Ur-humans, she had long suspected, than outright aggression or conspicuous gallantry. It did not fail her now. Visible fear would have attracted attention. They drifted among the myriad spaceborne forms, perhaps too strange a vessel to encourage ready attack; even hungry predators wisely select food they know.

"Do you think they will kill Leviathan?" Dawn asked.

"Mountains do not fear ants," Searcher answered.

"But they're gutting it!"

"They cannot persist for long inside the mountain. For the spaceborne, air in plenty is a quick poison."

"Oxygen?"

"It kindles the fires that animate us. Too much, and—"

Searcher pointed. Now curls of smoke trickled from the ragged wounds. The puffs of air had thinned but they carried black streamers.

"The skysharks can forage inside until the air makes

their innards burn." Searcher watched the spectacle with scholarly interest, blinking owlishly.

"The sharks die, so that others can eat the Leviathan?"

"Apparently. Though I suspect this behavior has other purposes, as well. The Malign has sent this little gesture, somehow—a feeler before the main assault."

"All this pillaging is just a feeler? It's awful."

"Yes. Many have died. But not those for whom this raid was intended."

"Who's that?"

"Us. Especially, you."

In the end it was like nothing she had expected or feared.

She lay on a vine mat in the Leviathan, alone, eyes closed. She felt nothing of it, or of her body.

And then she suddenly could not face the confrontation. Not this way. Not as a mere doormat.

She got up and fled the comfy confines the Supras had arranged. Moved silently through the Leviathan's thick, ropy jungles, using the forest way she had learned as a girl. Probed with her Talent. Avoided a hovering swarm that looked like a partial Captain. Sneaked by a few preoccupied figures, hunched over their devices.

Where was Searcher? The Talent could find nothing.

Softly she moved through fretted shadows. One of the transparent capsules hung on the Leviathan's pebbled wall. They were a lot like the pyramid she and Searcher had used to escape into space. She felt along the capsule's waxy surface, found an edge. Using the skills she had seen before, she unzipped the inner skin. It pried open, and a smartvoice said,

"Welcome. Which use do you—" and she cut it off as she squeezed in.

Lay back. Made her breathing regular.

Still— The struggle raged red through the landscapes of her mind.

Her link with the Supras, yes—she could feel those. Embedded, they helped smooth the harsh, glancing edges she felt coming to her through a medium she could not comprehend.

Minds were moving, somewhere. A seethe of thoughts, sensations, and something deeper . . . Ideas grown rank with time and experience, powerful, overbearing—

This cauldron of sensations was only a fragment of the broadening perspectives which, the Supras said, would open for her in the hours and days of the conflict. She shuddered at the thought.

These rode in the background of her mind. She had to ignore them. *Fly*, part of her said. Only by being *out of control* could she feel that this was part of her work. Her Original self would enter into this strange moment *as herself*, not as a Supra component . . .

Back to work. She struggled to get the bubble to let go of the Levathan hull. The chemical signals were complex and having watched Searcher call them up was not enough to get her through it. She tugged and tweaked and then had to bang on the walls to even get the bubble's attention. When she had the sequence right, she had no chance to savor the satisfying *pop*. She was among the roiling abundance of life and had to learn to navigate. Jove's amber scowl peered over her shoulder as she skimmed away along the Laviathan's skin.

The skysharks did not notice her, but something small and bullet-shaped did.

It arrowed at her, a spike emerging at its nose.

This lanced through the bubble in an instant. Orange mist puffed from it. The cloud's mere touch ignited flares in her nerves. Hurt reverberated in her nervous system in a searing echo.

She snatched off her belt and chopped at the spike. It broke. More of the orange fog spurted. Her skin shrieked. The stench was awful. The spike wavered, turned toward her as if it could see—and abruptly jerked back, slipping through the hole it had punched.

Her ears popped. The vacuum draft sucked most of the ornage mist away and then the bubble self-sealed. She was drifting outward from the Leviathan into a swarm of life.

And then something huge caught her up and swept her into a place beyond.

She had anticipated great flares of phosphorescent energy, climactic storms of magnetic violence. There were some, but these were merely sideshow illuminations dancing around the major conflict, like heat lightning on a far horizon.

For Dawn the struggle called upon her kinesthetic senses—overloaded and strained and fractured, splitting her into shards of disembodied perception. This was all she was capable of grasping.

Yet each splinter was intensely vibrant, encompassing.

She felt herself running, once. The pleasant heady rush of sliding muscles. Of speed-shot perspectives dwindling, of slick velocities—and then she was in cold inky oblivion, her sun blocked by moving mountains. These moist shadows coiled with acrid odors. Harsh, abrasive air thrust up her nostrils.

The ground—like a plain of lead-gray ball bearings—slid by below her invisible feet, tossing like

a storm-streaked, grainy sea. Sweet tastes swarmed
up her sinuses, burst wetly green—and she tumbled
into another bath of rushing impressions. Of receding
depths. And then of oily forces working across her
skin. It went on and on, a riverrun she could not
stanch or fathom.

But at times she did sense pale immensities working at great distances, like icebergs emerging from a
hurricane-racked ocean. Dimly she caught shreds of
a childlike mind, incomparably large, and recognized
the Multifold. It had prowled the solar system, she
saw, blunting the attacks of the Malign. She owed it
her life, for surely the Malign would otherwise have
found her on her outward voyage.

Beneath the ragged waves that washed her she
felt infinitesimal currents, tiny piping voices. She
recognized these as the recently grown Ur-humans,
unformed personalities.

They were all like elemental units in an enormous
circuit, serving as components which relayed messages
and forces they could no more recognize than a copper wire knows what an electron is.

And Searcher was there. Not the Searcher she knew,
but something strange and many-footed, immense,
running with timeless grace over the seamless gray
plain.

Or was it many Searchers?—the entire species,
she saw now—a kind which had come long after the
Ur-humans and yet was equally ancient now, a race
which had strived and lost and strived again, endured
and gone on silently, peering forward with a hollow
barking laugh, still powerful and always asking as life
must, and still dangerous and still coming.

And something more. She glimpsed it then, a corridor of ruin stretching back to the Ur-humans and
lined with the dead who had stood—single minds, alone

and finally afraid—against the fall of night. They had died to imprison the Malign and now their work lay in shreds as down that long passage of a billion years there now sped a vast shaggy shape, now compressing itself into this narrow inlet of a solar system—

"That's it, yes," she said to herself. For she did not know what this place was, transcending the dimensions of her world, skating somehow outside the brane of the ordinary. She was lofting now, high above a seethe that smoldered red and black.

"You want to make it come for me, to focus here," she said.

It is our only hope, Rin sent.

Dawn reached out and suddenly felt Searcher. The huge shape was engaged somehow at levels she could only glimpse. Searcher struggled in what seemed to Dawn to be a crystal sphere—luminous, living. Yet the mote glaring at the sphere's center was a star.

She felt the plasma beings then. Nets of fields and ionized gas slipped fishlike through blackness. They converged on the Jove system. Great slow-twisting blue lightning worked through the orbiting rafts of life there.

The mere backwash of this passing struggle scorched broad carpets of spacelife. Lances ruptured wispy beings the size of whole worlds.

The biting pain of it made Dawn twist and scream. Her eyes opened once to find her fingernails embedded in her palms, crimson blood streaking her arms. But she could not stop.

Her eyes squeezed shut against her will. A swelling seized her. She felt herself extended, warping the space around her as though she were herself a giant sun, bending rays of light.

She knew this meant she had somehow been incorporated into the Multifold. But instantly another presence lapped at her mind. She felt herself tucked up into a cranny, snug—then yanked out, spilling into hot, inky murk.

The Malign had her. It squeezed, as though she were moist fruit and would spit out seeds.

—an orange, crusty with age, browned and pitted, covered by white maggots sucking at the inner wealth—

She saw this suddenly, hard and vivid. Her mouth stung.

I see it now. She had to cleanse the slimy maggots before she could eat. She sent down fire and washed the orange in burnt-gold flame. Screaming, the maggots burst open.

—and the orange was a planet—

Seared and pure and wiped free of the very atmosphere which had sustained the soft maggots. Slugs singed to oblivion. They had been scaly, quick of mind. But not quick enough. They had barely comprehended what rushed at them out of the maw at the center of the galaxy.

I have to live it all. Dawn was the orange and then the fire and then the maggots and then, with long strangled gasps, the fire again.

It was good to be the fire. Good to leap and fry and crackle and leap again. Forking its fingers up at a hostile sky.

Better *by far* than to crawl and mew and suck and shit and die.

Better, yes, to float and stream and tingle with blue-white fires. To hang in curtains between the stars and be greater than any sun that had ever flared. To roar at the jeweled stars. Better to know and shimmer and reek. To rasp against the puny clots of knotted magnetic fields, butt into their slow waltzes. To jab and hurt and keep on hurting *because it is right they obey* when the magnetic kernels had ground beneath you, broken, were dust. Better to be a moving appetite again, an intelligence bigger than a galactic arm.

Pleasure seethed in its self-stink, more raw and muscular with every gathering moment.

It loved these hideous memories.

—and she broke away from it for a moment, into what seemed to be cool open space, empty of the skittering violence.

—*Oh!* she thought with buoyant relief.

But it was merely another part of the Malign. Oily and slick and snakelike, it slid over her. Into her ears. Up her vagina. A long, deep, snub-nosed probing for her ovaries. Down her throat, prodding with a fluid insistence. A scaly stench rose and bit into her. Its sharp beak cut and that was when she understood a flicker of what the outside struggle was about.

Suddenly she could *feel* abstractions. The partition between thought and sensation, so fundamental to being human, was blown to tatters by the Malign's mad gale. Trapped, she understood.

The Malign held that this universe was one of many expanding bubbles adrift inside a meta-universe. Ours was but one of the possibilities in a cosmos beyond counting. The great adventure of advanced life-forms, it believed, was to transcend the mere bubble which we saw as our universe. Perhaps there were civilizations of unimaginable essence, around the very curve of the cosmos. The Malign wished to create a tunnel which would prick a hole in our universe-bubble and extend into others.

And against it came the Singular. For they had ventured into the higher dimensions, learning to fold spongy space-time itself and make mass, to build castles beyond imagination.

They knew the Malign well, and came to kill it.

But somehow, in all this, she mattered . . .

Slimy blackness crept like oily fingers. Easeful ideas soothed into her.

Here are my works.

Bodies crushed and scorched.

Leviathans boiling away their guts into vacuum.

Gray moons melted to slag.

Bodies punched and seared and tumbling away into vacuum.

The Malign told her. Forced her to see through its eyes:

The Galactic Empire, she saw, had been a festering pile of insects. When she stopped to see them better they were of all shapes, chittering, filled with meaningless jabber.

Long ago some of these vermin had slipped away, she remembered, through the veils beyond the galaxy. Out, flying through strings of galaxies, across traceries of light. Spanning the great vaults and voids where few luminous sparks stirred.

Those Empire maggots had vanished, leaving dregs to slump into petrified cities on a desert world.

And elsewhere in the spiral arms, other races had dwindled into self-obsessed stasis.

But should the holy, enduring fire follow the Empire across the curve of this universe? Should the Malign pursue?

She knew instantly that such goals were paltry. *The stuff of maggot-minds.*

No—far grander to escape the binds of this universe entirely. Not merely voyage in it. Not simply skim across the sloping warp.

Follow those who had already lept free, into dimensions beyond the paltry infinity of this place. *Ah.*

Dawn struggled but could find no way through the cloying hot ink that oozed into her throat, that seared her bowels. Faintly she felt that these turgid sensations were in fact . . . ideas. She could not comprehend them as cool abstractions. They reeked and banged, cut and seared, rubbed and poked at her.

And on this stage ideas moved as monstrous actors, capable of anything.

She understood now—as quickly as she could frame the question—what the madness cloaking her wanted.

It desired to create deep wells in space-time. Compression of matter to achieve this in turn required the cooperation of many magnetic minds—for in the end, only intelligence coolly divorced from matter could truly control masses and their warps.

Such a venture risked the destruction of the entire galaxy. Fresh matter had to be created, carved and compacted. This could curve space-time enough to trap the galaxy into a self-contracting sphere, cut off from the universe even as it bled downward into a yawning gravitational pit.

Only in this way could the Malign escape the universe itself.

The galaxy could not accept such danger. The magnetic minds had debated the wisdom of such a venture while the Malign was confined. Their discussion had been dispassionate, for they were not threatened. Magnetic intelligences could follow the Malign beyond such geometric oblivion, since they were not tied to the fate of mere matter.

But the galaxy brimmed with lesser life. And in the last billion years, as humanity slept on Earth, life had integrated.

Near most stars teemed countless entities, bound to planets or orbiting them. Farther out, between the shimmering suns, the wisps of magnetic structures gazed down on this with a slow, brooding spirit. Their inability

to transcend the speed of light except in tiny spots
meant that these most vast of all intelligences spoke
slowly across the chasms of the galactic arms.

Yet slowly, slowly, through these links a true Galactic
Mind had arisen. It had been driven to more complex levels of perception by the sure knowledge that
eventually the Malign would escape.

So the magnetic beasts could not abandon the
matter-born to extinction. They had ruled against the
Malign's experiment before, and now they moved to
crush the new-risen malevolency before it could carry
out the phased and intricate compression of mass.

Dawn saw this in a passing instant of struggle, while
she swam in a milky satin fog—and then immeasurably
later, through sheets the colors of bloody brass. She
was like a blind ship adrift, with only the gyroscope
of her senses of any use.

The pain began then.

It soared through her. If she had once thought
of herself and the other Ur-humans as elements in
an electrical circuit, now she understood what this
could mean.

The agony was timeless. Her jaws strained open,
tongue stuck straight out, pink and burning. Her eyes
bulged, though still squeezed shut by a giant hand
which pinched her nose. She was terrified and then
went beyond that to a longing, a need for extinction
simply to escape the terror.

Her agony was featureless. No tick of time con-
soled her. Her previous life, memories, pleasures—all
dwindled into nothing beside the flinty mountain of
her pain.

She longed to scream. Rin! Muscles refused to
unlock in her throat, her face. Timeless excruciation
made her into a statue.

—and through her came a bulge, thickening in

her, a blunt momentum. She felt what it needed and *pushed*, letting the deep recesses of her mind gush out, letting the Multifold have the substratum of her Original self. It needed to know how her worn old mental machinery clanked and ground and flared forward. To use her as an ancient tool.

The pain was now exquisite. It sucked the strata from her. Her cramped way of seeing the world was a language in itself and she finally gave it forth. The *her* of her blew outward. Was sponged up. Gone.

Without this We could not traverse.

It was not any Supra. The voice strummed low and certain. She sensed a distant presence that was embroiled in a terrible vast struggle. A tiny fraction had come to her and taken what she could yield, what she could birth, and now went back into the fray.

Thank you, we give, to your kind. We leave you as we found you. Enjoy your simple self and do not try to be more. To be like this, ancient and quick, is enough. There are times when We wish we could be so again.

She heard a scream. Not aloud, but in the Talent.

It was a human. A Supra. Dying.

There came a moment like an immense word on the verge of being spoken.

And then it was over.

She sat up. The vines holding her were like rasping hot breaths.

She vomited violently. Coughed. Gasped.

Brown blood had caked thick and crusty at her wrists. Her fingernails had snapped off. The tips were buried in her palms. Numbly Dawn licked them clean.

"Have a rat," Searcher said and held up a green morsel on a forked stick.

Rin! She shook her head and was sick again.

"It's done," Searcher said.

"I . . . Who won?"

"We did."

"What . . . what . . ."

"Losses?" Searcher paused as though listening to a pleasant distant song. "Billions of lives. Billions of loves, which is another way to count."

She closed her eyes and felt a strange dry echo of Searcher's voice. This was Searcher's Talent. Through it she witnessed the gray, blasted wastes that stretched throughout the solar system. Worlds blistered, atmospheres belched into vacuum, countless lives gone.

"The Malign?"

"Eaten by us," Searcher said.

"Us?"

"Life. The Galactic Mind."

She still caught frayed strands of Searcher's ebbing vision. "You see it all, don't you?"

"Only within the solar system. The speed of light constrains."

"You can sense all life? On all the worlds?"

"And between them."

"How?"

Searcher pricked up her outsized ears. Waves of amber and yellow chased each other around its pelt. "Like this." More ear-flicks, and a grin.

"Well, what's that?"

"*This.*"

In a glimmering she saw in her mind's eye fragile, lonely Earth, now among the blighted worlds. Safe . . . for now.

Searcher shook one paw. She had just burned it on the cooking stick, and whimpered in pain. Dawn saw the hollows beneath Searcher's eyes. There was a weathered, wan look to the age-old racoon face— older, worn gray. Dawn sensed that the animal had suffered much since she last saw her, but there was no hint in its speech. "Human dreams can be powerful . . ." a breath, wheezed out, " . . . as we have just witnessed."

A moment hovered between them. Dawn saw that they would never be quite the same, she and Searcher. They had each been through something that they could not speak of, or know from the other's perspective. So it was with differing intelligences.

Maybe that was how it should be. Anyway, it was.

Other Supras came through the thick foliage.

Then she saw the body. They carried it between them in the light gravity. "Rin!"

Dawn asked a Supra man, "What happened?"

"He . . . gave . . . too much." The man-child's throat sounded raw and unused, as though he had seldom spoken before.

Dawn gazed into Rin's open eyes. A rosy pattern of burst veins gave them the look of small, trapped seas. Blood lakes. Ruin at a cellular level.

Dawn sighed. There was no pulse.

Dawn looked at Rin's troubled, fractured eyes and tried to imagine what he had finally faced. She knew suddenly, certainly, that he had somehow helped her when she was in the Malign's grip.

She had been the conduit, and he the guardian. And his cost had been to have his own mind burned away, the brain itself fused.

He had dignity in death. She felt a pang of loss. He had been strange but majestic, in his way. Searcher was wrong; the Supras were still essentially human, though she would never be able to define just what that meant.

✧   ✧   ✧

That night they did the ancient human thing: drank alcohol.

No matter how many millennia of chemical research had come and gone, something about that elemental chemical still resonated in the human soul.

Dawn did not mingle with the Supras. They kept to themselves anyway, and unlike every other party she had ever attended, she felt no need to go over and try to work herself into conversation with them. She let them be. Even the Supra men had no particular gravitational attraction for her. It felt good.

Instead, the childlike Ur-humans drew her. They were amusing, and their innocence she found touching. Their humor provoked her own giggles; and it was not just the alcohol.

Dawn looked around the room—actually, a bower the Captain had ordered to be worked forth from a vine cloister in the Leviathan—and felt an odd feeling creep over her. She knew humanity's role in the biome. Knew it in her gut. The mighty Supras did not; somehow she could tell. She very well might be the only person in the room who *felt* the meaning of that.

And her own retinue of her genetic identicals—they had not a clue.

Neither had she, until now. Until the long struggle with the Malign. Some Supra had noted, off-hand, that the battle had lasted seven days. It had felt like years. Dawn could feel the fatigue like an ache in her bones and knew that she would sleep for a week, once she closed her eyes. But not yet. Not yet.

She had to take it all in. There was so much to do now. The young versions of herself milled and spoke and tipped back their crystal glasses—after all, they were her, and she was doing a lot of that, too—all blithely adorable. Hers.

"We're going back together," she said to one of the young men. "Tomorrow."

"Really? Where?" he asked, blank-faced.

"Earth. Home."

"I dunno, we were all speed-grown in tanks, fast-taught, had a lot of time in the crucibles . . ."

"You need bringing up," Dawn said softly.

"Do we?" His face was open and could take any impression, she realized. The lasting imprint of a soft touch.

A strange form of adulthood beckoned to her. She would take these back to Earth and bring them up. They were of her kind, and she had to honor that. She would make a home.

And then, too, there was her father. He would help, she knew that somehow without asking. But he was a rover, too, and would be off to the great reaches of the sky in the long run.

Hell, in the long run, she would go, too. It was in the genes.

She felt a dawning wonder and joy. She finally had a place, a home to make. In forest or plain, no matter—a home.

Searcher came by, sipping suspiciously at a cup of a Supra punch. Dawn fell upon the procyon with glad cries. "You made all this happen! And I never thanked you."

"Not necessary. I was following my nose."

Dawn tweaked the long snout. "That must be easy; it's so big."

"I see you have gathered your kind," Searcher said pensively.

"All there are, right."

"Not all."

"But you said my kind were gone."

"Gone into the Singular, some of them."

"There are Originals in those branes of yours?"

"Yes—but they are not mine." Searcher eyed Dawn. "Nor yours. The higher dimensionals have incorporated humans, and those too fought in the battle with the Malign."

Dawn dropped her drink and it shattered on the stones. "My kin? How can I reach them?"

"That expedition would be more difficult than the one we have just finished." Searcher raised a skeptical eyebrow. "Are you willing?"

"Huh? Hey, first I have to get these kids back, find a place to live, make—"

"I know. There will be time for that. Shall I come calling in, say, three hundred megaseconds?"

"Uh, sure. But wait—last time we spoke, you owned up to being, well—"

"God?"

"Yes. But so are you."

"What?!"

"Of course, you need some polishing. But you show definite promise. I shall see you in a while."

Searcher walked away, still sipping.

"Wait! I don't understand!"

"Welcome to our society of the happily ignorant," Searcher said. And as Searcher departed, Dawn wondered whether she would ever see the remarkable beast again.

When it comes to the best
in science fiction and fantasy,
Baen Books has something for *everyone!*

IF YOU LIKE ...
YOU SHOULD ALSO TRY...

Marion Zimmer Bradley .... Mercedes Lackey,
Holly Lisle

Anne McCaffrey .... Elizabeth Moon,
Mercedes Lackey

Mercedes Lackey .... Holly Lisle, Josepha Sherman,
Ellen Guon, Mark Shepherd

Andre Norton .... Mary Brown,
James H. Schmitz

David Drake .... David Weber, John Ringo,
Eric Flint

Larry Niven .... James P. Hogan,
Charles Sheffield

Robert A. Heinlein ....Jerry Pournelle,
Lois McMaster Bujold

Heinlein's "Juveniles" .... Eric Flint & Dave Freer,
Rats, Bats & Vats

Horatio Hornblower .... David Weber's
"Honor Harrington" series,
David Drake's, "RCN" series

The Lord of the Rings .... Elizabeth Moon,
The Deed of Paksenarrion

IF YOU LIKE . . .
YOU SHOULD ALSO TRY . . .

Lackey's "SERRAted Edge" series .... Rick Cook, *Mall Purchase Night*

Dungeons & Dragons™ .... "Bard's Tale"™ Novels

Star Trek .... James Doohan & S.M. Stirling, "Flight Engineer" series

Star Wars .... Larry Niven, David Weber

Jurassic Park .... Brett Davis, *Bone Wars* and *Two Tiny Claws*

Casablanca .... Larry Niven, *Man-Kzin Wars II*

Elves .... Ball, Lackey, Sherman, Moon, Cook, Guon

Puns .... Rick Cook, Spider Robinson Harry Turtledove, *The Case of the Toxic Spell Dump*

Alternate History .... Gingrich and Forstchen, *1945* James P. Hogan, *The Proteus Operation* Harry Turtledove (ed.), *Alternate Generals* S.M. Stirling, Draka series Eric Flint & David Drake, Belisarius series Eric Flint, *1632*

SF Conventions .... Niven, Pournelle & Flynn, *Fallen Angels* Margaret Ball, *Mathemagics* Jerry & Sharon Ahern, *The Golden Shield of IBF*

Quests .... Mary Brown, Elizabeth Moon, Piers Anthony

Greek Mythology .... Roberta Gellis, *Bull God* and *Thrice Bound* Eric Flint & Dave Freer, *Pyramid Scheme*

IF YOU LIKE . . .
YOU SHOULD ALSO TRY. . .